Cathy Williams can remember reading Mills & Boon books as a teenager, and now that she's writing them she remains an avid fan. For her, there is nothing like creating romantic stories and engaging plots, and each and every book is a new adventure. Cathy lives in London. Her three daughters—Charlotte, Olivia and Emma—have always been, and continue to be, the greatest inspirations in her life.

When **Emmy Grayson** came across her mother's copy of *A Rose in Winter* by Kathleen E. Woodiwiss, she sneaked it into her room and promptly fell in love with romance. Over twenty years later, Harlequin Mills & Boon made her dream come true by offering her a contract for her first book! When she isn't writing she's chasing her kids, attempting to garden, or carving out a little time on her front porch with her own romance hero.

FORBIDDEN
YET CLAIMED

CATHY WILLIAMS

EMMY GRAYSON

MILLS & BOON

First published in Great Britain 2024
by Mills & Boon, an imprint of HarperCollins*Publishers* Ltd,
1 London Bridge Street, London, SE1 9GF

www.harpercollins.co.uk

HarperCollins*Publishers*, Macken House, 39/40 Mayor Street Upper, Dublin 1, D01 C9W8, Ireland

ISBN: 978-0-263-32035-0

12/24

This book contains FSC™ certified paper and other controlled sources to ensure responsible forest management.

For more information visit www.harpercollins.co.uk/green.

Printed and Bound in the UK using 100% Renewable Electricity at CPI Group (UK) Ltd, Croydon, CR0 4YY

SNOWBOUND THEN PREGNANT

CATHY WILLIAMS

MILLS & BOON

CHAPTER ONE

ALICE WAS BEGINNING to wonder whether this was going to be the day she finally met The Big Guy Up There— the very one her dad preached about in his sermons every Sunday.

The cold on her face stung, and even through the layers of protective ski-gear she could feel the whip of the freezing blizzard doing its best to turn her into an ice sculpture. She could barely see in front of her.

She had no idea how much time had gone by since she'd left the chalet where she and her three friends were staying: an hour? Three hours? Fifteen minutes? A year and a half? She'd forgotten her fitness watch in her hurry to leave and her phone was embedded so deeply into one of the pockets of her under-layers that to stop and unearth it would risk instant hypothermia.

Of course, she should never have ventured out, but hindsight was a wonderful thing, and at the time she'd just *had* to get some air: it had felt like the most straightforward decision in the world.

Bea had been proudly showing off her engagement ring, a surprise revelation she had been keeping up her sleeve for the right 'Ta da!' moment. Out had come the champagne; the popping of the cork had been punctuated by lots of squeals of delight, a flood of eager questions and excited talk about bridesmaids' dresses. Just like that, Alice had felt the world closing in on her.

She'd sat there, smiling and twirling the champagne flute between her fingers, thinking back to her own broken engagement eight months ago. Everything had been ticked on her 'ideal for permanent partner' checklist... and yet, Simon had just not been right, had just not been *enough*, had just not been what she'd wanted after all. Everything about him had made sense yet, in the end, none of it had made any sense at all.

So what if she'd been the one to screw up the courage to do the breaking off? She still had scars left from the whole sorry business, and those scars had suddenly flared up, raw and painful, as she'd listened to her friends blown away by the thrill of an upcoming wedding.

She'd just had to escape, and hadn't been able to stay put, pretending that she wasn't tearing up inside, so she'd stood up and announced that she needed to have a breather. The fact that they had all instantly seen her upset and rushed to apologise for being thoughtless had only made the whole situation worse.

So here she was now, no longer skiing but moving clumsily at a snail's pace, because she couldn't see what was in front of her with thoughts of hypothermia and meeting her maker uppermost in her mind.

She was scared witless.

An hour, three hours, a *lifetime* ago there had been fellow skiers on the slopes, but now the vast stretch of white was empty. She had skied away from the buzz of people, wanting the peace of solitude on the more dangerous pistes, and when the blizzard had roared in as sudden as a clap of thunder she had been alone.

Now she was desperately hunting for any signpost or

landmark to orient her and show her a way back to civilisation, but the driving force of the snow was making it impossible. Panic was rising, but Alice knew that was something she had to block out, because panic in a situation like this equalled certain death. She was too experienced to go down that road.

A blizzard was the most dangerous condition on a mountain: people couldn't see and the snow and moisture in the air made them lose heat very quickly. Those were basic 'fun facts' that had been drummed into all of her class as school kids over a decade ago before they'd gone on their first ever school holiday to Mont Blanc. They were also the very same fun facts she had drummed into her newbies when she had done six months of ski instruction during her gap year, on the very same slopes, less than four years ago.

Basically, no one in their right mind wanted to be out on a mountain in a blizzard—yet here she was. She stopped, tilted up her ski goggles and surveyed a scene of endless, driving snow, blowing this way and that as though driven by a giant, high-speed fan somewhere up in the sky. She was gripped by a momentary wave of sickening fear because the wilderness of white was so menacing, so alien. She could have been on another planet.

Keep making your way down and you'll get to safety— law of averages and basic rule of thumb.

But, when it came to lessons learnt from this whole adventure, sudden attacks of emotion were only *ever* going to be given airtime in the comfort and safety of her living room, preferably with a tub of ice-cream to hand.

She breathed in deeply and propelled her way onward with the speed of someone with weights strapped to their ankles swimming in treacle.

She had no idea how long it was before, at last, she saw *something*: a light, just a flicker penetrating the wall of snow. It was barely visible, and it might have just been an illusion, her fevered brain playing tricks on her, but at this point Alice didn't really care. What were her choices? Illusion or no illusion, she was just going to have to go in that direction. There was no room for hesitation or fear because she was flat out of options.

Mateo was in the middle of preparing his evening meal when he heard something: the vaguest hint of something which was barely audible over the jazz music playing softly in the background. The angry howls of the blizzard outside had been reduced to murmurs because his chalet was triple-glazed to within an inch of its life. He stilled, turned off the music and tilted his head, every one of his senses on full alert.

Here on this gloriously isolated and tucked-away side of Mont Blanc, the chances of skiers dropping by for a cup of coffee were non-existent. This part of the mountain, with its treacherous slopes, was suitable only for experts and was usually so empty that it could have been his own private playground.

It had been a definite selling point when he had bought the place several years ago. He had no problem with the jolly troops of revellers who had fun in the many chic resorts on the mountain…just as long as they didn't come near him.

So he was banking on whatever he'd heard producing the thump against his front door being the whipping snowstorm outside. Some idiot lost in this treacherous blizzard would test his patience to the limit and Mateo really didn't want his patience being tested to the limit right now. Any other time, maybe, but here, now—no.

He was here for a week, seven snatched days. This was his one and only pure time-out from the gruelling business of running his network of companies and living life in the fast lane. He'd been here for two days and the last thing he wanted was any of the remaining five to be interrupted by a risk-taking fool.

Here, and only here, did Mateo come close to reconnecting with a past he had long since left behind, a past that contained none of the often tiresome trappings that went with the sort of wealth he had accumulated. It was important to him that he never forget his beginnings. He had grown up in this part of the world—not on this side of the mountain but in a village close to one of the cheaper resorts—in a small house with struggling young parents, both of whom had worked at a low-end resort for minimum pay. In the high season they'd depended on tips to top up the coffers and, in the low season, they'd taken summer work wherever they could find it. They hadn't been proud.

Lord knew, things would have remained that way for ever had his mother not died when Mateo was twelve. After that, his memories were a blur of sadness, confusion, grief and then, as one year had turned into two and then three, the dawning realisation that he was growing up on his own because his still-young father just hadn't been able to cope without his wife as his rock, by his side.

Mateo had watched from the side lines as his dad had managed to hold down a job at the resort for a couple more seasons. It had been a struggle, because drinking and drugs had begun to make twin inroads into his ability to work, and then eventually his ability to do anything at all—including his ability to look after himself, never mind his precociously bright teenaged son who had been left on his own to cope.

Mateo had quit school at sixteen to begin the process of earning money because his father hadn't been able to keep his head above water. He'd had to balance earning money to pay the bills, because no one else had been around to do it, with studying to make sure he never ended up poor and dependent on the goodwill of others to pick up the slack. Keeping his education on track outside of the school system had became the ultimate goal. He'd known he had a good brain—better than good. He hadn't intended to waste it, or to flush his future down the drain side by side with his father.

He'd begun working at a local boxing gym. For fun, he'd boxed as an amateur and had challenged himself to win every match he'd played but mostly he'd fallen into a routine of working by day and studying by night. He'd been smart—too smart for the online courses, too smart for the problems posed in exams, but smart enough to see where his talents lay and to take advantage of his gift for maths by entering the complex world of coding.

And from there to where he was now. From a seventeen-year-old kid developing a website for his coach, to the eighteen-year-old being paid to design for someone else, and then wanting more than just working for other people; wanting more than just standing still.

He'd saved and become a hunter, the guy who knew just where to find the next big start-up. The guy who turned everything he touched to gold. By his late twenties, he'd been invincible. Winning had become his goal and winning had got him the sort of wealth most people could only dream of.

That said, Mateo knew that it was easy to forget the road that had taken a person from rags to riches, and to forget that road was to risk forgetting lessons learnt along the way. Rags to riches could end up as rags again in the blink of an eye. All that was needed was a little too much laziness and a little too much complacency.

Being here on the mountain was a reminder. His father no longer lived here. Mateo himself lived in London, with places in New York, Hong Kong and Dubai, but this quiet corner on the slopes was a sliver of a distant past.

The merest hint that some clown might now invade his sanctuary filled Mateo with grim rage. Quite still, and ear cocked, he heard the bang on the door with a sinking heart, well aware that he could hardly turn away whatever dope might be shivering outside. Dope or *dopes*: lads who'd decided to play fast and loose with their own lives, safe in the misguided juvenile delusion that someone would magically materialise to save their sorry skins.

He switched off the stove and padded barefoot to open the door.

Alice was about to bang on the door for the third time when it was pulled open without warning and she stumbled forward, clattering clumsily on her skis, sagging with exhaustion and relief. She hadn't had time to clock who exactly had opened the door. She just felt herself being caught as she began toppling to the ground. Arms around her waist grabbed her, tugging her straight and then holding her upright, at which point she did take notice of the guy who was now supporting her.

Cold, narrowed eyes were staring down at her from a towering height. She was an unimpressive five-three and this guy was well over six feet. She blinked and the breath caught in her throat, because she was staring up at a man who was sinfully beautiful with perfectly chiselled features, sharp cheekbones, the oddest colour of green eyes and very dark, shortly cropped hair. He was wearing worn, faded jogging bottoms, an equally worn sweater and an expression of barely suppressed annoyance.

'What the hell are you doing here?'

'I…'

'You'd better come in, but only because I can't have you collapsing in a blizzard outside my front door!'

'I…'

'And you might as well bring the skis in too. Leave them out there and they'll be buried under the snow and, before you apologise for landing on my doorstep, I'll tell you straight away that the last thing I need is a complete stranger invading my privacy!'

Hard, green eyes bored into her and Alice, normally the sunniest of people, felt a quiver of anger. Today was definitely not her day when it came to letting her emotions get the better of her. She stood back, folded her arms and tried to ignore the bitter cold settling on her now that she was standing still.

'Well?' he demanded, scowling. 'You're letting the cold in.'

'I'm not sure I *want* to come in!' Alice shivered, her arms folded.

'What the hell are you going on about?'

'I don't like your attitude. I can't be too far from… from…civilisation, if you have a place here, and I'll take my chances if you point me in the right direction!'

'Don't be ridiculous!' He looked at her with even more narrow-eyed displeasure, then stared straight past her shoulder to the swirling snow now being consumed in darkness. 'Although…if you really want to take your chances? Approximately five miles south-east you might just stumble to the nearest very small town. Miss it, though, and you'll be spending a very cold night on the slopes and, despite your idiocy in being out here in the first place, my conscience won't let me send you on your way. So, if you still refuse to come in then I'll be forced to carry you in over my shoulder.'

'You wouldn't dare!'

'Care to try me?'

He spun round on his heels. Alice detached herself from her skis and tripped along hurriedly behind him, slamming the door behind her and breathing a sigh of blessed relief at the warmth that had replaced the biting cold.

She took a few seconds to glance around her. The place was cosy but utterly luxurious in an understated way. Wooden panelling and stained-glass windows splintered the fading light and the rug that covered the parquet floor was soft, faded and clearly silk. Two black-and-white photographs on the wall were signed by the photographer and looked vaguely familiar. She was ridding herself of her outer layers as he vanished into one of the rooms off to the right and, when she entered behind him, it was to find herself in a superbly fitted kitchen rich with smells that made her mouth water.

She cleared her throat and then reddened as he swung round to face her. The lighting in the hallway hadn't done him justice. Her mouth went dry as she took in his truly spectacular good looks. Her heart picked up speed and she frantically tried to get herself back to a place of righteous anger at his high-handed arrogance. Was she here on her own with him? she thought belatedly. Should she be concerned? What if he was dangerous? Strangely, she wasn't scared, but then again she was half-crazy with exhaustion, so her brain was probably not functioning properly.

'You're wet.'

His dark, cutting voice interrupted her wandering train of thought.

'That's because I've been out in a blizzard for hours. Okay, maybe not *hours*, but long enough.'

'Which is something I'll get to just as soon as you get out of those clothes.'

'I can't. I have nothing to put on. I forgot to travel with my suitcase.'

'You think this situation is funny?'

'No.' Alice had no idea what had come over her, because it wasn't like her to be sarcastic, and it certainly wasn't like her to be rude. 'And… I suppose I ought to thank you for letting me in to your house.'

'I had no choice.'

'Are you here…er…on your own?'

She blushed as his eyebrows winged upwards and he shot her a slow smile of cool amusement that transformed the sharp, arrogant edges of his face so that he went from drop-dead gorgeous to stupidly sexy.

'I'm afraid so,' he drawled. 'Absolutely no handy chaperones in the form of wife and kids but, before you have a fainting fit, I can assure you that you're one hundred percent safe with me. I couldn't be less interested in some fool who's ventured out in a blizzard thinking that it might be a bit of a challenge. Follow me.'

'Follow you?'

'You'll have to borrow some of my clothes.'

Alice laughed incredulously. She couldn't help it. 'You really think I'm going to fit into anything you have here?'

'You'll have to use your ingenuity,' he said, pausing right in front of her, close enough for her pick up the clean, woody masculine scent of whatever aftershave he was wearing. 'Spending more time in wet clothes isn't an option.'

'No,' Alice replied, hackles rising again. 'I suppose getting a bout of flu and ending up bedridden is only slightly less troublesome for you than me getting lost in a blizzard in search of a small town somewhere further down the slopes.'

'You said it.'

'That's not very nice!'

'I do "honest" over "nice".'

'I'd never have guessed.' She met his impassive stare and then sighed. 'I'm sorry. I'm being very rude, and that's not like me. Of course I'll borrow some of your clothes. I don't want to get ill because I'm too proud to accept your help.'

She smiled with genuine, tentative warmth. Why was she reacting to him like this—as though he had reached deep into part of her she hadn't known existed and turned on a switch that had sent her emotions into some weird, puzzling place? He was a perfect stranger, for heaven's sake!

Even when she had broken up with Simon, she had done so in a calm, measured way. They had talked. She had been upset, but she hadn't felt out of control; feeling out of control just wasn't in her DNA. She wasn't cutting or sarcastic by nature. She had grown up in a vicarage and had learnt from a young age to be thoughtful of other people.

Over the years there had been many, many broken people who had dropped in to see her father, who was the kindest man on the planet. She had learnt to be patient and to listen to whatever they wanted to say if her father happened to be busy at the time and hadn't been able to see them straightaway. She had sat serenely though more gossip about who was doing what to the flower arrangements than she could shake a stick at.

She was equable by nature. Escaping from the chalet to think had been impulsive for her, but maybe the conversation about engagements had tapped into a depth of regret she really hadn't known was there.

At any rate, the way she was reacting to this guy was a completely alien to her. Was it because he was so good-looking, so arrogant? So unlike any guy she had ever met in her life before? Had she surrounded herself so much with *ordinary* that this guy, so far away from ordinary, unsettled her in ways she couldn't deal with?

'I think it's time for introductions,' Mateo said gruffly. He shoved his hands in the pockets of the joggers, dragging them down just a bit so that now they rode low on his hips, and tilted his head to the side.

A woman, banging on his front door, criticising his attitude even though he'd *rescued* her from a blizzard by letting her in in the first place? Not at all what he had been expecting. He was so accustomed to obedience, and so tuned in to women who were always eager to please, that he had been lost for words at the sheer nerve of this unexpected intruder blown in on the wind.

Even more annoying for Mateo was the fact that there was an appeal to her that bypassed his justifiable displeasure at her presence in his chalet, in his *sanctuary*. She'd followed him into the kitchen and he turned around to a curvy little sex kitten who had stripped down to her thermal layers, none of which could quite conceal the fullness of her breasts or the narrow hand-span of her waist. She'd also dragged off the woolly hat to reveal a spill of long copper curls that tangled over her shoulders and made the breath catch in his throat.

He was in danger of staring, and that was a reaction that was both foreign and unacceptable to him. Mateo's life was highly controlled. As far as he was concerned, surprises were rarely welcome, particularly when it came to the opposite sex. No surprises at all really worked for him. He went for women who fitted a mould: leggy blondes who enjoyed all the things that money could buy and, even more, all the doors that a powerful guy like him could open: doors to a social scene that tended to bore him but usually thrilled them to death. They demanded no more than he was willing to provide: fun without commitment.

Right now, Mateo was taking a breather from relationships of any kind, so it was intensely irritating to find his eyes being drawn to a woman who wasn't even anything like the ones he usually invited into his life. Said woman was currently looking at him with guarded eyes, waiting for him to introduce himself, as opposed to standing and staring like an idiot.

'I'm Mateo. And you are...?'

'Alice. Alice Reynolds.'

'Right. Now that we've covered that, I'll get some clothes for you and show you to the bathroom...' He paused and raked his fingers through his hair as she continued to look at him with huge, almond-shaped hazel eyes that somehow managed to dredge up something inside him that had no place in his tough, aggressive personality.

'Look, I get that you might be a little alarmed at being in a strange place with a guy you don't know, and I don't want to be flippant about that—you're perfectly safe here. There's not much I can add to that; you'll just have to trust me on that front. You haven't told me what you're doing in this part of the world, or who you've come with, but I have excellent connectivity here, and if you let me have your phone I can connect you so you can get in touch with whoever's out there rustling up a search party to hunt you down.'

'Oh! Would you believe that hadn't even crossed my mind? Yes, please, that would be great.'

She smiled a smile of such open radiance that Mateo was temporarily knocked off his feet but he concealed it well. She was fumbling to fetch her phone and he deliberately didn't spare her a distracted sideways glance as he connected her to his Wi-Fi and then brushed past her to his suite, sensing her light tread behind him and trying hard not to conjure up her image in his head.

'I just want to say…'

He paused and glanced round to find her standing inches away from him, face upturned and still smiling.

'Yes?' he muttered gruffly.

'I just want to say that I know you don't want me here.' She grimaced and rolled her eyes, laughing at herself. 'Even if you hadn't said so yourself, I can tell that I've interrupted whatever down time you had planned, and I'm sorry about that. I'm afraid I was a little rude when I first…well…fell headlong into your chalet but I honestly had no idea the weather was going to turn when I set off earlier. I was so scared out there… I guess my head was all over the place!'

'That's…fine.'

'And then I made it here and I was just so relieved that I wasn't going to die out there on the slopes that I didn't even stop to consider that…that… I mean, you could have been *anyone*!'

'I… Yes, I suppose I could have been.' Mateo was fascinated by this long, meandering explanation which wasn't designed to grab his attention or capture his interest. He was so accustomed to coy advances that her open honesty was a little disorienting.

'You read about these things. And then there are all the movies…'

'You do read about those things and, yes, I suppose there are movies out there as well, although I don't do them. Look, I'll fetch some stuff for you. You can choose whatever you want, and if you leave your wet things on the floor of the bathroom I'll stick them in the machine.'

'That's very kind. I can't believe I ever thought you might have been an axe-murderer.'

'You thought I might have been an *axe-murderer*?' Mateo stared at her and she smiled back, blushing and sheepish.

'Like I said, I've seen enough movies in my time, although I guess the typical axe-murderer wouldn't rent a chalet like this…although, in fairness, perhaps I'm stereotyping axe-murderers.'

'I happen to own this!'

'Which makes the axe-murderer scenario even more implausible. And yet…did you say that you *don't do movies*? I didn't know there was anyone who *didn't* do movies.'

'We should continue this conversation…eh…later. Now,

there are three suites here so you can use either of the two spare and you can take your time…eh…freshening up. No need to join me for dinner if you'd rather go to sleep. I imagine your nerves are frayed.'

'Actually, I'm quite hungry.' She cast her eyes downward and then glanced back up at him and blushed. 'I keep meaning to go on a diet but somehow that never really gets off the ground.'

Mateo backed away as the silence thickened. She'd brought his attention bounding back to her shapely little body and he was perspiring as he reached the door and nodded in the direction of the bedroom suites off the broad landing.

His eyes flicked to her semi-damp layer that stretched lovingly over her generous breasts and sexy curves. He swallowed…and scowled.

'Right. I'll be in the kitchen.'

He left without further pointless pleasantries. He wished he could summon up the suffocating impatience he had felt when he had pulled that door open. Instead, the woman seemed to have distracted him, and as he stalked back to the kitchen, glowering at his momentary lapse in focus, the reality of the situation sank in.

His peace had been invaded. God only knew when the blizzard would stop but certainly he would be stuck with her for the next day, possibly more. And, instead of trying to think of ways in which he could somehow confine her to safe quarters so that they weren't actually sharing space, he was already resigning himself to the fact that that was going to be impossible. Worse, he wasn't quite sure whether that was a problem for him or not.

He returned to the business of cooking but his solitude had been interrupted. Images of her filled his head and he loathed that. Truth was, there were things that were contained within him, experiences best left buried. They'd remain buried just so long as his life didn't derail, but the appearance of one Alice Reynolds had derailed him completely. As he stirred the sauce, his disobedient mind wandered back to his youth and to memories usually kept under lock and key.

Mateo had been nineteen when he'd met Bianca. He'd been within touching distance of getting his degree a year and a half ahead of schedule. She'd shown up at one of his boxing matches and had knocked him sideways with her beauty. What red-blooded teenager could have resisted all that long, dark hair, flashing dark eyes and a mouth that had invited a world of sexual adventure?

He'd fallen hook, line and sinker...for about six months, before realising that no amount of hot sex could detract from the cold reality that the two of them were not suited. He'd had ambitions; he'd wanted to move on from website designing for other people to ruling the world single-handedly. He'd known it would take time but that he would get there. He'd been young, ambitious and insanely clever.

She'd wanted the fast riches to be made if he turned professional as a boxer. She'd craved the adrenaline that would have come with the limelight and the lifestyles of the crowd that might hang around him. She'd been impatient, and contemptuous when it had come to looking at the bigger picture and thinking long-term.

The body he'd lusted after had begun to bore him and his eyes had begun to wander. The happiness he'd felt when she walked through the door had turned to irritation and impatience.

On the brink of breaking up, she'd fallen pregnant and everything then had changed. Mateo had married her.

He'd been just twenty with a baby on the way and all his dreams of making it big in the world of start-ups and finance had started to dissolve, like dew on a summer's morning. Money had had to be made there and then and turning professional would have paid all the bills and more. Bianca might not have been right for him but he'd been determined to put his all into a baby he'd found himself secretly thrilled to have fathered.

He'd never know how that adventure might have turned out because a miscarriage at a little over three months into the pregnancy had thrown everything up in the air. They'd stayed together for another eight months. He, because he'd felt sorry for her, had seen it as his duty to stand by her at a time when she'd needed him, whatever his personal feelings; and because, for a while, he'd been crippled by a sadness he hadn't expected, adrift and unable to think straight. And Bianca, yes: she'd been upset, and had clung just for a while, but she was tough and essentially narcissistic.

'We can always have another; we're young,' she'd told him with casual insouciance. The thought of a lifestyle being married to a professional boxer still glittered for her like a treasure chest waiting to be opened. Not for a single moment had she doubted that he would continue on that track. It wasn't to be, and he'd been relieved when she'd finally walked out on him because he'd told her to forget it if she thought he was going to launch into a career in which he had no interest.

Mateo frowned now and resigned himself to the fact that his wayward mind was just going to carry on travelling down memory lane. Maybe releasing pent-up thoughts wasn't such a bad thing. Maybe every so often he needed to pull them out from whatever vault he'd stashed them in and examine them, remind himself why he was the person he was—someone who would never take on commitment again or think that love was something that actually existed.

Maybe it paid sometimes, such as when a perfect stranger somehow put him on the back foot, to remember the ex-wife who had resurfaced five years after their divorce to try and squeeze money out of him. He'd been on the up and she'd been pregnant with another man's baby but that hadn't stopped her from trying to emotionally blackmail him into handing over money to her.

He was just managing to get back in control, and beginning to be just a little amused by his own temporary bout of introspection, when he heard Alice clear her throat from behind him. He turned round to see her standing in the doorway and this time she wasn't in tight, wet ski gear. No snug thermals were lovingly stretched across a body that was sex on legs.

She was wearing his clothes and it felt incredibly intimate. He felt a rush of blood to his head as he looked at her from under lowered lashes. She wore black joggers, and a striped jumper, everything rolled, cuffed and tugged tight, yet still swamping her.

Jesus.

He felt faint.

'Smells delicious…and thank you for the clothes. Not quite my size but I actually feel like a human being again.'

Mateo watched as she smiled and edged into the kitchen, all tension from earlier gone as a naturally upbeat nature was revealed. He was lost for words.

'Sit.' It was more of a command than he'd intended and he flushed darkly. 'Make yourself at home,' he countered roughly. 'And then you can begin to tell me what brings you to this part of the world—by which I mean the wrong side of the mountain.'

He reminded himself that this wasn't a social visit and he wasn't playing the part of Prince Charming looking for the owner of a glass slipper. She'd landed on his doorstep through her own foolish risk-taking, and in so doing had interrupted his very much anticipated time-out here.

'Because, just in case you didn't know,' he went on, 'This part of Mont Blanc takes no prisoners. For future reference, it's easy to end up a casualty of nature here unless you happen to be an experienced skier.'

'And I will duly remember your words of warning.' She gave that smile again, this time pretending and failing to be contrite. Mateo frowned, irritated to be taken off-guard once again.

'I promise: Scout's honour. And now, before I explain why I ended up banging on your door, let me help you do something. I may not be the best cook in the world but I'm a dab hand when it comes to chopping stuff.'

She walked towards him and Mateo looked at her narrowly, taking in everything and finding it difficult to drag his gaze away.

CHAPTER TWO

'I CAN HANDLE ONIONS.'

'There's no need for you to earn your keep by helping, Alice. Sit, relax—recover from your ordeal.'

'Honestly, I like to help out.' Alice smiled when she thought about her parents. She had grown up with people coming and going; helping out wherever and whenever was ingrained in her, which was probably why she had become a teacher. She enjoyed kids, and enjoyed the business of having a job where she felt she might be making a real difference. 'Now that we've established that you're not an axe-murderer,' she teased playfully, 'can you tell me what you do?'

Out of the corner of her eye she could see his hands, strong and bronzed, as he expertly continued to prepare whatever meal he had been preparing before she had ruined his peace.

'I… I'm self-employed, you could say.'

'That's tough, but you're obviously good at what you do, if you can afford a chalet out here.'

'Tough?'

'I'd hate the insecurity—never knowing where your next meal is coming from. I teach. It's the most secure job in the world.' Her eyes were beginning to water and she blinked and stepped back a bit.

'You're a teacher? Shouldn't you be at a school some-where?'

'Half-term; I'm here with three friends. I can't tell you how relieved they were to hear from me! Anyway, we've been planning this trip for ages, and just going back to when you told me about being an idiot for skiing on this side of the mountain...'

She grimaced and looked sideways at him. 'I'm actu-ally a pretty experienced skier,' she confessed, resuming her work on the onions, but half-heartedly, because she was so conscious of him next to her. She was buzzing with curiosity but knew better than to indulge it. Who-ever he was and whatever he did, he didn't seem to be the sort of open, talkative guy she was used to. She felt way out of her comfort zone just being around him and that was weirdly exciting. She wondered whether she was getting on his nerves with her chat but then what else was she supposed to do? She was talkative by nature and the thought of standing there in a state of repressed silence filled her with horror.

Actually, she just didn't think she could do it.

'I taught skiing on these very slopes for six months... Well, not *these* very ones—the easier runs on the other side—before I started my teacher training course.'

'Right.'

'So I'm accustomed to difficult runs but that blizzard just dropped out of the sky like a snow bomb. By the time it hit, there was no one else around on the slopes.'

'Perhaps they'd wisely noticed the darkening skies, be-cause I'm really struggling to believe that a blizzard can strike within seconds. Somehow that seems to defy the laws of nature.'

'That's a possibility,' Alice conceded thoughtfully. She paused and then swivelled so that she was leaning against the counter, her hazel eyes pensive as she stared off into the distance. 'I'm normally really clued up when it comes to changes out here but...my mind was a million miles away. What seemed sudden may not have been quite as sudden as I thought.'

Mateo took over the onions. He looked down at her, primed to discourage any unwelcome outpouring of personal back-stories, but hesitated at the expression on her face, which was a mixture of sadness and resignation.

Something in his gut made him think that she was too young and too inherently upbeat to be sad and resigned. Suddenly he felt a hundred years old. He was thirty-three. He couldn't be more than a handful of years older than her but he felt jaded, cynical and ancient.

He knew how that had happened, and knew that there was nothing wrong with being cynical, because cynicism was a great self-defence mechanism. But for the first time he uneasily wondered what another road might have looked like. Disillusionment and the bitterness of divorce had taught him the value of being tough and keeping out the world, but what would that world have looked like if he had kept doors open to it? The openness of the woman looking at him seemed to encourage restless thoughts that had no place in his life.

Impatient with himself, he told her to go and sit.

'There's not much left to do,' he said shortly. 'Dinner will be ready in half an hour.'

'Okay.'

'And help yourself to more wine.'

He'd opened a bottle of red and poured them both a glass. She'd sipped her way through half of hers.

'I'm annoying you, aren't I?'

'What sort of question is that?' Mateo turned to look at her. She had subsided into one of the chairs at the table, a small thing bundled in clothing too big for her, nursing her glass and staring mournfully in his direction.

'I don't suppose you expected to end up having to cook food for someone you don't want in your chalet.'

'Life throws curve balls.'

'You don't strike me as the sort who does curve balls. A bit like you don't do movies.'

'Come again?'

'Doesn't matter.' Alice shrugged. 'I don't blame you for being annoyed that you're stuck with me. Hopefully this blizzard will die down tomorrow and I can be on my way.' She rose to stroll towards the bank of windows and peered through the wooden shutters that concealed the vast space outside. 'Doesn't look like it,' she said on a sigh. 'When you're in here, you don't think it's as wild outside as it is.'

'Your friends...' Mateo said awkwardly, sipping his wine and staring at her over the rim of his glass but remaining where he was, leaning against the counter, keeping a safe distance between them. He didn't like the way he was distracted by her. 'Is one of them your partner? If so, no need to be depressed about it. I'm sure this will blow over and I'll make sure you're safely delivered back to your lodge.'

'Thank you. I'm an excellent skier; I certainly don't need to be delivered anywhere safely by you! The days of damsels in distress needing to be rescued by knights in shining armour, who think they're better skiers than they are, are long over.' She grinned.

Mateo shot her a reluctant smile. He was tempted to tell her that he couldn't think of any woman who would have rejected his offer and a lot who would have tried to engineer that exact situation. However, something told him that any comment along those lines wouldn't go down well, which made the temptation to voice it even stronger.

'But what about the anxious boyfriend wringing his hands and waiting for you to show up? Is he as experienced a skier as you?'

Food ready, Mateo began bringing dishes to the table, proud of the way he had risen to the occasion without resentment and only a little bit of initial hostility. The woman might have something about her he found a little unsettling, but it hadn't put too much of a dent in his basic manners. He'd stepped up to the plate and not allowed his own personal annoyance at her invasion of his privacy get the better of him.

He wondered whether it helped that she was so straightforward and not interested in him as anything other than someone who had come to her aid. Maybe her sheer novelty value had lowered his defences, or maybe the unexpected situation had in turn generated unexpected reactions—unwelcome, uninvited but oddly energising, intoxicating reactions.

Alice's stomach rumbled. She didn't want to appear rude but she honestly couldn't wait to dive into what he had produced from some onions, tomatoes and other bits and pieces that would probably have confounded her. Her culinary skills were basic to say the least. She watched as he helped her to the breaded chicken and pasta in a sauce that made her mouth water. She saw a shadow of a smile on his face.

'That's quite enough,' she said hurriedly. 'I couldn't possibly eat any more.'

'What about some cheese?'

Alice hesitated. He was here on his own and he wasn't wearing a wedding ring, not that that meant much. But was there a girlfriend in the background somewhere—even a wife? Whoever he was going out with, she was pretty sure that person wouldn't have wanted to tuck into a plate piled high with food topped with a generous dollop of fresh parmesan on top.

'Okay but just a bit. For the record, I'm here with three girlfriends. I… I don't have an anxious boyfriend waiting for me anywhere.'

'So what propelled you to make a headlong dash to this side of the mountain without your friends?' He shot her an astute look that was discomforting, because it seemed to bore straight into her. 'If I were the sort to indulge in guessing games, I'd have said you would have shot down here because of boyfriend troubles.'

'I…'

'Not that I'm asking you to expand,' Mateo interjected smoothly. 'Your business.'

Alice reddened, again in the grip of embarrassment at the thought that she was boring him.

He was making polite chit-chat because he had no choice. The last thing he wanted to hear was about her life or about *her*.

'What about you?' she asked, going slowly with the food, which took a lot of willpower, because she was ravenous. 'I mean, why are you here on your own? Do *you* have anyone waiting up for you?'

'I don't believe my private life is any of your business,' he returned gently.

'It's not. But if you can ask questions about me then isn't it only fair that I ask questions about you?'

'Not entirely, considering this is my lodge and you happen to be in it through misfortune as opposed to invitation.'

'That's not a very nice thing to say!'

'I've sometimes been told that I'm not a very nice person,' Mateo returned with a shrug.

'Have you?'

'You sound shocked.' He grinned at her and Alice felt her skin prickle and a tide of pink wash her face.

'Don't you care?'

'No.' He raised his eyebrows, still smiling. 'But, moving on from that, like I said when you got here, no wife and no girlfriend. Not here or waiting anywhere for me.'

Alice sighed. 'You're a fantastic cook.' She changed the subject but was itching to return to him, to find out more about him, even though he was perfectly right to say that it was hardly her business to probe into his private life, as someone who had infuriatingly landed on his doorstep like a parcel delivered to the wrong address. She didn't even know what he did: 'self-employed' could cover a multitude of sins!

'What are you self-employed doing?' she couldn't resist asking. 'And I know it's none of my business, because I'm just here through sheer bad luck—at least, bad luck *for you*. Good luck for me.'

Mateo burst out laughing and pushed his plate to one side so that he could relax back in the chair and look at her, head tilted to one side.

'You have a way when it comes to asking questions.'

'Maybe it's because I'm a teacher. We're kind of trained to ask questions. So, what do you do? Are you a ski-instructor?'

He laughed again, this time with more amusement, and carried on looking at her, his amazing eyes as intimate as a caress as they rested on her.

'From axe-murderer to ski-instructor with nothing in between.'

'You told me you're self-employed and you... Well, you have a chalet here out on one of the more dangerous runs, so you must be an experienced skier. I'm putting two and two together.'

'You should avoid a career as a detective. No, I'm not a ski instructor, as it happens, even if I am proficient on the skis. I work in...tech.'

'Oh.'

'You look disappointed.'

'I always thought that IT people were geeky.'

'Not all.'

Mateo lowered his lashes.

Was this what it felt like to be anonymous, to blend in with the crowd and inhabit a place where no one around you knew who you were?

It was a long time since he'd been in that position. For most of his adult life, as he'd climbed the ladder at dizzying speed, he had become a recognisable commodity. He realised his world had shrunk to contain only people who moved in the same circles as he did. It was safe. Was it also limiting? It was something he hadn't really considered before, because 'safe' equalled 'controlled' and control appealed.

Wealth and power attracted wealth and power and, while he had never courted any social scene, social scenes courted him. He got invitations to prominent events: hobnobbing with the great and the good; parties for openings stuffed with celebrities; and of course all those essential networking dos where the rich and influential mixed with the other rich and influential.

This getaway here was a taste of sanity. Being here with her meant she had no idea who he was and that was beginning to feel a little like a taste of sanity: stolen… temporary…pleasurable. She might not be his type. He definitely didn't go for fluffy, small, voluptuous women who talked a lot, but he could write a book on the appeal of the unpredictable.

All taboo, when he thought about it. He shook himself free of the disturbing feeling of control slipping through his fingers.

'So no argument with your boyfriend has brought you here,' Mateo inserted briskly. 'You were overcome with a need for some fresh air.'

'Not as such.'

'What does that mean?'

He opened his mouth to tell her again that he didn't care whether she confided in him or not, that in fact he would rather she didn't, but some base-level curiosity got the better of him and he shot her an encouraging look.

'Well,' Alice confided in a hitched voice. 'My friend announced her engagement with lots of fanfare and champagne-cork-popping and I…well… I guess it just got to me. I was engaged eight months ago and… I broke it off. It's not as though I'm sad that it ended, but all of a sudden I just felt empty inside and I had to get away. So, when I say the blizzard swept in from nowhere, it might have been a case of being so lost in my thoughts that I didn't notice the sky getting darker and the snow getting thicker. At least, not until it was too late to do anything about it.'

Mateo shifted because, generally speaking, he disliked all this touchy-feely stuff. But then frowned as he saw tears begin to gather in the corner of her eyes. He hastily scouted round for something useful and settled on some paper towels on the kitchen counter, which he pushed over to her.

'If you ditched the guy then why are you shedding tears over him? It obviously wasn't much of a relationship.'

'How can you say that?' Alice rounded on him and vigorously dabbed her eyes.

'You dumped him.'

'Doesn't mean—'

'Doesn't mean what?'

'Doesn't mean it didn't hurt. Simon and I went back a long way. I'd known him since I was fifteen! He should have been the ideal guy for me.'

'Mmm.'

'What's that supposed to mean?'

Mateo shrugged. 'I'm the last person qualified to give advice on the makings of a good relationship, but if you'd known the guy since you were a kid, then maybe it was all just a little too cosy. Cosy,' he said wryly, 'is just a cousin once removed from boring, and who wants a boring partner?'

He looked at her with guarded appreciation and a little voice whispered to him, *what would it be like, this woman who is so different from anyone else you've ever known...?*

He shifted and cleared his head of the treacherous thought. It just didn't pay to have thoughts like that. Bianca had been *different* once upon a time, until she'd ended up being just the same.

'Simon was far from boring.'

'So did the excitement get too much for you?'

'I don't know why I bothered to say anything to you about this,' Alice muttered.

She met his gaze with fierce resistance but was thrown by the cool, amused, all-knowing, *worldly* look in the green eyes resting on her.

What must he think of her? She shouldn't care but suddenly she saw herself through his eyes: small, could lose a few pounds, way too talkative and willing to confide, even in the face of all his signals that he was not that interested.

He might be an IT nerd but, with his looks, she reckoned he could have anyone he wanted, and from what she had seen of his chalet he was also not living in penury. He was one of those IT nerds with cash and those were in high demand. So was it any surprise that he found her *amusing*, after his initial horror that she had ruined his holiday for one? He didn't see her as *a woman*. He saw her as a novelty toy: wind her up and watch her go. At least, that was her suspicion, and it was making her self-conscious.

'I'm sorry,' he surprised her by saying quietly. 'I don't mean to make fun of you or to somehow belittle what you've been through. It must have been tough, breaking off an engagement...'

'It was,' Alice said, drawn once again into his orbit and seduced into opening up, because there was something so compelling about him. 'Everyone expected us to end up together, and I felt awful, because Simon is the nicest guy in the world.'

But just a tiny bit boring, she thought with a rare flash of acerbity. *Way too cosy...way too much of a known quantity...* 'I know what you're going to say.'

'Do you? Enlighten me.'

'You're going to say that *nice* equals *boring*.'

'Ah, was I? Thank you for filling me in. Saves me the bother of saying anything.'

'You wouldn't understand. I bet you've never experienced a broken engagement before—never known what it was like to pin your hopes on something, only for it to dissolve at the last minute.'

The silence that greeted this stretched and stretched until Alice began to fidget and wonder whether an apology might not be in order, although it wasn't as though she'd asked him anything personal or been in any way offensive. He'd glanced down but now, as he raised his eyes to hers, they were cool and remote.

'Can I ask something?'

'What?' Alice said cautiously.

'How old are you?'

'Twenty-four.'

'Don't you think you're very young to be thinking

about embarking on love, marriage and the whole nine yards?'

Alice thought about her happily married parents, having met when they'd still been teenagers going to the same school. There had been a brief separation when they had gone to different universities but breaking up had never occurred to them.

She uneasily wondered whether she had thrown herself into Simon in a subconscious desire to emulate the example her parents had set. Or had she just been lazy in following a path that had been set for her without examining whether that was *her* path?

'You're never too young to fall in love,' she said vaguely.

'But you didn't, did you? You made a mistake.'

'Well...'

'Not my problem. But, if you want to take some advice from someone a little further down the road than you, then I would say forget about the "true love" business at the moment. You have your life ahead of you; plenty of leg room to see what's out there before you go looking for whatever it is you're looking for.'

'See what's out there?'

'Have fun and forget about the love,' Mateo murmured in a low, silky voice that made the hairs on the back of her neck stand on end.

Have fun... I bet you'd be a lot of fun...

The thought leapt out at her with such surprising force that she was briefly struck dumb. She stared at him, her colour mounting, taking in the perfect symmetry of his face, his blatant sexuality and the lazy drift of his eyes that never left her face.

Surely he wasn't flirting with her? That would be highly inappropriate, she decided.

At this point she felt that a jolt of alarm was in order. She should rise to her feet and say something about feeling tired and needing to get some rest. He wouldn't stop her because, if there was one thing her gut instinct told her, it was that this guy was a gentleman, despite the arrogant, self-assured veneer and the annoying way he had of getting under her skin by telling her stuff she didn't want to hear.

Instead, a buzz of forbidden excitement anchored her to the chair and she felt her pulse begin to pick up pace. Her body felt sensitive under the baggy clothes, *his* baggy clothes.

She fidgeted and then kept very still, just in case he noticed.

'I'll certainly have fun,' she said politely.

'Want some cheese? It's the only dessert I eat.'

'You have a lot of dos and don'ts in your life, don't you?'

'What do you mean?'

Mateo was efficient when it came to tidying up behind himself. One more didn't add much to the process. He brought three packs of exotic soft cheeses out of the fridge, along with crackers from the cupboard, and could tell that she was sorely tempted to join him but for some reason had decided that she would be ladylike and refuse.

How was she to know that he liked the way she enjoyed her food? He was also surprising himself with his tolerance when it came to her airing her views about this, that and everything under the sun, despite the fact that she surely must have read the room and noted that he was not the most encouraging person in the world when it came to people sharing their opinions *of* him *with* him. In fact, thinking about it, hadn't he already made that perfectly clear on a couple of occasions?

'I mean...' Mateo watched with interest as she leant forward. Her arms were resting on the table and her breasts were nestled on her arms. They were abundant enough to push against the baggy clothes and it was making his imagination go into overdrive. 'Mmm...?' he encouraged absently as he felt the stirring of an erection. It was disobeying everything it was being told to do, namely to stop saluting and stand down.

She leant forward a little more. He wondered what she would look like under his clothes: rosy nipples, taut, tender and waiting to be kissed; the weight of heavy breasts in his big hands; the glorious perfection of wet womanhood opening up to him like a flower...

He drew in a sharp breath and sank a little lower in his chair.

'You don't do movies.' She ticked off each point on her fingers in a very prim manner that was also something of a turn-on. 'You don't do dessert, which means you probably don't do chocolate or ice-cream; you clearly don't do sharing of confidences, and you probably don't do love and marriage either, because you prefer to have fun, no strings attached...'

'I admit that's a fair summary of me.' He grinned. 'There *are*, however, quite a few things that I *do* do.' He relaxed in the chair and realised that he was thoroughly enjoying himself. He took his time sampling some of the Brie and then pushed it over to Alice, gratified when she distractedly wedged some off with one of the crackers. He vaguely thought that it would be highly satisfying to take her to one of the terrific restaurants he went to in London and have her sample some of the finest food the capital had to offer. Not, he reminded himself, that that was on the cards.

'I *do*...' he tabulated on his fingers '...work hard and I *do*...' he looked at her from under sooty, long lashes '...play hard.'

Thickening silence greeted this remark. Mateo noted the heightened colour that stole into her cheeks. She had a wonderfully transparent face, devoid of all artifice and guile. It wasn't just the way she looked, though. It wasn't just the satiny smoothness of her skin, the luminosity of her hazel eyes or the fact that her perfect hourglass figure did something crazy to his libido.

Her appeal lay in more than that. She dared to be one hundred percent genuine around him and that was a novelty. She didn't play games—maybe because she didn't know who he was, but he wanted to think that she just wasn't a game player. He could spot those a mile off, whatever tactics they used and he could deal with them. In many ways, game players were a known quantity and when you were a billionaire, he figured they came with the territory. The woman who had just given him a stern critique of his failings was unique in all her differences.

He could tell from her expression that he had embarrassed her. Most women at this point would have fallen over themselves to explore his ambiguous rejoinder. She, however, was looking at him as though he had suddenly decided to do a striptease without warning her in advance.

'Apologies.' He held up his hands in a gesture of rueful surrender, belying the fact that his erection was still as hard as steel. 'Just a thoughtless, light-hearted remark.'

'No! No, no, no! Of *course* I understand that. When you're freelance and having to work every day to get a pay packet, because if you have a day off you don't get paid, then you need to let your hair down now and again.'

'My life isn't exactly that tortured.' Mateo had the decency to flush at this sweeping misunderstanding of his position in life. He could frankly walk away from it all tomorrow and still have enough money to cruise through life in a way most people could only dream of doing.

'And I can also understand,' Alice said with bald sincerity, 'why you were so annoyed when I banged on your door and you were forced to let me in, a complete stranger.'

'You can…?'

'You probably don't get heaps of time off.'

'I do work long hours, now that you mention it.'

'So you get your one week here, or maybe two, and it's interrupted by me. Can I ask…where is your permanent home?'

'I…' Mateo opened his mouth to say what came naturally to him, which was that he had several places. Although, he might be hard pushed to call any of them *home*, as such, which implied open fires and a dog somewhere, along with a partner waiting for him every evening with a hot meal and his slippers at the ready. 'I live in London.'

Her face lit up.

'So do I!' She looked at him sympathetically. 'I guess you probably don't live in the sort of place I live in.' She

smiled without rancour. 'If you can afford this as a holiday home then you're not broke, which is good. Poverty
can be a burden that pushes many off the cliff edge.'

'I guess you could say that I'm not penniless.' Mateo's
antennae vibrated because the last thing he wanted was
to get involved in a discussion about what he could or
couldn't afford, even though he could see that she was utterly guileless in her questioning. A fundamental caring
nature shone through everything she said. It was fascinating. The world he inhabited was dog-eat-dog and the
women he dated enjoyed the challenge of dating a guy
who lived in the fast lane. Right now he could be talking
to someone from another planet.

'Or maybe you rent this place out when you're not
using it? That would pay the overheads...'

'Indeed.'

'And then gives you enough to have somewhere modest, because honestly, getting onto the property ladder in
London is a nightmare, isn't it?'

'Total nightmare.' He thought of his six-bedroomed
house in Holland Park with its manicured gardens in the
front and rear and its own gym and swimming pool in
the basement.

'I have no idea whether I'll ever be able to afford anything bigger than a box on my salary.' She sighed. 'Anyway, I get you value your time here, and didn't want it
interrupted.'

'Well,' Mateo mused silkily, 'now that it has been, I
must tell you that I'm finding it far less onerous than I
ever thought possible...'

CHAPTER THREE

THE BLIZZARD ABATED but the snow kept falling, a steady sheet of never-ending white.

They stood outside surveying the scene.

He'd washed her stuff so she could get back into her thermals but, rather than don the whole ensemble when she wouldn't be going anywhere near her skis, Alice had opted to wear some more of Mateo's clothes. She tugged the sleeves of the jumper to cover her balled fists but, despite all the layers, five seconds outside made her exposed skin pinch with cold. Next to her, she could feel Mateo's warmth and the unsettling power of his proximity.

The night before seemed like a dream. Had she imagined the frisson that had shimmered between them, tantalising and forbidden? She remembered landing on his doorstep like an unwanted package. She remembered how antagonistic he had been when he'd opened the door and found her outside. He hadn't been downright hostile, but he'd made it clear that she wasn't wanted, that he was only taking her in because there was no alternative. On a scale of one to ten, his welcome had scored a paltry four.

His attitude should have got her back up but somehow he'd managed to get under her skin, even though he hadn't made the slightest effort to charm. She remembered all that.

But had she *misremembered* the way the evening had progressed? Of course, she'd talked too much; that was just who she was. She'd talked and laughed, wine had been poured and his attitude had relaxed. He'd obviously chosen to go down the pragmatic road of accepting the inevitable with as good a grace as humanly possible Those cool, green eyes had rested on her... and that was when it all got a little blurry. Had she imagined a flicker of heat there? Had she imagined a thread of electricity that had ignited between them, sizzling quietly under the patter of their conversation like a firecracker?

He worked hard and he played hard...

She remembered that and she remembered wondering whether he'd been flirting with her, just for that second. It was all so *blurry.* What *wasn't* blurry was the thought that had followed her to sleep and wakened her in the morning, and that was the realisation that something about the man *excited* her.

She didn't know why but he did. She'd woken groggily a couple of hours earlier and had lain perfectly still for a few minutes, indulging in a bout of utter mortification that she might just have made a fool of herself the evening before.

Had she misread signals that hadn't been there and said anything that could have been misinterpreted? She wasn't used to alcohol and she couldn't quite remember how much she'd drunk. On the plus side, she hadn't fallen off her chair in a drunken stupor. On the minus side, she just might have stared at him a little too avidly, like a starstruck teenager, or worse—a desperate woman craving attention from a good-looking guy, having just recovered from a broken engagement. She might have attempted to flirt, having misinterpreted something said in jest.

By the time she'd dressed and left the room, she'd decided that the best route forward while she was stuck here—because one glance outside her window had killed any hope of heading back to her chalet today—was to pretend that the evening before hadn't happened. To have no blurry memories of sparks that might or might not have been there. No trying to wade through and analyse whatever conversation they had had. No wondering whether he had flirted with her. And no constant chatting and over-sharing.

She had been unnaturally quiet as they had shared breakfast, and had politely insisted on doing the dishes while he'd dealt with whatever early-morning emails it seemed he had to do. When he had resurfaced an hour later, again with stunning politeness she had agreed that they should check what was happening outside.

It had been draining.

At any rate, here they were now, and she shivered and glanced sideways at him.

Unfairly, he was as devastatingly handsome this morning as he had been the day before. That was one instance where, unfortunately, her imagination had not been playing tricks on her.

'At least the wind's died down,' she said.

'Still snowing pretty hard, though.'

'It's a shame. I'd hoped it might have abated overnight.' She wondered whether anyone ever spoke like that, using words such as 'abated'. *She* certainly didn't; it felt unnatural. 'I'd hoped,' she continued, 'that I might have been able to ski back to my chalet this morning, and enjoy the rest of my holiday with my friends instead of being cooped up here, but I'm not entirely sure that's going to happen.'

'We should head back inside. No point freezing to death out here chit-chatting about how heavy the snow is.'

'Indeed,' Alice heard herself say.

He headed in and she followed, watching him as he preceded her and, much as she didn't want to, appreciating the lithe grace of his body as he cut a path through the snow to his front door, making it easy for her to follow in his footsteps.

He was in black: black roll-neck jumper, black jogging bottoms and a black waterproof which he wore with careless elegance.

If she'd made the mistake of flirting with him the evening before, then Lord knew he'd probably spent the night roaring with laughter in his head. Even if he did something as boring as work in tech, he was so good-looking that women would probably beat a path to his door.

It was wonderfully warm inside and she shed her outer layers with alacrity, stripping down to one of his long-sleeved tee-shirts and some of his jogging bottoms.

Then she stood back and looked at him for a few seconds while he stared back at her.

'Spit it out.'

'I beg your pardon?' Alice said.

'You've been acting a little odd all morning. What's bothering you? Is it the fact that you've realised you have no choice but to stay *cooped up here* for another day?'

Alice flushed. 'Sorry, I didn't mean to sound ungrateful. *Cooped up* isn't the right word. I was, yes, just hoping that I might be on my way, so you'll have to excuse me if I'm not my usual self this morning.'

'You barely had any breakfast. You must be hungry.'

'I had more than enough.' Alice drew herself up to her very unimpressive five-three height and sucked in her stomach.

'Right. Well, I suppose we should discuss how the day is going to unfold. More coffee?'

He headed off to the kitchen without waiting for an answer and Alice followed him. In the cold light of day, and freed from the aftermath of her near-death experience on the slopes in a blizzard, she had taken the opportunity to really look at the chalet properly.

It was very, *very* luxurious but in an understated way. There was nothing flash anywhere but she could tell that all the bathroom fittings in her *en suite* were of the highest standard. There was a lot of marble and the towels were the sort that must have cost the earth. And, again, the bedroom was understated luxury. The linen was soft and silky and probably had the highest possible threadcount. The cupboards were made of solid wood and the rug on the ground, like all the rugs in the lodge, was softly faded, with the sheen of pure silk.

The view from the windows was absolutely staggering: vistas of pristine white, a vision of another world uncluttered by houses, people, restaurants, shops or life at all, come to think of it.

Fixing people's computers or designing websites obviously paid big-time.

Looking around the kitchen, she could see that everything in it likewise carried the stamp of quality. She sat and smoothed her hand over the table and watched as he made a pot of coffee.

* * *

'So, do you do lots of skiing while you're here? You must be an excellent skier to tackle these slopes. Where did you learn?'

Mateo turned round, carried the coffee to the table and then sat opposite her, angling his chair so that he could extend his legs to the side, crossed at the ankles.

He'd had a restless night. It had never happened before, not here. Here, he could always bank on some solid, battery-recharging down time. But he'd gone to bed thinking of the woman sitting opposite him and wondering why she'd managed to get to him the way she had.

He'd found himself actively looking forward to seeing her this morning—crazy. And, crazier, the fact that she was off for some reason and that, too, was bugging him. It seemed he'd completely forgotten lessons learnt from past experience, from a tough childhood, an even tougher adolescence and a woman who had done a number on him. He just didn't get it. He'd could have given a master class on how to avoid the pitfalls of being vulnerable to anything and anyone…and yet this woman ignited something inside him. Uneasily, he knew that it wasn't just physical.

'I…have experience of these mountains. I learnt to ski here when I was very young. Start young enough, and you become a master before you hit your teens. Same with every sport.' He shrugged and was about to change the subject when she interrupted.

'Agreed. I learnt reasonably young when my class went on a ski trip. I absolutely loved it from the beginning. I just loved the way flying down those slopes made me feel free.'

Momentarily distracted, with a shuttered expression

Mateo watched her mobile, expressive heart-shaped face. Her eyes were bright and she was leaning forward, her unruly hair tumbling over her shoulders and her chin propped in one hand. Her natural sunny nature was coming through once again, and it was weird how satisfied that made him feel.

No harm letting the conversation flow, he concluded.

He didn't want her feeling down while she was here. That was simply because it would make for an uncomfortable atmosphere—not because he, personally, liked to see her smile and hear her laugh.

'Free from what?' he probed.

'Oh, you know, the usual stuff... I adore my parents, but I'm an only child, and even though they always made a big point of letting me do my own thing I still always felt them hovering in the background.' She laughed. He noticed her laughter rippled like water over stones. 'You know how parents are—they can be super-protective even when they don't want to be. What about you—are you an only child?'

'I am, as it happens.'

'Then I'll bet you get what I'm talking about.'

'Not entirely.' Mateo flushed darkly as her hazel eyes rested on him, curious but not intrusive, just gently questioning. Then, without thinking, he said in a rough undertone, 'My mother died when I was young—eight. I was raised by my father.'

'Oh, my word, Mateo, I'm so sorry. How awful that must have been for you.'

Mateo instinctively made to pull back as she reached out to him, but then he let his hand rest on the table and let his fingers be squeezed by hers.

'You're very emotional, aren't you?' he said gruffly. 'I'm not a great believer in all this kumbaya nonsense.' But, still, her fingers were warm and the feel of them stirred something in him. He remembered what it had felt like to look after his father, to be that amateur boxer fighting for money, to be working life out on his own. To be on a road no kid should have been on from the age of eight. To know, far too young, that the only person who could save him was himself.

'I'm not emotional, I'm empathetic. It must have been a horrible time for you, and lonely as well. I'm sure your father was wonderful, but sometimes the grief of adults can take over, leaving their kids stranded for a while.'

'I… I admit something like that did occur, but naturally I rose to the occasion and found a way out. It's in the past.' He tugged his hand free but could still feel the warmth of her skin against his. 'Something else I don't do that you can add to your list: I don't dwell. Only reason I mentioned it at all was to say that my experiences as an only child perhaps don't quite dovetail with yours. But, getting back to what we need to discuss: plans for how today is going to unfold.'

'How did you cope? Were there other family members around you to help you deal with the situation?'

'Now you're beginning to sound like a therapist on a mission,' Mateo said wryly. 'For the record, there were no aunts and uncles fretting and clucking. I coped with the situation the way I have always coped with all situations: on my own.'

Alice felt her heart go out to the guy whose face was so unrevealing of the hurt he must have endured as a child.

He was so commanding and so tough, yet underneath there surely must be a vulnerability there, a hangover from his childhood experiences?

'It must have been lonely. How long did your dad hide away, Mateo?'

'Whoever said anything about *hiding away*?' He clicked his tongue impatiently but her eyes never left his face. 'A few years,' he expanded. 'He took time off for a few years.'

'And you were left to pick up the pieces all on your own,' Alice murmured softly.

'Setbacks always make a person stronger.'

She didn't say anything. She just continued to gaze at him in silence then she nodded and took a deep breath. 'Of course, you're right: setbacks can make you stronger. So, today…'

He was proud. Taking this conversation any further was going to make him shut down and Alice got the feeling that, once Mateo shut down, he would never open up again. Of course, she wasn't going to be around to have any more deep and meaningful conversations with him about his past, but curiosity about him bit into her with sharp, persistent teeth.

Also, for reasons she couldn't fathom, she didn't want him to turn away from her because she was getting too nosey. She didn't know why it mattered but it did—maybe because they were confined here, so it was best for them to get along. Yes, that was it.

'About today…' Mateo drawled, picking up where she had left off and strolling to the coffee pot on the counter to get a refill. 'I usually catch up on my skiing when

I'm here but, considering there's no chance of that, I will spend my time catching up on work instead.'

'Really? You can do that computer stuff remotely?'

'Yes,' Mateo said gently. 'That "computer stuff" can all be done remotely.'

'And I suppose time is money when you're working for yourself.'

'Never a truer word has ever been spoken. I have an office off my suite, so you won't see me for most of the day. Sadly, there's nothing here I can think of to occupy your time, and in the absence of a spare laptop...'

'I can do stuff on my phone. I can plan out lessons for the remainder of the term. Do you have any paper— pens, perhaps?'

'Paper? Pens?'

Alice burst out laughing. 'Now you're making me think of some of my children at school,' she teased. 'They're experts when it comes to computers, but show them a pen and tell them to write an essay and suddenly I'm asking them to fly to the moon. I teach eleven-year-olds, and my mission is to remind them that the old school way of doing things is still important.'

Mateo grinned. 'Technology makes everything quicker.'

'Which is why it makes our brains lazy. If you can press a button and have all the information you need right there, then how are you ever going to learn the value of research?'

'The "click of the button" scenario leaves time for other important things to be done instead of sifting through old tomes in a library and highlighting sentences and fold-ing pages...'

'Both of which would incur a fine for destruction of public property.' Alice grinned back at him.

'I stand duly corrected.'

Their eyes tangled, the silence stretched and Mateo was the first to break it.

'And to answer your question,' he said gruffly, 'I happen to have both.' He stood up, suddenly keen to escape the confines of the kitchen, which now felt suffocating. One minute he'd been backing away from a personal conversation he hadn't encouraged but seemed to be indulging, and the next minute she was making him laugh.

He was suddenly keen to escape. He needed time-out. He would confine himself to his office and stay put until he got his act together. He left her sitting at the kitchen table and returned five minutes later with a stack of A4 paper and a selection of pens in different colours.

'You use this stuff?'

'The paper, yes. The pens were bought as a standby years ago, just in case the broadband went down and I actually had to…work on some designs manually.'

'Okay.'

'So…er… I'll leave these with you. If you need me, I'll be in my office, but don't count on me for lunch. Help yourself to whatever you want; the fridge is fully stocked. I'll grab something at some point. When I'm working I tend to forget the time.'

'Very bad for you, you know,' she returned absently.

'What's very bad for me?'

'Too much work.'

'Like I said, Alice Reynolds, I play as well as work…'

Alice was forcibly reminded of the evening before, when the conversation between them had felt dangerously close to the edge…politeness rubbing shoulders with the sort of sexual undertones she wasn't used to but which had electrified her.

She felt as though she'd entered a whole new world. Mateo was so different from any man she had ever come into contact with. He might have a boring job but he certainly was far from boring. He was sophisticated, cynical and had the sort of self-assurance that made her tingle all over. But more than that, and more than his stunning looks, there was a sense of complexity about him that had roused her curiosity...and, yes, *turned her on*.

Compared to this beast, Simon was a boy. It was disloyal, but she wondered what she'd seen in him, aside from safety. Just admitting that made her go hot and cold.

'So you mentioned,' she mumbled, thrown back into politeness as words failed her and he burst out laughing.

'Only bores repeat themselves. Am I sensing an insult in there somewhere?'

'No!' Alice reddened and bristled but then grinned sheepishly. 'You're teasing, aren't you?'

'Guilty as charged.'

Mateo appreciated the delicate bloom in her cheeks. He could have added 'teasing' to the list of things he didn't do. But he enjoyed the way she blushed. He'd forgotten what that looked like.

'I'll catch you later,' he muttered. 'If the snow starts to lessen, I'll probably try and do some clearing outside; get it as ready as possible for you to make your escape. There are several rooms towards the back you can use if you want privacy to do whatever you plan on doing... and, like I said, help yourself to whatever you want from the fridge.'

He left before another conversation could commence, luring him in in ways he knew vaguely he shouldn't really like but did.

But work—the thing that always drove him, the one thing that took priority over everything else—proved difficult as the day wore on. By the time he hit the space he used as his office, it was close to lunchtime. He took only a brief break to rustle up a sandwich some time mid-afternoon, with the sun already on its way to setting and the snow still falling thick and fast with no sign of letting up.

Where was Alice?

Having spent hours in front of his computer with very little to show for it, Mateo had a job not hunting her down. His chalet wasn't the biggest in the world but there were nooks and crannies to which she could have retreated, including her suite. He held off knocking on any closed doors but, by the time six rolled round and he'd had a shower and was heading downstairs, he was caught in unusual position of restlessly anticipating something, against his better judgement: *anticipating seeing her.*

She'd lodged in his head and there was no point denying the fact that he *wanted* her. His formidable self-control had deserted him, all because of a woman who just wasn't his type and frankly should have got on his nerves...*sexy as hell or not.* She was as wholesome as apple pie and as sweet as chocolate, and neither of those things were what he looked for in a woman. So what was going on? Was novelty that powerful?

Scowling at a train of thought that refused to go away, Mateo pushed open the kitchen door and then...stopped dead in his tracks. She was there, fridge door open, bending in search of something and offering a sight that made him break out in perspiration. She was in her thermal leggings and they were stretched tight across a peachy rear. The baggy sweater was his but it had ridden up, exposing a sliver of pale skin at her waist.

He was frozen to the spot, and thoughts about why he was so attracted to her were replaced by a series of graphic images that made him feel unsteady. How long had he been standing there staring at her like a horny schoolboy? When she straightened and turned round, he felt as though he'd been caught with his fingers in the till.

Alice hadn't heard him.

How had he managed that? For a guy who was so big, he moved with the stealth of a jungle cat. She blinked, caught completely off-guard. He'd had a shower. His hair was still slightly damp and he was in a pair of faded jeans and a rugby shirt, the sleeves of which he'd shoved up to the elbows.

How long had he been standing in the doorway looking at her?

She frantically tried to think whether she'd made an idiot of herself somehow, bending over to find something to peck on, something sweet and contraband but very much needed after a day of thinking about the guy standing in front of her and feverishly analysing every word they had exchanged.

'I—I…' she stuttered, not moving a muscle. 'I was just…um…looking for something to eat.'

She shut the fridge door but remained where she was as he strolled towards her. With every step closer, her heart beat a little faster, and the blood in her veins felt a little hotter, because there was *something* in that lazy, green gaze that was *hot*.

She licked her lips and stuck her hands behind her back.

'You shouldn't do that,' he ground out shakily.

'Sorry, you said I could help myself to...'

'Not *that*.'

'Then what are you talking about?' Alice raised her eyes to look at him. He was so close that with almost no effort she could reach out and flatten her palm on his chest, and right now there was nothing in the world she would rather do. It was confusing and bewildering, but felt stupidly *right*, as though there was some powerful electrical connection between them that had sprung from nowhere.

'Bend over like that,' he returned thickly. 'Any red-blooded guy would have trouble resisting...'

'Resisting what?' Just saying those two words felt like the greatest act of daring she had ever undertaken. The challenge of breaking off her engagement faded in comparison. Alice had never been bold like this. She hadn't been raised to ask sexually provocative questions.

A rush of liberating self-discovery flooded her. In not so many words, Mateo had laughed at the concept of a cosy relationship with a boring guy, had laughed at the idea of settling down at the tender of age of twenty-four, and naturally she had bristled in angry response. But this felt good. She was daring to stray from the straight and narrow and it felt great.

'Touching. Want me to spell it out? *Touching.* Because I stood there at the door and saw you bending over and all I wanted to do was touch you.'

He shook his head, raked his fingers through his dark hair and shot her a frustrated look from under his lashes. 'Apologies,' he muttered. 'Forget I said that.'

'Maybe I don't want to,' Alice returned then, stretching recklessness to the point of no return, she did what she'd been itching to do and rested her hand on his chest.

His chest was all muscle under the sweater. She felt faint.

'No?' came a lazy drawl. His hand covered hers. 'Then tell me, Alice Reynolds, what you *do* want...'

'You.'

Had she really said that? Yes, she had, and it was more than liberating...it was empowering!

'I want *you*, Mateo Whatever-your-last-name-might-be!'

'Are you sure, Alice?' This time his voice was utterly serious, giving her time and space to think, to reconsider, to walk away from something she might rashly have suggested. Alice appreciated that more than she could have said and she gave the question the consideration it deserved.

'I'm sure.' She met his eyes steadily, even though her heart was beating madly inside her and every nerve in her body was at breaking point. 'I've never done anything like this before,' she confessed in a staccato rush. 'I guess you could say I've led a sheltered life.'

'I think I'd already deduced that, which why I'm telling you right now that, if you want to walk away from this, then you can. I might have to take several cold showers to calm my erection, but so be it.'

'Erection...' She rolled that sexy word on her tongue and melted.

'Would you like to have a feel of what I'm talking about, Alice Reynolds?'

'You've probably slept with way more experienced women…'

'You mean as the ski-instructor I'm not? You turn me on. And I'm not lying when I say that I can't remember ever being turned on by any woman like this.'

'Really?'

'Too much talking!' He groaned.

He took her hand and guided it to the bulge under his jeans. Alice closed her eyes and just wanted to pass out. She fumbled with the zip, eventually managed to tug it down, then she hooked her fingers into the waistband and daringly lowered the jeans.

She looked down at the black boxers and then circled his erection through the light cotton. It was thick and impressively big. She was so wet for him that her underwear felt irritating and uncomfortable, but the connection felt too strong to break. She was turned on even more by his groan of pleasure as she reached into his boxers to feel the muscle and sinew of his hardness. Raw instinct and driving desire replaced her lack of experience. She began to stroke him in long, regular slow strokes, watching as she touched, wanting to take him in her mouth so that the connection could get even stronger. Wanting *him* to do the same to her, to touch her and take her in his mouth.

'I'm not going to be able to hold off if you keep doing that,' he said hoarsely and then he scooped her up and began walking towards his bedroom. He carried her as though she weighed nothing. It was downright thrilling. He kicked shut the bedroom door behind them and then gently laid her on his bed as though she were a piece of delicate porcelain.

He pressed a remote and the shutters came down on the scene outside of snowy, grey twilight, leaving them in shadow. She was still fully dressed but now she watched as he shed what remained of his clothes, the jumper and the boxers, to stand completely naked in front of her. He was all gorgeous, rampant alpha male and, for tonight, *all hers*—a looming, heart-stopping invitation to untold pleasure.

'Enjoying the view?' He smiled and moved towards her. 'My turn now...'

CHAPTER FOUR

ALICE WONDERED WHERE this passionate side of her had been hiding all her life. Simon had certainly not managed to locate it and yet she had never given that a second's thought; she had simply accepted that love was something calm and controlled.

Maybe it was, she thought now in a muddled way, thrilling to his approach as he settled on the mattress and began the business of *enjoying the view*.

Maybe love was calm and controlled but this thing she felt wasn't love—it was desire.

In hindsight, she might not have loved Simon, although she'd been super-fond of him. She'd certainly never *wanted* him, not like this, not with this feeling of her whole body going up in flames.

Mateo tugged down the lined leggings which she had worn, because she'd known that they'd hardly be visible under his sweater, which almost reached her knees. She was breathing quickly as the leggings were stripped off and she squeezed her eyes tightly shut to block out any rush of self-consciousness at the sight of her pale thighs exposed to his roving gaze.

He was so beautiful and she was so...*nothing to write home about*.

'Don't…' she heard him murmur softly. She opened one eye to look at him and saw that he was smiling.

He abandoned the striptease and moved to lie alongside her, then he manoeuvred her so that they were looking at one another, her breasts pushing against his chest, her bare legs against his.

'Don't what?' she asked, both eyes open now, but shyly.

'Close your eyes. How can you enjoy what I want to do to you if you're not looking at me?'

'You're so beautiful, Mateo.'

He burst out laughing and, when he looked at her next, his gaze was hot and the smile was still lingering there.

'So are you. And you're so refreshing…and sexy… and funny…'

'You're just saying that.'

'Open your eyes and enjoy the way I touch you…like this.'

Alice kept her eyes locked to his as he slipped his hand underneath the crotch of her underwear and wriggled his finger into her wet crease until he found the pulsing bud of her clitoris. She gasped, squirmed and then gripped his shoulders. The thick sweater was an impediment and her breasts felt heavy and sensitive underneath it.

'See how much better that is?' he purred with silky assurance. 'It's even better when we talk…and I don't mean make small talk about the weather; I mean something a little raunchier than that. Maybe we'll leave that for the moment. For the moment…just keep your eyes open. Let me see the expression on your face when I touch you.'

Alice was in a world she'd never known existed. An explosion of desire burst inside her like a firecracker and she fumbled, tugged and unclasped until not only the cloying sweater had been removed, but the vest and bra underneath. Her eyes were very much wide open as she took in his rampant, masculine appreciation at the sight of her breasts.

It was an out-of-body experience, something she had never imagined possible. She was no longer Alice Reynolds who had always stuck to the straight and narrow, and in whom principles of what was and wasn't expected had been embedded. She'd burst through those barriers into a whole different world and was, just for now, just in this instant, a reckless, wanton woman with needs that shocked her.

She groaned, writhed and kept looking as he straddled her and sank to explore her breasts with his hands, mouth and tongue. He took an engorged nipple into his mouth and tugged the straining bud until she was on the point of coming even though his fingers were no longer teasing her down there.

It was so erotic, so exquisite. There was no room for inhibitions of any kind as he suckled on her nipples and then explored further, licking a delicate trail down her stomach and finding the place he had found with his finger but this time with his tongue. The intimacy of it made her want to squeeze her legs shut but he parted her thighs and, when he began to lick her, she had to stifle the guttural cries of pleasure that wanted to find a way out of her.

The rise of passion bursting its banks was unstoppable and she spasmed against his exploring mouth, her whole body shuddering and arching. Her mind went completely blank and, when the final quivers subsided, their eyes met and he gave a satisfied smile. He fumbled to find his wallet and produced a condom, which made her think vaguely that this was a guy who took no chances.

Her body was still throbbing, gearing up for that final, deep satisfaction that would come from feeling him inside her, and she parted her legs and opened up to him with eagerness and rising desire.

He thrust into her and a reservoir of pleasure she hadn't even known she'd been holding back raced through her and she came again, her rhythm matching his, their bodies perfectly tuned, reaching orgasm at the same time.

It was joyful…earth-shattering and glorious. If she'd thought that the reckless, wanton woman would go back into hiding when the sex was over, then she'd been wrong. The door he'd unlocked was still wide open as he settled next to her, his arm shielding his face as his body began to unwind. She curved against him and gently rested her hand on his chest.

'How was that?' he murmured.

'Very nice, thank you.'

'And to think that I was looking for a more exuberant response.'

But there was laughter in his voice and she smiled against him. 'Is it always like that for you?' Alice murmured drowsily.

'It's been known. Want to have a shower? Head down with me so that something can be done about dinner?'

'I'd completely forgotten about that.'

'Sex does that to a person. Makes you forget what's happening out there in the big, bad world.'

That made Alice think of the big, bad world he referred to, otherwise known as *reality*. She would be back in school in a matter of days. She hadn't phoned her parents, but she would, just as soon as she returned home. Their gentle questioning and eager interest in how her holiday had gone would be a timely reminder that what she was enjoying now was very far removed from her day-to-day life. This flare of attraction had hit them both like a ton of bricks but it wouldn't do to forget that it had only happened because they were stuck here in his lodge, snowbound.

Would their paths ever have crossed otherwise? Not in a month of Sundays. Forget about how different their backgrounds were—they just weren't compatible on any level. She might have taken time-out here from the person she really was but that person would be back in just over a week: cheerful, dependable, easy going...and still looking for the guy of her dreams, who might not be Simon, but certainly could never be someone like this man who had made her body sing.

She would still want a guy who was dependable and steady, the sort of guy that Mateo might find boring, but who would be the guy who would stand by her through the years until they were old and surrounded by kids and grandchildren. She would still want *normal* but with a guy she adored rather than a guy she was fond of. *Normal* would still be the desired goal.

There was a reason people made such a big deal about the differences between love and lust: one was for ever and the other was for five minutes.

'Want to shower with me?' He broke through her thoughts, his voice low, husky and sexy.

'Really?'

'Never done that before?'

'Not as such.'

Mateo laughed. 'What does *not as such* mean? You

took your clothes off, tested the water and then told that guy you dumped that it wasn't the right temperature, maybe another time?'

'Very funny.'

'You're very sweet, Alice.'

'Is that a good thing?'

'It's an unusual thing, at least in my world. In my world, the women aren't sweet.'

'What are they?'

'They're…experienced. Blushing—which you do so well, might I add—is something they left behind before they hit thirteen. You're an only child… Where did you grow up—in London? What do your parents do?'

Alice hesitated. For the first time the thought of admitting that her dad was a vicar felt somehow a little embarrassing. She'd had a pretty idyllic childhood all told, but to this worldly guy, who dated experienced women and had had a tragic background, her relatively uncomplicated life might seem a bit dreary.

She laughed at herself for being silly.

'Well, I was born in a tiny village in Wales, but my family moved to Surrey when I was still quite young.'

'Quite a culture shock I'd imagine. Did you have relatives there? Did your father get a job transfer?'

'You could say it was a job transfer, yes…' She sighed and looked at him a little sheepishly. 'My dad's a vicar, you see.'

'Your dad's *a vicar*?'

'There's no need to sound quite so shocked,' Alice said defensively. 'Lots of people are vicars!'

He stared at her. In the darkness, she could make out

the glitter of his eyes and the shadowy angles of his beautiful face. What was he thinking?

'Makes sense.' His voice was neutral and his eyes were serious. 'There's an innocence to you.' It was his turn to sigh. 'This was a mistake.'

'What?'

'This…us…making love: a mistake.'

'Please don't say that,' Alice whispered. 'Didn't you enjoy it?'

'Of course I did. But, Alice, like I said, I date women with experience, women who know the score when they sleep with me, and by that I mean women who understand that I'm not in it for the long term. They have no illusions. They're not looking for any happy-ever-afters with me. I suppose I should have made that clear at some point before we hit the bedroom but…'

'Why? Why would you have wanted to make that clear?'

Alice forced a laugh, only to find it turning into a genuine one. Hadn't she just been thinking that she could never fall for a guy like Mateo? Weren't they on the same page, neither interested in anything but living in the moment? She didn't regret what they had just done, even though she knew that maybe she should. Or at least maybe she should ask herself searching questions about how she could have jettisoned the part of her that took the sanctity of relationships as given without any thought at all.

She had never imagined that the only guy she dated would be the one she married, even though it had almost turned out that way; but she *had* always believed that a person didn't just hop in the sack because they happened to be attracted to someone. She *had* always believed that relationships had to mean something.

'Look,' she said firmly. 'I know what this is all about. It's about sex. We're attracted to one another, but there are no strings attached, and I'm not going to be looking for anything once the snow melts and I get out of here.' She met his brooding gaze and grinned. 'You're *so* egotistical.'

'What are you talking about?' he said, frowning.

'You're good-looking and you've been spoiled. You feel you've got to give women a bracing talk on not getting over-involved because you're a commitment-phobe. You think that *every* person you sleep with is out for more than you're prepared to give! You'll just have to accept that I'm not one of them.'

'You *are* nothing like anyone I've ever dated,' he agreed, gently pushing her hair back and then letting his hand cup her face.

'I don't want anything from you.'

'And I like that.'

'I certainly would never be interested in any guy who was a commitment-phobe.'

'Wise game-plan.'

'Can I ask why, though?'

Mateo looked at her. She was so fresh-faced and, just for a second, he was tempted to spill out his life story. The temptation came as a shock. He felt as though he was being sucked down into something over which he had no control, a rabbit hole. Some crazy place where he was tempted to let go and see what happened next.

It was enough for him abruptly to step back. Control had got him where he was in life. He had controlled his time, his energies and his focused climb to the top. He had lived through the sadness and despair that had ruined his father when he had lost the love of his life. From his own place of quiet grief—with no one to turn to, because it had felt as though his father had been taken from him along with his mother—he had learned the value of never handing control of his life to someone else.

His love life, after the horror story of Bianca, had been even more controlled, if anything, and after she had showed up asking for money years after their divorce nothing in his life had been left up to chance.

The fact that he had already played fast and loose by allowing his physical attraction to the woman staring at him now to dictate his behaviour was an uncomfortable fact. He had no intention of compounding his lapse by launching into a self-indulgent revisiting of his past or contemplating rabbit holes full of unknown outcomes.

'You can go right ahead and ask.' He tempered the coolness of his voice with a smile. 'But I'll be sticking to "no comment" on that one. And, now that we've had this illuminating conversation, can I entice the sexy vicar's daughter into a little more mutual physical exploration, or will it be shower and something to eat…?'

'Food beckons,' Alice murmured drowsily.

'Agreed.' Mateo's voice was laced with amusement. 'It's important to have stamina when it comes to the business of making love…'

The driving force of the snow eased off but somehow it was agreed that two nights together would become two more.

'Why not?' They'd been in bed at one-thirty in the afternoon, lazy and content after making love, and Mateo's voice had been soft and persuasive. 'We haven't exhausted the passion between us yet, have we? I certainly haven't. I haven't even been tempted to go out there and put the skis on, which is a first for me. So phone your friends and tell them that the kindly family who rescued you from the blizzard want you to stay on until they leave.'

'I'm not sure I mentioned anything about a kindly family,' Alice had returned drowsily, but her mind had already been racing ahead, eagerly accepting his proposition and mothballing the little voice inside her warning her that she was playing with fire.

It had only been a couple of days but he had cast a spell over her. She'd never met anyone like him. She still didn't know that much about him, aside from the skeleton list of facts he had given her in passing, but she didn't care, because what she *did* know was that he was clever, thoughtful, witty and mind-blowingly sexy.

Could stolen time feel more glorious?

She'd made a something and nothing excuse about staying on to her friends, which might have been a little problem, given her limited amount of clothing, but that hadn't mattered because lots of the time was spent without any on at all.

'I'll make it up to you,' she had told Bea on the phone the day before. 'It's so rude, and I know we'd all banked on spending time together, but…'

But she'd discovered a selfish streak in herself and she just hadn't been able to face the prospect of saying goodbye to Mateo. Not yet, not when she didn't have to. And what was so wrong with grabbing this little window of fun and stepping out of her predictable comfort zone? That comfort zone would be waiting for her when she returned to London.

'I just feel that to ski back for the sake of a day before we all leave, well, it feels more recuperative to...er...stay put and recover from my ordeal.'

And she would have another two fantastic days here with Mateo... She was being selfish but it had felt like taking charge of her decision making.

And today they would ski to the little town he had mentioned when she had first landed on his doorstep so that she could replenish her wardrobe. It all felt very clandestine and exciting.

Taking the stairs at a quick trot, she stopped and just gazed at Mateo, who was scrolling on his phone by the door, all black ski gear, his ski sunglasses on his forehead. He was all sexy, gorgeous male.

Not for a second did she regret staying on.

He glanced up at her and smiled slowly.

He'd surprised himself by giving in to impulse and asking her to stay with him for the rest of the time he was at the lodge. Having spent years valuing the sanity and solitude he got here, he'd done a complete about-turn.

She'd said yes, and he'd found that he'd been holding his breath, desperate for her to concur.

'We could always drive. The snow stopped yesterday and the roads down to the town will be passable. No need to take to the slopes.'

He was talking, but mostly relishing the sight of her as she walked towards him. Her ski outfit hugged womanly curves that were still managing to keep him in a state of semi-permanent arousal. She'd tied her hair back and stuffed it into a colourful woolly hat, but tendrils had already escaped, and his fingers itched to twirl one of them round his fingers.

Frankly, he itched to do a hell of a lot more than that. He itched to release the weight of her heavy breasts straining against her stretchy top, to feel them in his hands, to lathe the big, blushing pink nipples with his tongue and mouth, to feel her responsive wetness between her thighs and hear her little cries when he touched her there.

'If we leave now...' he banished those pleasantly erotic images to savour when he could do something about them '...we can be there in twenty minutes and back here within a couple of hours. Lunch at one of the cafés might be nice.'

'We should take a backpack for whatever I buy.'

'Already thought of that. Let's go; if we stay here much longer, I'm going to have to put this little trip on hold and take you back to bed.'

Alice laughed and told him they should take to the slopes and not go by car.

He was a brilliant skier. The conditions were now perfect for skiing: light, steady snow overnight had led to a cushioned, pillowy path down, with just enough grip for her to handle the challenging turns. He kept pace with her and she knew that he was slowing himself down. She was experienced but he took experience to a new level.

They made it to the town in under half an hour and it was as bustling and charming as she had expected, with shops—expensive boutiques catering for the expensive tourist.

Alice had tried to stop him from shopping with her but he'd raised his eyebrows and insisted on accompanying her into the shops. All seven of them, from what he could count.

'You'll be bored,' she'd warned.

'I never get bored looking at you. You could do a few twirls for me. I like the thought of that. I could sit and admire the view whilst smoking a cigar.'

'You don't smoke.'

'True.'

Now, looking at her from under his lashes, Mateo knew exactly what was going through her head: the price of the things she was rifling through. The places here were all exclusive. The salespeople all resembled models and the shops were achingly modern and austere with the clothes arranged artfully on mannequins without heads.

'Let me get this.' He wasn't sure whether this was the right thing to suggest or not, but the embarrassed hesitation on her face and the way she couldn't quite meet his eyes stirred something fiercely protective in him.

'Don't be ridiculous!'

'I persuaded you to stay. If it weren't for me, you'd be back at your chalet with your friends and a suitcase full of clothes you'd brought with you.'

'There's no way I would accept anything from you, Mateo. I know you earn more than me; I'm not blind. But you're still self-employed and I know what that means. You could be earning good money now but you never know what's round the corner.'

'My corners are pretty predictable.'

'I still don't want you getting me anything,' she told him quietly. 'I can't afford much, but I don't need much, and I've already eaten you out of house and home.'

He'd watched as she'd turned away and chosen the

cheapest jumper on show and the cheapest waterproof trousers, along with one pair of grey jogging bottoms. It was such a novel experience, not paying for whatever a woman wanted, that he wasn't sure whether to feel terrible or oddly pleased.

Or deceitful, considering she was oblivious to how much he was worth. He ruled the last out because he wasn't deceiving her. He was simply living in the moment with a woman who was likewise doing the same. Within this scenario, what he earned or didn't earn was irrelevant.

'In that case,' he said, shopping concluded as they stood outside, both of them briefly admiring the quaint buildings and the pretty tree-lined streets, 'I insist on buying lunch. Like you said, I have more than you.'

He'd wanted to do more. He'd wanted to take her into some more shops, buy stuff for her, but knew better than to go near that suggestion.

A couple of hours later, they were back at his lodge, and he smiled wolfishly at her. 'Okay, you denied me the masculine pleasure of treating you to whatever you wanted...'

'I'm very independent like that.' Alice laughed, standing on tiptoe to kiss him.

'Didn't you let your fiancé buy things for you?'

Mateo stripped off, dumping outer garments on hooks and ski boots on the ground, watching her as he did so.

'That's different, and anyway, there wasn't much money flying around for unnecessary purchases.'

'So that's "he didn't treat me to little surprise gifts because he was thoughtless"...'

Alice burst out laughing, her eyes warm and alight. 'You bought lunch. I'll cook for you in return.' She looked at him, her expression trusting and open, a smile still playing on her lips. 'Or, at any rate, I'll give it a go.'

Mateo stilled. He had never done domesticity. He and Bianca had gone out, socialising with the glamorous crew that tagged along in the wake of successful sportsmen, and he had been a very successful amateur boxer with his admiring followers. But cosy nights in had been few and far between. Bianca had loathed cooking. They'd eaten out most nights, or else had takeaways, and in fairness he'd been living with his father when he'd been dating her. And post marriage they'd rented a place, but somehow the business of cooking for one another, watching telly and discussing long term plans had never materialised. They hadn't had that sort of relationship. She'd wanted to socialise, and had wanted the thrill of being admired. There had been no room for domesticity in that scenario and that was just the way he'd liked it.

Buried deep inside him were too many memories of what that domesticity had felt like once upon a time, when he'd been a kid and the house had smelled of cooking and rang to the sound of laughter and love. His parents had been so in love. Domesticity, he'd decided a long time ago, was the flashpoint where want became need, and need became the sort of vulnerability that could be your undoing.

Mateo had always made sure that women didn't get their feet under the table. That was always going to be the safe route. He could handle the woman who wanted glamour and the thrill of being envied and admired by other men. He could handle the women who were like his ex, because they were a known quantity. He liked it that way and the women he dated liked it that way as well. They enjoyed being treated to the very best money could offer and, as someone accustomed to being a loner, he was content with that. Enjoyment without emotional involvement: standard procedure.

He'd done the cooking since Alice had arrived, which was fair enough: his house, his food, his responsibility. But now, just like that, he realised how much he had confided in her, how much of himself he had exposed.

Suddenly he was gripped by an uneasy claustrophobia. Alice was chatting, moving to the fridge and whipping out stuff to make a meal. In the space of only a few days, she knew the layout of this kitchen as well as he did. Hell, when had that happened?

'Like I said, things were different with Simon,' she was saying. 'Although, in fairness, we pooled our finances. He wasn't thoughtless, although… Hmm; where do you keep the chopping boards, Mateo? I'm not up to your standard but I can produce something edible from what we've got in the fridge.'

'Alice…'

His voice was raw and he shifted uncomfortably, raking his fingers through his hair, not knowing what to do or what exactly to say, just knowing that he felt threatened, that somehow he had to escape.

She did things to him, stirred things inside him, and he didn't want that. He didn't need it. He wasn't going to start flinging doors open that led to places he'd spent his life protecting.

Alice knew from the driven urgency of his voice that whatever was on the tip of his tongue was going to be something she didn't want to hear.

'You'd rather cook yourself.' She laughed nervously.

She knew what this was about; of course she did. She could see it on his face. He'd warned her off and she'd... She only gone and developed feelings for him; only forgotten that this was time-out and that he was a guy who didn't want her around once they left this bubble.

She felt tears sting the back of her eyes. How could this have happened? She'd thought herself so sorted when it came to what kind of guys she wanted in her life. Had the very nature of her background played a part in what had happened in this hideaway? Had she been so sheltered and so cosseted that she had never developed the truly tough streak that could guide her when it came to men? Surely, if that were the case, then this wouldn't feel so *right*? If that were the case, then this would feel like lust, instead of which it felt like...

She lowered her eyes and breathed in deeply, then she looked at him without flinching.

'This is beginning to bore you, isn't it?' she said quietly.

'This is beginning to...become too complicated.'

'Why?'

'Do I need to have a reason?'

'No.' She could feel her heart hammering inside her and her limbs were turning to jelly.

'You deserve a reason,' he said roughly.

'I guess by "complications" you mean you think I'm getting too attached.'

'Aren't you?'

'Because I offered to cook a meal for us?' Alice cried, hands on her hips as she glared at him.

Dismay and downright terror at the thought that she really had serious feelings—*loved him, even*—made her fight back. He didn't want her. He might still *desire* her, but he no longer *wanted* her around. They were getting a little too comfortable with one another. Alice steadied her breath. What was wrong with getting comfortable with someone? Teetering on a tightrope of confusion and indecision, she took the plunge. Being open, honest and truthful was always the right way to be. She'd been taught that. It was embedded in her DNA.

'We get along,' she said with driving sincerity. 'Don't we? Or am imagining that?'

'I never said we didn't.'

'And the sex is great, terrific…the best. At least for me, and you seemed to enjoy the times we spent in bed making love.'

'Again, ditto.'

'Then why are you so scared that this is complicated? It's straightforward, Mateo.'

'Alice, you don't get it.'

'What we have could be something really good, really special! Don't you feel that as well? I mean, I'm not saying that we're going to end up walking down the aisle together or anything…' She laughed nervously again but actually, in her head, she was toying with the seductive notion of this beautiful man asking her to marry him. Her heart fluttered. 'But we could do it justice by seeing where it leads, don't you think?'

'Alice, I was married once before.'

Alice opened her mouth, closed it and stared at him in utter shock. The thought that he might have been married hit her like a bolt from the blue. She shuffled over to one of the chairs by the table, flopped into it and continued staring at him, open-mouthed.

'What happened?'

'What happened was a divorce,' Mateo ground out, 'after a short, unfortunate time together.'

'I... I'm so sorry. You never said.'

'Is there any reason why I should have? Alice, I told you that I wasn't interested in anything beyond what we have here and now.'

'I know.'

'I'm not looking for a relationship. I had one of those and I will never repeat the mistake.'

'But what about love?'

'Not for me. In time, when singledom becomes a place I no longer wish to inhabit, then I'll consider settling down with a woman like me—a woman who sees the practical side to a relationship and isn't looking for a fairy-tale romance. A companion, in other words, who is as practical as I am when it comes to the concept of marriage, or at least cohabitation.'

Their eyes met. What else was there to say? Alice was comfortable with what she'd done and, if inwardly he sneered at her for speaking what was on her mind, then so be it. Once she left here, she would never set eyes on him again, but at least she would leave with her conscience intact and no regrets about letting pride stand in the way of truth.

And at least she hadn't made a complete fool of herself by going the distance and actually confessing just how deeply ran her feelings for him.

'Well,' she said with a tight smile, 'just for the record, it's been fun. My mistake for thinking we could have a little more fun when we got to London. I'll go get my stuff together and I'll be out of your hair.'

'It'll be dark in an hour. You know you're welcome to stay here for the night.'

'You've seen how experienced a skier I am and the snow is good. I can make it back to my side of the mountain. The girls have gone, but it'll be easy to rent somewhere for the night, and I can change my ticket by paying a fee.'

She didn't give him the chance to prolong the conversation. She spun round on her heels and walked away.

Mateo watched her leave the kitchen. His stomach was knotted. Of course, this was the right thing. He'd taken his eye off the ball and allowed things to get out of hand. She wasn't like him. She lacked the experience to put things in perspective.

He thought about that soft, sexy body and sweet, sexy personality and tightened his jaw. The truth was that this was good for her. He didn't want to hurt her and she'd be hurt if she stuck around, if they continued this when they returned to London.

Reality had no room for it—not *his* reality. He couldn't love, wasn't interested in it, and it was always going to be better this way. He was never going to go down rabbit holes, so it was sensible to back away from their dubious, treacherous allure. So yes, maybe he'd felt something for her, maybe he'd had a moment of weakness because she'd caught him by surprise, because she was so different from his ex and every single woman who had come after his ex. But happiness was an illusion and he was way too cynical to trade in illusions.

He headed back out, back to the town. He'd get the cable up later when he knew she was gone.

CHAPTER FIVE

SITTING BEHIND HIS DESK in the impressive glass tower that dominated the London skyline, Mateo was in a state of shock. It was over six weeks since Alice Reynolds had disappeared from his life. He could recall that final conversation as vividly as if it had taken place five minutes before.

She had wanted more. She had wanted to continue their relationship when they returned to London. It had been a simple enough suggestion. As she'd told him, bemused and just a little bit pleading, *they got along, didn't they? And the sex was great, wasn't it?* She'd seen it through the straightforward eyes of someone whose life had never been complicated. Her back story hadn't left her cynical, her emotions sealed behind doors that would never be opened.

Yes, she'd left a broken engagement behind her, but it had been obvious from everything she'd said that the solid security of her very loving and protected background had fortified her against any bitterness that the broken engagement might have generated. She hadn't left her heart behind along with the engagement ring. She'd kept her dreams intact, emulating her parents, he expected.

It had been too much for him. He'd had to walk away.

He might have given her the speech about not wanting commitment, but the minute he'd seen her pottering in his kitchen, comfortable in the role of his partner, he'd realised that those warning words had fallen on deaf ears. Even if she herself hadn't realised it, she'd been well on the way to *wanting more*.

Torn between desperately wanting her to stay and knowing she should leave, he had headed back down to the town and, when he'd returned, she was no longer there. She'd airbrushed herself out of his life and, typically, he'd reacted by spending the night in the loving arms of some excellent red wine.

In the morning he'd woken groggily to the realisation that there was no way he was going to hang around a minute longer in the lodge and he'd left for London on the first flight back.

That episode in his life was over. Okay, so there hadn't been a single day when she hadn't crossed his mind, and sure, his attempts at distraction with another woman— a six-foot-tall raven-haired model with a figure that had men walking into lampposts—had flamboyantly failed, but that was because what he and Alice had had had come to a premature end.

It was no surprise that his thoughts were still wrapped up with her because his nose had been put out of joint. He was so accustomed to calling the shots and ending things when his levels of boredom had been reached that to find himself on the receiving end naturally had left a few lingering remnants of bitter aftertaste. It wouldn't last, and indeed it was quite amusing, really. It seemed his ego was bigger than he thought.

So fifteen minutes ago, when his PA had buzzed

through to tell him that an Alice Reynolds was in the foyer requesting a meeting, he'd been gobsmacked.

And satisfied; he couldn't help himself. Now, relaxing back in his chair with the busy streets of London sprawling twelve storeys below, visible through the massive sheet of floor-to-ceiling glass, Mateo savoured the taste of what was to come. She'd found out who he was. He had no idea how, but in this day and age sleuthing was easy. Maybe he'd left some form of identification lying around somewhere and she'd seen his full name.

It was disappointing that she'd decided to turn up, because he'd really thought that she lacked that materialistic streak that might let her see the financial benefits of dating a rich guy. She'd struck him as pure as the driven snow, the type of girl who really fitted the bill when it came to being a vicar's daughter.

But he couldn't be right all the time. She was here. She wanted to reconnect some way because he was a catch.

He would have to gently let her down. But he would also have a chance to *see* her and he couldn't deny that that was an exciting prospect.

There was a good chance that his mind had been playing tricks on him for the past few weeks and that the woman who had driven him crazy with desire would not be what he remembered in the cold light of day...

Alice was told to wait by a glamorous blonde woman, one of several receptionists manning the impressive granite desk in the foyer of the building.

She'd taken the morning off work, determined to be at Mateo's work place as early as possible to get the whole business out of the way.

She'd braced herself for what she was going to say, and had been reasonably calm on the Tube getting here, but now that she was actually *here* she could feel nerves tightening her stomach into knots. There was a buzzing in her ears that was making her feel faint. It was a while since she had seen Mateo. She'd laid her cards on the table, been knocked back and had made her way back to London, never expecting to set eyes on him again.

She winced every single time she thought of the night she'd spent crying in the tiny room she'd rented before taking the next flight out on her altered ticket. She'd left his lodge crying, had returned to London crying and, in between her tears, her misery and having to put on a brave face because she was back at work, it had never occurred to her that there might be anything else to worry about aside from a broken heart.

She hadn't noticed missing her period. They were a law unto themselves, anyway, so there had been no warning signal that something might be up until her boobs had started feeling sore and she had spent mornings feeling queasy.

Then, without really believing anything could possibly be amiss, she had taken a test. Sitting on a toilet seat in the staff bathroom at school, she had watched the stick foretell the vast change in life plan heading her way.

She was pregnant.

How? How on earth had it happened? He'd been careful, hadn't he? There had been a couple of occasions, during sleepy early-morning sex, when maybe he hadn't been able to resist entering her. But he'd remedied that, hadn't he? He had fetched protection in time, hadn't he?

She'd racked her brains, thinking back, but had barely

been able to focus because her mind was far too occupied with the life developing inside her: a baby she hadn't planned but a baby she wanted with all her heart.

Every maternal urge in her had kicked in the minute that little stick had given her the unexpected news. All life was precious and this baby inside her would be welcomed into the world with all the fanfare he or she deserved, even if there would be no proud father at the birth.

She would tell Mateo. There had been no hesitation in accepting that, even though the prospect of breaking the news to him filled her with dread. It had occurred to her that he hadn't wanted to continue anything with her to the extent that he'd made sure not to tell her his surname, but in fact she'd had no trouble finding out who he was. She'd simply phoned one of the ski-instructors she knew and asked if he knew who lived in that particular lodge on that part of the mountain.

Ski-instructors were a tightly knit group and Alice had kept in touch with a number of them. And, of course, everyone knew who had classy chalets on the slopes.

Mateo Ricci.

Lost in her thoughts, she came to when a middle-aged lady appeared from nowhere, looked at her with measured curiosity and told her to follow her. Alice wasn't surprised at the overwhelming and impressive surroundings: glass, marble, granite and huge plants artfully dotted around the sweeping foyer.

The minute she had found out Mateo's name, she had looked him up, and *that* was when she'd been surprised, because he wasn't the reasonably successful, freelance computer guy he had made himself out to be. He was the king of the jungle. He didn't work at the beck and call of paymasters—he *was* the paymaster. There were pages and pages of information on him, all relating to his meteoric business rise.

She'd skipped most of it. The one thing she'd taken away was yet more confirmation that she'd been nothing more to him than a few days of fun. She'd been bowled over. He'd been casual. He would have women queuing up for him, but he'd been there and she'd been there, there had been no queues outside his door at that particular point in time...so why not have some fun with the girl who'd been so enthusiastic?

She'd clicked on a lot of images of the sort of women he went out with and, as expected, none of them were built in her mould. He'd found her an amusing novelty toy, because the women he dated were models with legs up to their armpits, the sort of woman Alice would never look like no matter what she did.

She stopped abruptly when the woman in front of her swerved through a smoky glass door and stepped aside to let her pass, and then she was there, in the inner sanctum of the man who had stolen her heart. Even the air seemed more rarefied.

'He's a very busy man.' The lady smiled politely at her.

'I won't be long,' Alice promised. She drew in a deep breath and felt faint as the connecting door to his office was pushed open.

Mateo had moved to stand by the window as he'd waited for her. Now, as he heard the silent whoosh of the connecting door being pushed open, he slowly turned and there she was—hovering in the doorway, then stepping hesitantly into his massive office so that Julie could close the door behind her. She looked like a rabbit caught in the headlights, even though she was obviously trying her best to appear controlled.

She hadn't changed. Mateo's lips thinned with irritation as he felt the abrupt rise in his libido. Hooded eyes drifted down the incredibly drab outfit she had chosen to wear: black, thick cable-knit jumper, jeans, trainers and a bulky waterproof which was slung over her arm. If she had come with the intention of reconnecting with him, then she certainly hadn't pushed the boat out in her attempts to seduce. It should have been a turn-off but was the opposite, much to his annoyance.

He hadn't expected her to have the same effect on him as she'd had when they'd been snowbound in his lodge. He'd concluded that circumstances had contributed to his uncharacteristic out-of-control horniness, but here she was, not saying a word, and the horniness was still there and still out of control, drab clothing or no drab clothing.

'This is an unexpected pleasure.' He swerved round back to his chair behind the conference-table-sized desk and relaxed back, nodding to one of the leather chairs positioned in front.

'I suppose you're surprised to see me here?'

'I'm surprised you found me. How did you achieve that? Did you come across something in the lodge that had my name on it?'

She'd shuffled into the chair he'd indicated and carefully put her coat and backpack on the ground next to her. He realised that he'd forgotten how sexy she was. No wonder the raven-haired model hadn't been able to pass muster. It was because the small, voluptuous siren sitting in front of him still managed to occupy his head.

Who'd have thought that a fling prematurely ended could have such sway over him still? Who could have thought that reason and common sense would count for nothing in the face of a libido he hadn't been able to subdue? It was ridiculous, incomprehensible.

'No, I didn't. I would never have gone nosing around through your personal stuff to find out who you were.'

'But you were obviously still curious enough to find out by some other means, so I'm not that impressed, if I'm honest. But apologies; I'm being rude. Would you like something to drink? Tea? Coffee?'

'I…no. I'm fine, thank you.'

'So you were telling me how you managed to find me.'

'I… I asked around when I got back to London.'

'Enterprising.'

'Do you have to be so sarcastic, Mateo?'

'What were you expecting, Alice? An effusive welcome? The red carpet rolled out? Have you forgotten that what we had no longer exists?' His body was singing from a different song sheet, unfortunately, not nearly so cool as that particular statement. It might be true but what his body wanted was a continuation of what they'd had.

What if she offered to resume their fling and pick up where things had been left off? He felt himself harden at the thought of that gloriously sexy body, so soft and responsive to his touch. He remembered far too vividly for his liking the soft, sweet little noises she made when he caressed her, licked her and explored every inch of her.

His original plan to turn her down flatly and politely when she inevitably offered herself back to him began to fray a little round the edges. The best bet, he decided as pride swooped in to replace hesitation, would be to send her on her way as fast as possible.

For starters, it wouldn't pay to forget why he had decided to finish what they'd enjoyed: she risked being hurt. He had nothing to give and she wanted a lot, too much. He'd warned her and she hadn't listened. Their bubble had burst and that was a good thing.

That said…didn't the fact that she'd showed up here because she'd found out that he was wealthy put paid to his woolly ideas that she was somehow too sweet, too gentle, just too damned *nice* to risk getting wrapped up with a hard-edged guy like him?

'Who did you ask around to get the information?' He reverted to the original topic because he was curious to find out to what lengths she had gone to track him down.

'Remember I told you that I used to teach skiing to beginners on the mountain? I still know loads of the ski-instructors there and also the ones who've left and moved on. They knew who you were.'

'And now you've showed up because…no, let me guess. Having found out that I'm not the freelance tech guy you thought I was, but instead the guy who *owns* those freelance tech guys—and that's just the tip of the iceberg—you decided that it might be worthwhile to explore your options?'

'Explore my options?'

'Dump the innocent act, Alice. There's no need. In fact, if you come clean and admit you've come here to see if what we had can be resurrected, then a conversation is there to be had.' Why kid himself that he still didn't want her? It beggared belief but no amount of burst bubbles, warning talks being ignored about the best option being to send her packing could stifle the insistent pulse of his suddenly reawakened libido.

'You're truly the most cynical person I've ever met in my life, Mateo.'

'I find that's a trait that's always worked in my favour. Give people the benefit of the doubt, and invariably they let you down. So, okay, you're here. You know I have money, and a lot of it, and you want to reconnect. I admit, much as it's frustrating to say so, that I'm tempted by the proposition.'

Their eyes met.

Alice felt the race of her pulse, the hot pumping of blood in her veins. She'd dreaded this meeting and it was turning out that she'd dreaded it for good reason. He couldn't even be bothered to be polite. The warm, funny, sexy guy she'd fallen for when they'd been locked in by snow was now a stranger in hand-made shoes and a crisp white shirt, sleeves rolled to the elbows, with an expensive barely there logo on the front pocket.

A stranger who thought that she was a gold-digger. And yet, she had to reluctantly concede that she could see where he was coming from. Women chased men with lots of money. Throw looks and charm into the mix, and the combination would certainly attract gold-diggers in a million different guises.

No wonder he'd been livid when she'd turned up at his door! That lodge was probably one of the few completely private getaways he possessed, where no one was around to pester him because no one could physically get there.

But surely *he knew her*?

Yet she'd managed to find him and there could only

be one reason for that: that would be the conclusion running through his head.

Alice looked at him from under her lashes with a hint of impatience. She wished she could be angrier at his response but there was something so predictable, so *human*, in his defensiveness, something so weirdly vulnerable in his immediately jumping to that cynical conclusion, that she felt herself soften.

'You're tempted by the proposition, are you?' she queried wryly, allowing him to continue on his tangent just a little bit longer.

'I admit, I've been thinking of you.'

'Have you? I'm surprised.'

'You're incredibly sexy. I reckoned that it might have been the circumstances—the two of us trapped for days in my lodge. I don't have much time for romance, but I'd say that was pretty romantic. I assumed, actually, that that was why I couldn't quite manage to forget about it…us…*you*. That and the fact that it ended before it had run its course.'

'Hmm.'

'I thought,' he continued with searing honesty, 'that I might have been looking back to those few days through rose-tinted specs but the minute I saw you again… You're as sexy as I remembered.'

'I don't know what to say.'

'You don't have to say anything at the moment. You can let me do the talking.'

'Hmm.'

'I still want you and, if you've come here because you think I'm a good bet, then I get that. You wouldn't be the first to be attracted to me because of my bank balance and you won't be the last.'

'That's a very sad statement, Mateo.'

'What are you taking about?'

'Assuming that your bank balance plays a part in why a woman would want to go out with you.'

He spread his arms expansively. 'I'm a realist. You know that. And I'm not too proud to admit that I still want you. The weeks haven't changed that.'

He lowered his voice ominously. 'Although, the rules remain the same. I'm not up for anything but fun, be that fun for days or weeks. And, while we're having fun, the world will be your oyster. Whatever you want, you can have, no expense spared. Diamonds, pearls and sapphires, cars and clothes… You'll find that I'm a generous guy.'

'Diamonds, pearls and sapphires,' Alice murmured. 'What dazzling temptation.'

'Am I missing something here?' He frowned and Alice didn't say anything. She just met his frowning gaze steadily.

'I haven't come here to try and reconnect with you, Mateo. Believe it or not, I'm not the type of person who finds out someone's worth and then decides that they're worth cultivating.'

'I don't understand.'

'I've come here…'

'You maybe want me to donate something to your school?'

She laughed. It was too absurd. 'Well, St Christopher's could certainly do with an injection of cash, but I haven't come here to ask for funding. I came here to tell you… to tell you…'

'I'm all ears, Alice. Take me somewhere new and challenging that explains your presence here.'

He sat forward, shot her a darkly wolfish smile, rested his arms on the desk and in a rush Alice said what she had come to say.

'I'm pregnant, Mateo. I came here to tell you that I'm having a baby.'

A deathly silence greeted this. It stretched and stretched and she could see his expression moving rapidly from shock to incredulity to outright disbelief.

'You can't be! Why would you come here and tell me something like that? Absolute nonsense!' He stood up, his body as tense as a bowstring, dark brows furrowed in arrogant disbelief, every inch of him simmering with furious denial. 'I refuse to believe a word of what you're saying!'

Alice stared at him in silence. She'd wondered how he would react but complete denial hadn't been one of the options—although she'd been spot-on with the anger.

She took a deep breath to steady herself and offered him a tight, indifferent smile.

'Okay.'

'Okay? *Okay?*'

'I came here to tell you because it was the responsible thing to do.' She stood up and snatched her coat and backpack from where she had dumped them by the side of the chair. 'If you don't want to believe me, then no one's forcing you to. I didn't expect anything from you, anyway. Now, if you'll excuse me, I'm going to carry on with my day.'

'You'll do no such thing! You can't just waltz in here and drop a bombshell like that and then tell me you're leaving! Alice...*don't you dare!*'

Alice ignored him. She didn't look back. She began

walking briskly out of his office, leaving him rising to his feet behind his desk. She could feel the sting of tears behind her eyes, because if she were certain of one thing it was this: never in a million years had she dreamt of having a baby by a guy who not only wanted nothing to do with her, but didn't even believe a word she said.

What was the opposite of 'happy ever after'? Whatever it was, she was definitely now living in that world.

No one knew about the pregnancy yet, but she was already projecting forward to telling her parents and seeing their disappointment. Of course they would try and hide it, and of course they would be supportive all the way, but she had let them down and the thought of it put a pain in her chest.

She fled.

Standing behind his desk, for the first time in his life Mateo was immobilised. Shock had drained him of the ability to think in a straight line.

Pregnant? No!

Those were the first thoughts that had run through his head when she had detonated that landmine. She couldn't be! He'd reacted with swift, instinctive denial as his mind had shut down.

And then she was half-running out of his office and here he was, still shell-shocked, but his brain was actually starting to engage. Why would she lie? She wasn't a liar. It just wasn't in her nature. And why would she have waited until now to find out who he was? If she'd been a mercenary gold-digger who'd somehow got a whiff of what he was made of, then why hadn't she contacted him sooner? And why wouldn't she have used the straight-forward approach of trying to entice him back into bed?

She would have had to be crazy to make up a story about a pregnancy. She would have known that sooner or later she would be found out, and anyway, surely she must have suspected that he would insist on a pregnancy test, along with a medical examination and a DNA test?

And he knew, as well, that he had subconsciously been catapulted back to that time when a surprise pregnancy had forced him down a road he hadn't foreseen, with all the predictable disastrous consequences. He'd been knocked for six but there was only the truth: she really *was* pregnant.

Mateo didn't stop to think about the repercussions of what she had told him. There would be plenty of time for that later. He exited his office at speed and handed his PA the very unusual task of finding out exactly where St Christophers was located. Then he waited, impatiently, for the full twenty minutes as she went into action, checking online and making calls, calling in at least two favours from friends who were teachers, making sure that when he showed up there would be no obstacles regarding entry.

Alice had run away from him but there was no way he wasn't going to find her. No way he was going to hang around and wait until she decided to get in touch with him again—*if* she decided to get in touch with him again. She'd come to do the decent thing and he'd reacted in just the sort of manner that would have had anyone in her position running for the hills. She'd come to deliver a message and he'd decided in his wisdom to shoot the messenger. He'd allowed shock, horror and a subconscious kneejerk reaction to something from his past dictate his response.

He remained in his office for half an hour more, thinking, allowing his head to be occupied with the practical issues surrounding the shock news. He avoided digging deeper into his own feelings about the thought of being a father. He didn't want to confront the feelings of vulnerability he had had all those years ago, the yearning and thrill of having a child only for those hopes to be dashed.

It was another hour and a half and just after lunch by the time he made it to the school and was instantly ushered in, having had the head pre-warned of his visit. His PA had pulled some strings, but Mateo thought he would have been able to get in without that simply because he was who he was. His identity could easily be checked and he could have promised a sizeable donation.

He looked around at the shabby surroundings masked by cheerful banners and upbeat sayings printed boldly on bright pieces of card and artwork stuck on the walls in neat rows on either side of a corridor teeming with kids coming and going. An inner-city school in desperate need of refurbishment, relying on government funding and donations from strangers. These were the sort of surroundings he hadn't been exposed to in a very, very long time and when he thought of Alice, actually imagining that she might have to face raising their child on a teacher's wage, his heart squeezed tight. He would definitely be doing something to improve the place.

But all that for later. For now, Alice.

Alice was so absorbed in thinking about Mateo and his shock and horror at what she had told him that she kept losing track of what the kids were doing. Just now, four in the back row were passing notes between them and giggling. The rest had their heads down and were doing their best to ignore the unruly back row.

Clara, her teaching assistant, was sitting with three children around her, painstakingly going over some work which they were finding impossible to comprehend.

A normal day, but not for her. What happened next? She'd done what she'd known she had to do. She'd told Mateo about the baby, but it was clear from how he'd reacted that he wasn't going to take any kind of active part in its upbringing. He had his gilded life, a life in which long-term commitment was not allowed to intrude, and there was nothing more long-term than a child. So he'd gone into denial mode and she had to accept that he might just stay there.

When she thought about the nuts and bolts of having a baby when she earned a modest income and rented a place, she could feel a headache coming on. She would have to move back home and live with her parents until she found her feet.

With those thoughts buzzing in her head, she was only aware of someone at the door when the entire class fell silent. The four at the back, all girls, were staring at the door with their mouths open and, as Alice slowly turned around, she knew who was at the door. Only one person could inspire that sort of reaction, and it wasn't Mr Dennis the headmaster. He might inspire a bit of temporary silence but definitely no jaws on the ground.

Mateo.

He was lounging in the doorway, the very embodiment

of sexiness, his brooding, green eyes lasered on her, and she could feel bright colour surge into her cheeks.

They could have heard a pin drop.

'We need to talk,' he drawled from the doorway.

Someone from the back row piped up in a 'butter wouldn't melt' voice, 'Miss, is that your boyfriend?'

Alice leapt to her feet, threw a stern look around her, told them that she would be back in ten minutes and then walked quickly towards Mateo, eager to usher him away from her gawping pupils. They might struggle to remember some basic rules of maths, but they would have memories like elephants when it came to remembering *this*.

Alice felt a wave of anger rush through her. First he had told her that he didn't believe a word she'd told him and now, here he was in *her* territory! If he thought that he could pursue a conversation about her making stuff up then he was in for a shock.

She didn't glance behind her as she restrained herself from slamming the classroom door. Nor did she utter a single word as she dragged him down the corridor, quieter now that there was no change of class in progress, but still not empty.

There were three quiet rooms used for one-to-one teaching. She took him to an empty one now and shut the door behind her but she remained leaning against it while he turned to look at her.

'First of all,' he said before she could lay into him, 'I want to apologise.'

CHAPTER SIX

'SIT.' SHE POINTED to one of the chairs ringed round a small square table, the surface of which was scuffed with the markings of pens over the years. He dwarfed the room and oozed the sort of expensive sophistication that emphasised the shabbiness of his surroundings: bare green walls in need of repainting, a couple of posters with inspirational quotes from well-known books and a weathered low-shelving system that was stuffed with various educational books and leaflets.

Alice looked at him and felt that familiar lurch in her stomach, a purely visceral awareness of him as a man, as someone who had made love to her, a guy who appealed on the most basic level—whatever her head had to say about it.

'You had no right to come here.'

'I had every right to come here. You detonated a bomb in my life. This isn't the place to have this sort of conversation. Have you had lunch? I can take you somewhere a little less…confined…and we can at least relax and discuss this situation in a bit of comfort.'

'I thought you'd already made yourself perfectly clear on where you stood with *this situation*.'

'I apologise. I…may have overreacted but it wasn't something I was expecting. Alice, let's get out of here.

Someone is going to barge in at any minute, and neither of us is going to be able to give what has to be discussed the attention it deserves if we're listening out for someone pushing that door open.'

'I haven't finished for the day.'

'Then finish.'

'Don't think you can come here and tell me what to do!'

Mateo didn't answer. He stood up and began heading towards the door.

'Where are you going?'

'To the staff room. I have a good idea where it is. The teacher who showed me to your classroom helpfully gave me a little tour of the school. I may have mentioned that I was interested in making a financial contribution.'

'You can't go to the staff room!'

'I can when you consider that I'm going to explain the situation to your fellow colleagues. I'm sure they'll understand why we may want a little privacy to discuss this development.'

He looked at her and she returned his calm, level gaze with biting frustration.

'You're...*impossible*!'

'That's what I call a massive overstatement, all things considered,' Mateo returned coolly. 'So, what are you going to do?'

'Wait for me by the front doors.' Alice gritted her teeth. 'I'll join you in ten minutes.'

She rushed to the staff room, said something about a personal situation arising out of the blue and made it to the front doors of the school before her time was up.

Mateo was staring through the glass doors and she stopped abruptly and took a few seconds to look at him.

Her heart was beating like a sledgehammer. He'd hunted her down and she could feel some of the heavy weight of uncertainty lift from her shoulders.

Whatever the state of their affairs, it could only be a good thing for him to acknowledge his child. Good for him, but mostly good for this baby they had accidentally created. As a teacher, Alice had seen many times the effect on children of broken homes, absent parents and just mothers or fathers unwilling or unable to provide the security their offspring needed.

She had seen it all. It was one thing if a parent had died, or even if a couple had loved and tried but lost the battle and divorced. It was another thing completely if one parent had just decided to walk away from their own flesh and blood and not look back. That was the sort of thing that always came out eventually and could cause lasting damage.

He might have reacted forcefully and negatively to what she had sprung on him, but Mateo wasn't running away, and she felt as though some of her faith in him had been restored. She grudgingly conceded that, if he had gone into instant denial mode at what she had thrown at him, then it was only to be expected. He was a guy who controlled every aspect of his life. Of course he wasn't going to embrace the least controlled event ever to have happened to him with open arms and a warm, trusting smile.

She powered herself towards him as he turned to look at her.

'I've ordered a cab to take us somewhere a little more private.'

'I know this is a shock, Mateo, but I couldn't think of any other way to do it.'

'You realise I'll be taking nothing on trust. I'll want you to have a full medical examination so that I have all the facts at my disposal.'

'What sort of facts? Are you still going with the theory that I showed up at your office pretending to be having your baby?'

They walked to the black cab waiting by the kerb and she slid into the back seat, making space for him next to her. Every nerve in her body was stretched taut with anxiety and tension…and a dark, feverish excitement she couldn't shake.

'I'm not going with that theory,' Mateo said seriously. He angled his body against the car door so that he could look at her levelly.

'Ah, I see. You think that I've been sleeping with someone else and now I'm trying to palm their child off as yours so that I can… I don't know…force you into parting with your precious cash for a baby that isn't yours?'

'These things happen,' Mateo muttered, but as their eyes tangled he could see the senselessness of that misplaced caution. She wouldn't do that. He might be primed to distrust, but to distrust *her* would be downright offensive…

He was going to be a father!

There was no point harking back to those dark days when impending fatherhood had forced him down a path he wouldn't have taken, and when gut-wrenching disappointment at Bianca's miscarriage had cut so deeply. This was the here and now and positioning himself on the opposite side of the fence to her was not a good way to start.

He unconsciously glanced at her stomach, wondering what it would feel like to see it expanding with his child. He refused to succumb to the thrill of anticipation. He remembered what that had felt like, the vulnerability that had come with it and the anguish when things had collapsed. He had withdrawn behind his barriers then, but he'd always known that he'd taken it a damn sight harder than Bianca had.

'I don't understand how this happened,' he said in low, calm voice. 'Precautions were taken. I'm a very careful man.'

'Not *all the time*,' Alice reminded him uncomfortably. 'Once or twice things got a little out of hand... One morning, very early, we were both half-asleep... You reached out and...'

'I remember.' He flushed darkly. He'd never felt passion like he had for those few days when he'd been marooned with her in his lodge...and, yes, once or twice contraception had been an afterthought.

'Or maybe it was just a genuine accident...a tear in a condom. It happens.'

'Look, we'll be at my club in a few minutes. Let's park the details until we get there. How...how have you been?'

'Wonderful.'

'And your parents? Were they worried when you told them about your little adventure?'

'I thought it best not to mention anything although, now that I'm having a baby, I suppose I'll have to confess to what happened.'

'You haven't told them yet?'

'It was only right, as the father of this baby, that you were the first to know and I only found out about the pregnancy myself a couple of days ago.'

'It must have been a shock.' He could only admire her calmness. She had done what she thought was the right thing to do and hadn't showed up at his office with accusations, blame or demands for money. 'All right, look, there will be no tests to determine paternity. Of course I believe you. It was the shock talking. What we have to do now is decide what the way forward is going to be.' He glanced past her. 'We're here. We can talk about this once we're inside. This is as private as it gets.'

The cab had slowed in front of a door in a wall. Alice frowned, confused, because this wasn't what she'd been expecting.

'Your club?'

'Probably the most private place in London and numbers are strictly limited. This is where the world is run.'

'You're kidding.'

'Only slightly.'

She fell back as he pulled out an old-fashioned metal key and let them in, standing back so that she could precede him. Inside, the corridor was dark, cool and silent, a space of flagstone tiles and panelling that ran halfway up. The lighting was subdued and, when she began to wonder where the heck they were, they turned left into an open space guarded by a weathered guy behind a desk who nodded at Mateo without moving.

'Sir.'

'Fornby. Doing well?'

'As well as can be expected, given the times we live in.'

'All a man can ask for.'

They'd left the madness of London behind and somehow entered a different place in a different era. This, Alice thought, trying hard not to gape, was what extreme wealth bought: perfect privacy. Somewhere where a person could be a direct descendent of Zeus and no one would glance in their direction.

It was tough not looking around at the clusters of deep

sofas and tables discreetly set apart. Some were occupied. A glance at one of the occupants relaxing with a newspaper revealed a personality who had been in the news for the past fortnight, a man in charge of fractious talks with certain nations in the Middle East. Two showbiz personalities were talking and eating food, and there was a small group of two women and a man, all besuited, poring over a bank of documents with a bottle of wine on the table between them.

No one looked at Alice and Mateo as they settled into two deep chairs with a circular table in front of them. A man appeared from nowhere with a bottle of sparkling mineral water. Mateo ordered a carafe of 'red wine': obviously the kind of red he liked had long been noted, presumably with no deviation unless told otherwise.

She murmured something about the water being fine. 'Wow,' she whispered. 'I never knew places like this existed.'

'Most people don't. London is full of exclusive clubs but this one thrives on being very much under the radar.'

'It's definitely more private than the room at the school.' It was quiet and dark, with rich, old furnishings and the sort of carpets that looked as though they belonged in the age of the Tudors. The men serving food and drinks had a palpable air of expertise and discretion.

They sat back as a tray of canapés was brought for them. Frankly, Alice would have liked to carry on surreptitiously staring around her, but reluctantly she returned to Mateo, who was now looking at her with a certain amount of amusement.

But it didn't last long. 'I think we should both be as professional as possible in the way we approach this situation,' he opined.

Alice focused. Of course, this was exactly the right way to deal with the situation. They'd had a fling but, beyond that, it wasn't as though he had feelings for her. It wouldn't do to forget that, when she had suggested carrying on with what they had to see where it would lead, he had firmly closed the conversation down and sent her on her way.

If they handled this in a *professional* way, then they could remain friends, which was what would be necessary as time went on. They would have a bond that would never go away, whatever their changes in fortune.

And yet her heart constricted at all the consequences that lay down that road. She'd have to watch as other women came and went in his life, knowing when that *someone* he had talked about came along—that woman with whom he would want to share his life, who wouldn't be under any illusions that he was going to fall in love with her—Alice would wave goodbye to their daughter or son and watch him drive away with someone else in the passenger seat.

'Neither of us expected this to happen,' Mateo started, 'but I intend to pull my weight every inch of the way. First of all, there will never be any need for you to worry about money. My child will want for nothing. I knew what *want* was when *I* was a child, and it's a miserable hardship that I'm only grateful my own flesh and blood will not have to endure. And, as his mother, you will likewise want for nothing. You will both have the best.'

'I'm not asking for anything for myself, Mateo,' Alice said faintly.

'You don't have to. It goes without saying that you can give up your teaching job, which I imagine doesn't pay the earth.'

'That won't be happening.'

'Your thoughts on that might change. You might find that you enjoy being a hands-on mother when you no longer need to go out and earn a pittance teaching. On the subject of which, you were right—your school could do with an injection of funds from the looks of it. Before we part company, I'll get details the name of your admin person so that I can do my civic duty.'

Alice was beginning to feel as if she had suddenly jumped on a rollercoaster and was now whizzing madly across the universe.

'Well, I'm sure the principal would be grateful for any financial help... Fund-raising can only get so far, so thank you; and, yes, it would be nice knowing that our child will be financially secure.'

It was all so matter-of-fact. They could have been discussing a business deal, she thought sadly. The intense physical chemistry between them had been wiped out and replaced with this run-of-the-mill conversation about their future.

'I don't suppose this was what you'd spent your life looking forward to,' Mateo said roughly.

'I'd always planned on having children.'

'But not like this—an unplanned pregnancy with a man you never banked on having a future with.'

'And who never banked on having a future with me.'

'Or with anyone,' Mateo qualified. 'But, love and marriage aside, I want you to know that you can expect one hundred percent support from me.'

Alice picked at the wonderful canapés and wondered why they tasted of cardboard. Why did she feel so miserable? He was being terrific. She couldn't have asked for more. Was it because, for her, having a baby had always been wrapped up with love and marriage? Just something she'd always taken for granted?

Or did this businesslike approach hurt because here she was, carrying his baby, and she wanted so much more than financial support. Once upon a time, she had dimly seen Simon in this position. Now she knew that what she felt for Simon had not been love. She'd had a narrow escape but, from the frying pan she'd fallen straight into the fire, because, yes, what she felt for this wonderful, elusive, complex guy sitting within touching distance was love in all its glory—but love that wasn't reciprocated. He was offering her emotional support, and she knew that he would be there for her, but only *because of the baby*.

'I appreciate that,' Alice said politely.

'Can I…see it?'

'See what?'

'The baby. Now.' He flushed darkly. 'A scan.'

'Don't tell me you still have doubts about that?'

'I don't. I just want to…'

'Okay,' Alice agreed in a husky voice. 'I'll get it arranged.'

'And then we can fine-tune all the details. I don't know where you live, Alice, but I'm guessing it's not a palace. And before you tell me that you don't need a palace to raise a child, you're going to move from wherever you are to something suitable, and that is non-negotiable. Also non-negotiable is that you use the money I intend to deposit into your account. The only thing that's negotiable there is the sum, if it's not enough. Like I said, I intend to take care of both of you in style.'

'I'm very grateful, Mateo.'

'Then why are you looking at me as though I'm the Grinch who stole Christmas?'

'Because it all sounds so much like a business deal...'

Mateo glanced down, lush lashes concealing his expression, making him a closed book.

It did, he privately conceded, but wasn't this the best route forward—the one that avoided a future that would probably be filled with messy complications? Hadn't he raced into a youthful marriage because of a pregnancy without foreseeing all the chaos that would result from his hasty decision? Had he and Bianca had that baby, wouldn't the whole thing have come unstuck in an ugly and predictable way? Yes. And the ugly unravelling of a marriage would always impact a child far more than two parents who liked and respected one another and worked in unison for the good of the child they had created without aiming for what was never going to be achieved.

Mateo knew that he had locked away his heart, just as he knew that it would be unfair to encourage Alice to do the same with hers, which was what would happen if they made the mistake of marrying. For him, marriage would be something that might or might not happen one day and, when that day arrived, it would be a choice made with his head.

Alice deserved better. She deserved to have the best she could find and that would be to marry someone for love and not through necessity.

He thought of her with another man and bit down a rush of jealousy. It was an emotion so foreign to him that he almost didn't recognise it for what it was.

'What are you thinking?'

Mateo looked at her thoughtfully. 'Isn't that how it

should be, Alice? I know we had…a good time for a while but that wasn't about love. That was about sex. What you want for yourself isn't to be with a guy you don't love who is as cynical as you are optimistic…' He smiled crookedly at her.

Again he felt that sharp pang of something strike deep into his core when he thought of her with another man. It went against all the cool logic that had been the bedrock of his adult life and he refused to let it in for closer inspection. It unsettled him. In his head, vulnerability like that led to love, and love led to loss. He would never invite the possibility of loss back into his life.

'Of course you're right, and I'm really glad you're being so…accommodating about this. I know it's the last thing you need.'

'I can arrange for you to have a private scan,' Mateo inserted in a rough, uncertain voice. 'Please.'

Alice's smile was slow and genuine. She would have to face certain facts, however hard it was going to be. He didn't think she had feelings for him but she did: deep, strong feelings that had wrapped around every bit of her heart. However, he had none for her, aside from feelings of responsibility now. He would take care of her because she was carrying his child, and of course he was right: for her, marriage without love would be awful. So the conventional situation she had always envisaged for herself was not to be…

But he *had* come to terms with impending fatherhood much quicker than she could ever have hoped. Not only that, for him to be so keen on a scan showed that he was facing up to this sudden bomb dropped into his well-ordered life full-on, without trying to distance himself from it. And that was to be celebrated.

A lot of men would have turned their backs in a scenario such as this.

'Yes, sure.'

'And then we can really sit down and talk about what exactly happens next…'

The scan was arranged for the following week— a private scan, in a private hospital. As Alice was ushered through to where Mateo was waiting for her, she was afforded a glimpse of life that happened on the other side of the wealth divide. The hospital was quiet and luxurious. There were no trolleys spilling out of corridors and no sense of frantic urgency with patients, nurses, doctors and consultants racing through corridors, white coats flying and noise and bustle everywhere.

Mateo turned around. She paused as their eyes met and he rose to walk towards her. He'd phoned her every day since their last meeting. He'd asked her about her day, how she was, what she'd eaten. Alice knew that his concern was for the baby but she was treacherously becoming accustomed to seeing his name pop up on her phone and hearing the dark, velvety sound of his low, sexy and hypnotising voice.

He'd come from work and was in a suit, a cashmere tan coat draped over the chair next to him. Her heart skipped several beats as he neared her, and just for a few seconds it was easy to pretend that this was a normal relationship, a loving relationship with the man who was to be father of her child.

He gave her a peck on the cheek. If there was any reminder needed that their relationship had changed, then this was it. A peck on the cheek was a far cry from the hot lust that had made it impossible for him to keep his hands off her.

'This is like a five-star hotel,' Alice whispered, eyeing the neatly turned out consultants occasionally walking past and the cool, unruffled receptionists waiting to usher them to the right place.

'No need to whisper.' Mateo drew back and looked down at her. 'And it's a taste of what you'll be getting used to.'

'I'm fine with the health care the state provides.'

'Again, this is one of those non-negotiables. Have you cleared your diary for the day? I'd like to take you for an early dinner so that we can discuss some of the finer details of what comes next for us. Not my club—we can skip that—somewhere more casual.'

'Yes, I've taken the afternoon off.' Alice was trying to digest the way things had changed between them. They were as polite as strangers. The peck on the cheek had had the sting of indifference. He was no longer attracted to her and the teasing familiarity between them that had built so quickly and effortlessly when they'd been snowbound was a thing of the past.

And this was what she would have to get used to. He generously wanted the best for her, and had approached what had been thrown at him in an adult and thoughtful way. She should be grateful, not quietly devastated.

'Good.'

It was said in a clipped voice, with polite, unreadable gaze and kind smile. She wondered whether he had moved on from her and was seeing someone else. A bit of background reading on him had told a story of a guy who had a healthy appetite when it came to the opposite sex.

They were escorted to the maternity ward and to the bank of quiet, comfortable rooms where scans were done. Her mind was still on Mateo and the business of getting used to this version of him as she lay on the couch, suddenly self-conscious as the procedure began. He'd seen her naked. They had made love many times and he had touched her in all her most intimate places. Even so, lying on this couch in a darkened room, with the machine beeping and the radiographer about to see what was happening inside her, Alice felt oddly nervous and vulnerable.

But all of that was forgotten when she saw the little speck on the machine, the fierce pumping of a tiny heart, the beginnings of a boy or girl. The radiographer was talking, and Alice excitedly asked a couple of questions, but it was only when they were wrapping up the scan that she realised that Mateo had not said a word. He'd been completely silent and, as they were left on their own to digest what they'd been told and gaze at the black and white picture printed out for them, she suddenly felt her heart drop.

She couldn't meet his eyes as she hurriedly hopped off the couch and straightened her clothes. 'It's all very real now, isn't it?' she said in a high, light voice. She backed away so that she was pressed against the couch, arms folded, her eyes locked with his.

'Come again?'

'It's okay to discuss the ramifications of a baby but, now that you've actually seen proof of the pregnancy with your own eyes, I guess all those ways your life is going to change are really being rammed home to you.'

He was pale. Good intentions were easily washed away, she thought miserably. He'd been great talking about what an active parent he was going to be, but was he now considering the consequences in a slightly different way? A living, breathing little human would take up a disproportionate amount of time and it was a responsibility that would never end.

Was he now back-tracking on being hands-on and heading down the 'financial support only' route?

Surely not? And yet, why on earth was he not saying anything?

'If you've changed your mind about…about everything, then that's fine. I understand,' she said in a rush, grabbing her coat and back pack and walking briskly to the door whilst making sure to keep plenty of room between them. Get too close, and whatever vibe he had just went right through her, scrambling her brain and turning her body to mush. Right now, she wasn't interested in either of those things happening.

'Well?' The silence from him was agonising. 'Have you—changed your mind? Because you can come right out and say it.'

'Let's get out of here. When it comes to conversations, a hospital is only marginally better than a box room at a school.'

'I'm not going anywhere until you tell me what's going on, Mateo. If you're having second thoughts about getting involved with this baby, then that's fine, but I'm not going to go for dinner so that we can discuss your change of mind over a three-course meal.'

He was already heading out and Alice tripped along next to him, every nerve in her body braced for news that was going to be so disappointing. If thinking about a future with him involved in her life at some level had been bad, thinking about a future with him *not* in her life, just depositing money into an account to make sure she was okay, was a million times worse.

'You're right.' Mateo finally spoke when they were outside and a black cab was slowing for them. 'Slight change of plan. In the cab, Alice. This isn't an email conversation, I'm afraid, or anything I want to rush because you're suddenly in a hurry. Restaurant chit chat with a waiter interrupting us every three minutes isn't going to do—not quite the venue for the conversation we need to have.'

He stepped aside, waiting until she had no option but to slide into the taxi. While she grappled with the near impossibility of remaining silent, he stared, first at her, with cool, assessing eyes, then straight ahead.

Alice fumed and simmered in silence as they cleared through late afternoon traffic, stopping and starting before cruising past the crowded streets into a hushed residential setting where towering Georgian houses were set back from the road by a wide pavement. Rows of precise, black wrought-iron railings stood guard outside each of the impressive properties.

'Where the heck are we, Mateo?'

'My house.'

'No way.'

'I'm not having an argument in the back of a cab, Alice, so hop out. You're free to argue with me when we get inside.'

'That won't be happening because I won't be getting inside.'

But, agonisingly, she knew that she would because she needed to hear what Mateo had to say. Running from a problem never helped when it came to solving it. A baby was on the way and neither hurt feelings nor stubborn pride should be allowed to get in the way of deciding what to do.

His house was testimony to his immense wealth. In comparison, his lodge on those snowy slopes had been a positive shack in comparison. Alice winced when she thought of her kindly remarks to him when she'd thought that he was no more than an averagely well paid IT guy who might only be able to afford a nifty ski lodge if it was rented out when he wasn't there and who probably didn't own his own place in London.

She stepped into a glorious sea of white marble, bold abstract paintings on the walls and rich, expensive rugs underfoot. A very modern staircase of metal and glass carved its way upstairs, dissecting the open area into two halves. Wide-eyed, she gazed around her. To the left, an impressive archway led to various rooms. On the right, an arch that mirrored it led to yet more rooms. Why on earth did one guy need so many rooms? she wondered.

Her gaze finally settled on him and he raised his eyebrows and told her that they could chat in the sitting room.

'You have a lovely…er…house, Mateo. Or maybe I should say *palace*.'

She blinked when he burst out laughing, and then blushed, because the sound of that laughter, rich and amused, was at once familiar and filled her with nostalgia.

It was also a timely reminder of the silence that had settled over him ever since the scan. Which in turn brought her right back down to earth with a bump.

'So…' she ventured as she was ushered into an amazing sitting room with low, cream sofas and a warm, rich rug that covered most of the floor.

'So…'

Mateo raked his fingers through his hair and looked at her gravely as she edged towards one of the chairs and sank into it. He sat facing her and leant forward, arms resting loosely on his thighs.

That scan had changed everything. He and Bianca had married in haste when she had only just become pregnant and there had been no scan. The usual confirmation tests, yes, but no scan at that stage...and then the miscarriage had changed everything. Plus he'd been so young, already tough, but not nearly as tough as he was now. He'd thought about fatherhood, and had known that he would always do the right thing, but the whole concept of a baby and the reality of it had been abstract and woolly—something that would happen down the line.

But seeing that little scrap of life eagerly waiting to enter the world... Mateo had felt the fierce tug of possessiveness that had wiped out all good intentions about stepping back because he didn't want to pull her into the loveless marriage she wouldn't want. No. He had seen his baby and in an instant had known that anything less than marriage wasn't going to do.

It had been naïve to think otherwise but then he was so accustomed to boxing up his emotions that he hadn't expected to feel the overpowering jolt he had felt in that room. Nothing could have protected him from it, not even the hard veneer he had cultivated over the years. More than anything else, he'd seen that tiny beating heart and had known that keeping Alice safe, keeping their baby safe, would be his lifelong mission, and to do that he would not be able to step back. Detachment was no longer an option.

How could he ever have thought that he could allow another man to enter her life and join in decision making about *his* child's future? How could he ever have imagined that anyone but him could be involved with this baby of theirs?

He looked at her carefully and knew that, having approached the situation with the emotionalism of a robot, he was going to have to win her over. He'd magnanimously told her that he would be a hands-on father but in the capacity of one who lived a separate life—that she needed to fulfil her dream of finding someone to love and he would give her the freedom to do that.

He was going to do a complete turnaround and already he wondered why he hadn't gone down this route in the first place. He'd remembered Bianca, remembered the foolhardiness of rushing into marriage for the sake of a pregnancy and then all the attendant problems that had resulted from his hasty, emotional decision. He'd then obeyed his instinct and turned away from making a similar mistake.

But Alice wasn't Bianca. They might no longer be together, but the relationship hadn't been poisonous. He and Alice could make a go of it, but he would have to persuade her. Somehow he would have to make her see that there was life beyond love. No way was he going to walk away from the one hundred percent commitment that now beckoned.

'Well? Are you going to say anything, Mateo? Like I said, I didn't come to your office because I wanted anything from you. If you've had a reality check now that we've had that scan, then just come out and tell me.'

'I've had a reality check, Alice.'

'And…'

'And this is going to play out slightly differently. We're going to get married.'

CHAPTER SEVEN

ALICE LOOKED AT HIM in shock. The shock was then followed by confusion. Was this the same guy who had, only days before, banged on about the situation requiring a businesslike approach? Since when had marriage been *businesslike*? Weren't *business deals* more along the lines of shaking hands and signing a contract?

'I can see you're surprised.'

'Not what I was expecting, no.'

'Seeing our baby, Alice, brought it forcibly home to me that this isn't something that can be dealt with the way I would deal with a work problem.'

'Well, Mateo, you don't say.' But her heart was beating like a sledgehammer. *Marriage!* It was everything she had dreamed of. The guy she loved…their baby…

She had sneaked a glance at Mateo in that small, darkened room and her heart had swelled with love as she drank in the beautiful lines of his face cast into shadows. Then she had looked at the small, living, breathing baby they had created together and the longing for them to be a family unit, a *real* family unit, had been so overwhelming that she'd had to breathe in deeply to control the rush of emotion.

And now, the prospect of marrying this guy was being

dangled in front of her like a carrot. She thought of them bringing home their baby, buying stuff for their home together, stuff that wouldn't be white or include any marble. She thought of them watching telly, going to the shops together, having friends and family to dinner…

When she blinked, what she saw was über-luxury all around her and a man who lived firmly in this world. A world that was a million miles from the dream world she had just concocted in her head. So much about this picture was right but so much more was wrong.

If the promise of normality with Simon had not been enough for her in the end…if she had, in fact, wanted something more extraordinary…then at the very heart of her, she knew that it would only be okay with a guy who truly loved her. What she'd found was extraordinary without the love. She longed for this extraordinary man but with the wonderful *ordinariness* of love. In the end, love was what made the small trivia in life oh, so amazing.

Mateo had been moved by seeing his own flesh and blood on that scan, just as she had. Now he was prepared to go a step further and offer her the one thing she knew he would never, ever have offered in any other circumstances: a ring. However much she longed to take that ring and slip it on her finger, how could she do it? How could she turn his world on its head and live with herself? He didn't love her. Would she be able to cope with that for ever?

How long before they started wandering around this big, palatial house like two strangers bound together for the sake of the child they shared? How long before the isolation of doing the small things on her own began to eat away at all their noble intentions about being united for the sake of their baby? Would either of them be happy?

'That's not going to work, Mateo,' she said gently. 'Although I appreciate the offer.'

'I realise this was never your Plan A, Alice, but it makes sense and I should have seen that from the very beginning. Let me get you something to drink: tea? Fresh juice? Water?'

'Let's just talk this out, Mateo. No, you're right, I never thought that I'd be having a baby out of wedlock, for want of a better way of putting it. You know, it just wasn't something that was ever on the radar.' She sighed wryly. 'That along with spending a few torrid nights with a complete stranger.'

'But now we're here and I feel that we need to both put our Plan As to one side and consider what's best for the baby. And that's both parents on board, married and united in making joint decisions and providing stability and security.'

'Love is what makes a marriage work, or else it's just as good for us to live apart and amicably share in this baby's upbringing. We can like one another and get along without tying ourselves together. We both know the tie would break eventually, anyway.' She sighed and looked around her, this time more slowly, before resting her eyes on him.

'That's not what you said when we were at my lodge,' Mateo countered with silky assurance. 'If I recall, you said that you wanted to see where our relationship led when we returned to London.'

'Yes, well, that was then. That was before…'

'Yes, things are different now, but what we had… Let's be honest, it's still there, isn't it? It is for me. When you showed up at my office, when I saw you again, I wondered whether that thing I'd felt might have disappeared… that *charge*.'

'Mateo, this is beside the point…'

She watched with alarm and excitement as he rose slowly from where he'd been sitting and sauntered towards her, dragging a foot stool which he placed so close to her that she could feel the heat emanating from him.

'Is it?'

His eyes were dark, questioning and gently probing and they stirred a longing in her that was dangerously familiar.

'What does it matter if this so-called charge is there or not?' Alice whispered a little shakily. 'Would you have done something about it if I'd shown up to ask you to pick things back up with us?'

'I would have tried not to.'

His blunt honesty hurt but it showed a side of him that was to be commended. He didn't play games. What he said would always be the truth.

'Because you're so attracted to me, right?'

'Yes, as a matter of fact.' His eyes were lazy, roving over her flushed face in a leisurely, sexy scrutiny. 'I would have been tempted but I would have probably reacted with my head and not that other unreliable part of my body. I would have known that I couldn't offer you the long-term relationship you wanted. Even when you told me about the pregnancy, when I knew that I had to allow you the freedom to find a man who could give you what you really wanted in life, even then, I wanted you. But I resisted the urge to touch, to try and seduce you… to tempt you back into my arms.'

He edged closer fractionally, leaning slightly into her. 'But things are different now. Now I want to offer you a long-term relationship.'

'I never said I wanted a long-term relationship with you. I said we could carry on having fun when we got back to London. I always knew you weren't the kind of long-term guy I was looking for.' Alice looked away and licked her lips. Her eyes strayed to the knees almost touching hers and the strong, brown hand hanging over one knee.

Mateo pressed his thumbs to his eyes and then looked at her, deadly serious. 'Having fun? No. I knew that would have been a bad idea. I'm not the sort of guy you would want to have fun with. You'd end up getting hurt.'

'Who's to say *I* would have been the one getting hurt?'

'I'm well-insulated when it comes to women having that sort of effect on me. But who knows…?' His green eyes darkened with wicked amusement. 'Think you might have been the one to make me cry, Alice?'

'I guess we'll never know!' She went bright red.

'At any rate, things have changed. This isn't about fun. This is about the baby we've made. I thought I could live with a situation whereby we shared this baby as friends, nothing more, but I can't. Seeing our baby moving inside you, that small speck…' He shook his head. 'We could work, Alice. I respect you, I like you, we get along and then…' he brushed her cheek with his finger '…there's this.'

'Mateo…' Alice heard the husky tremor in her voice and half-closed her eyes, tilting back her head, utterly unable to resist the pull of an attraction that was too powerful for her. His finger on her cheek was soft and gentle and the breath caught in her throat when that finger found the contour of her lips and delicately traced them.

'Kiss me,' she heard herself groan and he did. He kissed her. She'd forgotten just how sweet and beautiful the feel of his mouth was on hers. Cool lips and the slide of his tongue roused her until she was squirming and wet for him. When he rested his hand on her thigh, she immediately parted her legs, wanting more. Instead, frustratingly, he pulled back and looked at her gravely.

'We have more going for us than a hell of a lot of starry-eyed couples who start off with nothing more than the hope that a bit of fairy dust is going to last a lifetime.'

'A little fairy dust never hurt anyone…'

'Until it turns to shards of glass.'

'You're so cynical, Mateo.'

'Realist. And realism is what is going to work so well for us. Marry me, Alice. You'll find that I can make an excellent father and husband.'

Alice looked at him. There was so much going for what he had said—a stable life for a child who had not asked to be conceived. He would be a good provider and she knew that he would be an attentive husband. Her parents would be overjoyed; they were traditionalists through and through. And, yes, there was the sex. It would fade away, of course, and without love would slide into a sort of brother-sister amicability.

Inevitably, he would discreetly fool around. That went without saying. Duty would bind him to her but mutual respect, liking one another and having a child together would only go so far when it came to tethering him. He would be able to deal with the intensity of desire and the searing urge to protect what he would see as his, but would he be able to deal with the everyday normality that every relationship needed? Or would that bore him? Could an extraordinary man ever know the value of ordinary? And, however much she knew that she wanted and needed some extraordinariness in her life—that *some-*

thing that was all wrapped up with *love*—didn't she also know that normality was also needed to be in the mix?

Her heart would be crushed on a daily basis and, whilst Alice knew that she should put their child first, the thought of her own projected misery filled her with panic and apprehension. Maybe if she stood back she might be able to build her own inner reinforcements to protect her from that. Would she get stronger and more immune to his pull over time? Wasn't time supposed to do stuff like that?

'I'm not willing to make such a big commitment just yet, Mateo.'

'I'm not following you. Is it the love angle? Alice, there's more to a successful marriage than love. We have all the ingredients to make it work, and that's not even taking into account the fact that we're still hot for one another.'

'It's not that. Maybe when you first decided that we were better off apart, free to see where life took us while remaining committed to our child, I thought about it and realised that it made sense.'

Their eyes tangled and she saw that in that instant Mateo knew that he had lost the argument. If he wanted marriage, he was going to have to win her over. And the only thing she wanted was the one thing he couldn't give her.

Alice was flicking through the paper in the staffroom three weeks later when she froze.

Three of her friends were busy marking papers and she was waiting for Mateo to show up because he wanted to show her something. He wouldn't say what.

She'd done her best to curb her excitement because she hadn't failed to notice that, ever since his heady marriage proposal, all had gone quiet on that particular front. She'd backed off and he'd immediately respected the distance she had insisted on keeping between them.

No more talk of the burning desire that simmered between them and no gentle persuasion for her to come round to his marriage solution. Had he actually been serious when he'd told her that he still fancied her, wanted her? Or had he decided that that was the best route to take because he had changed his mind and wanted to put a ring on her finger?

The uncertainty tormented Alice but she knew that the best thing she could do for their relationship was to ignore it. If he had changed his mind, then there was nothing she could do about it and, in every other aspect, he was turning out to be the responsible guy he had held himself out to be.

Besides, if the pull of that intense, crazy desire was snuffed out, then wouldn't that be all to the good? Wasn't that one complication removed?

He called her daily, saw her at least a couple of times a week and had insisted on relocating her from her rented place to somewhere more suitable. Alice had not objected, and the new place was so much more magnificent that she was quietly grateful that he had taken charge and stampeded through her weak protests that she was perfectly happy where she was. He'd also deposited a startling sum of money into her account, which he had labelled 'petty cash', and had opened several accounts for her at some of the high-end department stores.

He was as respectful and charming as any woman could have hoped for from the father of her unborn child and Alice struggled not to absolutely *hate it*. It was an adult, civilised relationship and she treacherously longed for the passion which had disappeared. No amount of bracing mantras could ease the anguish of having the man she adored so close and yet so far.

It hardly helped that when they had gone to see her parents, to jointly break the news to them, he had somehow managed to charm them into accepting what was presented as not marriage, but something sensible, loving and transparent—just as good in many ways.

The perfect guy. Except now, staring down at the pictures in the weekly gossip rag in front of her, the reality of their relationship was hitting home—because there he was, at some networking bash or other which he had attended the week before. And next to him, gazing up at him, was just the sort of leggy blonde he used to date before she'd come along.

She didn't want to keep staring at the pictures, looking for clues, so she slapped the magazine shut. But the images were imprinted in her head and they were still there, churning around, when Mateo buzzed her fifteen minutes later to tell her that he was waiting outside.

Mateo was lounging against his car, waiting for Alice to emerge. Winter had morphed into spring and there was a pleasant hint of warmth in the air. It was a source of wonder as to why she insisted on remaining in her job when there was no need.

'I like the people I work with,' she had told him doggedly, when he had probed her on that point. 'And I enjoy the kids, even though they can sometimes be unruly and stubborn. I love what I do and you can't expect me to give it all up just because I don't need the money any longer.'

Mateo was discovering what it was like to be with a

woman who wasn't impressed with what he could provide. He'd steered clear of returning to the subject of marriage. He figured that, the more he made of it, the deeper she would dig in her heels, and maybe she would see sense if he resorted to the art of subtle persuasion, but he was beginning to wonder whether it was a ploy that was going to work.

Accustomed to getting his own way in everything, it went against the grain to play the long game but he could see no other way. He was dealing with a woman who was completely different from any woman he had ever known and in this instance he was on uncertain territory.

He'd had to back off, and back off he had. He'd ditched all talk of marriage and had been scrupulous when it came to not touching her or giving her any reason to think that he wanted to revive the physical side of their relationship. It felt as if he was starting from scratch, playing an urgent courting game, the rules of which he was not wholly sure about.

She had principles. Having met her parents, he could see where that had come from. He could see that what she wanted was to emulate the quiet love her parents shared. The more he thought about that, the more hopeless he felt about his quest to convince her that there were alternatives, and that those alternatives were workable and satisfactory—that within the framework of marriage lay a host of different ingredients; that there were no hard and fast rules that applied to everyone.

He saw her push through the glass door of the school and he straightened. She wore loose dark-grey trousers, a dark-grey jumper and serviceable flat shoes. It was the outfit of a working woman who put comfort above appearance and who had certainly done nothing in the way of dressing to impress because he was picking her up.

He walked towards her and had to resist the temptation to tuck some of those loose strands of hair behind her ears. The physical chemistry he felt buzzed like a live wire just beneath the surface of his polite conversation. Again, he was questioning his vow not to touch her. Was torturing himself like this even the right way to get what he wanted?

'How was your day?' he asked, relieving her of a backpack that seemed far too heavy for someone in her condition.

'Good, thank you. And yours?'

Mateo flicked her a curious, sideways glance as he picked up something in her tone of voice that was a little off-key.

'The usual,' he drawled. 'Stuck behind a desk making a shedload of money.'

'Anything else you've been doing recently?'

'Throw me some clues so that I can see where that question is going, would you?'

'It's not important. Where are you taking me? I hope it's nowhere fancy because I won't be changing into any party outfits. I'm tired after a hectic day at school, and honestly, all I really want to do is go home, have a shower, mark some homework and then go to bed.'

'Why on earth are you hanging onto that job? You're pregnant. You shouldn't be working your fingers to the bone.'

'We've already been through this, Mateo. I'm a normal person who enjoys doing a normal job. I'm not one of these glamorous types who thinks it's okay to swan around doing nothing but going to beauty parlours and attending fancy social dos.'

'Where the hell has *that* come from?'

'Nowhere,' Alice muttered. 'I'm just tired. Tell me where we're going.'

'It's a surprise but I'm hoping it'll be a pleasant one.'

He held open the door of his black BMW and she slid into the passenger seat.

Before he started the engine, he turned to her. 'Okay, spit it out. What's bothering you?'

'Nothing's bothering me.'

'Think I don't know you well enough to know when something's on your mind?'

'Honestly, Mateo, I'm just tired.'

She was the first to look away, and suddenly Mateo felt the vice-like grip of panic wrap around him. Was this a sign of her pulling away from him? Who knew what those friends and colleagues of hers talked about? Was she slowly being persuaded into taking the hard line that there was no way she would ever consider marriage?

He thought he'd left that door open for her to consider, to come to her senses. But had he? Should he have kept hammering home to her that marriage was the best solution, best for the baby? Should he have played hardball and seduced her into bed with him, put her in a place where walking away would have been a lot more difficult? Should he have ruthlessly exploited the fact that the chemistry wasn't just confined to him?

Maybe there was someone there, some teacher she was interested in, one of those touchy-feely, sensitive types providing a shoulder for her to cry on.

Unused to such flights of imagination, Mateo didn't quite know what to do with his thoughts. It took an effort for him to grapple his way back to a position of common sense. He shrugged and started the engine into life, and his powerful car purred away, cutting through the London traffic, heading south away from central London. When he glanced sideways at her, she was staring through the window. He wanted nothing more than to reach inside her head and find out what was going on in there.

They drove in silence, and it was only as they cleared the congested roads of London that she perked up and looked a little more curious about where they were going.

'I want to show you a house,' Mateo said, breaking the silence.

'A house?'

'You can't live in a rented place for ever. I've personally had a look around this place, and I think it's a good find. Although naturally, if you don't like it, then that's that.'

'We don't have the same taste in houses.'

Mateo heard the underlying cool in her voice and gritted his teeth.

'You like lots of white and marble, stuff with sharp edges—not very toddler-friendly.'

'My bachelor pad,' Mateo returned drily, 'wasn't meant to be toddler-friendly. I've always found I can manoeuvre round table corners without bumping into them and I rarely spill ice lollies on the white marble.'

'Not funny, Mateo. You might say your lifestyle isn't toddler-friendly.'

'Are you determined to pick an argument with me, Alice? And, if you are, then maybe you could explain why so that I can defend myself?'

He pulled away from the main drag and began manoeuvring through the picturesque lanes and streets that circled the sprawl of Richmond Park.

Looking at him, Alice could feel the tension stiffening his shoulders and she knew that she was being unfair. So what if he was out there having a good time? So what if he was doing what he normally did, networking with beautiful blondes? She'd built up an entire scenario around a few photos in a stupid rag and had then needled away at him in a manner that was shamefully passive-aggressive—not like her at all.

He didn't deserve that. He'd been open and honest with her from the beginning and she could hardly find fault with whatever activities he decided to get up to in his own time. If anything, seeing those photos should have reminded her of his unsuitability long term. The player could never be taken away from the game for too long, and Mateo was a player at heart. Had he reconciled himself to that? The fact that they were in a 'no touching' place pretty much said it all.

Determined to be less emotional, she paid attention to where they were and, when he finally pulled up in front of a red-brick Victorian house in its little plot, she was open-mouthed with surprise.

'Not a single slab of marble in sight,' Mateo murmured, circling round the car to open her door for her. 'No sharp edges. Extremely toddler-friendly.'

'I'm sorry,' Alice said, looking at him and resting her hand on his arm. 'I haven't exactly been great company this afternoon.'

'To be discussed. Come in, have a look around and tell me what you think.'

Alice forgot about Mateo padding along slightly behind her as she explored the house. It was cosy, with little nooks and crannies leading to rooms in a topsy-turvy, charming way. There were wood floors throughout, and in the downstairs sitting room parquet flooring reminded her of where she had grown up in the vicarage. Outside, the garden was as tangled and charming as the inside had been, a broad stretch of lawn with fruit trees at the back growing against an old brick wall.

'It's perfect...' Alice breathed, finally turning to Mateo and smiling sheepishly. 'And not at all what I was expecting.'

They were walking back to his car and she glanced over her shoulder, already knowing that this was where she wanted to be. The sun was starting to lower in the sky, and her heart warmed when she looked sideways at Mateo, impressed at how he had managed to get something as big as this just right.

'I'm a guy who's full of surprises. I've booked a table for an early dinner for us so that we can discuss the place.'

'You assumed I'd like it?'

'I'd assumed even if you didn't that we would have a lot to discuss.'

As he circled the small courtyard in front of the house heading out towards the town centre, Alice murmured, 'I haven't said how great it is that you've taken all this in your stride.'

Mateo looked at her in silence for a few seconds.

He'd made sure to take a step back as she'd looked around, wanting to gauge her reaction without her being aware of him gauging her reaction. She loved it, as he'd known she would; subtle persuasion had been his game plan. Now, he was in the process of gauging something altogether different—namely whatever had prompted her mood earlier on.

'You can move in as quickly as next month, but it will entail quitting your job. I can't see the commute working.'

'Mateo…'

'If you want to hang on at the school, then be my guest, but the seller wants to get rid of the house as soon as possible and there are already three offers under review. I'll outstrip them all, but only on your say so.'

'Can I think about it?'

Mateo shrugged. 'I'd say you have little more than twenty-four hours to do that.'

'I'm just so attached to the school and to all my friends there.'

Mateo gritted his teeth and tried to check resurfacing notions of some fellow teacher laying it on thick about Alice's situation, mopping up her tears of sadness that she hadn't found true love with the father of her baby. Jealousy didn't usually feature in his life but he was having a hard time fighting it. When he thought of her pouring out her disappointment to some other guy, he literally saw red.

'What was all that about?' he ground out, before clearing his throat and trying to sound as composed as possible, given the weird feelings tearing through him.

'What was all what about?'

'Your mood earlier on.'

'I…'

'Don't be shy—it's not your style. I'm too accustomed to you saying exactly what you think so, like I said, spit it out.'

'If you must know, I saw a picture of you—actually, several pictures of you.'

'No idea what you're talking about.'

'I happened to be looking through the paper in the staff room and there you were, at some do or other last week, with a blonde.'

'Ah. I see.' He did see, quite a bit. In a heartbeat he thought…to heck with the long game. He should never have denied the man he was, the guy who'd literally fought to get where he was, the guy who'd always known that all was fair in love and war. 'I think I remember the occasion—a bash for a charity dealing with mental health issues in youngsters.'

'And was the woman with you?'

'That's not really your concern, now, is it, Alice?'

Had there been a blonde woman there? More than likely. Expensive charity fund raisers with high-profile guests usually attracted a very pretty crowd, and a lot of them tended to gravitate towards him.

'No, I know that. I was just a little curious, that's all.'

'But curiosity about who I may or may not be going out with doesn't enter the equation, not now.' He slowed down and pulled into one of the spaces close to the restaurant and waited for her to digest what he had just said for a few minutes, then he opened the door for her, and they walked to the place he had booked for them.

'If you had chosen to accept my marriage proposal,' he told her as soon as they were seated and water had been poured, 'then you would naturally have had a right to that kind of curiosity, but you chose another road, and that road has a different set of rules.'

'Forget I asked.'

'No, I won't. You *did* ask and now's a good time for us to discuss this. If I happened to have gone to that bash with a woman, then I don't have to answer to you for that decision, because what we have here, right now, is something that exists purely for the sake of the baby inside you. I want you to look a little into the future when our baby starts growing up and I want you to get used to the idea that there will be women in my life and then, eventually, just the one woman, because as a father I will no longer be interested in playing the field.'

'I've already thought about that, Mateo.'

Mateo chose to ignore her because some keen sixth sense had picked up a thread in her reaction that was the very same thing that had been bothering him. The tone of her voice when she'd asked about the woman at the party had given a lot away and he intended to use that to his advantage.

She wanted love, but she didn't want *him* to find it. She would have been happy for him to remain celibate in the background, even though she would realistically know that that was never going to happen. If she'd thought about him moving on, then it had been in an abstract way. until now…

'And that may happen sooner rather than later,' he told her gravely. 'I take my responsibilities seriously, and a woman by my side is something I would find desirable.'

'That's so different from what you said when I first told you that I was pregnant.'

'I… I had my reasons for being wary of jumping into marriage because of a pregnancy,' Mateo said with driven honesty. He raked his fingers through his hair and looked at her, jaw clenched as memories took over.

It was so rare for him to lose control of the narrative when it came to his private life that he floundered and only picked back up the thread after a few seconds of silence. She wasn't urging him to open up and he appreciated that.

'When I rushed into marriage with Bianca, it was because she was pregnant. It was early days, but I was keen to do the right thing, even though we'd been on the point of breaking up. It was a mistake. Bianca miscarried three weeks after we married, but we were locked into a situation by then that was never going to work out. I gave it my best shot but it was a harsh lesson in how the head should always rule the heart. If I'd used my head, I would have worked out that our relationship was fundamentally flawed and would never have survived even if a child had been involved.'

'I'm really sorry, Mateo. That must have been such a painful time for you.'

'Life happens. We divorced.'

'But you should never have married,' Alice said slowly. 'And then along I come, telling you that I'm pregnant, and of course you don't want to repeat your mistake. So why the change of heart?'

'The minute I saw our baby on that scan, something kicked in,' Mateo admitted truthfully, in a rough undertone. 'It was different with Bianca. I was very young, and the baby was more of an abstract reality, but seeing that baby move…the heartbeat.'

He glanced away and clenched his jaw. 'So here we are,' he continued in a cool, measured voice. 'I will meet someone, Alice. I will marry. My first choice would be to marry the mother of my child, but failing that I will not remain a bachelor playing Dad from a distance. If you want the cottage, I intend to have a place of my own also in Richmond, which I will share with the woman I make my wife, and there will be more than just the two of us then in the family unit. So the blonde lady? I may have a little fun for a while, but not for long, I predict.'

He looked at her and then said, without bothering to beat around the bush, 'You don't like the thought of me having another woman dangling from my arm, do you?'

'It's not that. I wouldn't want any child of ours to be exposed to a dad who plays the field.'

'Which, I assure you, I won't be doing by the time any child of ours is old enough to cotton on to anything like that. So I'll ask you one more time and then the question will no longer be posed—do you want to finally accept the benefits of marrying me, or are you aiming for the blended family, because you still think that love is really the one and only thing that matters here?

'I'll repeat for your benefit: Bianca and I were a mistake before we tied the knot. You and I? We're not. This chemistry between us... We can be lovers again and, if we're both honest to ourselves, isn't that what we want? Tie this knot, Alice, and it remains tied. You'll never open a sordid magazine to find me pictured with a blonde on my arm again, ever. Your choice.'

CHAPTER EIGHT

ALICE HAD SAID YES: that had been seven weeks ago. Since then, things had moved fast. In two days' time, they would be moving into the house she had looked around. He'd seemed startled when she'd asked him, some time back, if it wouldn't be be too modest for his taste.

'We come from very different worlds, Mateo,' she had told him when she had accepted his marriage proposal. 'Whichever side of the tracks you've come from, you've ended up on the side where the pavements are lined with gold, and I'm not sure if you're going to find somewhere as unassuming as that cottage up to your current standards—especially if you'll be living there with me full-time, not visiting once a week from your über-modern mansion on Mount Olympus.'

He'd grinned. 'I'll prove you wrong,' he'd asserted, with such ease that she had been reassured and surprised at the same time. But, sure enough, he hadn't looked back.

He had left the bulk of the soft-furnishing shopping to her, and had got a heavy-duty team of contractors on board, who had set to work turning one old and slightly dilapidated Victorian house into a work of art, while keeping every single original feature intact. It had been done at speed because no expense had been spared.

The wedding date had been set: a quiet affair with just close family and friends, to be held at the very parish church where her father preached. The small village was abuzz with excitement and her mother had swooped in with commendable enthusiasm for every part of the process, from picking out flowers to organising the choir.

Amidst all this, she expanded as the baby had grown, and there was not a single moment when she didn't feel Mateo's deep and honest involvement with the tiny human being maturing inside her. But he would never love her; of that she was now sure, having heard the rest of his story when it came to marriage and, as it turned out, pregnancy.

Everything about his relationship with his ex-wife explained the man Mateo was now. Not only had he rushed into marriage way too young but the marriage had been propelled by a pregnancy neither he nor his young girl-friend had planned.

However hardened he had been back then, he had obviously still been romantic enough to hope for a positive outcome. Maybe he had secretly thought that whatever love they'd shared at the start could be resurrected with a baby on the way. But the evolution of that relationship—the divorce, then the woman returning years later to try and fleece him for money—had opened his eyes to the bitter fact that not only had that love been little more than an illusion, but the very business of opening himself up a fraction could be disastrous.

Roll the clock on and Alice knew that, while she might love Mateo, he would only ever return love with, at best, affection mingled with a sense of duty. He wasn't a guy who ignored learning curves and he had had his fill of them.

But she had had a glimpse of what her life would be like if she let him go. Forget all her high-minded principles of not wanting to suffer the pain of being with a guy who didn't love her. The truth was that seeing him with that blonde woman had shown her that the pain of actually seeing him move on would always be hard for her to bear.

She would just have to plaster a smile on her face when she was with him, always keep a careful guard on her emotions and love him from afar, knowing that to be open about how she felt would risk turning him off.

And who knew? There were always surprises round every corner. He might not come to love her in the way that *she* defined love, but he could come to *need* her, and that would be a step up from affection.

Want and need were close companions, weren't they? And he wanted her. It was there every time he glanced at her, or looked at her until her body was raging with an urgent, primal burn. One that matched his. Oh, how glorious it was to be able to feel that hard, perfect body once again.

She'd made her choice at his ultimatum: marriage and the knot tied for good, lovers once again. Since then, permission granted, they had fallen back into each other's arms with the exquisite satisfaction of two people who knew each other intimately, who revelled in the pleasure of touching.

There was no question how he felt for her on a physical level: he wanted her. Honestly, whatever doubts she might harbour about this situation, one thing was absolutely clear: this part of their relationship worked and who knew if this one thing might not grow into more?

One day he might need her. *Need* would make it harder for him to stray when the physicality between them eased away and he no longer wanted to touch her the way he wanted to touch her now.

Right now, getting done the final touches before she left for the leaving party her friends at the school were throwing for her, Alice blushed at the thought of those touches, that *physicality. She* would never tire of the way he could make her body sing and even now, with it swelling and getting bigger, he was still turned on—more so, if anything.

She didn't get it. When she thought of that woman she'd seen in the picture, leggy, skinny and tall enough to look Mateo in the eye instead of roughly somewhere in the region of his chest, Alice could only wince at the unfavourable comparison. She knew that she was marrying the most gorgeous, eligible bachelor on the planet through default and she had to fight to overcome the occasional burst of insecurity that generated in her. Yet, when he traced the contours of her swollen belly with such tenderness, she had no doubt that he wasn't put off by her expanding girth.

Sometimes, at night, she wondered how things might change after the baby was born, which was no longer in the distant future. Would the romance of an unborn child and the adventure that represented turn into the more prosaic business of sleepless nights and exhausted days? Would he still be turned on by a tired, yawning wife who didn't have time to look after herself because of the demands of an infant? Would temptation elsewhere begin to beckon as the mysterious pull of her pregnant body no longer existed?

Since she had no answers to those questions, and since she knew that speculation would only end up with her in a place where she probably wouldn't want to be, Alice boxed up those concerns, to be considered some other time in the future.

She stepped back and looked at her reflection with a critical eye. She could see the change in her shape, the small but distinct roundness of her expanding belly. Possibly not a great idea to go for bright, summery colours when she was short, genetically plump and a few months' pregnant. But, then again, she looked cheerful, which was exactly how she felt as she saw the beep on her phone: Mateo's driver outside and waiting for her. She flew out, grabbing her bag and her lightweight jacket on the way.

She would miss her friends, but would still keep in touch with many of them socially, and, if she was finishing a tiny bit ahead of the usual maternity-leave schedule then that was fine. Deep down, she could see the sense of taking it easy and relaxing before the baby came along rather than trying to prove a point about independence when she really didn't need to work. She would enjoy herself and then look forward to the new chapter in her life in a couple of days, when they moved in to their new place together.

Right now, she was still in the rented apartment Mateo had moved her to and Mateo had said he was making sure that as many complex deals were completed as possible before the baby came along. Alice hadn't protested and, while she trusted him, she knew that there was no such thing as certainties in life, so she made damn sure not to go near any gossip pages just in case.

But tonight wasn't for any anxious thoughts. Tonight was for enjoying herself.

* * *

Mateo had no idea why he had decided to surprise Alice at the school where her leaving do was being held. Things were exactly as he had hoped for: she had accepted his marriage proposal.

He was guiltily aware that a certain amount of tactical economy with the truth had played into that decision. He'd painted a nicely vivid picture of what Alice could expect when he found another woman. He'd allowed her to think that, having had his proposal turned down, he was already easing himself back into the dating scene... even though he hadn't looked in the direction of another woman since Alice had returned to his life. But he had no regrets about those creative liberties. He'd got what he'd wanted and it was for the best.

What could beat two parents united and together when it came to bringing up the child they shared? What could beat the fire between them? He'd resisted her for as long as he could when he'd been waiting for her to come to him, but he had prodded and she had come to him, and it was damn near wonderful not having to deny what his body wanted—what both their bodies wanted!

There was no way she could deny that they got along. He'd been nothing but accommodating—the ideal husband to be and father in the making. But he was beginning to think that proving himself was a vain pursuit, because she honestly didn't seem to notice all his hard work.

For instance, she had no idea how much grit it had taken to accept the wedding taking place in weeks rather than hours. He had nodded, murmured something or other and battled the instinct that had pushed him to firm things up while he still had her, because the longer they delayed walking down the aisle the more time it allowed her to reconsider.

For the guy who'd never given marriage a second's thought in years, he found himself in the challenging position of desperately wanting it now.

He hadn't raised an eyebrow when she'd made noises about the house he'd bought being too modest for his taste. True, he would have gravitated to something bigger and more impersonal, but he'd been quick to appreciate that that would never have been to her taste. Besides, as she had pointed out, infants were allergic to too much white and too many hard edges. So he'd left the choice of whatever décor she wanted to her.

He'd likewise listened with interest as she'd rambled on about resuming work locally once the baby was born. He didn't see the point of that, but he was determined to prove to her that she hadn't made a mistake when it came to giving in to him and giving up on whatever romantic dreams she still clung to.

Yet, he had caught glimpses of her when she hadn't realised he'd been watching her and her expression had hardly been one of undiluted joy. At times like that, his gut instinct was to touch her, because on that one front he was perfectly secure.

Her body curved to his as natural as a flower keening towards the sun, but he had to resist that because it was a cheap fix; he knew that. They could still lose themselves when they were making love, get to a place where nothing mattered and there was no sadness, thoughtfulness or anything at all but enjoyment of the moment, but more and more he found that he wanted more than just passing enjoyment.

He wanted her to smile *all the time*. He just didn't know how to get there with that.

So he'd decided that he'd surprise her at her staff party—maybe remind her somehow that he was there for her and the baby. Show her that the life she was leaving behind wasn't one that she should file under the heading of 'whimsical nostalgia for the good times'. If she conditioned herself to think of her past as a sacrifice she'd been obliged to make, then there would be no chance of her ever really accepting the present without wondering whether an alternative would have been better.

He could have told her to expect him but he favoured the element of surprise. It was only as his driver neared the uninspiring building that he realised something: part of him was curious to see her in her natural habitat rather than his.

He knew the code to the door. With the agreement of the other members of staff, she had been allowed to share it with him. Mateo thought that his hefty financial contribution to the school finances might also have had a little something to do with that particular decision, but had tactfully refrained from pointing that out. Time had shown him that she was naive when it came to her accepting the unpalatable truth that money bought pretty much everyone and everything. Probably because she was the one exception to that rule.

He'd been to the school on a number of occasions and knew the layout pretty well, although it felt a little eerie to wander around without the noise of kids everywhere. Lord only knew why they'd chosen to have a party at the school, but Alice had been thrilled. She'd wanted it to be informal and private. And besides, she had confided at the time, her memories were all there, which was important to her. She hadn't wanted lots of waiters and staff faffing around, serving them, with a deadline for them to leave and no music allowed.

He followed the noise. Only essential lighting was on in the corridors and the doors to the classrooms were all firmly shut. It wasn't a big school, serving kids between the ages of eleven and sixteen, with a sixth-form college standing on other grounds not far away. If he'd somehow looked at it through rose-tinted specs, he would say that it was as cosy as a functional, unimaginative concrete and glass block could possibly get. That was thanks to sheer ingenuity when it came to filling the unappealing wall space with posters.

Mateo heard old-school 80s music as he nudged open the door to the staffroom, which was adorned with balloons, a banner and a long table groaning under the weight of food ordered in for the occasion.

And there she was: Alice.

She was chatting in a group, jigging about merrily and laughing.

Mateo drew in a sharp breath and remained standing where he was, framed in the doorway but not immediately noticeable in the dim room crowded with so many people—a huge turn-out for a popular teacher.

The door was angled in such a way that someone would have had to twist round to make him out, and no one was doing that. Everyone was too busy having a blast. At least thirty-five people were there. Most were dancing and there was a lot of laughter, talking and screeching.

Watching, Mateo felt as though he'd been hit in the chest with a sledgehammer, because what he saw on Alice's face was absolute joy, and that absolute joy was something he hadn't seen for a long time. He'd seen abandon when they'd made love, and appreciation for his thoughtfulness when they'd gone out for meals or visited the house they'd be sharing.

But that *absolute joy*? No.

He pushed himself into the room, feeling as out of place as he'd felt in a long time. She instantly spotted him.

In the middle of turning to fetch herself some more of the nibbles on the table, Alice stilled. The last person she had been expecting to see was Mateo.

She'd become so used to guarding her feelings around him, hiding her love because she knew that it wasn't returned, because she wanted to protect herself as much as she could. She stole glances at him when he wasn't looking, like a thief stealing a cache of gold to be inspected later in privacy, but she made sure to school her expression when she was with him. She couldn't let all her defences slip. Where would that leave her? As helpless as a turtle deprived of its protective shell.

He'd asked very few questions about the leaving party and she'd got the impression that he hadn't been all that interested. Why should he have been? she'd asked herself impatiently. The leaving party didn't involve the baby. The leaving party involved *her* and he wasn't interested enough in her to ask for details.

He came alive when he touched her, and his eyes lit up whenever they rested on her swollen stomach, proof positive that it was the baby he wanted. But otherwise he was kind, unfailingly attentive but keen on keeping some distance. Physical distance…no. Emotional distance…yes.

At least, that was what it felt like to Alice.

She drank the remainder of her lemonade, knowing that he'd been spotted from the awed reaction from everyone, and walked towards him. The conversation which had stopped for a few seconds picked back up again around her as she propelled her way forwards.

'What are you doing here?' was the first thing she asked when she was standing in front of him. 'I thought you said that you were going to be working late this evening.'

'Thought I'd surprise you, join in the fun. Are you disappointed that I've come?'

Alice hesitated. Disappointed? How could she ever be disappointed to see Mateo? He thrilled her to the bone. He looked sexy as hell, indolently leaning against the door frame, staring down at her in ways that made her whole body feel as though its primary mission in life was to fire up in readiness for him.

It was such a frustrating reaction that she reddened and scowled. 'Surprised. Come on through.'

She began turning away, but then saw that he wasn't immediately following suit, so she reluctantly turned back round to look at him.

'Wait. I… I don't want to interrupt your good time, Alice.'

'Why did you come, Mateo?'

'I came because…'

'Did you want to see how the other half live?'

'Of course not,' he said shortly.

'There are no waiters and waitresses here with great platters of expensive food and there's no champagne. Everyone put money into a kitty towards the food. Sarah, the dinner lady, did the spread. And we all brought some alcohol and soft drinks, and James is the DJ for the evening.'

'Why are you getting hot under the collar? Have I said anything about coming here because I wanted to see *how the other half live*?'

'No, but you weren't exactly very interested when I told you about this leaving do.'

Alice heard the hurt petulance in her voice with dismay. She was punishing him for not taking the sort of interest in her that she wanted him to, seeing his surprise arrival here as patronising rather than interested, and she was ashamed of the pettiness.

So far she hadn't involved herself in his social life, although in fairness he had invited her to an opening only a week before. Mateo might have come from a rough background, might have had to fight tooth and nail to get where he had, but now that he'd got there he blended in with the highest echelons of society as though he'd always belonged there. He knew how to do that because he didn't care.

Hormones suddenly seemed to surge through her. In a rush, she felt self-pity for having fallen for a guy who didn't return her love, and for her own blasted body, which reacted to him mindlessly every time he was within a metre of her. It all seemed hopeless as she stared down the barrel of a future of want, need and love, too much for her to contain but with nowhere to go.

She thought of how her life was going to change and it was really the first time she had given this thought house room. She would no longer have this cheerful crowd of friends around her every day. She would be mixing in a world that was going to be very different, and she had a moment of panic that she was just never going to be able to fit in.

'You shouldn't have come here,' she said sharply. Her hazel eyes flashed with misplaced anger as she stared up at his beautiful face, noting the way the shutters dropped.

'I wouldn't have,' Mateo returned tightly, 'if I'd known that the reception was going to be as hostile as it is. Why's that?'

Alice was steaming full ahead. Maybe it was just the fact of seeing him here, on the last day of life as she'd known it. She didn't know. She just knew that everything seemed to have piled up on top of her and this was where it burst its banks.

She glared at him, and in return he raised cool eyebrows and stared right back at her with unflinching aloofness.

'You don't get it!' she snapped miserably, half-stepping out of the room and then drawing the door behind them so that the world wasn't witnessing this stupid spat that had sprung from thin air.

'Tell me what I don't get.'

'I feel…' Alice left the sentence hanging in mid-air because she wasn't quite sure what she did feel. Things were not ideal but she thought she'd reasoned her way past the business of being in a loveless marriage. She knew that it was the right thing to do. So why all of a sudden was she miserable and tearful?

Was it because he had showed up here unannounced? Was he a reminder of the world she'd be entering in stark contrast to the one she would be leaving behind? Was there a part of her that was just pretending to accept the situation because she was afraid of the alternative? It felt unfair that love could be so painful.

She looked at him in mute, misplaced anger and then glanced down.

'Talk to me, Alice.'

He put one hand on her chin and tilted her face to his. When their eyes met, his were gentle and curious, which actually didn't make her feel much better.

'I don't want to talk,' she said with a defensive toss of her head.

'What do you want to do?'

'I'd quite like to make love to you.'

She watched the way his eyes darkened and the flush of simmering heat that stole into his face.

She didn't want *polite* and if this was the only way to get *passion* then, right now, it was a ploy she wasn't averse to using.

'I don't think an empty hall outside a staff room where there are forty people celebrating your imminent departure is going to do the trick, do you, Alice?'

'We could leave.'

'No, we could not.'

'Don't you want me? Don't you want to make love to me?'

'Where the hell is all this coming from?'

Alice shrugged, dealt him a challenging, provocative stare from under her lashes and felt a kick of power. However polite he might be in his role of perfect husband to be, nothing could hide the flare of passion he still seemed able to provoke. How much longer that would last, she had no idea, and she knew that this uncertainty was just something else that unsettled her.

She sighed and looked at him ruefully.

'I'm just kidding,' she said. 'Come on through. It's fun in there. Everybody's really put themselves out and you know they all like you.'

'It was a mistake coming here,' Mateo returned roughly. 'But it's obvious something's on your mind and I want to know what that something is. I'll wait up for you.'

'You'll wait up for me?'

'I'll be at your place and, Alice…don't overdo it to-night.'

'Because I'm pregnant?' she couldn't help but ask sweetly, immediately spotting his area of concern which, of course was for the precious cargo she carried. 'Staying up late isn't going to damage the baby, Mateo. I'm pregnant. I'm not ill!'

He didn't say anything. He gave her one final look before turning on his heel and walking away and she followed him with her eyes until the door had shut behind him.

Mateo was sprawled on the sofa in Alice's apartment and was consulting his watch for the eighth time in less than an hour when he heard the sound of her key being inserted in the door.

He'd left her over three hours ago. It had been a mistake to surprise her at her leaving do. He hadn't been invited for a reason, and the reason had become patently obvious the second she had spotted him. He'd seen the dismay on her face, noted the way the laughter had died on her lips and had known that she hadn't asked him along because she hadn't wanted him there.

He'd never been in a position like that in his life but

Mateo was already growing accustomed to the fact that there was a Mateo that had existed before Alice and one that existed post-Alice. The post-Alice version could take nothing for granted and was conscious of the fact that at any given moment he might find himself in alien territory without any signposts and no idea what lay round the corner.

He certainly hadn't foreseen being dismissed in not so many words. As soon as he had walked out of the building, his imagination had gone into overdrive. He'd remembered the happiness on her face before she'd spotted him and then he'd tried to think who she'd been with in that little group.

Had there been any men there? Mateo had always prided himself on not being jealous. In fact, he'd never cared about his girlfriend's exes and had never had the slightest concern about any of them playing the field behind his back. Why should he? Few could match what he brought to the table and the women he dated had always been grateful to go out with him. He'd grown lazy, it had to be said, and Alice never failed to remind him of that.

But as he waited for her, nursing one drink for the entire time and unable to focus on anything but the crazy scenarios in his head, he did his best to try and recall who'd been there.

Had she been having a few last flirtatious encounters for the road? She was pregnant, for God's sake! Mateo didn't know where his runaway brain was going with that scenario but, once it took root, it refused to budge.

Was there some teacher there who had had a crush on her before the whole pregnancy thing had happened? Before she had found herself in the position of having to seek him out through sheer decency, only to find herself embroiled with him because he'd given her as little choice as he could get away with? Because he had played on her driving need to do the right thing?

Was that a great place for him to be? Since when had a ruthless need to get what he wanted trumped generosity of spirit?

Maybe the time for talking had finally come—and this time he would have to accept whatever outcome it led to.

CHAPTER NINE

MATEO VAULTED UPRIGHT as soon as Alice was through the door. She looked surprised to see him, even though he'd warned her that he'd be waiting for her in her apartment.

'You're here,' she said, walking through and dumping her bag on the table, along with a sack of unopened presents wrapped in brightly coloured paper.

'I told you I would be.'

'Mateo, I'm honestly not in the mood to talk.'

'Was it a good leaving do?'

'The best.' She sighed. 'You shouldn't have waited up for me, Mateo. I'm dead on my feet.'

Mateo watched her as she struggled out of her light-weight coat and kicked off her shoes.

He looked at her stomach and gritted his teeth in frustration at the sudden disarray of their carefully formed plan. He knew that he should back off but he'd hated to do it. He didn't want to stress her out but he was breaking up inside.

'I expected you back a little earlier than…' he made a show of consulting his watch '…nearly twelve-thirty.'

'You're not my gatekeeper, Mateo—plus twelve-thirty is hardly the early hours of the morning. We were all having fun; we started playing games at eleven, and it was so riotous that the time just flew past.'

She was still in a mood and that cut him to the quick. He didn't understand. Where did they go from here? How long was she going to be in a mood? Was it hormone-driven—understandable nerves as the due date galloped towards them? Or cold feet before a wedding she hadn't wanted in the first place? It didn't pay to forget that she had already been engaged once and had broken off that engagement... He wasn't the only one with a back story.

Suddenly, the conversation staring him in the face felt bigger than before. He'd barely asked her about that broken engagement. She had mentioned it in passing the very first time they had met, and had vaguely brushed it off as the reason she had fled her friends and taken to dangerous slopes in that fast-gathering blizzard that had thrown them together.

Now it felt imperative that he find out what happened there. Could history be about to repeat itself? Mateo suddenly felt sick with panic.

The baby; this was all about the baby and the fact that he wanted what was best for their child, wasn't it? This was his highly developed sense of responsibility kicking in and he would have it no other way. He was sure of that.

Sudden uncertainty drove him towards her. He moved to reach out, felt her stiffen for a few seconds and then the predictable melting of her body as it reacted to his.

'Remember you told me that you wanted me...?'

Alice buried her head into his chest. He hadn't changed. He kept a stash of clothes at the apartment, as she did at his, but he was still in the trousers he had showed up in and his white shirt, which was rolled to the cuffs, although the hand-made Italian shoes were off and he was barefoot. It was a breathtakingly sexy combination at nearly one in the morning, she couldn't help but think.

She felt her belly pushing against him and felt her clothes a barrier between them although, as her body surged into shameful life, it was a barrier she didn't think was going to be there for much longer. Jeez, was it always going to be like this—one touch and all self-control down the drain?

She moaned softly as he slid his hand along her back; there was no zip. The dress was softly stretchy and very easy for him to ease up, scraping it against her thighs and then over her stomach until he could flip it over her head with a bit of help from her eager, scrabbling hands.

He stood back and looked at her. The lighting was subdued. He'd been lounging in semi-darkness while he'd waited for her.

'Take the bra off,' he commanded shakily, and Alice was only too happy to oblige, reaching round to unhook it and then sighing as she was freed of the constraint. She'd always been generously endowed, and her breasts had gone up a size since the pregnancy.

'God, you're beautiful,' Mateo said in a strangled voice and he moved to her, gently guiding her to the sofa as though actually reaching the bedroom hadn't even been a consideration.

Alice subsided onto the sofa, which was huge and very comfortable. 'The bed would be a whole lot more comfortable,' she murmured.

'Ah, but starters can be served here, my darling...'

Alice smiled. She knew his touches so well and yet every time they made love it felt new, wonderful and special.

He knelt at the side of the sofa and she twisted so that

she was lying on her side, making it easy for him to nibble at her breast, and then separate them with his hand to suckle gently on her nipple, which had darkened and grown, and was so sensitive that the slightest lick was enough very nearly to take her over the edge.

He knew that and continued to torment her with his tongue, which flicked darts of exquisite sensation through her. His hand on her belly was tender and gentle, as were his lips, and then, moving between her legs, the idle flick of his tongue slipped into her wetness and drove her insane.

He knew how to make her forget everything but the moment, and Alice barely realised when they left the sofa and made it into the bedroom. She was so conscious of the weight she'd gained, maybe because she hadn't been a slip of a thing in the first place, but Mateo was still strong enough to sweep her off her feet and carry her through to the bedroom as though she weighed nothing.

The love-making was slow and gentle. He touched her as though she were as delicate as a piece of porcelain, despite her constantly telling him that she was actually as strong as an ox. Deep down, she couldn't deny the lovely feeling of feminine helplessness at his protectiveness. It was just one more thing to add to the list of reasons for loving him.

Would that all disappear once the baby was born and he was no longer bothered about her fragile status? The disturbing thought drifted through her head, but she pushed it away, and then it was easy to do what she always did and sink into his caresses, letting her body get carried away on a tide of love, passion and fulfilment.

Her body was tingling all over, über-sensitive and on fire, when she finally climaxed, arching up against him and wrapping her arms around his neck so that she could pull him towards her, losing herself in him.

'Now I really am tired…' She yawned, stretching out and then squinting as he slid off her and lay flat on his back with one arm flung over his eyes.

'It was unfair of me to distract you when it was already so late.'

'You didn't do anything I didn't want to do, trust me.' Alice laughed and curved onto her side to look at him.

'Get some sleep, Alice.'

'You too.' She peered at him, although her eyelids were already beginning to feel heavy as she reached for her underwear on the ground and then smiled as he brought her the baggy tee she was accustomed to sleeping in. 'You wanted to talk?' she said reluctantly.

'It can wait. I'm going to try and get some work done. I'll make sure I don't wake you when I come to bed…'

Mateo nudged open the bedroom door at just after eight the following morning. She'd been sound asleep when he'd finally joined her in the early hours of the morning, snoring gently and curled on her side, wrapped around a pillow which supported her bump. They'd made love and, for a while, he'd forgotten the unsettling feelings he had had when he'd surprised her at the leaving party. Making love tended to do that. Unfortunately, uncomfortable notions could only be pushed to the side for so long before they popped back up, demanding to be acknowledged.

He had made her breakfast. It was something he had never done for a woman before, but he needed to clear the air, and getting her onside with some toast and coffee didn't seem too big an ask.

'Surprise,' he announced, dropping the tray deftly on the table next to the bed and then straightening to look at her as she shifted into an awkward sitting position with the pillows propped behind her.

She was pink and ruffled, her long hair a chaotic tangle that somehow made her look a lot younger than she was, a mere girl instead of a woman on the brink of having a baby.

'You should have woken me, Mateo. I know it's the weekend but, now that I won't have a job to wake up for on Monday, I don't want to get into the habit of just lazing around in bed until mid-morning.'

Mateo smiled. 'You happen to have a very good excuse.' He poured her some coffee and handed her the cup, then he arranged the tray to the side of her and pulled up a chair next to the bed. 'Besides, from tomorrow, you're going to be busy with the house move.'

Mention of the house they would be moving to was a reminder of a conversation that needed to be had. But now he found that he was happy to put it off, happy not to hear her tell him that this wasn't the life she had banked on.

He'd got his own way with the marriage but it seemed that there was more to life than getting his own way.

'Delicious toast, Mateo.'

'I'll make sure to contact the bakery to congratulate them on the quality of the bread. I'm sorry I showed up last night, Alice. I…hadn't meant to. It was something of a spur-of-the-moment decision.'

'It's okay.' Alice reddened.

'Want to know *why* I decided to unexpectedly show up?'

'Yes,' Alice said cautiously. 'Maybe.'

'It's a big step—moving in together, getting married.

And it may have seemed more distant, when these things were agreed between us, but time's moving on. House move next week and then, before you know it, we're married and a new chapter begins.'

Working her way through the toast, Alice looked at Mateo warily from under her lashes. 'What does that have to do with you turning up at my leaving party?' she asked with genuine curiosity.

She felt at a distinct disadvantage. She knew that she was rumpled from having just woken up, and her baggy tee-shirt wasn't exactly the sort of power outfit required for a conversation that sounded serious.

He, on the other hand, looked bright-eyed and bushy-tailed in black jeans and a black jumper that fitted him like a glove. Nerves slammed into her and all of a sudden the toast tasted like cardboard.

'I think I ought to get dressed,' she said, clearing her throat. 'I don't think that a bed is the right place for us to be having a serious conversation.'

'Okay. I'll wait for you in the living room. Want some more coffee?'

He was already standing as she shook her head and pushed back the duvet. She felt a vice-like grip around her heart. So it was going to be a serious conversation. How much more serious did conversations get than ones that included a marriage proposal—except, perhaps, one where it was retracted?

She waited till he had left the bedroom then had a quick shower and dressed hurriedly in loose jogging bottoms and a loose top, stuff she could move around in, because anything with a waistband was out of the question.

He had deposited a pile of money in an account for her but so far she had bought nothing for herself with any of it, despite his gentle reminders that it wasn't there to gather cobwebs.

'I've got things for the baby,' she'd replied vaguely.

He'd laughed and said, 'The money is for you as well. You're going to be my wife. You'll need a wardrobe of clothes that aren't just serviceable, Alice. Feel free to buy whatever designer things you want, and that includes whatever designer things you find to accommodate your beautiful, growing shape.'

'That's a waste,' she'd responded politely, reminded of the new role her brand new life was going to entail as wife of a billionaire, 'When they'll only get used for a matter of a few weeks.'

She emerged into the beautiful, spacious sitting room with an air of quiet defiance.

He was waiting for her. The apartment was completely open-plan with only the bedroom and the bathroom enclosed. Unlike Mateo's own enormous house, this apartment was modern but informal. It had come furnished with comfortable sofas, and the wooden floor was scuffed but gleaming, proud testimony to all the people who had enjoyed the space.

Alice paused and looked at him for a few seconds, trying to decipher what was going through his head from the thoughtful expression on his face. His beauty never failed to shock her. Maybe that, along with everything else, had piled up on top of her recently, making her pensive and cautious around him.

Had he picked up on that? Was that the reason for his sudden urge to have a serious conversation with her?

They'd made love but he hadn't forgotten that he still wanted to talk to her. Making love wasn't a panacea that encouraged forgetfulness, not in this instance.

She took a deep breath and joined him, curling up on the sofa next to him and laboriously positioning herself so that she was looking straight at him; he, in turn, did the same.

'Why am I nervous?' she opened with a little laugh.

'Are you?'

'You're sitting there as though you're about to interview me for a position in your company.'

Mateo laughed. 'I'm struggling to think of anyone who might be less interested in working in my company. Since when have you expressed any interest in the nuts and bolts of what I do?'

'It's not because I'm not interested.'

'Yes, it is, and I like that. I can't think of anything more boring than coming home to a wife who wants the details of what deals I managed to put away.'

Heartened by that, Alice smiled and relaxed.

'I suppose,' Mateo said thoughtfully, 'as the time goes on I'm curious about…well, to name but one thing…your broken engagement. You haven't told me a huge amount about that, about what happened there. You've mentioned it in passing, and I've let it go, but now…tell me what happened?'

Something must have occurred to him and he frowned. 'I've never been a guy who believes in a lot of hand-holding and confidence sharing, but it's suddenly occurring to me that I've shared a lot more with you than you have with me.'

It was an uncomfortable realisation and he flushed darkly and shot her a fulminating, vaguely accusatory look from under his lashes.

'So?' he prompted.

'So it just didn't work out. It wasn't that it ended on a bad note. In fact, I can't really recall what sort of note it ended on—an amicable one. Which is probably why, when I told you about him, told you that it was all very friendly in the end, you immediately concluded that he must have been boring.'

'Did I conclude that?'

Alice shrugged and smiled. 'You did. "Nice but dull" was the way you summed him up when I told you that I'd ended the relationship.' She frowned. 'If you want to know, it was something I sleep-walked into. At least, that's what it feels like looking back. I was young and we were good together: friendly; no highs and no lows... We got along, and I suppose I never thought I'd do anything but end up with a nice guy in a solid relationship and Simon seemed to fit the bill. You were right, though. He wasn't for me. I didn't analyse at the time what I wanted but I just knew that I wanted more. All history.' She shrugged.

'I surprised you at your leaving party because I wanted to see you in your own comfort zone.' Mateo abruptly changed the subject and Alice looked at him, startled at this admission.

'And? You surprised me but then you didn't join the party. Everyone wanted to know what happened to you, why you showed up and then just disappeared.'

'What did you tell them?'

'That something had come up with the house. You had to make a decision about something and needed my input but you couldn't get through to me on my mobile and you were in the area.'

'And they fell for that?'

'They were too busy having fun to go into a question-and-answer session.'

'And you were as well.'

'Meaning?'

Alice felt that they were going round in circles and, because she knew that Mateo was a direct person who couldn't be bothered with conversational niceties, she couldn't stop a tremor of nerves.

He'd implied that they were still going to be married. It was crazy but, having dug her heels in to start with at the whole marriage idea, she had given in the minute she had seen that picture of him with another woman. It was as though the reality of an alternative situation had hit her hard enough for her to put things in perspective. She had accepted his proposal even as she'd accepted that it wasn't ideal and had told herself that nothing in life was ideal. She'd kept her love guarded, but there had been a sadness behind the acceptance that it was a one-sided relationship and would probably always remain that way.

She knew that she'd been skittish around him recently, and she wondered whether he'd picked up on that. Uncertainty swooped through her, shaking her to the foundations. For good or bad, she knew that she *wanted* this man, *wanted* to be married to him and damn the consequences; she would live with them.

'Alice…' Mateo's voice was low and quiet. 'I looked at you at that party and you were laughing.'

'I was having a good time.'

'That's my point. What we have here…' He spread his arms wide to encompass the room they were in, the apartment, everything around them. He raked his fingers through his hair and vaulted upright to pace the room in restless, jerky strides while Alice remained where she was, following him with anxious eyes and wondering where this was going.

'What we have here is duty and obligation, based on mutual respect and a healthy sex life as a foundation for a union.'

'There's nothing wrong with any of that. You yourself said so from the start!'

Her heart picked up speed. She wanted to spring to her feet and dash over to where he was still prowling the room so that she could hold onto him. But then would that just be taking refuge in physical contact again?

She looked down and clenched her hands into balls, willing him to just shut up and overlook whatever blip had recently happened between them instead of dragging it out into the open and analysing it. Since when had he been the guy who liked having heart-to-hearts? Couldn't he just do them both a favour right now and return to type, scorn this chat he insisted on having?

'And when I said that I meant it, but time has a habit of changing everything,' Mateo returned in a low, driven voice. 'I see now that, whilst I can be perfectly happy with those ingredients, unlike you I'm not the sentimental sort. You broke off your engagement with Simon because you wanted more than he could offer. Maybe he offered you the sort of neutral love that wasn't enough; you wanted more. The *more* you wanted then will always be the *more* you want now—the *more* that I can't give you. Alice, I saw you laughing with your friends. You don't laugh like that with me.'

Mateo's words hung in the air between them and there was nothing Alice could do to deny the truth in them.

He was so right, because Simon had never been quite enough, had never offered the love her heart craved. He had never been anywhere close to Mateo, this difficult, complex, proud, caring guy who had everything she wanted but would never give it to her.

There was a reason she hadn't laughed in a while. Laughter would come again but it had been in short supply as she had grappled with circumstances that gave so much and withheld so much more. Grappled with a union where the sex was so sweet and the caring nature of Mateo so undisguised...and yet a union in which the love she so desperately wanted, the love that only he could give her, was not forthcoming. Putting her guard up had made her cautious, and caution had kept that open, honest laughter in check.

And then all sorts of other thoughts had swirled in her head of late, exacerbated by hormones and sudden apprehension at the future awaiting her.

Looking at the shadows flitting across her face, Mateo almost cursed himself for having said anything. What he had just said had made him sound vulnerable. He wasn't the vulnerable sort, but the words were out there, and he couldn't retract them. He didn't know whether he even wanted to.

Just like that, clarity came to him with sudden, shocking force.

A chance meeting: he'd opened his door to a woman lost in a blizzard and he hadn't realised that, in doing so, he had also opened the door to a world of emotion he had thought to be beyond him.

As realisations struck him, he could do no more than

make for the nearest chair and sink into it. Frankly, if it wasn't so early in the day, he would have been seriously tempted to see if a slug of whisky might not help things.

Suddenly released from their restraints, his thoughts ran rampant, coming at him from all directions as the silence built up between them. Snowbound on those slopes, he'd thought that he was enjoying was some harmless fun with a woman who was way too sexy to resist. He'd gone to his lodge to escape the frantic, high-voltage world that occupied him for fifty-one weeks of the year. He'd taken his usual week off to recharge his batteries and remind himself that, in life, it paid to remember your roots.

He'd gone for peace, solitude and some edge-of-his-seat skiing…and instead he'd found Alice. They'd lived in a bubble for a while, marooned in his lodge and discovering one another. What he'd thought was just going to be a week of unexpected fun had turned into something completely different, and just how different that something was now hit him with the force of a sledgehammer.

He'd fallen in love with her. How and when, Mateo had no idea, but it was something that had crept up on him as stealthily as a thief in the night, overthrowing his defences and leaving him powerless.

They'd parted company, but how could he not have realised what had happened when he'd returned to London only to find his thoughts consumed with her? He knew now that if she hadn't contacted him he would eventually have been driven to seek her out. He might have used some feeble pretext or other, but he would have pursued her because he would have had to. Love would not have given him the option of remaining detached.

When she had showed up at his office out of the blue,

he couldn't have foreseen how circumstances were going to change for him. Yet, even as he'd waded through the shock of her announcement, he had failed to feel anything but a certain gut deep pleasure at the thought of fatherhood suddenly thrust at him.

Why on earth hadn't he immediately insisted on marriage? He'd gone into a position of instant self-defence, holding himself back from the ultimate commitment, because he'd been there before and had arrogantly presumed to know that it might just be a case of making another mistake, of stepping into a raging fire, because of a pregnancy.

He'd let his past determine his present and he had paid a steep price—because here they were, and he knew that she was having second thoughts whether she said so or not. He'd seen her happy, had seen that look of joy on her face when she'd been surrounded by her friends and colleagues, and he knew that she was wondering what she was doing.

Would she actually say anything—express doubts? Probably not. She'd made up her mind and she would stick to doing what he had persuaded her was the right thing to do. She'd seen some stupid picture of him with a blonde, had been spooked and he'd used that as an opportunity to drive home to her what it would mean if she didn't marry him. She'd paid attention and gone against the grain. She'd given up her hopes of finding true love in favour of following his line of argument.

That his argument was valid didn't seem to matter to Mateo just at the moment. What mattered was that look of joy on her face—a look that would never be spared for him. He could give her the world, but it would never be enough because she didn't love him and, more than that, she wasn't impressed with his wealth.

He'd never been one for looking back over his shoulder at things that had come and gone. Lessons were learnt and time moved on. Now, though, he looked back and saw a life conditioned by his experience dealing with a father whose future had collapsed when his wife had died and who had needed propping up by a son too young for the task. He saw a life with his ex, a woman who had cared for money more than she had cared for him, and him being happy to go along with that because giving money had been a very different thing from giving his heart. He had given his heart to Alice and had fought tooth and nail to deny that because his drive to protect himself from hurt had been stronger than anything else. He couldn't do it. It was impossible. He could never let himself be vulnerable: down that road lay pain.

'Are you going to say anything?'

Mateo looked at her with a guarded expression. 'I'm going to say that I feel I've forced your hand when it comes to marrying me and there's still time for you to take a step back and really think about what you're letting yourself in for.' He shielded himself from the stab of pain that roared through his body like an arrow.

Alice felt the blood rush to her cheeks as she gazed in dismay at Mateo's serious face.

He was letting her go. One minute he'd wanted her, the next minute he didn't. It was as though their timelines were all wrong. No sooner was she on his page than he was turning his back on that and moving on, and she was struggling to keep up.

But she couldn't pretend that he was wrong and that everything was just great. He would see through that in an instant, and she didn't want him to turn her away for her own good because he'd suddenly had an attack of conscience. This was a time when she should tell him how she felt, about her doubts, which were only to be expected. She would reassure him that things would work out, remind him of the bigger picture. She felt sick when she thought of him having second thoughts.

'I admit I've been feeling a little nervous recently,' she said on a deep breath. 'And I guess, when I was at the leaving party, it was all brought home to me.'

'Explain.'

'Everything...' Alice sighed. 'I was having fun, letting my hair down and when you showed up. I guess I saw what my old life looked like and what my new life was going to look like. But in all honesty it had hit me before that the world you live in is very different to mine. Remember I told you that, when you bought the cottage which would then become somewhere for both of us and the baby and not just me? Remember I told you that you might find it all a little cramped?'

'I remember,' Mateo said heavily.

'Mateo, I'm going to have to dress differently, go to things I've never gone to and present the sort of persona that will fit in with your lifestyle.'

'And of course, were we not to be married, that would not be a problem.'

'I suppose it wouldn't,' Alice agreed thoughtfully.

'No having to mix in my boring world,' Mateo said softly. 'No having to wear clothes you don't want to wear or make conversation with people you don't want to make conversation with. Would you prefer that?'

'I...'

* * *

'I know we've told everyone that we'll be getting married and things are in motion but…'

Mateo shook his head and glanced off into the distance. He'd tried. She'd wanted a relationship that had love at the centre of it rather than a baby, and he'd told her flat out that if she was looking for love, then he wasn't the guy who could give it to her—but, of course, she hadn't been looking for love with *him*.

His ego had been in the driving seat when he'd jumped to that conclusion. Seeing her letting her hair down, not wearing that wary look on her face that always seemed to be just there, just under the surface, ever since they had ironed out the whole marriage situation, had been the game changer.

If he loved someone, he shouldn't harness them to his side because of what *he* wanted. If he loved someone, he'd allow them to go to find their own destiny, even if he personally thought that their destiny was to be glued to his side.

Giving Alice the house of her dreams and more money than she could shake a stick at was never going to cut it, even if on paper it all made perfect sense, and even if he'd managed to get her round to his point of view that there was no viable alternative.

'I'm releasing you, Alice.'

'Sorry?'

'You don't have to go through with a marriage you originally had no interest in.'

He stood up but he couldn't meet her eyes. He didn't want her to see what was in his. Instead, he remained standing there in silence for a few seconds.

'I'll leave you to mull over what I've said. I want you

to know that, aside from your freedom which I am returning to you, everything else will remain the same and that includes my unwavering commitment to you and to our child. I'll be with you every step of the way. You can count on me financially, and of course emotionally, until such time as you see fit.'

'Until such time as I see fit?'

'Correct.'

He began making for his coat and retrieving his mobile from where he had put in on the table in front of him, looking around vaguely as though he might have forgotten something.

Then he gave her a final look, brief and remote but not unkind.

'I'll be in touch. The move is in a couple of days. I'll be there to make sure everything goes smoothly—if, that is, you still want to live there and not closer to where your friends are?'

'And, if I went for the "closer to the friends" option, what would you do?'

Mateo shrugged. 'It wouldn't be a problem. A house is a house and the fact that I've already bought it would be immaterial. I'd hang onto it and then sell it.'

'Life's easy when money's no object.' Alice half-smiled but the eyes that met hers were as remote as ever.

'On the contrary,' Mateo murmured, turning away. 'Money just makes the issues more manageable on a practical level. Everything else remains the same.'

CHAPTER TEN

WHAT THE HECK was going on?

Alice sat in a daze for a while.

She felt as though she'd suddenly been flung onto a roller-coaster and, now that the ride had come to a stop, her head was still all over the place.

Slow anger began to build inside her. Ever since she had skied her way to Mateo's front door in search of help, her easy, predictable, pleasantly normal life seemed to have gone off the rails. Nothing was straightforward any more. And now, having steered herself to some kind of acceptance of what the future would look like, here he went, derailing everything all over again.

While she sat here and stewed, where was he? Back off to his fancy house, where he would probably lose himself in work and put her out of his mind, to be fished out again only when it suited him. Probably when he had to think about supervising the house move.

Was she going to sit around moping, coming to terms with Plan Three Hundred and Three?

No way. She changed her clothes, stuck on something more public-friendly than what she'd shoved on earlier and hunted down a cardigan. Outside, it was a lovely day, blue skies with teasing hints of spring in the air. She decided against public transport and instead called a cab to take her over to Mateo's house.

She'd been there so many times that it no longer impressed her. She'd breathed a sigh of relief that he had never, not once, suggested that she move in with him before the cottage he had bought became available. Maybe he'd known that the soullessness of his house didn't appeal to her on any level.

Or maybe it was a place he saw as his and his alone. It wasn't as if he'd ever intended to get rid of it even once they'd married and were living together in the cottage. He'd said something about its convenience for work purposes, and the added bonus of providing somewhere for clients to stay that wasn't as formal as a hotel if any confidential deals had to be hammered out.

Ha! Had he subconsciously decided to hold on to it because it was back-up for a relationship that might very well fail despite all his upbeat, persuasive chat about it being the ideal solution?

Thoughts occupied her as the taxi made steady progress through the congested streets. She didn't want to go down any rabbit holes or get too absorbed in doubts, questions and uncertainties. She was angry with Mateo for putting her in that place.

She felt a flutter of nerves as the cab came to a stop outside the house. She could see the driver glancing at the impressive property with a certain amount of awe, and she nearly rolled her eyes, because it was such a predictable reaction.

Was it any wonder that the damned man waltzed through life with such overwhelming self-assurance that it was nearly impossible to say *no* to him? Growing up on the wrong side of the tracks had taught him how to be tough and making it to the top of the pile had taught him invincibility. He hadn't got where he had by taking a back seat and being courteous. He'd got where he had by putting himself ahead of the pack and tenaciously making sure he held on to the lead.

The grand house was a spectacle of white, set back from the road and protected from it by wrought-iron gates and an intercom for entry though Alice had a code for the little side gate so there was no need for the intercom. She also had a key to the front door, which she had never used and which she wasn't going to use now. Instead, she rang the doorbell, not even contemplating the fact that Mateo might not be home. Her anger wasn't going to allow that little setback.

She heard the sound of his footsteps and then the door was pulled open and there he was. The flutter of nerves disappeared. She glared at him, hands on her hips, and met his eyes squarely.

'How *dare* you?'

'Come again?' Mateo said, frowning and belatedly stepping aside so that she could sweep past him before spinning round on her heels and resuming her hands-on-hips stance.

'You think you can show up at my leaving do and then get it into your head that because I happened to be *laughing* it was time for you to rethink the whole marriage scenario?'

'Can I get you something to drink?'

'I don't want anything to drink, and don't think you can stand there and *prevaricate*. What I do want is for you to tell me why you think you can act like a puppetmaster. One minute, there's no marriage; the next minute, you're persuading me that marriage is *the only possible solution* and then, when I've bought into that, getting used to the idea, you decide that you're going to do a U-turn and call the whole thing off!'

'It's not as simple as that.'

Alice followed him as he headed off towards the kitchen, bypassing doors that led to stunningly beautiful rooms, most of which were devoid of colour. White walls were interrupted by priceless works of art, and just as priceless rugs were strategically placed on the blonde wooden floors. The whole house soared with space, light, clever windows and arches that made the area seem as vast as a football field, yet there was nothing there that could ever be called *personal*. It was the sanitised space of a billionaire without intimate connections to anyone.

He had a complicated coffee machine which he now started up and it was only after a while, when the coffee was poured, that he sat facing her at the metal-and-glass table, long enough to seat ten and about as homey as an ice-pick.

The flutter of nerves returned and Alice knew it was because of the depth of her feelings for him and because of the way his sheer beauty got to her.

'You don't get to do this, Mateo,' she said tightly.

Mateo raked his fingers through his hair and looked at the plump, sexy woman quietly simmering opposite him. He wanted to scoop her up and carry her off to the bedroom cave-man style, but of course that was the last thing he was going to do. She must have dashed out of the apartment, hot on his heels, because he hadn't been back that long.

'I hope you haven't been using public transport,' he said with a frown, suddenly distracted by the thought of her being jostled on a crowded Tube.

'What does that have to do with anything? And stop changing the subject.'

Mateo lapsed into silence, because this was the last thing he'd been expecting when he'd opened his front door. Yes, he could see why she had stormed over here to find out what was going on, and could see why she felt he'd been pulling her strings and getting her to dance to his tune. What he couldn't understand was why she couldn't see that he was releasing her from an obligation she had never wanted in the first place.

'I'm doing this for you,' he eventually muttered.

'You're doing this *for me.*'

'How many times have you told me that we're not suited? That what you saw in your future was a man who was your soul mate?'

'Things changed when I found out that I was pregnant.'

'Things changed when you saw a picture of me in some trashy magazine with a blonde.'

'Maybe,' Alice admitted uncomfortably.

'Maybe? There's no doubt about it. You thought I'd gone to that function with a woman and I let you believe that because…because I felt that marriage was the best solution. If I got there by exploiting a moment of weakness in you, then all was fair in love and war.'

Mateo flushed darkly and shot her a brooding, challenging gaze.

'What do you mean?'

'I have no idea who that woman was. Someone must

have trying to get her mug shot in a magazine. I haven't looked at another woman since…since you.'

'You haven't?'

'Why would I?' He glanced away. He could feel the steady thud of his heart and the racing in his veins as he peered down into an abyss of the unknown.

'Because…'

He heard the faltering in her voice and knew that she was utterly confused. He couldn't blame her, considering he was pretty confused himself: confused by emotions that had overwhelmed him. Confused by an indecisiveness that was so unlike him. Confused as to what to do next.

'I was jealous,' he admitted roughly, and when their eyes met he saw with no great surprise that she was even more bewildered by his impulsive confession. 'I think I've always been jealous when it comes to you and, seeing you there at your leaving party, I wanted you to laugh like that with me. I didn't want you laughing like that with anyone else…but me. I realised that that was something you hadn't done in a while and I knew why.'

He held up one hand although she hadn't interrupted him. Her mouth was half-open and she was openly gaping. But, now that he had started down the confessional route, Mateo intended to lay his soul bare and complete the journey.

'You'd been coerced into a situation by me. How could you be carefree and light-hearted when you were doing something you didn't really want to do?'

'Don't speak, Mateo. Let *me* do the talking. Honestly, for someone so smart, you can sometimes be so…so… *not smart*. I wasn't light-hearted because I was scared! I was scared that you might see just how much I wanted to marry you! I was so caught up in the effort of trying to hide my feelings for you that it was impossible to be carefree. When you said that I'd wanted more from Simon, you probably didn't know just how right you were. Simon was a shadow, and I know now that any life with him would have been a half-life: a half-life *for me*.

'Mateo, you're the bright light that makes me feel alive! I don't know who I was before I met you, but I wasn't this person—I wasn't this person who felt whole and wonderful and giddy with a thirst to see everything life holds for me, but only with you by my side! I wouldn't have rushed over here like a bat out of hell to find out what the heck was going on if you didn't make me feel the way you do.'

'Alice,' Mateo whispered. 'Everything you've just said...my gorgeous girl...'

'I *want* to marry you, Mateo.'

'And I want to marry *you*, Alice.' He sucked in a shaky breath and met her gaze with steady conviction. 'I want to marry you, and not for the reasons you probably think. Yes, I truly believe that two parents are better than one. Yes, I sincerely think that for the sake of the child we have created it's better for us to be together than apart. And yes, I admit that I was a blind fool, and for far too long didn't look beyond those reasons to unearth the real reason I want to marry you...which is that I love you.'

'You *love me*?'

'You fell through my front door to get out of a blizzard, and in that instant my life changed for ever. I just didn't realise it at the time and, even when it should have been obvious, I ignored it because I'd lived my life assuming that love wasn't something I was capable of feeling. I watched my father disintegrate when my mother died and, even though I loved him, something in me died then and that something was trust in the power of love.

'When Bianca lost the baby we were going to have, I understood how much pain love could bring, because I loved that unborn child. So, Alice, by the time we met I had well and truly built a fortress of steel around my heart, and I was so sure that no one could ever get past it. Yet you proved me wrong. You got past all my barriers as easily as if they had never existed. I just didn't see it at the time.'

'Oh, Mateo.'

Had Alice been expecting this? Not in a million years. Joy flooded her and she leant towards him with bright eyes.

'I've been hiding,' she whispered. 'I fell in love with you after two minutes, and ever since I came round to the idea of marriage I've been hiding my love, protecting my heart, because I thought that if you knew how I felt you'd be appalled.'

'Talk to me. I want to hear.'

'Okay, so, to start with I felt that it would be just too painful being married to you, living with you, loving you and knowing that you were never going to return my feelings. But then when I thought of you with someone else…another woman…'

'A woman I had no idea I was supposedly dating…'

Alice smiled and blushed. 'Well, that's *your* fault for not denying it.'

'Guilty as charged.'

'Well, I knew in a heartbeat that that would be a lot more painful than being with a guy I was crazy about who wasn't crazy about me.'

'So, my darling…' Mateo curved his hand on her cheek

and smiled with such tenderness that her heart wanted to burst. 'Now that we've established we need each other and love each other…can I ask for your hand in marriage? A real marriage with love and affection and all the happy-ever-afters I never thought would be on the cards for me. Because I can't live without you.'

'I can't think of anything else in the world…' Alice breathed. 'Anything else on your list of demands? Because, for the record, my answer is *yes*.'

'Now that you mention it…' His voice was low, loving, wickedly sexy.

'Anything.'

'I've discovered that all the money sitting there in my bank account means nothing, because all I want to do is spend it on you, and you've consistently refused to be persuaded into accepting anything from me.'

'Not true!' Alice protested, laughing and delivering tender kisses on his cheek, the side of his mouth and against his neck. 'Okay, largely true.'

'A small church wedding is fine but, before we do that, I want to sweep you off to the Caribbean. Call it a honeymoon before the marriage, because after we're married you might feel just a little too uncomfortable to travel.'

'Well, you've already swept me off my feet, so who am I to object to a little more of the same…?'

Within days, Alice realised that all those signs of opulence—the club where the hush of the fabulously rich had had her gaping, the small but perfectly formed ski chalet, his palatial house in the best postcode in London—all paled in comparison to the black, sleek private jet that flew them to an island in the Caribbean where the wealthy and famous had their discreet, intensely private bolt holes.

From private jet they went on his own small, private yacht to a villa that sat within walking distance from a beach with pale, soft sand that melted into turquoise sea that was calm as a lake. He'd told her to pack light and, so she had, taking the bare minimum, floaty dresses and a hastily purchased maternity swimsuit.

She'd left the tentative warmth of spring to bask in the perfection of tropical heat and enjoyed a week of doing absolutely nothing. She paddled, sat with the warm water lapping around her and watched as Mateo struck out towards a blue horizon, as frighteningly good in the sea as he was on the slopes.

She lay by the side of his infinity pool, shaded by trees with the Technicolor vibrancy of flowering bushes and plants all around, and drowsily listened to the call of birds and the lazy buzz of insects. There was a personal chef who prepared all their food before disappearing at the end of the day, leaving them together to sit on his sprawling veranda with velvety darkness all around them and the sound of the rolling ocean in the background.

And, of course, they made love.

She knew he adored her pregnant body; he explored every inch of it, transporting her to a world of sensory excitement, leaving her sated and complete.

And when after a week they headed back to London, as he helped her into the Range Rover waiting for them at the airfield, he murmured that she was his queen and she could expect a whole lot more of the same in the years to come.

Could anyone have asked for more?

EPILOGUE

MATEO WALKED THROUGH the front door to the sounds of
kitchen chaos and smiled. For a few minutes, he stood
in the hallway and breathed in the glorious, heady scent
of domestic bliss: cooking smells, toddler smells and the
aroma of a house lived in, which was so unlike the mansion he had once owned, where everything had felt so
sterile in comparison. He'd hung onto that for a couple
of months after he and Alice had married, after the most
amazing pre-wedding honeymoon a guy could ever have
asked for, and had then promptly sold it.

Thoughts of using it if and when he needed to be closer
to the office, or if and when he might want to work with
a client in privacy, had vanished because, to put it simply, he was quite unwilling to spend a single minute away
from his wife if he could help it.

He looked around at the comfortable furnishings: the
warm paint on the walls, the clutter of shoes by the door,
the tiny yellow wellies with smiley faces, Alice's per-
petually mud-splattered green ones and a half-opened
umbrella. This was home—the warmth and comfort of
family life which he had never envisaged for himself.

He walked towards the sounds of chatter and smiled
from the doorway at just the scene he knew would be

waiting for him. Isabella was protesting vehemently at being trapped in a high chair. She was squirming and glaring, her pudgy fingers covered in food, her curly dark hair a cloud around an angry, determined face that was similarly covered in food.

He caught her eye and she stopped, protesting immediately, raising her arms and delivering the sort of beaming smile that got to Mateo every time.

'How do I always know when you're here without having to see you?'

Alice turned to him and her heart swelled with love. They'd been married for two years and the impact he had on her remained the same—had grown, if anything. It wasn't simply because he was just so devastatingly handsome, standing there in a pair of fabulously tailored grey trousers and a white shirt cuffed to the elbows, jacket discarded somewhere between front door and kitchen doorway. No; her heart beat quicker every time, swelled with love and tenderness every time, because when he looked at her it was with such undisguised adoration.

'Tell me,' Mateo drawled, strolling towards his daughter and scooping her up into his arms, regardless of the food that was now going to be deposited on his white shirt or of the little carroty fingers patting his face.

'Whenever Izzy goes silent, I know it's because you've appeared. She knows that she's about to be thoroughly spoiled.'

'If you mean rescuing her from a fate of squished-up vegetables, then I can't deny it.'

He padded towards his wife and looked down at her with adoring eyes, while his daughter did her utmost to get his attention before subsiding against his shoulder with a little gurgle of pure contentment.

'Not that much longer,' he murmured with satisfaction.

'Tell me about it. Was I ever this tired with Izzy?'

Mateo placed his hand protectively on the bump that signalled baby number two. As with Izzy, neither had wanted to find out the sex.

'Probably going to be a boy,' he predicted with a grin. 'Then I can have back-up with you women.'

He pulled her towards him and kissed her as thoroughly as he could with a toddler's head on his shoulder.

'Have I ever told you, my darling, how much I treasure you and how much I thank everything there is to thank that you skied into my life?' He drew back and lovingly stroked her cheek with his thumb. 'I don't know what I'd do without you or this little scrap nodding off on my shoulder. The life I lived before was no life. I've only begun living since I met you.'

'Just what I want to hear,' Alice said approvingly. 'And, now, you'd better go and change before you find your clothes ruined beyond repair with squished up vegetables.'

She reached for their daughter and saw from the flare in her husband's eyes that desire was building in him, a desire she was happy to return.

She grinned. 'And then let's get this evening over with and have some fun. Because in the blink of an eye we'll be back, my darling, to sleepless nights.'

'I can't wait…'

* * * * *

DECEPTION
AT THE ALTAR

EMMY GRAYSON

MILLS & BOON

To my mom,
who helped me bring this enemies-to-lovers story
to life and gave Juliette a voice.

And to four spring souls lost far too soon.
You will always be remembered.

CHAPTER ONE

Gavriil

WALKING INTO MY father's will-reading seven minutes late is satisfying. The old man, selfish as he was, was a stickler for punctuality.

I glance to my right as I walk in. The staggering sight of hundreds of skyscrapers clustered together on a tiny island never ceases to take me aback. New York City, with its gleaming steel and frantic energy, is a far cry from Malibu, where I currently live. Alessandra Wright, my father's estate lawyer, offered to fly to California or even to Greece, where my older half brother, Rafael, lives. I don't know what reason Rafe gave for declining her offer. We talk, yes. But it's usually work. Drakos Development, the largest property development firm in the world, is the glue that binds us together.

Blood certainly doesn't. That was my reason for telling Alessandra no. I've carved out a nice life for myself in Malibu. A mansion on three acres with its own beach, a private jet that can fly me from Los Angeles to anywhere in the world, and a professional reputation I earned through hard work and even harder dealings. I took the North American division of Drakos and transformed it from passable to powerhouse.

I want nothing of Lucifer Adomos Drakos anywhere near

my personal paradise. Including this damned will. Family lore says my grandfather named his only child after the devil because my grandmother died giving birth to him. Whatever the reason, he more than lived up to his moniker. He was greedy and brutal. The world is a better place without him.

I turn away from the view, the towers and high-rises like jagged teeth stabbing into the sky, and focus on the two people sitting near the far window. Rafe is reviewing a thick sheaf of papers, his back ramrod straight. His black hair, combed back into submission from a broad forehead, accentuates his narrow face and sharp chin. My mouth twists into a slight grimace as I draw near. He looks more like our father every day, a point I know he wouldn't appreciate. Neither of us had any love for the man who sired us.

He glances up. Pale blue eyes meet mine. The one and only characteristic we share. It marks us. Rafe rarely displays emotion, so I have no way of knowing if it haunts him the way it does me; looking in the mirror and seeing the eyes of our father staring back.

I hate it.

"You're late."

"I am." I circle around the desk to where a tall, slender woman is standing to greet me. "Alessandra."

She smiles slightly and accepts my kiss to the cheek. The woman could have been a model, with auburn hair falling just past her shoulders and a jawline that could have been carved from marble. Instead, Alessandra Wright became one of the youngest and most sought-after estate lawyers in the world.

"You look stunning. If you're free this evening, we could have dinner. Strictly business," I add with a suggestive smile.

Alessandra rolls her eyes as she takes a seat in a straight-backed office chair. For all our teasing and flirting over the past few months, nothing would ever happen between us. Not only do I not mix business with pleasure, but she's not my type. One day, Alessandra will want—and deserve—a husband and a family. She's got *long-term relationship* written all over her.

"As promising as that sounds, I'll have to decline." She glances down at her watch and frowns. "Hopefully Michail will join us sooner rather than later."

I tap my fingers on the plush leather armrest once, twice. Michail Drakos. Another half brother. One neither Rafe nor I have ever met. We learned of his existence this morning after a revised will was delivered by courier. It didn't escape my notice that our recently discovered brother bears the moniker of a celestial being, just like Rafe and me. Lucifer had a nasty sense of humor.

I'm sure Rafe had an entire dossier put together within an hour of receiving the will. I, on the other hand, spent the last few hours pretending like Michail didn't exist. No different than the last thirty-two years of my life.

My chest hardens. It hadn't surprised me that there was another child.

But *Theós*, it hurt.

My father had called eight days before he died. The last time we ever spoke. I almost didn't answer. I still don't know why I accepted the call. But I answered. The raspy weakness of his voice cut me deeper than it should have as he whispered "Hello, *yiós*."

My father was dying. He was dying and, for the first time in years, he'd called me. He'd called me *son*.

For one moment, the world stood still. I waited, letting threads of hope creep in. Hope for words of apology, of pride, of something other than the decades of scorn that had chased me.

Then time slammed back to its regular breakneck pace with his next words.

"There's someone I need to tell you about."

Thinking that Lucifer gave a damn about his bastard son was a moment of weakness. I knew better. When you care about someone, you give them power. The power to control, to manipulate.

To hurt.

Like realizing that my father's last words would have been about a son born after Rafe but before me. A son invited to today's will-reading, which means he's getting something even though he didn't survive a childhood with Lucifer criticizing his every move. Reminding him that he was less, would always be less.

I brush aside my juvenile pain. Lucifer can bequeath whatever the hell he wants to Michail. As long as it doesn't involve anything with my share of Drakos Development. I'll fight that to the highest court in any country and win.

A knock sounds on the door. My fingers tighten into a fist.

"Enter," Alessandra calls.

A man strides in, barely restrained anger radiating off his large frame. Taller than Rafe or me, with thick shoulders and a tense jaw. The only thing that confirms he's a by-product of Lucifer's numerous affairs is the eyes.

Pale blue and snapping with fury as he sweeps his gaze over Rafe, then me, then Alessandra.

His step falters. Just a moment, but I see it. My head snaps between him and Alessandra. But she doesn't bat an eye. She simply regards him with a professional expression bordering on bored. Maybe he's surprised by Alessandra's stunning looks.

Or maybe he's just a misogynistic idiot like his father.

"Mr. Drakos." She stands and offers her hand across the desk. "Thank you for joining us."

He eyes her hand like it's poisonous.

"My name is Sullivan." His voice is gravelly. "Not Drakos."

"Don't know where you're from, *adelfós*," I say casually, "but it's usually polite to shake someone's hand."

Michail's head swings around. He stares daggers at me. I give him a small smirk in return. Wit is a weapon I wield well.

A weapon and a shield.

"Who the hell are you?"

I settle deeper into my chair as my smile grows. "Your baby brother. Shall we hug, or does the occasion of our reunion warrant a familial kiss on the cheek?"

He snarls. The man actually snarls.

"Boys."

Alessandra's voice rings out, icy enough to quell even my humor. She starts to turn away. Michail's hand stabs out and grabs hers, his mammoth fingers swallowing hers in a tight grasp.

"Sorry, Miss Wright." Michail's voice comes out strangled, as if he can barely choke out the apology. "I don't want to be here."

"Then why are you here?"

Rafe finally speaks. Cold, with a thread of steel woven through his words, as usual. The man isn't known for his warm and fuzzy feelings. But the one thing he does care about? Drakos Development. If he sees Michail as a threat, God help our half brother.

Michail releases Alessandra's hand and stalks over to a window on the far side of the room, then leans casually against the glass with America's most populated city at his back.

"My reasons are my own."

Alessandra sighs as she eases into her chair.

"If you're all done seeing whose is bigger, let's proceed."

She shoots me a glance that tells me to keep the joke on the tip of my tongue to myself. I respond with a wink, which nets me another roll of her eyes and the tiniest quirk of her lips.

"Gentlemen, I will now read your father's final will and testament. Please reserve any questions for the end."

Any trace of humor disappears. I stay reclined, keep my slight smile. But inside I'm coiled tight. I know I'll survive, no matter what the will says.

But losing my life's work will be like a death. Unlike my mother, who preferred her own grief to raising her son, and my father, who cared too much about himself, Drakos Development gave me something back for the work I put in. The hours I put in, the research, visiting properties, uncovering what it was my sellers coveted and putting their dreams within reach as I netted sale after sale, all of it came back to me. Wealth, prestige, recognition.

It's filled the void left by my parents' neglect. It's been the one thing I've been able to rely on my entire life.

Well, aside from the fact that Lucifer could yank it away at any moment.

"'I, Lucifer Drakos, being of sound mind and body, declare this to be my final will and testament.'"

She starts with Rafe. Aside from inheriting thirty-five percent of Lucifer's shares in Drakos Development, he receives several luxury properties, a substantial monetary inheritance and—oddly—the contents of the library from the villa on Santorini. Our father also includes an edict that Rafe retain his position as head of the European and Asian divisions of Drakos Development.

Something tightens in my chest. He being granted his job in the will is a good sign for me.

But not a guarantee.

Hatred twists in my stomach. I'm fully aware that the last ten years of my life are hanging on the whim of a dying old man who cared only for himself and his bank account.

When Alessandra reads off similar conditions for me, including my keeping my position over the North American offices, the band that's been wrapped around my heart for the past twenty-four years since I learned who my father was loosens. Even Lucifer's death didn't alleviate the tension I've lived with since I was eight years old, standing in the midst of a wealth I couldn't comprehend as a man I'd never met stared down at the child he'd never wanted with disgust.

It's done.

I have my share of Drakos Development.

After Alessandra reads that Michail is inheriting the remaining thirty percent of Lucifer's shares, a couple of American properties and something about a bequest for Michail's mother, I stop paying attention as I mentally review the upcoming months. Some would find my anticipation of the next steps in my life odd, even inappropriate, in the wake of my father's death. But they wouldn't understand the sense of peace that fills me. The power I now have to make decisions without wondering if it could all be yanked away at any given moment. Now, when I think of my schedule, it's with confidence, excitement. The press conference tomorrow in Malibu to announce the latest West Coast projects. The evaluation of the Mississippi River warehouse development. Then, a meeting in Paris with the board of directors in three weeks.

And after that, I think with a smile, a long weekend. Two or three days in Italy with a woman would be the perfect way to celebrate—

"'As to the conditions…'"

I snap back to the present moment and sit up.

"Conditions?" I repeat.

The vise winds itself back around my chest and tightens until it traps my breath in my lungs. Alessandra looks at me with a glance I can only interpret as apologetic before she resumes reading.

"'I have learned, too late, the value of family. Of legacy. Which is why Rafael, Gavriil, and Michail must marry within one year of the reading of this will and stay married for at least one year, or forfeit everything I have bequeathed to them.'"

CHAPTER TWO

Juliette
Two days later

MY MOM TOOK me to a butterfly garden when I was four. The summer before she died. When we walked into the outdoor mesh tent, a swarm of butterflies flew up and around us. Their bodies brushed my skin, their wings soft, their movements frantic.

As I watch people filter into the ballroom, I can feel that same movement now, except it's in my stomach. A flutter of anticipation and determination, underlined with a sharp sliver of doubt.

Anticipation for facing a Drakos once more. Determination to follow through on what might be my last chance to take back my family's legacy.

And doubt. Doubt that's been plaguing me ever since Texas. That's where it first started. I had hesitated in a moment that mattered more than anything else had in my life. Where I came face-to-face with the fact that we are all capable of being monsters.

An ugly, sluggish sensation fills me, drags me down. That doubt has only grown, chipping away at the motivation that had driven my career ever since my first exposé. When I learned of Lucifer's impending death, my determination dimmed even further, leaving me adrift. That the man I hated more than anything in the world had been part of the foundation of my professional life was a cold truth I hadn't been prepared to confront.

Stop. I'll address my own hang-ups later. Right now, my mission isn't just making sure Lucifer Drakos's cruelty stopped with his death. No, it's a chance to reclaim what he stole from my family fourteen years ago. To give back something to a woman who carved out a piece of heaven for me to live and thrive in even as my life fell apart. Lucifer's death has put that possibility within reach.

If Lucifer's sons and heirs are following in his footsteps and I just happen to uncover another story in the process of achieving my own goals, so be it.

People start filtering into the ballroom. I lean against a pillar, watching, mentally cataloging those in attendance. My initial plan had simply been to observe Gavriil Drakos's press conference, to hear if any of his future plans for the North American division included a certain section of coastline in Washington State.

Specifically, my family's home that Lucifer stole for pennies on the dollar from my reckless father.

The worst part is that, in the years since Lucifer bought Grey House, he visited it once. I saw him arrive in a limo with a tiny blonde woman on his arm. They walked around the property. The wind carried her voice down the hill to where I spied on them from the bushes. I couldn't hear everything, but I heard enough. She wanted a house on the coast, yes, but not in a backwater town that only had two coffee shops and a scattering of restaurants. Never mind that people traveled from all over the world to the peace and quiet elegance of Rêve Beach, or that two of those restaurants had won national awards. All she'd seen was the lack of glitter and, like so many who lived privileged lives, turned her back before she'd truly looked.

I never saw Lucifer at Grey House again. The house was repaired. I watched the new roof being put on, the exterior being sanded and painted.

And then it sat. Empty, lonely, taunting as my father and I squeezed into the tiny gamekeeper's cottage left over from the early days when Grey House had hundreds of acres and a staff that included a butler and a head housekeeper. I watched my father stand at the fence that marks the line between cottage and mansion day after day, pining for what he had lost. His wife. His business. The second woman who loved him even when he couldn't love himself.

By the time I left and moved to Seattle, he had nothing. Nothing but an empty shack and an endless bottle of vodka that served as his only companion when he walked off the edge of a pier and into the cold waters of the Pacific Ocean.

Heat threatens to take over, licking at the edges of my control with a seductive whisper. So tempting to track Gavriil Drakos down, grab him by his tailored collar and vent my fury on him.

But that would accomplish nothing. I'd feel better in the moment, sure. I'd also ruin any chances I have of figuring out if Gavriil knows about Grey House, if he has plans for it or if he might be open to righting his father's wrongs. Not just for my father and myself, but for the woman who had become my second mother. To give her more than a tiny cottage to live out the rest of her life in. A cottage that, when she experiences one of her multiple sclerosis relapses, is impossible for her to navigate in her wheelchair.

Grief rubs against the anger, raw and bleak. The word *stepmother* used to conjure images of the villainess in Cinderella, with her crazy hair and evil cat. But then my father met Dessie three years after my mom passed and I realized that while I would always love my mother, it was possible to love someone else, too. Dessie hadn't pushed her way into my life or ignored me in those early months of her relationship with my dad. She slipped in as much as I would let her, reassuring me when I would feel angry or guilty, stepping back when I needed space.

It's funny how much the little things matter. I walked out one day, late for school, to find a strudel warmed up and waiting for me with my raincoat laid out. It probably took her all of five minutes. But as she looked up and smiled at me from the living room, coffee cup in one hand and our cat Jinx purring on her lap, I realized how well she fit into our lives.

A woman like her deserved the best. Not a man who wasted away after making a colossal mistake. They never married, but she was there, a piece of our lives until my father's desperation and pride drove her out of his life. But not mine. Like clockwork, every other weekend she drove from Seattle to Rêve Beach to see me. When my father could barely take care of himself, let alone his teenage daughter, she stepped in and took me away.

She deserved to have a home of her own. Not the loss of her job that sent her back to Rêve Beach to live with me three years ago. Not a disease that randomly yanks her out of her life for an unknown length of time and, for now, has her living in an assisted-living facility I can barely pay for.

I inhale deeply through my nose, purse my lips, and slowly breathe out. There's far too much at stake for me to give into my emotions. I have to play this carefully. There's nothing illegal about what Lucifer did. He bought the property. He just happened to do it at a fraction of its estimated value, preying on my father's gullibility and desperation as his own business dwindled. It was hideous, horrific.

But not illegal.

Until five years ago when I uncovered something criminal. Not with my father. But someone else. Another victim. One subjected to coercion, force, payouts. I hadn't hesitated then to put together the story that, when it was published a year later, made my career and unveiled Lucifer to the world as the monster he truly was.

A murmur rises as a group of people walk out of a doorway and mount the stage. The first is Rafael Drakos, tall, cold, face sharp like it's been hewn from a glacier. Seeing him—with the same distinct features and icy arrogance as his father—catapults me back to the last time I spoke to Lucifer in person. I'd paid him a visit after he'd stepped back from his role as CEO of Drakos Development amid the fallout. I'd slid my father's picture across the table, knew the moment Lucifer recognized the man he'd conned.

The ice in my spine spreads, fills my veins as I remember the way Lucifer looked at me, eyes dark and lips twisted into a cruel smirk as he offered to sell it back to me at market value. Six times what he had bought it for all those years ago.

Before I'd been able to utter a retort, he'd smiled. "It would be a shame, wouldn't it, to fight me on this? Who knows what might be revealed?"

My father's drinking. His gambling. Grey House meant the world to me. But not enough to sacrifice my father's already tortured memory. To go to court and risk thousands of dollars. I may have won the battle against Lucifer and taken away something he valued. But the war between us was far from over.

Today, though, I have another chance. Unlike five years

ago, there's far more at stake. This phase of Dessie's multiple sclerosis has lasted for over a month now. The longest we've ever experienced. We're both wondering the same thing, not wanting to say it out loud. Has the disease progressed? Will she ever have another period of remission again where she can walk without assistance? Live on her own?

Dread builds in my chest as Rafael takes a seat to the side of the podium. I need Grey House. Not, as I once dreamed, to live in, but to sell, to make the kind of money I need for Dessie and me to survive. The thought of it breaks my heart. But I'm out of options. I make decent money as a reporter, but not enough to pay for the care Dessie will need if this is permanent.

As much as I don't care for Rafael and his brooding, superior attitude, he's not my target today.

My gaze shifts to the man moving behind the gleaming podium. Awareness flickers low in my stomach. Broad-shouldered, with mahogany hair and a confident smile he aims like a weapon out over the crowd. Thick head of hair combed back from his face? Check. Square jaw? Check. Chiseled cheekbones I secretly envy? Check. It's not fair for a man like him to be as handsome as he is.

We've interacted over the years, mostly at press conferences. Unlike his father, he's never shied away from my questions or threatened to have me thrown out. As head of the North American division of Drakos Development, he's the most likely holder of Grey House.

The question is, how far does the apple fall from the tree when it comes to Gavriil Drakos? Does he have plans for Grey House? Does he even know it's in his family's roster of holdings? From what I've observed, he's obsessive about details and can quote company facts for days on end. But will a Victorian house on the remote Olympic Peninsula have attracted his attention?

I need to find out if he knows and, if he does, what his plans are so I know what angle to approach him from. Will he do the right thing and pay up the difference of what Grey House was actually worth? Sign it back over to me? Or will I have to go public and unveil a scandal he can't afford as he seeks to show the world he's not like his father?

Our eyes meet. His grin widens, a dare that pisses me off even as it sends an illicit thrill through my veins. I squelch it. I will not be distracted. I will do whatever I have to do to get Grey House back. To provide for Dessie.

I smile back at him. Knocking Gavriil Drakos and his enormous ego down a peg or two is just a bonus.

Gavriil

She stands on the fringes of the ballroom amongst a sea of people, eyes fixed on me with a confident smirk on her lips. Reluctant admiration warms my chest as I arch a brow at her.

Game on, Grey.

I flew from New York to Malibu right after my meeting with Alessandra. Stepping off the plane and into the embrace of the California sunshine did nothing to ease the tension that had slithered under my skin and lay coiled like a snake about to strike ever since learning about Lucifer's ultimatum.

Tension exacerbated by learning that Juliette Grey, the reporter who is the only person in known history to bring my father to his knees, would be in attendance at today's press conference.

I have nothing to hide. But that doesn't mean she hasn't discovered something illicit, something Lucifer did before his death that could bring Drakos Development to the edge once more. I can't think of a single article she's published in the years since her bombshell exposé that didn't include a reference to Drakos Development. Her obsession is the last thing I need to worry about right now, especially when my first priority needs to be finding a wife who will stick with me for a year and satisfy that damned clause.

Unlike the rest of the crowd milling about the ballroom, dressed mostly in name-brand labels and upscale clothing, Juliette is wearing a white T-shirt underneath a cheap-looking gray blazer and simple black pants, with her dark hair pulled up into a ponytail. I rake her casual clothing with my gaze and raise a brow. She returns the gesture and gives me a thumbs-up.

My lips twitch. She's got guts, I'll give her that.

I look away. Confident or not, she's still a threat. I want her to see firsthand how I reassure investors that Drakos Development will not only continue after my father's death, but will flourish.

I do a quick visual sweep of the room. The chandeliers catch the afternoon sunlight filtering in. The massive windows on the far side offer views of the impossibly green grass, soaring palm trees and the Pacific Ocean beyond. Elegance. Prestige. Wealth. Everything my share of the company embodies.

Selecting the grand ballroom of The Royal for the conference was a good choice. Not only is the Malibu seaside hotel renowned for its opulence, but it was my first success when I ordered the North American branch to break into the hospitality industry. My father called me a foolish bastard.

Literally and figuratively.

I included a bottle of Rémy Martin cognac with the first year's earnings and occupancy report. The handwritten note suggested he pour himself a glass before reading. The old ass never replied, but I didn't need him to. I'd made my point.

Now, with him gone, Rafe and I can finally take the company beyond the selfishness and scandals my father flowed to taint his legacy in his final years.

No longer his legacy. I smile. *Ours.*

Thankfully, Michail wants no part of it. After doing a quick read-up on his company, Sullivan Security, it's clear he has no need for the billions generated every year by our company. He has plenty of his own.

I spare a glance at Rafe standing just to my right. He returns my gaze. Nods. I face the audience, mentally burying my deep-rooted hatred for the man who sired me, and speak.

"Good morning, ladies and gentlemen. It is with profound sadness and yet immense pride that my brother and I stand before you today."

Liar. When Rafe called to tell me the news, I released a pent-up breath. Then I smiled. I kept on smiling as I poured myself a cognac and toasted to his demise. There are plenty who would be shocked by my callousness. Accuse me of being heartless or cold.

They're right. My heart was ripped out twenty-four years ago when my mother died, alone and poor, while my father lived like a king just a few miles away.

I rattle off the speech written for me by someone in Drakos's public relations department. It's drivel, with sappy lines honoring my sire's accomplishments and supposed testimonies from people who knew him. My fingers tighten on the podium every time I say his name.

Anapnéo. I fill my lungs with a deep breath, then slowly release it as I force myself to find a place of calm. This is a minor detour. Right now, my focus needs to be the future of Drakos Development North America.

A future without Lucifer.

With that thought to comfort me, I focus on the microphone.

"Our father's legacy will live on through the continued expansion of Drakos Development."

I finish the maudlin portion of the speech and dive into why I'm really here: my division's growing list of projects along America's West Coast. A buzz whips through the room, feeding my confidence and my ego as I share the three properties I'm most proud of. The three that will mark the beginning of a new era.

"The Serpentine, luxury condos on Catalina Island. The Cooper Industrial Park next to the Port of Los Angeles. The renovation of the Edgware Warehouse Complex in Seattle."

I recite the names and locations from memory as I sweep my gaze over the hotel's grand ballroom. Concept drawings flash on flat screens placed around the room. Appreciative murmurs ripple over the crowd.

My eyes flicker back to the woman leaning against the pillar. Her arms are still crossed, one leg crossed over the other. A casual pose to go with that casual smirk.

But something's changed in the last ten minutes. Her body is no longer relaxed but tight, her shoulders tense beneath her blazer, her pointed chin slightly lifted. Despite her petite stature and huge eyes, she looks anything but innocent. She's been dragging Drakos Development through the mud for years. It's gratifying to see her riled up.

I incline my head in her direction. A deliberate provocation. Instead of glaring or flouncing off, one corner of her mouth curves up. Awareness pricks my skin. I don't like it.

Or her. I prefer women soft, warm and willing. Not hard, stubborn, prideful creatures like Juliette Grey.

I face the audience and smile. "Questions?"

Hands shoot up. I answer most of them myself, deferring to Rafe on a couple about our European and Asian markets. The energy in the room is palpable. It fuels me as I smile, laugh and converse with reporters, local legislators and community members.

And then I see it. *Her* hand, slowly easing up, her fingertips waving at me. My first inclination is to ignore her, which annoys the hell out of me. I don't run from a fight. I haven't since I was four. I'm not about to now.

"Miss Grey."

The conversations subside. Most everyone in here knows Juliette. She's made quite the name for herself, appearing on major news networks, podcasts and videos to discuss the results of her investigative reports. She'll disappear for months at a time, only to reappear with a jaw-dropping report on embezzlement, money laundering, fraud, or—my father's specialty—bribery. She's cost companies billions in fines and lost revenue.

Not mine. Not this time.

"First, my condolences on the loss of your father, Mr. Drakos."

Tension tightens my neck. Responding to people's sympathies is hard to do when you have none of your own. But for once, there's no subtle smirk or hidden intention in Juliette's words. She actually appears sincere.

"Thank you," I force out.

"You mentioned several large-scale projects in major metropolitan areas. Any plans for Drakos Development to expand in smaller circles?"

She knows something.

Even from across the ballroom and the few dozen people standing between us, I can feel her emotions. Feel the anticipation, the excitement as she hunts something new.

The problem is, I'm not sure what she's after. None of our plans over the next five years include anything but projects in large cities or tourist destinations.

"Not at this time."

The room seems to hold its collective breath, waiting for her to deliver a customary Juliette Grey follow-up question that will unveil her newest target, wreak havoc or both.

"Thank you."

Surprised, I can only stare as she smiles, nods her head in my direction, and walks out of the ballroom.

Silence reigns for a split second before conversations break out, voices rising as everyone wonders what Juliette's little performance was all about. Many of them cast curious eyes in my direction or, for those with a vested interest in Drakos Development, concerned faces.

I grit my teeth. Perhaps that was her game. To get her name linked to Drakos once again. Put the world on alert that my company was back in her crosshairs.

I don't glance at the door she left through. I'll deal with her later.

Once and for all.

I turn and give the audience a small smile, like I'm letting them in on a little secret.

"Next question?"

CHAPTER THREE

Juliette

SHORTLY AFTER THE press conference adjourns, Gavriil walks out of the ballroom with his brother. I watch them both from a small alcove off to the side and note the similarities and differences between the sons of Lucifer.

The eyes are the same. Both tall, both broad-shouldered. But Rafael's face is sharper, harder, compared to Gavriil's square jaw and quick smile. Gavriil's hair is dark brown compared to Rafael's jet-black, his beard more like a well-groomed shadow. Rafael's is cut to precision. They both command respect, making heads turn as they walk into the main hall.

Gavriil is stopped by a slim blonde woman with a figure shown off to perfection in a navy sheath dress. Natalie, if I remember right. Natalie White, a financial reporter based out of New York. Based on the photos I've seen of Gavriil with his various women over the years, she's just his type.

She throws back her head and laughs as she lays a hand on his arm. He smiles down at her, his teeth flashing white against tan skin. Natalie pulls a card out of a leather folder she's carrying and slips it into the breast pocket of his jacket. He leans down and whispers something in her ear that makes her grin widen and a blush tinge her cheekbones.

An uncomfortable sensation spears through my chest.

Being on the shorter side with dark hair and very defined features, I'm the opposite of the blonde and delicate type men like Gavriil and Lucifer prefer. Men don't look at me the way they look at Natalie. It's not something that's bothered me much over the past few years.

But as I watch Gavriil, the charm and focused attention on a woman he finds attractive, I can't deny the envious tug deep in my chest. A tug that turns into a pull as Natalie croons something up at him that makes his smile deepen.

He's a playboy, I reassure myself. *Good-looking, sure. He's also exactly the opposite of what you want or need.*

Natalie gives Gavriil one last steamy glance before walking away. The flirtatious smile disappears as he leans toward Rafael, replaced by an intense focus that hardens his face. They hold a whispered conversation in the middle of the hall. Their bodies are angled just enough that I can't read their lips.

My phone buzzes in my lap. I look down and my stomach drops. An automatic text reminder that Dessie's bill is due. A bill I can make, but just barely, and only because my best friend Catherine is giving me a generous discount. A discount I don't want to accept. But as Catherine lovingly but bluntly reminded me last week, I don't have a choice. And if this relapse continues and turns into secondary-progressive multiple sclerosis, the bills will only continue to climb as Dessie declines.

Unless I can get Grey House back.

I look up just in time to see Gavriil walking toward an arched doorway. I mentally pull up the map of the hotel. The doorway leads to a flight of stairs that descends to the lower level of the hotel. A heated indoor lap pool, the hotel's spa and a walkout to the cliffside pool.

It takes less than a second for me to make my decision. I

had hoped to approach this with more care. Do some additional research, talk to people at Drakos who could give me insight into Gavriil, into any whisperings about Grey House.

You're out of time.

I stand and walk purposefully to the archway. I pass a couple holding hands and a group of women wearing pink sashes on the way down. As I reach the bottom of the stairs, I see Gavriil turning a corner just up ahead. I pass by the glass double doors that lead to the spa and continue. The light dims, overheads giving way to wall sconces covered by aquamarine glass to add a sense of mystique to the white-tiled walls and black floors. Soft music plays from hidden speakers, a slow, deep jazz that lingers over the skin.

I reach the door to the lap pool. I glance back over my shoulder, my senses tingling. There was no other place Gavriil could have gone. I know from my research he's active and usually does something physical at least once a day. But he wasn't carrying a swimsuit or a towel.

I reach into my bag and grab my recorder, flipping it on before I grab the door handle and slowly ease it open. Smooth ivory pillars hold up a mosaic ceiling, the vivid tiles a kaleidoscope of deep blue, glittering gold and alluring red. The lap pool snakes through the floor. Steam rises from the surface. Loungers have been arranged, some at the edge of the pool, others tucked into private alcoves.

I wait, listening, watching. The steam blurs the room, creating a foggy dreamworld that, coupled with the music drifting on the air, invites one to sit, to relax, to forget.

My fingers tighten around the recorder. A fantasy, nothing more.

After two minutes, there's nothing. No furtive movement, no whispered conversation. My heart sinks. Perhaps

I missed a side door. Or perhaps Gavriil continued out to the cliffside pool.

Or maybe you created your own fantasy.

I curse under my breath. Yes, I wanted Gavriil to be up to something. Wanted to find him conducting a clandestine meeting I could record and use to do what I do best.

Bring arrogant bastards to their knees.

I glance around the lap pool room. The last time I stopped to relax was five weeks ago when I met Dessie for a spa day, a break I was so grateful I took when she relapsed just three days later after a fall outside the cottage. Dessie and I opted for matching manicures, and when she chose scarlet, I didn't have the heart to tell her I preferred pale pink or nude. Something that wouldn't draw attention.

I frown down at my nails. The edges are chipped, my real nails showing through at the bottom. I love the idea of indulging in myself more. I just don't have the time.

Neither does Dessie.

My heart catapults into my throat at the thought. I cast one more look over the room. Maybe we could do a road trip in a month if she gets better.

When she gets better, I firmly tell myself.

Take the coastal road and stop off in Crescent City, then continue on down here to Malibu for a long weekend. It would cost more than a penny, sure.

But how much longer does she have?

I swallow my grief and commit to the plan. I click off the recorder and shove it in my pocket as I turn to leave.

Something moves behind me. I start to whirl about, but an arm winds around my waist and yanks me back against a broad chest. Adrenaline kicks in, along with my self-defense training and a healthy dose of fear. I jab my elbow back, but my attacker is quick and strong, only letting out a grunt as

I land my blow. Another arm wraps around me just below my breasts, pinning my arms at the elbows.

I open my mouth to scream. The arm around my waist loosens and a split second later a hand slaps over my mouth.

Damn it.

CHAPTER FOUR

Juliette

"RELAX, GREY."

I stop struggling as his voice sinks in. Dark, smooth, laced with his lilting accent.

Gavriil-freaking-Drakos. My body responds to his voice, my heart ticking up as warmth pools in my belly even as my mind snaps at me for letting a spoiled billionaire playboy get the drop on me.

"Are you going to scream?"

His lips brush my ear. I stiffen as the muscles in my thighs clench.

You haven't been on a date in months. Or had sex in... months. I frown as I count back. *Okay, a year and a half. Totally normal reaction.*

I shake my head. His fingers start to loosen, then tighten once more over my jaw.

"I don't know. I rather like it when you can't speak."

Ass.

I force my lips open and graze my teeth against his palm, a threat of what I'm willing to do. The action startles him enough that he loosens his grip. I sag in his arms. He swears and stumbles backward. I lean forward, breaking his hold, and then whirl around to face him.

"Don't ever sneak up on me or touch me without my permission," I snap.

He rights himself and stares me down. He's nearly a foot taller than me. Steam swirls around him. With the dim lighting and his dark suit, he looks like a demon lying in wait.

I reach into my pocket and hit the button on my recorder.

"You're the one who followed me, Grey."

"Which I think you wanted, Mr. Drakos."

He arches a brow, the one with a small scar bisecting the dark hair. "Oh?"

"Or perhaps I interrupted an assignation?" I smile sweetly at him. "Is Natalie White joining you?"

His lips curve up. "Jealous, Grey?"

I manage not to snarl at him. "I don't have any interest in another woman's leftovers."

His amusement disappears as his mouth flattens into a grim line. "Keep your speculations about my private life out of your gossip rag."

That he didn't deny a personal relationship with Natalie bothers me for reasons I don't care to examine. That he calls my work *gossip* infuriates me to the point I almost lose focus and lash out.

Stay on target.

"Gossip implies the facts have not been verified, Mr. Drakos. I always verify."

"And ruin people's lives in the process."

Men like Gavriil have no idea what *ruin* means to the average person. Have no idea about the children left behind, the women with broken hearts, the families without a penny to their name. All they care about is their own wealth, their reputations.

"I'm not in the business of ruining people. I reveal them for who they really are."

"Then you should know that my brother and I are not like my father."

He's got me there. In all my research on the Drakos men, I found little to suggest that Rafael and Gavriil were close with Lucifer. The subtle venom in Gavriil's voice makes me wonder what happened before he grew up, those early years that are still a mystery. If there's something there that can be used to further my cause.

However, as I've learned the hard way, the words that come out of someone's mouth, the expressions of grief or outrage or sympathy, all of it can be twisted, manipulated. I've talked with Gavriil less than a dozen times over the years, all in a professional capacity. I don't know him nearly well enough to know if he's lying right now. If his supposed disgust of his father is real or an act.

"We'll see."

Gavriil's eyes narrow to slits. "The man was cruel, arrogant and greedy."

"Agreed."

"And I don't begrudge the first story you published about him."

I blink in surprise. "You read it."

"It was well researched. Lucifer was wrong."

I mentally note his use of his father's first name.

"He threatened and harassed an eighty-year-old grandmother of seven into nearly selling her property for a fraction of its worth, or face having her house condemned by the county."

His jaw tightens. "Like I said. He was wrong."

I tilt my chin up. "What if you found out you and your brother were now in possession of property that had been obtained in a similar manner?"

He moves before I can blink, stopping with mere inches

between us. My breath catches in my chest as I look up. I try to keep my face professional, try not to let this man see the physical effect he has on me. It would give him power over me. Power I have no doubt he would use to get what he wants.

But it also irritates me. I've never been the type to fall for a handsome face. I'm not about to start now with the son of the man who ruined my family.

"What do you know, Grey?"

"I know a lot of things."

He leans down. *Damn it.* I take a step back, not wanting to let him get *too* close. But it's too late. That sensual awareness that I felt back in the ballroom slams back into my body and curls through me, leaving me breathless and unfocused as my gaze lands on his mouth.

My back hits the wall. His hands come up on either side, pinning me in.

"You know something about one of the properties."

I cock my head to one side, faking a bravado I don't feel as my pulse pounds even as my mind screams at me to slow down, to not let lust get in the way of what I need to do. I inhale, acutely aware of the barest brush of my breasts against his chest. His eyes flare as his lips part slightly.

Focus!

I mentally reach out and manage to rein in my racing thoughts. Judging by the underlying question in what he just said, the balance has just tipped in my favor. He doesn't like the idea that I might hold some knowledge of his father's illicit doings over his head. Maybe even fears it.

"Yes."

"What did he do?"

The rawness in his voice catches my attention. Gone is the silver-tongued heir who dominated the podium in the ballroom. Standing before me is a man who knows the truth about the man who fathered him. A man who, judging by the pain and fury in his blue eyes, is tortured by that knowledge.

I never thought I'd feel a kinship with Gavriil Drakos. Every time I've seen him, talked to him, he's come across like an arrogant jerk who knows he's handsome and wealthy and could care less about what his father's done.

But right now, as he stares down at me, our breaths mingling with the steam and creating shapes out of shadows, I realize how much this man is hurting. Hurting because of decisions made by someone else.

The truth hits me. He doesn't know about Grey House. Knows nothing about Simon Jones, his wife, or the woman he later loved. His daughter. And I'm using his lack of knowledge, his embarrassment over his father, to get what I want.

Shame weighs down my heart. I'm doing what so many have done before me. What I promised myself I would never do, especially after Texas. Even knowing there's a purpose to it doesn't make me feel any less ugly inside. Doesn't stop the knife that was shoved into my conscience all those months ago from twisting a little deeper.

"I don't think here is the place—"

"Cut the crap, Grey."

I blink. "Excuse me?"

"You know something. What are you planning?" He leans down further. "Blackmail?"

My empathy evaporates. I curl my fingers into my palms, the nails digging into my skin, to stop myself from slapping him across the face.

"Blackmail was your father's specialty, not mine."

"Don't think for a second you can drag Rafe or me down with him."

I stand up on my toes, bringing our lips within a breath of

each other's. Do I imagine his sharp intake of breath? Probably. Despite our moment of attraction earlier, men like him prefer women like Natalie White. Glamorous, fair, voluptuous. Not short, skinny, nosy reporters who have exposed his family's secrets for the world to see.

"If you have nothing to hide, then you have nothing to worry about."

His hands come up and grab my shoulders. The heat from his palms seeps into my skin. "I do worry. I worry far too much about you, Grey."

Shocked, and more aroused than I've been in…well, ever, I swallow hard. His touch is possessive, his fingers searing my body through the material of my blazer. A brand. It should disgust me. I should be bringing my knee up and ramming it into his groin. The man is arrogant, rude, conceited and a Drakos.

But I don't. I don't because for one moment, I'm not thinking about revenge or illness or the depths of human depravity. I'm savoring how it feels to be wanted, desired. Indulging in a yearning I've never experienced before with a man who tests the limits of my patience even as he has earned my grudging respect for doing what his father never had the courage to do and go head-to-head with me.

Carnal images fill my mind, remnants of dreams I've suppressed and imaginings that make me blush even as they make me crave. It takes my very limited reserves of self-control to stop myself from rising up on my toes and pressing my mouth to his.

He lowers his head. God, I can feel his breath against my lips.

Just a taste.

A sharp peal of muted laughter sounds off to my right. A moment later the door swings open. The women in pink sashes stream through, still wearing the sashes but now sporting swimwear. A couple of them cast glances at Gavriil and me. Some keep their eyes focused on him, not bothering to hide their appreciation of his impressive physique. Others shoot me an envious glance. One even winks at me and gives me a thumbs-up.

Gavriil releases me and steps back, nodding to the passing women with a smile that could kill. They titter and preen as they head toward the first set of lounge chairs clustered at the edge of the lap pool.

That uncomfortable feeling when I saw him with Natalie hits again, harder and deeper after our intimate moment. I did what I haven't done since I started my career—I let myself be swayed by a handsome face. Whether he was genuinely attracted to me moments ago or was just faking his response to distract me, I don't know. But his ability to step away so quickly, to smile at another woman like she's the best thing he's seen all day seconds after nearly kissing me, reinforces the rule I almost forgot.

Men like Gavriil—like Lucifer—don't care about other people.

Be careful, sweetheart, I can hear Dessie murmuring as she brushed my hair before a school dance. He turns his back to me, the smile disappearing as it's replaced by a dark brooding that sends a shiver down my spine. *A handsome face can hide an ugly heart.*

"Goodbye, Mr. Drakos."

His eyes harden as he starts to reply.

"If she's turning you down, I'm free, sexy!" one of the women calls from the edge of the pool. "I could use a date for the wedding tonight." The women around her alternate between laughter and groans.

I shoot her a grin over his shoulder. "He's all yours. And I've heard he loves to dance."

He glares daggers at me. The sight boosts my mood and I incline my head. "Mr. Drakos."

"This isn't over, Grey. Not by a long shot."

"On that, Mr. Drakos, we agree."

I leave the pool, walk past the spa, and ascend the stairs, my body tense as I listen for the sound of footsteps behind me.

Nothing. He's letting me go.

Good.

I reach the main floor of the hotel.

Time to regroup. Strategize.

The next meeting will be in an office setting, preferably one of my choosing. I'll have research, notes, everything I need to make my case.

That and an iron grip on my wayward desire. He didn't even hesitate to shut down his reaction to me when the bridal party came in, to engage in flirtation with another woman as if we hadn't just been about to tear each other's clothes off.

It hurts. My throat tightens as I hit the top of the stairs. It hurts and I hate that it hurts. That I let myself be swayed for even a moment by the chemistry between us. Even though I tell myself I won't let things go that far again, I make a promise as I move toward the main doors of the hotel to never let myself get that close to him again, especially in a dark room that blurs my inhibitions and tempts me to the edge of reason.

No matter how much I might fantasize otherwise.

CHAPTER FIVE

Gavriil

I STARE AT the storm-lashed beach from the driver's seat of my convertible. Rain drums on the leather roof. It's thin enough I can see the sea, steely gray waves churned white in places by nature's fury.

My fingers tighten on the wheel. I know the feeling.

Why, of all places, my father decided to steal a house from a tour boat operator on the coast of Washington State is beyond me. The sand here is dark. Pine, fir and spruce trees cover the craggy mountains, casting shadows. As soon as I arrived in Seattle, I was met with rain.

That was nearly three hours ago.

My glance slides from the gloomy landscape to the house just beyond my car. It sits on a bluff with a good view of the ocean. Architecturally speaking, it's beautiful. A Victorian manor painted dove gray with dramatic touches like a wraparound porch, tall arched windows on all three floors and at least two towers I can see from this angle. The lawn surrounding the house is lush green and trimmed.

I have a hard time believing Juliette would care for the house like this. She's methodical in her work. But she's also brash, bold. If the house was hers, I'd expect overflowing flowerpots with no rhyme or reason to the blooms, and the siding painted in a bright shade as if to let the whole world know she was there. Organized chaos.

Which leaves me with the ugly conclusion that Lucifer maintained the house to this level of immaculate perfection simply to taunt Juliette that it was no longer hers.

I breathe in. What I'm about to do could cement my future. Ensure Drakos Development survives while also taking care of one pesky reporter. All good things. Doesn't mean I don't feel like I'm about to sentence myself to hell.

Proposing to one's sworn enemy tends to do that.

It was Juliette who gave me the idea. When she deserted me at the pool with lust pounding through me like a sledgehammer and the single bridesmaid—who I swear licked her lips as she batted her eyes at me—her last words had crawled under my skin.

I'm not the kind of girl a guy like him goes for. And, she'd added with that brazen smile I couldn't get out of my head, *vice versa.*

I'd gone to my suite that night alone with the weight of Juliette's insinuations pressing on my chest. That and a throbbing need to fill myself with her, to tug at the ties pulling back her hair and watch it tumble free around her shoulders before I buried my fingers in it. To taste her skin as I drove myself inside her. I'd stroked myself in the shower that night, and the morning after, to rid myself of the desire that had sunk its claws into me. Even after giving myself a release, it hadn't fully taken the edge off.

So I'd changed my focus and turned to business. Starting with a thorough investigation into Juliette. I'd anticipated creating a stronger foundation for myself as I tried to figure out what hold she might have over me. I hadn't foreseen the shocking ties she had to Lucifer, or how far back her connection to Drakos Development went.

I'd sat on my private balcony twenty-four hours after the press conference, golden sand just beyond the railing and rich blue ocean past that, with a brandy in one hand and my tablet in the other as I read through the report provided to me by the private investigator I kept on retainer. Knowing the deepest secrets of my business associates—and my enemies—had come in handy more than once.

As it had this time. Learning that Juliette's first report on Lucifer had been based on a vendetta dating back to her childhood instead of the good girl persona she presented to the world had been deeply satisfying. She'd always struck me as black-and-white. But she had her own shades of gray layered beneath her confidence. A complexity I couldn't help but find intriguing. Coupled with how much willpower it had taken not to kiss her in the spa, she had become something of an obsession. A threat, yes, but also a mystery to unravel.

My lips curl back from my teeth in a snarl. I have no need to know her on a deeper level. Don't need the temptation that offers, especially when I've woken up the past three mornings with the scent of her filling my head and my fingers burning from the memory of her skin beneath my touch. Yes, she's sexy and complex, more than just a damned moral crusader fighting against her so-called villains.

But I don't care. I don't care about her reasons. I don't care about her backstory. The only thing that matters is getting her to agree to be my wife, stay married for a year, and then go on her merry way. The snarl smooths into a smirk as I think about how her name will forever be tied to mine, even after the divorce. Even if she chooses to target Drakos Development in the future, any stories will be easily dismissed as the bitter writings of an ex-wife.

I get out and walk quickly through the cold rain to the

cover of the porch. I glance down at my watch. Thirty minutes until she'll be here. I texted her last night requesting a meeting and included the address. Nearly an hour had passed before I received her one-word reply: Fine.

It had been deeply satisfying to picture her face, brows raised in shock, eyes narrowed in anger at me figuring everything out. I'd held on to that image throughout my trip, especially the long drive from civilization to the middle of nowhere.

I walk up and down the length of the porch. A quick glance into the windows confirms the rooms are devoid of furniture, but the flooring has recently been stained a dark gray. White trim gleams despite the shadow of the storm. I start to pull the key out of my pocket. The drumming of rain on the porch roof softens. I turn to see it abruptly give way to a light mist. Despite my preference for sun and warmth, the effect is not unpleasant.

Curiosity drives me down the steps and out onto the wet lawn. I circle around the house. There's a veranda off the back that overlooks the ocean. Empty garden beds sprawl across the backyard, a defiant plant pushing up through the soil here and there.

In my mind's eye, I can picture the house as it could be. Gardens lush with native plants that would thrive in the wet, cooler climate. The veranda dotted with cozy chairs and subtle lighting for the darker days. Still not my preferred setting. But it could be a nice one.

Still doesn't answer the question of why. Why my father snatched this property away from one Simon Jones, father of Juliette Grey. Why he kept the house maintained, at least on the outside, but did absolutely nothing with it.

But Lucifer never did need a valid reason to indulge his cruel nature. It could be as simple as Simon bragged about his house and Lucifer decided he had to have it. Like a spoiled child who always wants what others have. Never satisfied.

I move past the gardens toward the cliff. A wooden fence runs the length of the property on the south side of the lawn, marked by a small gate. The plateau the house sits on slopes down at the fence line. The hill is fairly steep and falls out of sight. But I can still spy a glimpse of a roof at the bottom.

A roof of a cottage that, way back when, belonged to a gamekeeper back when Grey House presided over hundreds of acres. A cottage that now belongs to Juliette.

Not liking the sudden uptick in my heartbeat, I turn away from the sight of the cottage and focus on the ocean. No reason to be on edge. She had the upper hand back in Malibu. She knew it, and I can't help but respect her for how she played it. But the tide has turned, and I'm back in control once more.

Satisfaction heats my blood despite the brisk wind pulling at my coat. Juliette is the key I need to move forward, to be free from Lucifer's hold once and for all and ensure Drakos Development's success for decades to come.

I won't leave until my ring is on her finger.

I stop within a dozen feet of the cliff. The sea has settled, the waves still choppy and capped with white, but smoother, more graceful. The mix of pine and evergreen trees covering the slopes shift from craggy and peculiar to regal as the fog abates. Further down the coast to my right is the small town of Rêve Beach. A cluster of houses, shops, wineries, cafés and restaurants, with a luxury resort and a couple small hotels. Not my idea of a vacation enclave, but my research showed it did well enough.

It's where Simon Jones ran a tour boat that had brought in a modest income until a year before my father bought

Grey House. That was when his finances took a nosedive as the occasional sports bet had turned into reckless gambling. He took out a second mortgage on the house at an exorbitant rate, sold his business, and then finally sold the house.

Three months later, he was found dead in a rock-strewn cove near the north end of town.

I eye the edge of the cliff, the sharp drop-off. The dark beach lies sequestered at the bottom. The coroner's report had included suspicions of suicide. But with witnesses testifying that Simon had imbibed far too much at a local bar before insisting he could walk home himself during a rainstorm, it had officially been ruled an accident. The life insurance, a mere twenty-five thousand dollars taken out four weeks before his death, had been bequeathed to his only child. A child who had disappeared off the face of the earth for the next four years, until she'd reappeared as Juliette Grey at a university in Missouri renowned for its journalism program.

When I first read the report, sympathy snuck in. I know what's it like to lose a parent as a child. Juliette had been six years older than I was when my mother passed. But still a child, one who had lost a mother at the age of five and then her father less than a decade after that.

Had she gone to live with family? Been put into the foster system? I hadn't dug too deep on that score. It had been irrelevant to my initial goals. But now the questions poked me. I'd learned so much about her in the past two days. The missing gaps added to the mystery of the woman who dared to spar with me, who had driven me to a level of sexual frustration I hadn't experienced in…well, ever.

Yet there is still so much I don't know. I had respected her for years as a reporter, then loathed her for the exact same reason. She is a paradox.

And that, I remind myself as I take one last look at the sea, is what I need to keep in mind. There's nothing special about her. When she says yes to my proposal, we'll spend time together as needed. But there will be no more intimate settings that threaten my control. No more near-kisses that torment me. Gradually, the mystery of Juliette will give way to familiarity, which will lead to indifference and apathy. The traditional cycle of many a relationship.

Awareness prickles over my skin. I glance to my left and she's there at the gate. I wondered if she would show up early, perhaps even be lying in wait on the porch.

My thoughts dissipate as a gust of wind catches the long dark hair she normally wears in a bun and pulls tendrils over her face. She doesn't brush them aside. No, she simply stands there, strong and impervious, watching me.

My gaze slides over her. It's not just the hair that's different. She's wearing a dress underneath a tan shawl, a long-sleeved burgundy gown that hugs her slender torso. With a heart-shaped neckline and little buttons between her breasts, it softens her, makes her look both fierce and feminine.

A combination I respond to as my body tightens. A warning whispers in my mind. The attraction that surged between us in the grotto was unexpected. So, too, is this side of her I've never seen.

But then I remember the late-night call from a buyer after her article went live. The frantic flurry of emails from my public relations department. The sidelong glance cast my way by an investor. All of my hard work threatened by a few words from this woman.

My lips tilt up. Not only will my proposal solve multiple problems, it will also be incredibly satisfying. I can handle an aggravating attraction if it means her silence with a side of retribution.

"Good morning, Miss Grey," I call out.

"It would be a better one if you weren't here."

I can't help the smile that crosses my face.

"Tell me how you really feel."

She cocks her head to one side. "You know."

"I do."

She doesn't reply, simply watches me.

"Are you keeping your distance so you don't give in to the urge to strangle me?"

"This is your land. I don't want to trespass."

She states it matter-of-factly. So succinctly I nearly miss the glint in her eyes, the edge to her words.

"It used to be yours."

"Used to. Now it's not."

Her gaze shifts to the right. Longing flits across her face. Even as I experience the quick thrill of knowing my proposal will be an easy sell, I can't dismiss the uncomfortable sensation of empathy. I know what it's like to be within reach of what you want. To see it day after day, thinking that perhaps tomorrow you will finally have it within your grasp.

I can give Juliette what she wants. I'm good at giving people what they want. A talent born from being denied what I wanted for so long. I cling to that thought and dismiss the sliver of guilt that's slipped beneath my skin and rests there, small but sharp.

"You went after my father because of what he did to yours."

"Initially." One eyebrow quirks up. "He provided more than enough reasons for me to keep an eye on him."

Satisfied at hearing her confirm my suspicions, I move toward her with measured steps. She doesn't back down. No, instead she squares her shoulders, her body tensing as if bracing for me to push her away from the gate.

"He set you on the path to becoming a reporter."

Her face darkens.

"I became a reporter because it's what I wanted to be."

"Touché. And because you're a good reporter, you know I am nothing like my father."

She tilts her head as she regards me, a Mona Lisa smile touching her lips. "I know there's no evidence of bribery, coercion or extortion."

Some of my good humor evaporates, replaced by quiet anger.

"But?"

"But you're still relentless. Borderline ruthless."

"The same could be said of you."

Darkness flares in her eyes, a sorrow that speaks to something deep inside me buried beneath years of pain. Then it's gone and she raises her chin up in the air.

"Perhaps. But pair those qualities with astronomical wealth, good looks, and a silver tongue, and you have the conditions for a man who could be very dangerous."

I smile. "You think I'm good-looking."

That brow shoots up again. "You know you are."

The wind kicks up over the edge of the cliff, gentler this time as the storm continues on its path just north of us. A stray lock of hair drifts across her cheek. I mentally curl my fingers back into my palm to stop my first inclination of reaching up to smooth the strand away.

"So you're prejudiced against handsome, wealthy men."

"Wary. Given my history, as you've discovered," she says with a nod to the house behind me, "you can understand why."

"I can understand why you had an aversion to my father."

"Him. Damian Ruthford. Alfonso Adams. Peter Walter."

She steps forward until she's pressed against the gate.

Damn it, I don't want to like her. But my esteem for her climbs up as she says the names of the men she's brought to their knees with the power of her pen.

"Yes, Mr. Drakos. I have an aversion. An aversion to men who abuse their wealth and power and leave nothing but suffering in their wake."

I hear it, the slight catch in her voice.

"How did you suffer, Grey?"

Her throat moves as she swallows. Her eyes flick once more to the house, then back to me. All trace of yearning disappears as she meets my gaze.

"I didn't suffer. I grew stronger."

It's not just respect that fills my chest. Not just lust that lurks in my veins. No, it's recognition. Like me, Juliette faced down the impossible at a young age. We could have surrendered to our losses, our grief. But instead of letting it beat her, she fought back. We combatted instability, uncertainty, and rose to achieve our own forms of success. To carve out our places in the world and take pride in the roles we created.

I look back at the house. A few beams of watery sunlight break through the clouds to touch the fresh paint, making the railing of one of the second-floor balconies gleam white.

"You grew up here."

"The house was in my mother's family for five generations."

"Grey House." I glance around. "Aptly named."

"Not everything has to be glittering gold."

I turn back to see her look across the sea. Her face softens into a smile that makes my body tighten. These glimpses of the woman behind the reporter are unnerving. I can handle her determination, her confidence, even the attraction that sizzles between us, no matter how strong it may be.

But the softness…that's a different beast. One that beckons, invites me to give in to that temptation to unravel the mystery of who this woman is, to get to know her better.

I don't want that closeness. Not with her. Not with anyone.

"There's beauty in everything." She nods toward the retreating clouds. "Even storms."

I think back to another storm, one where cold rain poured in through cracks around the window as I curled against my mother's side, listening to the death rattle in her chest as she gasped for air between bursts of thunder.

"Not everything."

Her head snaps back to me and the softness disappears, thank God.

"Did you just come to make conversation, or are you here for a reason?"

"I'm here to propose a mutually beneficial arrangement." I smile at her again, the smile I wield before I offer people what they desire. "One that would include me signing over the deed to Grey House."

Even the air seems to still as she stares at me. Then she inhales sharply and time resumes. Her lips part as her eyes move between the house and me.

"What price are you asking?"

"A reasonable and affordable one."

I reach into my pocket and pull out a black velvet box. The confusion on her face would be amusing if so much didn't hinge on her saying one specific word.

"What…"

Her voice trails off as I flip open the lid to reveal a ten-carat diamond set into a platinum band decorated with smaller, but no less fine, diamonds.

"Your hand in marriage."

CHAPTER SIX

Juliette

THIS HAS TO be a joke. There is no scenario in this universe where Gavriil Drakos would propose to me.

I stare at the ring. It's so opulent it's almost comical.

"Is that fake?"

Gavriil glares at me.

"It's a million-dollar ring, Grey."

I'd laugh at the offense in his tone if I wasn't still shell-shocked.

"Is there a hidden camera somewhere?" I look around. We appear to be alone on the bluff, but Gavriil could have easily paid for cameras to be secreted around the property. "Is this some elaborate prank to embarrass me? Punish me for looking into your family?"

He frowns at me like I'm an idiot.

"It's a proposal, Grey. I'm asking you to marry me."

"Why on earth would you want to marry me?"

He gives me a lazy smile, which stirs some of the warmth that's lingered ever since our near-kiss in the grotto. I hate that he has that effect on me.

"I don't want to marry anyone. But I have to."

"Come again?"

He sighs. "We may not see eye to eye on some things, Grey. But on the subject of my father, we can both agree he was a bastard." His lips twist into something menacing that makes my chest clench. The fury flickering in his eyes as he snaps the lid shut on the ring box gives me far deeper insight into just why he's so successful at what he does than any research I could have done. For all his pomp and flash, Gavriil Drakos has a dark side. One that sends a not unpleasant shiver down my spine as I see a glimpse of the dominant leader behind the mask of amused arrogance he so often shows to the world.

"I shared at the press conference that Rafael and I inherited our shares of Drakos Development. What I neglected to mention was that inheritance is contingent upon my marrying and staying married for a year."

My jaw drops.

"What?"

The snarl disappears as the amused glint I'm used to reappears.

"I had similar, if not more colorful sentiments, when I learned about it three days ago."

"What happens if you don't get married?"

The fury returns, hardening his face as his fingers curl around the ring box like he might crush the diamond in his grasp.

"Then I lose everything."

It sounds absurd, like the plot of one of the cheesy yet swoon-worthy romance novels I read when I have time. Yet the stunning viciousness of it is what hits me hardest of all. I know firsthand how malicious and selfish Lucifer could be. But to hear he inflicted that emotional brutality on his own sons makes my heart ache for the seemingly impervious man standing in front of me.

"That's sick."

One thick brow curves up. "On that we can agree."

"What's the purpose? Did he doubt your ability to lead?"

He glances over his shoulder at Grey House. "You know how cruel and capricious he was. Did he need a reason to torment his sons from beyond the grave?"

There's a story there, seething beneath his supposed apathy. A story that, for once, I want nothing to do with as I shove away my sympathy once more. I don't want this personal detail of his life. I don't want to see the pain of his childhood, to feel sympathy for him.

But why?

The question passes through my mind and freezes me in place. Why am I so determined to believe the worst of Gavriil and Rafael Drakos? Because they're related to the man who ruined my father's life? Because they're wealthy? I was furious when Gavriil accused me of being prejudiced against rich people.

Except…he's right. I've spent my career exposing the lies and hypocrisies of the rich and powerful. I've dedicated my life to ripping the masks off predators who hide behind money and power. But now…now I'm wondering if I've gone too far. Focused so hard on the people I'm chasing that I've been blind to the innocent people between myself and my own goals. People like Gavriil, who might be an arrogant bastard, but who is nothing like the man who fathered him.

Gavriil is offering me what I've wanted ever since Lucifer stole it: Grey House. More than that, he's offering me a chance to help Dessie, to secure the future she deserves even if he doesn't seem to know about the woman who held my life together.

Except this choice isn't as black-and-white as the first one I made when embarking on this journey—to reveal Lucifer for who he really was to the world and ensure he could never hurt an innocent person ever again. This choice is layered with pitfalls, such as sacrificing my integrity as I marry a man whose values center on the two things I detest the most: money and power.

One year ago, the answer would have been simple. No matter how badly I wanted Grey House, it wouldn't have been worth it.

But now, it's not just about me. And as I stare at the familiar pillars and turrets of the home I grew up in, I also know that the career I've poured my heart and soul into is no longer the driving force behind my existence.

It's a punch to the gut. One that leaves me breathless and adrift.

"So?"

I blink and refocus on Gavriil.

"So what?"

He holds up the ring. The massive stone glints in the weak sunlight fighting through the clouds. It looks nothing like a ring I would wear. Ostentatious, over-the-top. Even if Gavriil is nothing but a brazen billionaire, his preference for the finer things in life is off-putting.

"Why are you asking me? We don't even like each other."

He splays a hand on his chest.

"You wound me, Grey."

"With what? Honesty?"

He chuckles. The sound is surprisingly warm, deep. It rolls through me, leaving a trail of wanting in its wake. My hands tighten on the gate. The wet wood is a necessary contrast to the heat I can't seem to get rid of since our encounter in the spa. That heartbeat of a moment where I felt beautiful and sexy and desired.

"This has nothing to do with liking or attraction. It's a practical decision."

"For two people who don't like each other to get married to satisfy the requirements of an asinine clause?"

"I have something you want."

I can't help it, can't stop my eyes from drifting over his shoulder to Grey House. When I came back after I graduated college and took up residence in the cottage, it had nearly killed me to see the house every day. To remember which window I sat at with my mother when a winter storm lashed the town. To close my eyes and envision sitting on the balcony off my parents' room as spring drifted in and warmed the wood beneath me. Aside from Dessie, it's the one thing I have left of my family, my childhood.

And now it's within reach. But Gavriil lied. The price is not reasonable. A year with him is a very steep cost.

"I'm sure there are any number of women who want something you could give them."

"True. But none of them have something I want, too."

My skin grows cold beneath the warmth of my wrap as his grin flashes white.

"Which is?"

"Your name on a contract swearing you'll never write a poisonous word about Drakos Development again, or you'll forfeit ownership of Grey House back to me."

I rear back before I can stop myself. I knew there had to be more to this proposal. Hearing him state it out loud, as casually as if we were discussing the weather, infuriates me.

"You're trying to bribe me."

"No. I'm offering an incentive."

"You're splitting hairs, Drakos," I spit out.

"Call it what you want, Grey." The amusement vanishes, replaced by the steely-eyed businessman I've heard so much about but never witnessed firsthand. "We both know your research for the past four years has revealed no wrongdoing on my part. You have nothing but a vendetta against my father, driving this relentless campaign against my family. The fact that I have to offer you anything to get you to back off and leave us alone is a testament to your lack of professionalism."

My lips part in shock. I flounder for a moment as his words stab straight into the heart of my doubts and insecurities.

His smile returns, but his eyes remain hard.

"So accept my offer. Live a life of luxury and glamour. Give your pen a break. Move back into your childhood home." He looks back over his shoulder. "You've wanted it for years. It can be yours again."

I bite my tongue. I'd heard rumors and firsthand accounts of what made Gavriil so good at what he did. The man has a knack for identifying people's deepest desires and then making them happen. Easy to do when so many want money, or something money can buy them, and he has it in abundance.

I never would have thought myself capable of accepting any deal. But...

"What's holding you back?"

His voice is silky now, dark and tempting. I avoid his gaze as I stare at the familiar pillars and curves of Grey House. I can't tell him what's truly holding me back. I don't want to share that fear is making me pause: Fear that he's right and I'm incapable of letting go of my vendetta. Fear that if I accept his offer, I'm giving in to someone who may not be the monster I imagined him to be, but still represents so much of what I don't like about this world. Fear that if I don't, I'll never have another chance like this to solidify Dessie's future.

My phone buzzes in my pocket. I pull it out and stifle a groan. My alarm reminding me about the social at Dessie's facility. Catherine told me Dessie's been sleeping more and more. Each day that passes when she can barely get out of bed, when her legs collapse beneath her and she won't use the walker or wheelchair, spikes my fear higher and higher that she won't come back from this.

Dessie...

My eyes snap back to the house. An idea appears. One that is most definitely selfish, as it will give me something I want even as it solves my most pressing problem. But one that also gives me back some of the control I've lost.

"Will this be in name only?"

A corner of his mouth twitches. "No sex required."

It shouldn't bother me how easily he agrees to no sex. *Whatever.*

"Then I agree."

I detest the satisfied smile that spreads across his face.

"I'll have my lawyers—"

"I agree," I repeat, "for Grey House and two million dollars, payable before the wedding."

The smile disappears. Any satisfaction I would have derived from it is eclipsed by the icy cold that stills his features. I can feel the disapproval emanating from him as much as I can feel the renewed wind sweeping up from the sea.

"Everyone has their price." He cocks his head to the side. "I didn't expect yours to be so mercenary."

I think of Grey House. I think of Dessie sitting on the patio in the summer with a raised garden bed that will accommodate her wheelchair if her prognosis worsens. I think of turning the empty guest bedroom into an office where I can work. Of not having to worry about money ever again, no matter what hurdles Dessie's condition may throw in our path.

These are the thoughts that keep me from smacking the judgmental look off Gavriil Drakos's handsome face. He may not be a criminal like his father. But he is a selfish creature who has no problems enjoying his own wealth even as he judges others for wanting a better life for themselves and the ones they love.

"Do we have a deal?"

He stares at me for one long second before nodding. I stick out my hand.

"Oh, no." His eyes gleam. "A deal of this magnitude requires something more than a handshake."

He flips the lid open on the ring box and takes the ring out before he grabs my left hand. I freeze as his fingertips warm my skin, barely hold back a shiver as he slides the ring on. It's cold. Feels more like a shackle than the most expensive piece of jewelry I've ever worn.

"What happens now?" I ask as I cross my arms over my chest.

"Now you plan the wedding of the century."

My jaw drops.

"What?"

"We have to convince the world that, after years of acrimony, we're suddenly in love and desperate to get married."

My brilliant idea now sounds brilliantly stupid as I stare at the man I've just bound myself to for a year. I thought we'd take care of this quickly and quietly: a simple ceremony, sign our names, then live out the rest of our sentence separately.

"Why not just go to the courthouse—"

"No."

"Why not?" I ask, not bothering to hide the frustration from my voice.

"It's not my style."

"What if it's mine?"

"My offer, my rules. Two," he continues, his voice hardening, "there is to be no hint, not even a whisper, of the real reason for our wedding."

"I take it I'll be signing more than just a marriage license," I reply dryly.

"An ironclad nondisclosure with the condition you'll forfeit anything I grant you if you end the marriage early or tell anyone about the will."

"What if I pinky promise?"

The brooding scowl disappears as he throws his head back and laughs. A deep, rich laugh that makes my skin tingle with the pleasantness of the sound.

"I don't think that counts as legally binding."

I sigh and wrap my arms tighter around myself, partly to ward off the lingering chill and partly to comfort myself.

"So you're wanting this…circus to convince people we're marrying because we love each other?"

"That's part of it. No one who knows me would expect me to go to a courthouse. And," he adds with a wicked grin, "there's something satisfying about having you play the role of blushing bride."

I roll my eyes, then curse as my phone vibrates again.

"I have to go."

"I'm staying at the Seaside Inn through tomorrow morning. I'll have my lawyers fax over the paperwork." He reaches out and catches my arm as I start to turn away. "Come by later and I'll have the hotel print them off for you to sign."

"I'm busy tonight. Maybe tomorrow."

His body tenses.

"Busy doing what?"

I tug my arm away, not caring for his tone. "Busy doing

something I already had scheduled before you decided to invade my home and bribe me."

"I neglected to mention that dating or seeing anyone else is off-limits until our divorce is finalized."

"Is that a two-way street?" I snap.

An image appears in my head, vivid and unbidden, of Gavriil rolling around naked in bed with some tall, glamorous model. It's an extremely unpleasant vision.

Not because I'm jealous, I reassure myself.

"Adultery is not a habit I indulge in."

Dear God, he almost sounds offended. Right after he just insinuated that I would be entertaining men on the side during the course of our so-called marriage.

"No," I reply with a sweet smile, "just a new woman every week."

He returns my smile with a slow curving of his full lips that draws my attention down to his mouth before snapping my eyes back up to his amused gaze.

"Jealous again, Grey?"

"Nothing to be jealous over. We're not in a relationship."

He reaches out and grabs my hand once more. This time, however, his touch is firm but gentle. My breath catches in my chest. His fingers wrap around my wrist as he slowly raises my hand so that my palm is facing him. The diamond glints back at me, large and dazzling and mocking.

"Hate to break it to you," he says, his voice low yet no less powerful as it ripples over my skin, "but this ring says otherwise."

CHAPTER SEVEN

Gavriil
Four weeks later

PEOPLE MOVE ACROSS the lawn, Chanel dresses and Louis
Vuitton suits sparkling under the twinkling lights strung up
in the trees. The setting sun casts a rosy glow on the crowd
made up of movie stars, platinum-award singers, bestselling
authors, fellow billionaires and politicians. Waiters dressed
in black tuxedos move through the crowd with silver trays,
offering crystal flutes of champagne and some rare oyster
only found in a river in France.

I tasked Juliette with creating the wedding of the century. She delivered.

Four weeks ago, I slid my ring onto her finger. She showed
up at the Seaside Inn the following morning, agreed to a
wedding one month later and vanished just as quickly as
she'd arrived. I heard nothing else from her the rest of the
day.

I got the first bill the following day. Sarabeth DeLancey,
the premier wedding planner in the country, orchestrated
the weddings of A-list actors, platinum-selling singers and
the children of presidents. She would also be coordinating
ours. Sarabeth was the first in a long line of bills that had
crossed my desk in the past month.

But Juliette's wanton spending seems to have done the

trick. The engagement, and the buzz surrounding our luxurious wedding, has been positive. No one has questioned it. The enemies-to-lovers angle has made Juliette and me a regular feature on West Coast news outlets and social media. That we are turning down every interview request has only increased the hype and speculation about our wedding.

It's been a week since I've seen or spoken to her, other than through text messages. She's played her part well at the events we've attended together, including an engagement dinner hosted by some business associates and their spouses. Every time I'd looked over at her during the evening, she'd smiled, laughed, even laid her hand on top of mine. To anyone watching, all they'd seen was a young woman in love. Exactly what I asked of her.

I thought I had some grasp on who she was, some understanding of her character. Yet she's spent my money as if she'd been born to wealth instead of supposedly loathing it for years. To see how easily she slips into the role of lovestruck fiancée, as well as how quickly she sheds it once we're in the privacy of my car or plane, is unnerving. So is realizing the extent that she's using me. As much as I am her.

Which probably makes us perfect for each other, or at least for the next year we're trapped in this arrangement.

When we're alone, she slips into silence and all but ignores me. The first time it happened, it struck me as petty. But as it continued, over and over every time we were alone, I started to slip back into the past, into a tiny, stuffy room and my mother staring at the wall, ignoring her child in favor of reminiscing about her lost lover.

The lover who had given her five thousand euros when she'd told him she was pregnant and then abandoned her.

The more the past overshadowed my present, the terser I

got with Juliette, until we were both practically snarling at each other on the few occasions we talked. The only thing that still lingered was that damned sexual heat. Every time Juliette placed her hand on my arm, dressed in gowns that made her understated beauty shine, I wanted to hide her away, to snap at the men leering at her that she was taken.

Nights have been the hardest. I wake up with a throbbing need pounding its way through my body and phantom moans rippling in my head. I've kept it under control so far. Easy to do when she's been spending her nights elsewhere.

But when she's just next door…

I curl my fingers into a fist and let my nails bite into my palm.

Just two more weeks, I remind myself.

After tonight, we'll fly to France for a two-week honeymoon to keep up appearances. I've booked us suites in Paris and on the river cruise to keep us apart as much as possible when we're alone. When we return to the States, the spotlight on our relationship will die down and we'll go our separate ways for the rest of our farce of a marriage.

We just have to make it through the ceremony first. Juliette's played her part well so far, at least in public. But I won't feel completely settled until she's said *I do* and the countdown to my owning Drakos North America free and clear has officially begun.

I watch as the guests below start to drift toward the beach and the rows of ivory chairs lined up on either side of the aisle. I heard nothing but compliments as guests were welcomed into the foyer of my mansion and escorted into the backyard for preceremony cocktails. There've been no whispers about the will, no speculation about this being an arrangement. The only ugly stories I've seen are the ones theorizing that Juliette is marrying me for my money.

Which, I remind myself grimly, she is. My money and a house.

Unfair for me to feel angry about that. I made the offer of the house. But her asking for money took the image I had of her as a feisty but independent reporter and dismantled it until all I was left of was a woman who, sadly, was just like everyone else.

I had one moment on the flight home from Rêve Beach when I wondered if I was judging too harshly. My mother's absence, both in life and death, had left a gaping hole. As a child, I had hoped the hole might be filled with family, namely my father and brother. When both of those failed, the hole widened until I felt like an empty shell.

A shell that only started to feel complete when I made my first million. When I experienced satisfaction at realizing what I had accomplished on my own. Pride at finally being recognized for what I had achieved. I didn't need love or family. In my experience, those things were fleeting, unreliable.

Juliette had experienced the same loss, the same struggles over the years. She had reached out and grabbed an opportunity with both hands, just as I had.

Yet as I watched her go through the same motions, it seemed...hollow.

Then the bills for the wedding started to roll in. The overblown spending turned my discomfort to antipathy. Yes, I told her to spend. I have the money. I indulge.

But even this is excessive for me.

I glance at the arch at the end of the orchid-lined aisle, draped in gauzy white fabric and wrapped with the same lights strung up in the trees. The only bill that didn't cross my desk was for her wedding dress. A designer probably donated a gown for the chance to be seen at what one news outlet dubbed the most anticipated wedding of the decade.

I move away from the window and walk to the mirror on the far side of my room. The tuxedo, a dark navy with a black satin collar and matching bow tie, are hand-stitched and fit perfectly. Everything is going according to plan.

So why, I wonder as I stalk back over to the window and shove my hands into my pockets, *am I still unsatisfied?*

The door opens behind me.

"Guests are being directed to their seats."

Rafael joins me at the window in a matching tux with a slim tie. My eyes are drawn to a bear of a man stuffed into a suit moving along the edges of the crowd. Anger stirs, but I squelch it. I'm not wasting emotions on him.

"Michail came."

Rafe leans forward and watches him. "I thought he declined."

"He did."

I watch as he approaches Alessandra. The smile disappears from her face when she sees him. Those two have a history. I'm not sure what it involves, although I can make plenty of guesses as I watch her say something that turns his frown into a glower before she whirls around in a swirl of emerald silk and stalks off.

"I'm surprised you invited him."

I shrug. I don't like him. I don't like what he represents. I despise that our father cared more about telling me about the son he barely knew instead of trying to mend the fractures between us.

But the world now knew about Michail Sullivan Drakos, private security millionaire in his own right and secret son of Lucifer Drakos, thanks to a belated press release arranged by Lucifer before he died. The old bastard just had to have the last word. Leaving Michail off the guest list would have looked petty at best and undermined my image.

A mercenary approach. But I don't make decisions based on emotions.

"Are you sure you want to do this?" Rafe asks quietly.

I smirk. "If you really wanted an answer to that, you would have asked it four weeks ago when I asked you to be my best man."

Silence reigns between us.

"I don't always know what to say."

I glance at Rafael in surprise. My brother is a block of ice. I've never once heard him admit to anything that could resemble a weakness.

"You always know what to say."

"For business, yes." He leans forward, his eyes sweeping across the lawn. "When it comes to personal matters, I'm more of a failure than our father."

I frown. "Are you drunk?"

He laughs, the sound rusty as if he hasn't used his voice for that function in a very long time.

"Sadly, no. Merely reflective."

He looks at me then with that sharp gaze I know so well. Except right now it's tinged with a brotherly concern I've never experienced. It cuts me, unexpected and sharp. When I found out I had a brother, a stubborn flame of hope had flickered to life. Despite my mother choosing heartache over life, and my father dismissing me as if I were nothing more than a bug he'd stepped on, the concept of a sibling—a *brother*—had made me hope one last time.

A hope that died the moment Rafe had walked in on a break from university, said hello as if he was greeting a stranger on the street, and then continued on to his private rooms on the second floor where he stayed until he went back to London a week later.

He was never cruel or rude. His indifference was almost worse.

But I grew up. I shoved all of those hopes and desires for something more, for a family, out of my mind as I hardened my heart.

That a single glance and a few words can shake my resolve makes me feel...weak. Weak and angry that he would choose now, after all these years, to try and be a brother.

"I have concerns about how quickly you rushed into this. And who you're rushing into it with."

"That's the beauty of this arrangement, Rafe." I slap him on the back. "She's agreed to cease any investigations into our company. After we're divorced, even if she does try to write anything, it will look like pettiness from an ex-wife."

"But we don't have anything for her to write about." That look of concern intensifies. It's almost unnatural on a face that's usually as smooth as stone. "We never have, and never will, be like him."

The way he says it with such conviction digs deeper into my heart. I pause, waiting a second for my emotions to settle before I speak. It's nice to hear, sure.

But it's too late. I'm not opening my heart to anyone again.

"Doesn't mean she won't try to drum up something to get back at Lucifer."

Rafe's brows draw together. "I've wondered why she focused on him so hard. I should look into her background."

I nearly tell him then, about Grey House and her father. At the last second, I bite it back. No matter what I think of her, it's not my story to tell. That's what I tell myself as I ignore the protective instinct that rises.

I glance back out the window, then smile as I see a familiar blond-haired woman moving through the crowd, shoulders thrown back with confidence as she navigates with the use of her forearm crutches.

"Tessa's here."

I can practically hear Rafe's neck snap as his head whips around and he moves to the window. Interesting. I think this is the most emotion I've ever seen him display. His eyes zero in on the petite figure dressed in blue. His wife.

"You invited her?"

"She's family."

There. An almost imperceptible flinch before he regains control.

"Yes. Of course."

He doesn't offer up anything else so I steer the conversation back to my own nuptials.

"Don't worry about Juliette. She's signed the contract." The majority of guests have moved to the beach and are taking their seats. The sun is just about to graze the horizon. In a matter of minutes, I'll be a married man. "Drakos Development is safe."

I can feel Rafe's gaze on me, but I don't look. I've had enough surprises for one evening.

"Business isn't everything, *adelfós*. I hope you learn that before you lose something important."

"I have something important." I look at him then and arch a brow. "My share of the company. I would do anything for it. Including marrying to ensure its legacy." I make a show of glancing down at my watch. "Speaking of, it's time. Shall we?"

I don't bother waiting for an answer. I stride toward the door. A moment later, I hear his footsteps behind me.

As we walk downstairs, Sarabeth materializes at the bottom. With her black hair pulled into an elegant twist on top of her head and a violet-colored sheath dress, she could pass for a guest if she wasn't sporting a headset and a tablet.

"Mr. Drakos, please proceed to the ceremony site. We'll begin the processional in ninety seconds."

I salute her as I pass. The woman would have made a phenomenal drill sergeant.

The quartet reserved for the cocktail hour and ceremony are playing a lighthearted tune as Rafe and I walk down the elevated aisle. I nod to guests and smile, aware of the photographer catching my every move. The photos, and our only interview, have already been sold to a national magazine. An additional investment in making sure the right story is told about our relationship while reaping extra publicity for Drakos North America.

Rafe and I stop before the arch and face the crowd. A flower girl in a blush-colored dress prances down the aisle, scattering scarlet rose petals with an abandon that makes me grin. Catherine, the mother of the little girl and a good friend of Juliette's, follows in a bridesmaid gown the same shade of seductive red that makes her dark brown skin glow. She smiles for the cameras, but I don't miss the sharp glance she serves me as she takes her place on the opposite side of the arch. I only met her for the first time last night at the rehearsal, and Catherine has suspicions.

Smart woman. Fortunately, in the one conversation I had with Catherine, it doesn't appear Juliette has broken her promise. Yet. But Catherine, who has known Juliette for years and has some connection to Juliette's family, isn't buying the whole suddenly-in-love angle. As long as Juliette adheres to the contract, Catherine can cast me all the suspicious looks she wants.

A moment later, the traditional wedding march begins to play as the officiant gestures for everyone to stand.

And then I see her.

The world fades away. My vision becomes a tunnel, my focus solely on the stunning woman at the opposite end of the aisle. Long sleeves made of lace offer tantalizing glimpses of her skin. The low cut of the bodice leaves her shoulders bare and follows the lines of her waist before cascading into a full skirt that makes it seem like she's gliding down the aisle towards me.

The subtle, sexy touches blend with elegance and her natural beauty. Gone is the severe bun or the efficient braid. Her hair flows, dark and wavy, down her back, just like it did that day on the bluff. A veil trimmed in the same lace as her sleeves flutters behind her like butterfly wings. Blush highlights her cheekbones. Her lips, painted a vivid red, are tilted up into the barest of smiles as she nods to some of the guests.

I blink in surprise when I see the woman by her side, moving down the aisle in her wheelchair with one hand on the control and the other wrapped tightly around Juliette's. She'd mentioned someone special was walking her down the aisle but that they had been indisposed for last night's rehearsal.

The woman looks at me, and recognition slams into me. Desdemona Harris. Simon's ex-girlfriend. Silver streaks through her blond hair. The slight wrinkles by her eyes make her appear kind. Her gaze, chocolate brown, is warm but nervous, as if she's not sure what to make of all this. She turns her gaze to Juliette, who looks down at her and smiles with such reassuring warmth it makes me lose my breath.

The tension in their grip pulls me back from my fantasy.

Juliette looks back up. Our eyes meet and I see nerves, apprehension.

Beautiful.

I nearly mouth the word to her, to ease the tension in her gaze and build a bridge between us.

But then she shifts, her chin rising as her eyes harden and she stares at me with something akin to disgust even as she smiles so sweetly it makes me want to growl. In that moment I regret the horde watching our every move, the cameras clicking away. I want it to just be the two of us so we can finally rip the gloves off and shout at each other. Something raw and honest, not this brittle chasm that widens with every encounter.

An alarm sounds deep within my mind. I freeze. I can't remember the last time I wanted something messy, craved reality instead of the precise existence I'd crafted for myself. The woman walking toward me, the one I'm about to pledge my life to for the next twelve months, has made me want…more.

I don't want more. I want what I've forged for myself, with no one but me at the helm.

I slip back into the familiarity of my role and shoot Juliette a confident smile as I rake my eyes up and down her body. A different heat is kindled as my gaze lingers on the swells of her breasts above the bodice of her dress, the flare of her hips beneath the gown. A heat made all the more pleasing by the warning look she shoots me as she draws near.

My smile grows. We agreed on no sex. But no one said anything about not looking.

Juliette passes her bouquet to Desdemona and then joins me in front of the officiant. My chest tightens as I wrap her hands in mine, my thumb brushing against her ring. She blinks rapidly as I trace a lazy circle on her skin before tensing in my grasp as I gently press down. I try, and fail, to hide my slight smile as her mask slips and I see the raw need in her eyes.

"Repeat after me, Gavriil."

I repeat the vows spoken by the officiant. No one else seems to notice the slightest hesitation before she repeats her own.

"You may kiss the bride."

I smile at her as my hands settle at her waist and pull her close. My fingertips brush bare skin. Blood surges as my body hardens at the realization that her back is naked.

I lower my head and seal my lips to hers.

Too much. The thought flashes in my mind, then disappears, smothered by the craving ripping through my body. It's too much for a first kiss. The first kiss between man and wife. The first kiss ever between two people.

But it's happening. It's happening and, *Theós*, I can't stop.

Her taste fills me. Fire licks up my hands, my arms, then flashes down my spine as I press my lips more firmly against hers, tease the seam of her lips with my tongue. Not just to tease, no, but to claim. Even if this is a charade of a marriage, I want everyone to know this woman is *mine*.

I should let go, should be done with it, need to stay in control—

Her lips part. I feel her inhale right before she kisses me back, our parted lips deepening the intimacy between us for a mere second before she suddenly pulls back. I stare at her, my gaze fixed on her face. Her eyes are dark, her breathing heavy. She felt it just as much as I did. That pulsing need, more than desire or mere lust.

What have I done?

Over the roaring of blood in my ears, I hear the cheering of the crowd, the whoops and congratulations.

"I now pronounce you man and wife," the officiant proudly declares.

I recover first and tug her around to face the guests. Their smiles blend together as my mind tries to process what just happened.

I married Juliette Grey. I married her and then I kissed her and now my world feels like it's been tilted off its axis.

I inhale once, exhale slowly. Then I slip an arm around her waist and pull her against my side. She stiffens but doesn't turn away. A quick glance out of the corner of my eye confirms that she's at least trying to smile. But the stretching of her lips looks more like the grimace of someone about to face a firing squad.

I lean down, my lips brushing her ear and sending a shiver through her.

"Smile, Mrs. Drakos."

CHAPTER EIGHT

Juliette

I LEAN AGAINST the marble banister, a glass of champagne in my hand and a glimpse of stars above me. The lights of the Queen's Necklace, a collection of opulent homes and buildings on Malibu Bay, glow against the darkening navy of a summer night. Even though I prefer my mist-covered Olympic Coast, it is beautiful.

I smile at the dark waves of the Pacific rolling lazily up onto the beach. Given the sheer size of the ocean, it's odd how it can still feel like a comfort, a familiar friend amidst so many strangers milling just a few dozen feet away.

My moment of peace drifts away as someone laughs behind me. Just one hour ago, I said "I do." Now my gargantuan ring has a mate, a silver monstrosity that has even more diamonds shoved into the band. Its sole purpose is to draw attention to the wealth that purchased it.

Which about sums up my husband in a nutshell.

When Gavriil told me his reasons for wanting an outrageous wedding, I was furious. The man wanted to humiliate me, to put me on display not just for that stupid will, but to show me who had the upper hand in this arrangement. That he would also be showing the world, again, how much money he had was just a bonus.

Two can play at that game.

I take a drink of my champagne. The bubbles dance on my tongue, leaving behind a taste of citrus blended with honeysuckle. The best champagne I've ever had. Given what it cost, it should be. I wondered if it would be one those luxury items everyone raves about because it's so rare when it's actually terrible.

I'd never heard of king protea flowers or phalaenopsis orchids before I let Gavriil slide that monstrous engagement ring onto my finger. But I made it my mission to do exactly what he said: spend and let the whole world know just how much money he had. But I did it in such a way that even he would be irritated at the amount of money spent.

Judging by the irritation furrowing his brow when I'd handed him the final bill for the catering, I'd accomplished my mission.

He could afford it. I'm comforting myself with knowing Sarabeth worked with Dessie to identify local care centers that would wake up to lavish flowers, carefully packaged Belon River oysters from France, and leftover triple-chocolate cake with raspberry sauce and buttercream frosting. It takes some of the sting out of having just spent over three million dollars on an event that won't last more than eight hours.

A sigh escapes. The question drifts through my mind again—will this marriage, this farce, be worth the price—even though I know it's too late as I avoid looking at the rings.

I also know the answer. All I have to do is look at Dessie to know it was the right choice. Ever since I told her that Grey House would be mine again, and that I wanted her to move back in with me, she's been on cloud nine. Catherine, whose daughter Whitney served as the flower girl, told me Dessie's been putting more effort into her physical therapy appointments and getting out of her room again.

Those reports came in between concerned questions from

Catherine about my engagement and upcoming wedding. Aside from Dessie, she's the only other person who knows why I loathed Lucifer Drakos with every fiber of my being. She's not convinced about this sudden whirlwind romance with Lucifer's son.

But even if I hadn't signed the contract, I would have kept my word. No matter how much I wanted someone to talk to about this crazy scheme I'd landed myself in.

A scheme made all the more ridiculous by my insane attraction to a man I can barely stand. My cheeks heat as I relive that fateful kiss, from the burn of his fingers against my back to that intimate, playful swipe of his tongue against my lips.

Another gulp of champagne fails to cool me off. Not when I'm thinking about how I kissed him back. Just for one second, but the damage was done. That moment when our breaths mingled, when the world around us stilled and we were the only two people caught in the eye of a storm that had been swirling ever since we'd known each other's names.

What am I going to do? I had envisioned the attraction between us as simple, a little more intense than the couple previous relationships I've had, but nothing I couldn't handle.

Except I can still feel his hands on my waist. Can still feel that moment his body went hard and still when I returned his kiss, as if I'd surprised him. Can still see his eyes when we pulled apart, wide and shocked like his world had just been rocked as mine had.

Until he'd turned to face the crowd. Any hints of his true feelings were gone beneath that perfect mask as he'd ordered me to smile.

I'd made it down the aisle and to the cocktail hour with what I'd termed as my *elated bride* face intact. I'd eaten one smoked trout croquette, greeted a handful of people who had a look of importance about them as Gavriil rattled off names I barely heard, given Dessie a hug, and then disappeared into the night with my champagne before she or Catherine could see past my charade.

I have no idea where my husband is. Which is better all around. After our mandatory two-week honeymoon, I'll be able to come up with plenty of excuses to keep my distance for the remainder of our contract. My work, overseeing renovations to Grey House, traveling with Dessie once she's feeling up to it. Anything to keep distance between us, to prevent another kiss from happening.

The salty scent of the sea drifts to me on a breeze. I inhale, my breath a shudder as I admit what I will never confess to another living soul: that Gavriil Drakos, a man who stands for everything I've fought against for years, has the power to consume me. He's the kind of man parents warn their daughters to stay away from. The kind who pulls you so high you know you can fly.

Until they let go of your hand and you plummet back to earth. Alone. Broken.

I press my fingers against the cool stone of the banister. I've seen the women left behind by powerful men, the discarded toys that mean nothing once the novelty's worn off. I may have sold my hand in marriage.

But I refuse to sell my soul to the son of the devil.

Awareness prickles the back of my neck. Above the alluring fragrance of orchids and sea salt, I smell amber and smoky wood. A shiver teases its way down my spine as I fight to keep my face toward the waves.

"You disappeared for so long I wondered if I had a runaway bride on my hands."

His voice slides over my skin.

"Just needed a break. Lot of people."

He moves to the banister next to me. I don't look at him,

but I can feel him. Feel the heat of his body, feel his sheer presence.

"Our first dance is in eight minutes."

My lips quirk. "Sounds like Sarabeth found you."

"Found me and gave me marching orders. I should hire her."

I can't help but laugh. I feel him tense beside me, then slowly relax as a chuckle escapes him. Warm and casual, a sound that fills my chest before I can guard myself against it.

"That's a beautiful dress."

Now it's my turn to tense as I finally look at him. The one thing that is mine and mine alone in this sham of a wedding is my dress.

The pissed-off side of me argued for going to the splashiest dress boutique in California and plunking down a hefty sum on a designer gown. Except everything I tried on felt…wrong. Constricting. Fake. I was drawn back time and time again to the cedar chest tucked into my closet in my little cottage. The one my father gave to me before I left to move in with Dessie. The one with my mother's initials carved in the lid.

I have only the flimsiest memories of my mom. They're more impressions than images. Cool glass beneath my hand and the warmth of her body at my back while we watched rain splash the windows of Grey House. A laugh, boisterous and full. A soothing voice when I came home from preschool crying because my best friend played with someone else. But when I pulled out her wedding dress, I felt her. Relived those wonderful, warm memories as her floral scent, mixed with the faint hint of cedar, drifted up from the lace.

"It's my mother's."

His eyes widen slightly before a shutter drops over them.

"A surprising choice, given your other selections for tonight."

I shrug. He doesn't need to know that I had never envisioned wearing it as my own gown. I'd talked about using part of the train as a veil, or perhaps wrapping a strip of lace around my wedding bouquet to honor my mother. But when I'd pulled it out of the chest, felt that warmth wash over me, I knew I would need that connection today, that remembrance of love, as I walked down the aisle and into a loveless marriage.

"Haven't you heard? Vintage is in."

His eyes narrow, as if he's trying to decipher some puzzle. I'm about to open my mouth and tell him not to bother when Sarabeth materializes out of the darkness.

"There you are!" She taps a finger on the clipboard. "You should have been lined up two minutes ago. Let's go."

Gavriil's lips tilt up. Amusement lights his pale blue eyes as he inclines his head to Sarabeth before extending a hand to me. I ignore him and toss back the rest of the champagne before setting the glass on the banister.

"Charming," he murmurs under his breath as he grabs my elbow and pushes me toward the dance floor.

"At a thousand a bottle, I didn't want to waste any."

His grip tightens and I suppress a satisfied smirk as he leads me to the dance floor. If the man is going to parade me around like a monkey in his personal circus, I'm not going to waste an opportunity to get under his skin.

We near the patio, strung with twinkling lights and surrounded by stunning pots overflowing with the ridiculously expensive orchids and dramatic roses. Tables draped in black tablecloths and topped with smaller clusters of the same flower arrangements form a C around the dance floor, with the orchestra on an elevated platform at the far end of the patio.

"Ladies and gentlemen, Mr. and Mrs. Gavriil Drakos!"

The crowd cheers as Gavriil leads me onto the dance floor. I think I'm smiling at the sea of faces blurred by the lights and my own nervousness. The fear that they'll see right through me.

"It's a wonder you managed to gain the reputation you did."

My spine snaps into a straight line as I shoot a steel-laced smile his way.

"Oh?"

He pulls me close, one arm tight about my waist, a hand resting on my naked back and the other wrapped around my fingers.

"For someone with your renown, I expected you not to wear your heart on your sleeve." He leans down, his breath tickling my ear. "At least look happy for your first dance with your new husband."

I smile then, a bright, brilliant beam as I stop myself from stomping on his foot.

"Of course, darling," I croon.

He presses me closer, his eyes flaring as he whisks me into a turn. I grit my teeth against the traitorous pleasure that zips through my veins at the feel of his body against mine. Lights streak by as music fills the air. With the way he's looking at me, the masterful way he's waltzing me about the patio, and the gentle brush of lace against my skin, it would be easy to fall into the illusion. To think that the magic of one gilded night could be carried into the next day and beyond.

I focus on a spot over his shoulder. I just need to get through this dance, and then I'll sit down with Dessie or Catherine.

"Everyone's been telling me they haven't attended a better wedding."

His voice breaks through my thoughts, a touch of cold edging his tone.

EMMY GRAYSON 81

"You don't sound pleased."

He shrugs before he raises my hand up and spins me into a turn that has my skirt flaring out. The guests applaud and I swear I hear someone swoon. His palm lands once more on my bare back, making me silently curse myself for asking for a "touch of sexiness" from Catherine's seamstress-friend, who did the alterations.

"I didn't say that."

"You didn't have to."

I can feel him watching me for what can't be more than a few seconds but feels like forever.

"You confuse me. You spent thousands on flowers and champagne. But you wear your mother's wedding dress. You work with one of the most lauded event planners in the country, yet invite less than a dozen guests of your own to our wedding. Your father's ex-girlfriend walked you down the aisle." When my head snaps up, he grins down at me. "Dessie spoke very highly of you when I introduced myself during the cocktail hour." He leans down and I swallow hard, vividly remembering the last time his lips were so close to mine. "You're a puzzle, Juliette. One I want to figure out."

"You don't have to figure me out."

I regret the words almost as soon as they're out of my mouth. Something flashes in his eyes, fleeting but no less potent in its pain.

I've hurt him, and for no other reason other than I want to keep distance between us. I open my mouth, grappling for the right words of apology. But before I can speak, he continues.

"True." He shrugs his shoulders. "This is a business arrangement. Not a relationship. You have the house you want. And the money." He says that with the slightest of sneers in his voice as his words slice through me. "And I have what I want."

"Your share of Drakos Development." I say it almost bitterly, as if I expected something more.

"Yes."

"It's so important you would risk marrying your sworn enemy?"

"I would do anything for it."

I glance around us then, at the people watching us dance. Some look starstruck, others calculating, as if they know something's off, can sense the story we've spun is pure fiction.

"And what if someone finds out? About the will and why we got married?"

"If they agree to keep a private family matter private, nothing." His eyes sharpen to chips of pale blue ice. "But if they threaten me, I'll destroy them."

He watches me, his head cocked to the side, as if waiting to see how I'll respond to this display of power. I'd be lying if I said it wasn't intimidating. But in some twisted way, I'm grateful for it. One kiss made me swoon. His frank words, the reminder of why he married me, help cool some of my desire.

If I can just keep playing his words over in my head, a daily mantra to keep me grounded, I can survive the next two weeks in France.

The music starts to wind down. As he takes me into a final turn, he leans down.

"I do, however, propose one adjustment to our contract."

The glint in his eyes puts me on guard. "Oh?"

"Given how well our first kiss went, perhaps we could do both of us a favor and revise the no physical intimacy clause."

My heart stops. I bite down on my lower lip to stop myself from saying the first word that comes to mind. I can imagine it all too easily: hot, sweaty bodies joining together on top of mussed sheets, questing hands and frantic gasps. An inferno that would ignite every nerve as it destroyed reason and left only pure pleasure in its wake.

Applause sounds like a thunderclap and yanks me from my vision. Gavriil smirks down at me, confident of my decision. The sight of it infuriates me that he would assume I could be swayed by one kiss.

Enrages me that I would be tempted by one kiss.

I slide my arms around his neck and rise up on my toes. Fire flares in his eyes as I draw near...

Then shift at the last minute and brush my lips against his cheek as I steel myself to say what needs to be said. To prevent me from compromising my beliefs any further.

"There will be no revisions," I whisper into his ear. "And if you suggest it again, contract or no, I will walk away from this marriage."

His shoulders tense. He draws back, his gaze hard. He grasps my hand and spins me out. My heart leaps into my throat. Have I gone too far?

"My wife, ladies and gentlemen," he announces in a booming voice. I can hear the promise in his words, the threat. He's got his ring on my finger. He's not letting me go anytime soon. And as much as I want to fight him, to shout out the truth and be done with it, I can't. Not when Dessie is sitting on the fringes next to Catherine with color in her cheeks and hope in her eyes.

His fingers tighten on mine a fraction. I incline my head toward our guests as my body grows heavy.

This is going to be a very long year.

CHAPTER NINE

Gavriil

THE EIFFEL TOWER juts up into the summer sky, proud and dark against a light blue. Some might call it cliché or boring. But for me, the Eiffel Tower is a symbol of longevity, of history and pride.

Yet despite my appreciation for the historic landmark, I've barely glanced at it more than half a dozen times in the three days I've been in Paris. Juliette and I spent our wedding night in the King Suite at The Royal. The bellhop had scarcely closed the door before Juliette cleaved off and walked into the guest room, firmly closing the door behind her. I hadn't bothered to follow. Not after her threat on the dance floor. One that still makes my blood boil thinking about how casually she turned and smiled at the crowd as we walked off the dance floor.

I told myself I could simply shut my desire off. Anger simmered on our wedding night and kept the lust away. Business gave me something to focus on for the first leg of our flight from California to New York. We had just passed over the Rocky Mountains when I got the call I have been waiting for. Louis Paul was contemplating my offer for an entire block of New York City real estate just outside of the Financial District.

Juliette dozed off on the leather couch in my private jet

shortly after we took off across the Atlantic. I looked up from a finance report to see her hair slipping loose from her bun and framing her serene face. Need had jolted through me, along with that word that had reared its head during the ceremony.

Mine.

If it had been a simple case of the attraction not being reciprocated, the decision would have been easy. But as I've revisited her threat over the past few days, I realized there was something lingering behind her words. Something buried beneath her bravado.

Fear.

She intrigues me. Entices me. The dichotomies of her character, from feisty reporter and bold mercenary to kind-hearted daughter and sentimental dreamer. Learning she had worn her mother's dress, that she had asked her father's former girlfriend to walk her down the aisle, had taken everything I had been thinking about her during our short engagement and turned it on its head. It had also opened the door for the attraction I'd been fighting to surge through.

An attraction she refuses to acknowledge. We're bound together for a year. Why is she dedicated to celibacy when we clearly have something between us worth exploring and enjoying?

But I also know the value of biding my time. Of watching and waiting. The image of impulsivity and brashness I portray is an illusion, one that has served me well time and again while helping me keep my distance. Without that detachment, I wouldn't be nearly as successful.

So we passed most of the flight in silence. A limo whisked us from the airport to the Shangri-La Paris. There was a brief flicker of excitement on Juliette's face when she saw the Eiffel Tower for the first time. But before I could ask her about it, she lapsed back into silence, her gaze distant and focused on anything but me. I let it go.

For now.

I set up my office on the terrace of our penthouse suite, which included views of the Eiffel Tower, the River Seine and the buildings that made up Paris's 16th arrondissement. The first day, I took her to brunch at a glass-roofed restaurant. Yesterday we went on a private tour of the Louvre after closing. Photos of us entering the museum through the contest pyramid in the main courtyard had already made the rounds on various media circuits, my arm around Juliette's waist as she appeared to glance demurely at the ground.

My jaw hardened. Fortunately, I seemed to be the only one who knew she was doing her best to avoid me, even when we were side by side, being shown some of the rarest and most expensive art in the world.

Other than those two outings, we'd kept our own agendas. Juliette flitted in and out of the suite, sometimes with her camera, sometimes with a shopping bag. She never joined me for meals on the terrace. In fact, she rarely came out at all, except at night right before she went to bed. She'd walk out on the far end of the terrace, arms crossed over her chest as if she were keeping something out, and watch the sparkling lights of the Eiffel Tower at night. Then she'd glance my way, nod, and go back to her room.

I've given her more than enough space and kept our excursions to a minimum. It's time for us to be seen together in a more romantic frame, to refocus the spotlight once more on Gavriil Drakos and his enemy-turned-bride.

And to remind her of what could be between us.

A soft creak sounds behind me. Surprised, I turn in time to see Juliette emerge from her room. *Theós*, she's beautiful. Wet hair, slicked back from her forehead, makes her look younger, more vulnerable. She's wearing a short, white robe and moves through the room with an ease that tells me she thinks it's empty. I did leave earlier to meet with a business associate eyeing a housing project next year in the Hamptons. But when I came back, I thought she was out and would stay out the rest of the day.

I watch her for another moment, the casual confidence of her movements, the relaxed ease of her shoulders as she drifts over to the radio and turns it to a jazz station. You'd think that a fluffy bathrobe would deter sexual fantasies. But the sight of her long legs bare beneath the far too short hemline creates visions of those legs wrapped around my waist. I harden faster than I can suck in a breath.

"Good morning."

Her head snaps to the side and her eyes widen momentarily before she smooths out her features and nods to me. Like a queen nodding to her subjects.

I fight to keep my mouth straight and not let her see that I find her confidence so damned sexy.

"Good morning." She tightens the sash of her robe. "I thought you were still out."

We stare at each other for a moment. Her eyes dart from me to the door. I take pity on her and gesture to the table.

"Would you like some coffee?"

She hesitates, then blinks and gives the tiniest nod of her head.

"That sounds nice. Thank you."

I pour her a cup of coffee and watch as she doctors it with a dash of honey, a generous splash of milk, and a spoonful of sugar.

"I was out. Now I'm back." I top off my own cup as I nod toward the cityscape laid out beyond our balcony. "Enjoying the view."

Her head swings in the direction of the Eiffel Tower. The hint of a smile teases her lips as she gazes at the iron lattice, the blur of shapes behind the metal as the more adventurous climb the numerous steps on their way to the top.

"I've been up since sunrise," she finally says softly.

Her words conjure an image of her waking with golden light filtering through the windows, hair mussed as she rises and eyes heavy with sleep. I raise my cup to my lips as I internally vow that before this honeymoon is over, I will be in her bed one morning to wake her up, to rouse her with deep kisses and slow strokes until she's crying out for me.

"Working?" I ask, my voice only a touch gravelly.

She shakes her head. "Sort of. More of a personal hobby I once enjoyed." She shrugs. "Maybe it'll turn into something."

"Oh?"

Her gaze refocuses on me, her eyes narrowed, as if she's trying to determine if I'm genuinely interested or if I have an ulterior motive in mind. I maintain her gaze. Yes, I want her to agree to amend the damned contract. But I'm genuinely curious as to what she'll do next if she truly plans to honor her commitment to not pursue any more stories about Drakos Development.

"Something new. Nothing to do with corporations," she adds with an arched brow.

"I feel safer already."

Her barest huff of a laugh fills me. I don't want to have as strong of a reaction as I do, to be as aware as I am of the little nuances and subtleties of her body language. But I can't help it. I'm not just enjoying the chase. I'm enjoying her company. And she seems to be enjoying mine. Perhaps convincing her to spend the afternoon out where we can be seen and play up the lovesick honeymooners won't be so challenging.

"Can you talk more about it?"

She dips her head. Pink changes her cheeks. It takes me a moment to realize it's not coyness but shyness. She's nervous about whatever the special project is. That hint of vulnerability tugs at me.

"Not yet. It's still in its infant phase."

She looks at me then. Her unexpectedly sweet and self-conscious smile stabs straight into my chest. Her fire, her passion, even her determination, all of it intrigues me. Coupled with this unexpected softness, from the way I saw her check in on Dessie throughout the wedding to the shy excitement adding a sparkle to her eyes right now, is alluring in a way I've never experienced before. I've never been interested in looking past the surface.

Until the woman sitting across from me caught my attention with her daring in standing up to Lucifer. The first person outside my family I'd ever seen risk his wrath.

"Are you moving away from investigative reporting?"

Some of the light dims.

"I don't know. My last job…" Her throat moves as she swallows hard. "It was more challenging than I expected."

I watch her as she raises her coffee to her lips, her gaze distant. I start to ask more, but my phone rings. I glance down. Anticipation zings through me as I recognize the number for Paul Properties offices in New York City.

I glance up. She's looking at me now. I've never hesitated in taking a work call. But after what she's just alluded to, I pause.

"Go ahead." She smiles. "I'm okay."

I move into the living room and take the call from one of Paul's numerous lawyers. The property I want to buy is in a neighborhood that most people have written off. But I had seen the early signs of rejuvenation. The investment in local businesses, the efforts of residents to organize neighborhood watches, community gardens, and other activities that bolstered the rate of people moving in while reducing crime. There are still problems, but there's a lot of potential.

Unlike my early years in the slums of Santorini, I now had both the money and power to turn that potential into something concrete. Something that hasn't become a focus until recently. My only objective when I first started with Drakos Development had been to make as much money as possible. But that goal has evolved, especially in the last year or so as the money hasn't brought as much contentment, as the sensation of wielding power and influence has dulled. My goals now include bettering the communities surrounding my properties. Maybe it will do nothing.

But maybe it will make a difference for someone. Someone like my mother who had someone like me who loved them, despite their numerous faults. Someone who, with the right support, might be able to do what my mother failed to do and climb out of their pit.

I'm not ready to share this new focus with the public. Not yet. Knowing it's rooted in my own painful past is a vulnerability I'm not ready to share. Six minutes later, after answering numerous questions I know were more designed to test me than to divine any information, I hang up and return to the terrace.

Just in time to see my wife with her head tilted to one side as she reads the file I left open on the table.

I freeze, watching as she cranes her neck to read more. Betrayal rips through me so fast I barely contain my snarl. I stalk over, reach down, and snatch the file from under her nose.

"It didn't take you long to break our bargain."

She stares up at me with a wrinkle between her brows and an innocent expression on her beautiful face.

"What are you talking about?"

I dangle the folder from my fingertips.

"Tell me, did you decide to marry me because it might give you access to some of the corporate bigwigs you've been trying to take down? Or was that just a side benefit in addition to the two million dollars?"

Her face pales.

"Do you truly think so little of me? That I wouldn't stand by our contract?"

"The story is the most important thing to you."

She sets her coffee cup down with careful precision, stands and walks to the edge of the terrace. Her shoulders are tense, her chin lifted. But beneath the bravado is a painful sadness that pierces my anger and leaves me feeling like an ass. She looks away from me and out over the rooftops of Paris.

Damn it. I don't know why she was reading the file. But it's not like I walked in on her trying to break into a safe. She glanced at papers I left out on the breakfast table. Instead of asking like a sane person, I jumped to conclusions and lashed out.

I walk up next to her and stop a couple feet away. An apology doesn't seem like enough.

I follow her gaze down to the road below us. A couple walks down the sidewalk, a blond man in a T-shirt and shorts with his arm wrapped about the waist of a red-haired woman. They stop on the corner. The man grabs her close and dips her back, kissing her laughing lips as if he doesn't have a care in the world.

My gaze moves back to her face. She's still watching

them, and in that moment I feel more like my father than I ever have before. I'm being cruel, pushing her away because for two minutes we had a conversation that stirred something more than lust or the casual apathy I've coasted on the past twenty-four years, and this made the sense of betrayal that much harsher.

"Perhaps the story is the most important thing."

My gaze sharpens on her face. She continues to watch the couple below.

"But when I care about the story, I care about the people in it, too." She whirls around suddenly, and jabs a finger toward my chest. "I don't care about the payday or what I could buy. I care about justice, about giving a voice to those who have been silenced by people like your father."

Frustration and anger wipe away most of my guilt. Does she think I'm blind? That I didn't pay attention to the numerous bills crossing my desk, to what she's been doing while she's here in Paris?

"You don't care about the payday, but you ask for two million, spend nearly double that on the wedding, and came back yesterday with a bag from Louboutin?"

Instead of dissolving into tears or slapping me across the face, she merely leans back and cocks an eyebrow in my direction, all traces of shyness gone. And damn it if that casual confidence doesn't shoot straight down into my groin and make my blood pulse.

"Coming from the man worth billions and wearing a three-hundred-dollar Hermès tie to drink coffee on a terrace, that insult doesn't carry the sting you want it to."

Frustrated, I rake my fingers through my hair.

"I don't want to insult you, Juliette. I told you before, you confuse me and I reacted—"

"Like a jerk?"

"I was going to say *gáidaros*, but close enough."

She doesn't back down. No, she tosses those shoulders back, the robe partially falling aside and giving me a glimpse of the swells of her breasts. Unlike that tantalizing neckline of her wedding dress, though, there are no layers of lace, no buttons. Nothing but air between me and the woman I'm longing to possess.

The woman I need to touch, now, even if I'm damned for it.

I close the distance between us. She watches me, her body poised to flee. But she doesn't. I reach out. She freezes but doesn't pull away as I glide the back of my hand down the curve of her face.

"What are you doing?" she whispers, her chest rising and falling as a blush twines up her neck.

"Touching you."

She inhales, her eyes burning into mine. "Why?"

"Because you make me hunger." I wrap my arms around her waist and slowly pull her against my chest, savoring the anticipation. "Because no matter how much you confuse me, I can't stop thinking of your lips beneath mine. Of how you felt in my arms." I stop, hovering my lips just above hers. "Tell me to stop, Juliette."

I wait for her to push me away, to remind me of her threat from our wedding day or call me a name and storm off.

But it's Juliette, so she does the last thing I expect. She throws her arms around my neck and kisses me.

CHAPTER TEN

Juliette

I'VE MADE A MISTAKE. I know it as soon as our lips crash together. Mingled harsh breaths, his heartbeat racing beneath my palm as I rest my hands on his chest and press myself against him. I've never done this, never thrown myself at a man because I either had to kiss him or go up in flames.

Our wedding kiss, as unexpected as it was, had the tether of being in front of hundreds of people. It could only go so far. Even our excursions around Paris, as we held hands at the café or he slid a possessive arm around my waist at the Louvre, had been for the benefit of anyone watching.

Here, there's only us. No excuses. And as I respond with an aching need that makes my whole body throb, I have no regrets. Not when his arms are around me like bands of steel, his groan filling me, his hard length pressing against my hips. I'm acutely aware that there's only my robe and the fabric of his pants between the most intimate parts of our bodies.

I slide my hips up and down just a fraction. The friction on my sensitive skin makes me tremble.

"Theós."

He growls it against my mouth as he spins me around and pulls me into the privacy of the penthouse. Cool air kisses my skin and I glance down to see my robe parted, revealing my breasts. It should make me feel self-conscious, embarrassed.

But when I look up and see Gavriil staring at me like he's starving and I'm the only thing that can satiate his hunger, all I feel is a reckless boldness urging me on.

I step back. Need a moment, just a moment to think. Gavriil's hands tighten momentarily on my waist before he releases me, the tendons in his neck straining as he sucks in a shuddering breath. Seeing his restraint, his respect even as he devours me with ravenous eyes, pushes me through that last moment of hesitation.

I surge forward again, my hands sliding up over his chest as our mouths meet. It's not a kiss but a branding I feel through my chest, through the pulsing in my core, all the way to my toes as his tongue sweeps inside my mouth in an intimate caress that makes me moan.

His hands dive into my hair, anchoring my head as his lips trail over my jaw before he nips my neck. The graze of teeth on sensitive skin makes me cry out and arch against him. I press my hips against his, pressure building as wetness slicks my thighs.

"Gavriil…"

He nudges one leg between mine as he holds me against him. I shift, the friction of his pants against my bare skin making me pant. His mouth descends to the curve of my shoulder, then farther down. One tug and my robe falls open, baring my naked body to his gaze.

"Ómorfi."

The word ripples through me. I don't know any Greek, but I don't need a dictionary to feel the meaning. To feel beautiful. Seen.

Before I can claw back enough of my sanity, Gavriil

dips his head and sucks my nipple into his mouth. Sensation spears out, heated energy whirling through my body as my fingers slide into his hair.

"Gavriil!"

His tongue swirls over me. His hair, thick and silky beneath my hands, is a lifeline as I spiral upward. He keeps one arm banded around my waist as his other hand cups my other breast.

He pulls back. I moan, not wanting this to be it, to live with this unbearable pressure seething beneath my skin, electricity crackling through my veins as if I might combust unless I find some kind of release—

He sweeps me into his arms and stalks over to the couch. I take advantage of my proximity to his neck and repeat what he did to me, kissing his heated skin before I run my tongue over the hollow at the base of his throat.

A growl rumbles in his chest before he sets me down on the couch facing him. He grabs my knees and spreads my legs. I should be embarrassed. I should stop. I should definitely stop.

Not a chance.

His next kiss is fierce, one I return with my need growing to unbearable proportions. I don't know why I'm responding to him with such wild abandon. Maybe it's because I have no vengeance to achieve, to focus on to the detriment of everything else. Maybe this is the distraction I need as I try to figure out the rest of my life.

Or maybe it's simply this man. This man who infuriates and impresses and seduces.

I tense as he glides one hand up my leg, pauses at the top of my thigh and taps out a teasing dance with his fingertips.

"Please, Gavriil."

I don't care that I'm begging, that I'm letting him see just how deeply he affects me. All I care about is being touched, feeling wanted by this man I'm married to.

His hand skims higher. His fingers gently stroke, light touches that tease and stoke the flames higher as he uses his other hand to pull my robe down to my waist and move his mouth down to continue his sensual assault with tongue and teeth on my other breast.

"You're so wet."

I cry out as he slides one finger inside me. It only takes a few long, slow strokes for the peak that's been building since he stalked toward me on the terrace to burst.

"Oh, God!"

It shatters through me, tiny peaks of light spiraling from my core throughout my body. He continues to make love to my breasts with gentle kisses as I drift down from my peak. The soft press of his lips against my skin makes my eyes grow hot. I hadn't imagined such gentleness from him. It shouldn't matter.

Can't matter.

As the pleasure slips away, intrusive thoughts try to break through. Reminders to keep my guard up, to not let this become a habit and risk sliding in deeper. I shove them away as he eases me back to rest against the back of the couch. A lazy smile curves my lips as I recline against silk. For right now, I'm going to focus on feeling. Enjoying.

My eyes fly open as Gavriil pulls my robe back up. I look up to see him watching me. For a moment, there's something in his eyes. Something that kindles a different spark deep inside my chest.

And then it's gone, replaced with his usual languid expression of superiority.

"Should I take this as your agreement to amending the contract?"

I stare at him. Humiliation burns away the lingering tendrils of desire. For one horrible moment, I think I might cry.

No.

He's not worth it. He might not be the lawbreaking bastard I had suspected him of being. But he's still a bastard, incapable of anything but arrogant humor and pompous pride.

I stand, taking vicious pleasure in watching his eyes slide down to the bared skin of my chest. I take my time pulling the lapels of the robe closed and belting it, never taking my eyes off him. I run a hand through my hair and give him a cool smile.

"I don't think what just happened counts as anything meaningful. So, no."

His face tightens. Perhaps in anger or chafed pride. I don't really care. His ego deserves a beating.

"Enjoy your coffee."

I walk to my room and close the door softly behind me, not bothering to lock it. He won't come after me.

I tell myself it doesn't matter. I insist on it even as tears burn the backs of my eyes.

CHAPTER ELEVEN

Juliette

I STAND IN front of the mirror and smooth my hands over the skirt of my dress. I've always paid for good quality clothing. But I've never indulged in luxury before. I never understood why people bothered to spend hundreds or even thousands of dollars on a shirt or dress that would end up with a stain on it the next day.

But right now, standing in front of the oval mirror with the lights of Paris at my back, I understand a little. I was walking down the Champs-élysées earlier this morning when I passed a boutique store. It was so unlike the other gilded storefronts lining the historic road. The dresses in the window were simple yet elegant.

The dress I'm wearing now, with a Queen Anne neckline that adds a touch of regalness to the simple silhouette, was front and center. Colored a periwinkle blue, with a full skirt falling from the waist and a deep V in the back that bares my skin. Combined with the pearl studs I brought from home and my own hair twisted up into something as close to a chignon as I could get, I feel beautiful.

Beautiful.

The word flickers through me, brings back that moment this morning when he whispered that word and it pulsed through me like a heartbeat.

My eyes grow hot and I turn away from the mirror. When he kissed me, when he…touched me, I felt alive. Sensual.

The bastard had ruined it all with one of his casual quips. A reminder that what happened between us had been simple pleasure. Yes, he obviously found me attractive. But I have no interest in going to bed with someone who treats sex so casually. I most definitely have no interest in sleeping with someone who doesn't trust me and, I suspect, doesn't even really like me. *A mutual feeling*, I remind myself as I move toward the door. I don't trust him either. How could I when he moves in the world he does, with money ruling his decisions? When he's made it clear his bank balance is the pinnacle of his existence?

My father thought the same thing in the last year of his life. His obsession pushed away the two women who would have loved him to hell and back.

I wasn't trying to be sneaky when I read that file. I'd glanced down as I'd reached for a spoon. The name at the top of the paper had jolted me into action.

Louis Paul. The same man who had been staying at Peter Walter's mansion in an exclusive gated community outside Dallas seven months ago when my investigation led to a raid on the warehouse. A raid that resulted in the rescue of nearly half a dozen human trafficking victims.

Paul came out clean. He'd known Walter for years but had never done business with him. There was no evidence of Paul being involved. Even though I hadn't been actively investigating Paul, I'd kept an eye on him and noted two more trips to Dallas in the past year. Those trips, however, were much more discreet. Paul flew commercial, arrived and left in taxis instead of his usual limo and disappeared into the Dallas suburbs instead of a ritzy hotel downtown.

Yet I couldn't connect him to anything. And then Lucifer had passed away and Paul faded to the back of my mind. Seeing his name on a possible business deal with Drakos North America was jarring. I thought about telling Gavriil when I saw Paul's name on the file. That is, until he stormed in and accused me of using our marriage as an espionage tactic.

Fine. If he doesn't want to bother digging into the backgrounds of people he does business with, then he can suffer the consequences. Just confirms what I suspected all along, too. Gavriil doesn't care who he does business with so long as it gets him what he wants.

My breath rushes out. Even if I'm not confident in my future career, the habits I've developed won't let me back down. That and an irrational desire to not see Gavriil connected to someone who might be a different kind of a monster than his father, but a monster nonetheless. I don't know why I care. Only that I do. Which is why I sent a few texts to my most reliable sources. It's probably nothing, but I've never left things like this up to chance.

And if you do find something? What then?

I don't know if Gavriil would even believe me if I do uncover something. His accusations before our interlude on the couch showed me exactly how little he thinks of me. But he doesn't seem the type to ignore hard evidence, even if he doesn't like the findings. I've also caught glimpses now and then of a different side of him. The tender respect he gave Dessie after I introduced them after the ceremony. His genuine happiness when I saw him chatting with his sister-in-law Tessa during the reception. The man likes to act like he has no soul. From what I've seen, though, he has one. He's just buried it so deep under what I can only suspect is years of hurt and rejection that most people don't see it.

I stalk to the window and lean my forehead against the

cool glass. I don't want to see these glimpses. It twists my feelings for him up in knots, complicates what should be a case of simple lust and adds an edge to it. A very dangerous edge that can only lead to heartache.

My phone buzzes and my stomach drops. My fifteen-minute warning before I have to present myself like the dutiful wife and accompany my husband to whatever activity he's planned for us to be seen by the general public.

The brunch had been casual but delicious, a welcome reprieve after being cooped up in a plane for hours on end. The private tour of the Louvre had also been fascinating. I'd kept my face passive throughout, not wanting to do something that would be untoward for the wife of a billionaire and betray that I was a complete and total fraud, like tear up at the sight of the headless winged goddess guarding the top of the Daru staircase or let my mouth drop open at the sight of *the* Mona Lisa.

No, the scheduled activities haven't been excessive. While I've done my best to maintain the bored façade I'm sure most people in my position would assume, I've enjoyed our excursions, even if it irks me to admit it. But it still makes me feel like an experiment under a microscope.

After our encounter this morning, I got dressed and left the penthouse as quickly as possible. It took me a good hour of wandering up and down random streets for my heart to quiet and some of the ache to lessen. I spent the next hour with my camera, taking shots of the winding streets and shops. I snapped a dozen or so portraits, too, mostly of Paris residents, but a couple expatriates and a group of tourists.

The more time I've spent with my camera, drafting passages about the people I've met and the stories they've shared, the more I've felt my heart respond in a way it hasn't in a long time. When I was younger, before Lucifer Drakos came to Grey House, I wanted to be an author. In middle school, I fell in love with photography. Sure, I took some of my own photos for my investigations, but that wasn't the primary focus.

I glance at my camera. It's nearly time to join Gavriil for whatever he has planned for this evening. But I can't resist flipping the camera on and toggling through the photos. An old man with bronzed skin and a face covered in wrinkles sitting outside his coffee shop. A clay mug full of coffee brewed with cinnamon and sugar, steam curling up from the surface. Two kids standing with chocolate ice cream dripping down their hands as they smile in front of the crowds lining up to see the restored Notre-Dame Cathedral.

There are stories here. The everyday people I'd missed so much of in my quest to bring down the criminal elite. The shop owner emigrated from Mexico over forty years ago after he fell in love with a French woman on a trip to see Sinatra sing in Las Vegas. The two kids are here with their mother and grandparents after losing their father in a car accident. It's the first time, their mother confided in me with tears in her eyes, that she's seen them happy in nearly a year.

A part of me still clings to the possibility of jumping back into my investigative work. It doesn't seem possible that something that has been such a huge part of my life, all the way back to my last years of high school when I started working for the school newspaper and applying for scholarship after scholarship, is over.

But as I turn the camera over in my hands, anticipation flickers through me. Not the demanding urgency of my investigative reporting. Not the thrill of elation when I knew I'd caught someone, a thrill that had turned into something ugly. My version of wealth was the knowledge I hoarded and the power I used to bring them down.

My fingers lightly trace the dials and buttons on top of the camera. This excitement is different. Innocent, new. Something wholly mine. Even if there are fewer jobs and less pay in the areas of photography and photojournalism, I don't want this next chapter of my life to be rooted in money. I want it to be founded on something more than death and revenge.

I switch off the camera and tuck it back into its case. I still have time. Almost a whole year. Even after the renovations I'll be making to Grey House, I'll have a tidy sum left over that, with the right investments, can keep Dessie and me going while I try to figure the rest of my life out.

I walk toward my closet where I have some sensible flats tucked away. My eyes stray to the gold shopping bag, the red tissue paper peeping over the edge. I pause. The trip into the Louboutin store was a spur-of-the-moment decision following a text from Catherine that Dessie had started a new round of physical therapy and had already shown marked improvement. Her relapse appeared to be subsiding this time. I bought her a pair of blush-colored ballet flats with cute straps that wrapped around the heel and the signature red outsole.

And yes, I think with no small amount of acrimony, I bought a pair of heels for myself. A dress and shoes. Anyone would have thought I'd spent another three million dollars by the way Gavriil had snapped at me earlier.

The man really is a pompous jerk. The thought propels me across the room to the bag. I bought them with my money. Would I have bought them without two million sitting in a high-interest savings account? No.

But I bought them for me using money I had before I

agreed to this ridiculous arrangement, and I'm going to wear them because I want to. If he doesn't like it, I can just slip off a shoe and jab him with it.

A highly improbable scenario. I'm not going to jail over him. But it brings a smile to my face nonetheless as I set the bag on the bed and reach inside.

I pull out the heels, nude leather with the sole and stiletto heel colored red. Thankfully the store offered a variety of heel heights. The assistant who helped me, an older man with a thick silver beard and a kind smile, had helped me try on several before I found one I semitrusted myself not to tip over in.

I slip the heels on and stand. I glance at the mirror again. I've always believed vanity to be one of the worst sins, especially with how much I've seen it in the people I've investigated over the years.

But as I look at my reflection, I don't try to stop the rush of pleasure and confidence. I look good. No, I look great.

With a smile on my face, I open my door and nearly walk straight into my husband.

"Good eve…"

His voice trails off as he rakes me from head to toe with a searing gaze. I clutch my handbag with both hands, willing myself not to feel anything at his blatantly appreciative appraisal.

"Ready?"

"Yes." I strive for an indifferent tone, as if he hadn't just had his mouth on my breasts a few hours ago. "Where are we going?"

"It's a surprise. The limo's waiting downstairs."

I give him the ghost of a smile. He holds out his arm and I slide my hand into the crook of his elbow as he escorts me out of the suite. I force the smile into something a little more lovesick when the elevator doors open to the lobby. Most people glance at us and look away. A few, though, stare. One pulls out their phone and snaps a photo.

My breath rushes out once we're in the limo, the tinted windows giving me at least a few minutes' peace. Gavriil takes the seat opposite me. He leans back into the leather and drapes one arm across the top as he stares at me, his gaze assessing.

"Relax, Grey. It's not a bad thing to be seen with your husband."

I shrug. "For all intents and purposes, Drakos, you're not my husband. We're business acquaintances. I know these… field trips have a purpose. I'm just not used to the scrutiny."

I say the words, even if my heart twists inside my chest at the lie. Feeling like a bug under a magnifying glass is draining. But so is trying to keep my walls up. Especially after what happened between us earlier. I need to back away. Maintain the distance I'd established during our wedding and kept up until this morning.

"Many people would enjoy this."

"I'm not most people."

"No, you're not." Something that looks astonishingly like regret crosses his face. "I have no excuse for earlier. What I said was crass and rude, both before and after we kissed. Let me make it up to you."

I almost ask why. Why did he say something so horrid?

But asking for a reason, giving him a chance to explain, could take me back to that line I'd straddled this morning. Reintroduce the traces of emotional intimacy that had developed during our coffee on the terrace.

It's not worth the risk. So I simply nod, telling myself I can stay strong even as my heart whispers a warning.

CHAPTER TWELVE

Juliette

TEN MINUTES LATER, my jaw drops open as the limo crosses the arches of the Pont d'Iéna. The Eiffel Tower literally sparkles against the backdrop of a rose-streaked night sky as the limo pulls up to the curb.

"I saw it the other nights, but up close…" My voice trails off as my heart surges in my chest. "I wanted to come here before we left."

The limo driver opens the door and we step out onto a sidewalk teeming with people. Some are posing for photos with the Tower behind them. Others are kissing or simply ogling the sight of one of the most iconic structures in the world. Between the massive iron legs holding its incredible weight aloft, I can see the green park on the other side dotted with picnickers.

"Is the restaurant off the Champ-de-Mars?" I ask as Gavriil puts a guiding hand to my back.

"Not quite."

We walk through the crowds to the south pillar. A short set of stairs leads inside.

"Inside the Tower?"

My voice sounds breathless, but I don't care. I've heard of the restaurant, seen the reviews, the mouthwatering photos of gourmet cuisine on Instagram.

"Yes."

He sounds amused, but when I glance up at him, he's smiling down at me like he's pleased with my excitement. I brush aside any self-consciousness as I commit to enjoying the evening ahead of me.

An elevator whisks us up to the restaurant, located on the second floor of the Tower. Our table is right by the window. Boats drift down the Seine. The wings of the Palais de Chaillot on the other side of the river are lit up with golden light. In the distance, I can see the dome of the Basilique du Sacré-Cœur de Montmartre.

A waiter in a dark suit approaches our table and greets us in French as he hands us menus.

"*Bonjour* and good evening," Gavriil replies.

"Good evening and welcome. May I start you off with a glass of wine?"

"*Un verre de rosé, s'il vous plait.*"

I smile as Gavriil looks at me in surprise before ordering himself a glass of merlot, in French as well.

"Dessie insisted I take a foreign language in high school," I say in response to his unasked question after the waiter takes our orders for the seven-course tasting. His brows draw together. "I fell in love with French and kept it up in college."

My phone vibrates in my handbag.

"I'm sorry, do you mind if I check that?"

At his nod, I pull my phone out. Alarm skitters through me.

"It's Catherine."

"Go," he says as he stands, waiting for me to leave before he sits back down.

I walk away from the dining area as I answer.

"Catherine? What's wrong?"

"Nothing's wrong." My friend's voice is practically vibrating with excitement. "I'm sorry, you're probably out to dinner or something naughty—"

"Cate!" I break in with a laugh as my heart rate steadies. "What's going on?"

"She's walking again."

My vision swims as tears fill my eyes. I blink them back and take in a deep, shuddering breath as relief swamps me.

"Thank God."

"That's all. She asked me to call, she was exhausted after physical therapy and went to sleep almost as soon as we got her back to her room. But she's better, Juliette. She's getting better every day."

We say goodbye. I linger in the vestibule for a moment. Dessie's getting better. We'll have a follow-up with her doctor when I get back and learn more about what the future may hold. But right now, in this moment, Dessie's walking. I'm in Paris dining in one of the most incredible restaurants in the world. And, shockingly, I'm enjoying Gavriil Drakos's company.

That's enough right now.

I'm not going to question it. I'm simply going to enjoy the evening.

I return to the table. Our wines have been delivered. Gavriil is looking out the window, one hand resting on the stem of his glass, his handsome profile in stark relief against the encroaching night.

My breath catches.

Focus on the moment. Just tonight. Nothing else.

"Everything all right?" he asks as I sit.

I nod. "Just an update on Dessie's physical therapy."

The waiter delivers the first course: beets folded over blue cheese and Greek yogurt, sprinkled with cilantro and pumpkin seeds, and served with toasted crackers.

I take my first bite and barely bite back a moan.

"Is this how you eat all the time?" I ask as I force myself to go slow and savor every bite.

"Believe it or not, I like burgers, too," he replies with a grin. "You said Dessie insisted you take a foreign language. Did you live with her after you disappeared from Rêve Beach?"

Thankfully, I had just slid a cracker into my mouth, giving me a moment to think about how much detail I want to share. He already knows so much about me.

On paper, I think as my chest tightens at how he looked down at me with disgust right before touching me so intimately.

Good enough for a quick fling, but not good enough to spend his money or trusted to keep my end of our bargain.

Stop. I'm not going to let anyone else ruin my evening. He's playing nice right now. I can do the same.

"When things with my dad went downhill, I moved in with Dessie in Seattle."

His lips flatten into a line. "I'm sorry."

I shrug and focus on my food. "It was a long time ago."

"Doesn't mean it doesn't still hurt."

I stab a beet with my fork. This isn't the conversation I want to be having. I want to enjoy my meal, the sight of Paris at twilight, the knowledge that Dessie is doing better.

I look up to tell him just that…

…then falter at the faint glimmer of pain in his eyes. A pain I know all too well.

"Who did you lose?"

He blinks. For a moment I think he's going to make a joke or dismiss the question.

"My mother."

I've never heard so much conveyed in just two words. Grief, loss, anger, regret. Emotions that take my assumptions about Gavriil Drakos's childhood and turn them on their head.

"I'm…" My voice trails off and I swallow hard. "You're right. There are weeks and even months where everything seems fine. And then you see something or smell something or hear something and it takes you right back."

"What takes you back?"

Don't.

My heart shouts at me to stop, to keep myself intact. But he's looking at me now with a different kind of hunger lurking behind his mask. A need to connect with someone who understands. I know deep in my bones this is not something he has revealed to many, if anyone.

"Popcorn." My eyes burn and I look back down, stirring crumbles of blue cheese around my plate. "When I was little, I would get scared of the storms. I thought the rain and lightning would drag Grey House into the sea." I pause, giving myself a moment to let the wave of anger and anguish crest, subside. "So Dad would make popcorn. We'd sit in my window seat and watch the storm until it passed like it was a movie."

His eyes burn into mine. "My father took that from you."

My throat tightens. "He did. But my father didn't do himself any favors. His obsession with making it big started him down that road in the first place."

Gavriil's lips part slightly as understanding dawns. That it's not just his father who created my fixation, but the actions of my own, the greed that drove him away from his daughter and the woman who loved him.

Needing to get back on firm ground, I ask, "What takes you back?"

He blinks and looks out over the city. He stares so long at the lights flickering on as night drifts in I wonder if he's going to answer.

"Scratching."

I frown. "Scratching?"

"In the walls. On the floor at night." The twist of his lips is quick, harsh as he glances at me. "Rats."

The horror of his answer has me reaching for him before I can stop myself. I nearly lay my hand over his when the waiter arrives with our second course. I snatch my fingers back just in time. But it doesn't stop the physical ache inside me, the hurt for what he must have endured in those lost years before arriving at Lucifer's villa.

The waiter sets bowls of squash soup topped with green onions and a swirl of coconut milk in front of us. China clinks in the background. Someone laughs. Soft, seductive jazz plays from hidden speakers. Gavriil recovers first, picking up his spoon as he shoots me a casual smile, as if apologizing for sharing something so terrible. I start to reassure him, but he speaks first.

"Tell me more about Dessie."

Right now I'd tell him almost anything. Anything to take his mind away from the hell of his past.

"Like what?"

"Like why your father's ex-girlfriend accompanied you down the aisle."

"She's a second mother to me. The one constant I've had in my life. I wouldn't be who I am today without her."

"She loves you."

There's a tinge of envy to his voice, an underlying heartache that further cracks the vision I've carried of Gavriil for so long—impervious, cavalier, uncaring.

"She does. She gave me a home when I needed it the most. And now I can give her one."

The jolt is so small I nearly miss it, a flash of tension through his body as his eyes widen.

"Everything okay?"

"Yes." A slight shake of his head. "I haven't revisited my past in a long time. It threw me off."

The first things that come to mind all sound trite, bland words that don't come close to addressing the bits and pieces he's revealed.

"I can't imagine," I finally say softly.

"Most can't."

The salad arrives. I glance down, registering the artful arrangement of asparagus, mushrooms and artichokes on top of a bed of greens glistening with vinaigrette and flecked with Parmesan. How can I eat like this, be surrounded by this kind of luxury, when the man across from me has just shared something I can't even begin to comprehend?

Gavriil was eight when he went to live with Lucifer. Which means what should have been some of the happiest years of his childhood were spent in hell. A hell that, judging by Gavriil's borderline hatred of his father, Lucifer continued in his own twisted way.

"Money can corrupt."

My head snaps up. Gavriil is watching me, his expression languid except for the sharpness in his gaze. His fingers trail up and down the stem of his wineglass.

"It can." I release a pent-up breath as I reconcile this glimpse into Gavriil's childhood with his obsession with wealth. "It can also be used for good."

He nods, his shoulders relaxing a fraction. "Agreed. Or it can be the one thing that gives back. The only thing."

My heart cracks.

"What about your brothers?"

His chuckle is a dark, sinister sound that nevertheless rolls through me, stirring the embers left from the morning when I bared myself to him.

"I met Michail at Lucifer's will-reading. The same day I

learned my father had tied all of my hard work to his own obsessive need to control everything, even in death. And Rafe has always preferred his own company."

If Rafael Drakos was in front of me right now, I would toss my very expensive wine in his face. He's ten years older than Gavriil, which means he would have been eighteen when Gavriil went to live with Lucifer. More than old enough to take a little brother who'd just lost his mother under his wing. To protect him and give him at least a taste of family.

"Just as bad as Lucifer."

Gavriil slowly shakes his head. "Unfortunately, no. It would be so much easier to hate him if he was. But Rafe is just…cold. Straight down to his icy heart. As much as I sometimes want to punch him, I can only imagine what turned him into what he is."

He shakes his head then and signals for the waiter. He orders us each a glass of pinot noir before changing the topic to what my favorite exhibit was at the Louvre, then skillfully guiding the conversation to the traveling I did for my job. He does it so well I almost forget the rips in our souls we've bared to each other as we eat our way through rosemary risotto topped with beef fillet and shaved truffles. When Gavriil feeds me a bite of chocolate ganache topped with a roasted strawberry, I see the heat in his eyes as my lips part for him.

My body responds to his desire without hesitation. Things have changed between us. The intimacy of sharing so many secrets, of feeling his support and compassion, has built a bridge between us.

I'm now terrified I won't be able to stop myself from crossing it. Even if it means I leave this marriage divorced and brokenhearted.

CHAPTER THIRTEEN

Gavriil

NIGHT HAS FULLY settled over Paris. The last sparkling lights of the Eiffel Tower fade.

Midnight. The witching hour.

I've never given much credence to the concept of magic. But after my dinner with Juliette, I now understand the meaning of the word *bewitched*. Only magic could have made me confess what I did tonight. Some details, like the rats, I've never shared with another living soul.

Magic or lust. It has to be one of the two that made me reveal what I did.

Or guilt, I amend.

I knew as soon as she belted her robe this morning and went back into her room after she'd come apart in my arms that I had made not one, but two horrible mistakes. The first had been accusing her of using our marriage to further her career. No, she shouldn't have looked. Yet I caught her doing what anyone would have done in that situation; glancing at a piece of paper laid out on the table. She hadn't rifled through private papers or even opened a closed folder. I had still jumped to the worst possible conclusion. Then, just minutes later, I'd let my need to keep myself emotionally removed trump kindness when I made light of the intimacy we had shared.

I was already tense from our interlude this morning and my pervading guilt when she'd come out tonight looking like a goddess in that dress and her damned heels. When she shared what she had about her father, it had awakened something inside me. The need to not only show her she wasn't alone, but to reach out to someone, just for a moment, who understood what it was like to lose a parent you loved and despised in equal measure.

I hadn't thought about that noise in a long time. The scratches in the wall, the softness almost worse, making me strain to hear if they'd infiltrated the barren room my mother and I shared. The occasional heavy weight on my legs as the bolder ones scurried across in search of food.

The one time one had bit me on the leg and I'd cried out. My mother had sobbed that night when she'd seen the tiny red welts, the blood staining the dirty sheet. The weight of her guilt had still not been heavy enough to spur her to action.

Well, hell.

Not the way I pictured spending the third night of my honeymoon. Remembering some of the worst moments of my childhood. This is what came from giving into one's emotions. It took those cracks one had worked so long to patch up and wrenched them wide open. Plenty of room to let old hurts and insecurities crash back through.

Intimacy complicates that, although I was the one who had pushed that button this morning. I enjoy sex. I enjoy women. Never have I felt more like a god than I did when Juliette's cries filled my mind, when the barest of touches pushed her over the edge into uninhabited pleasure.

But it was that sweet smile on her face, that touch of innocence mixed with womanly sensuality as I'd laid her back on the couch that had reached into my chest and wrapped its fingers around my heart. Never once did I think about that physical passion coming with the claws of feeling something more than casual affection for her.

It was there, though. No matter how much I wanted to pretend otherwise. The admiration I felt when she had stood up to me, the regret of knowing I caused her pain with my senseless attempt to put distance between us.

And respect. Respect for how she continued on through the worst of circumstances. I don't know which is worse—having the love of a parent and then having it wrenched away? Or growing up and watching those who have it with envy? Envy and the ever-present question of what you did wrong to not at least have a little taste of that love.

At least one good thing had come out of that. I'd channeled that envy into the motivation I needed to climb out of the hellhole my mother had thrown me into, the same hole my father had then tried to bury me in. I fought my way to the top and finally achieved what others could only imagine: incredible wealth, an international reputation that opened doors wherever I went, and the envy of some of the richest people in the world, who never would have glanced twice at a street urchin from the slums of Santorini.

I'd given Juliette a piece of power tonight. No one, not even Rafe, knew the depths of what I'd suffered those first few years.

But Juliette hadn't looked at me with pity or disgust. No, it had been empathy, compassion, understanding for the dichotomy of emotions I'd hinted at when it came to my mother. I saw a different side of the reporter, the side that made someone feel heard as they shared the harsh circumstances inflicted on them by people like my father.

Even though I had hated the attention her report had brought to Drakos Development, I'd always admired her for facing down the devil and appreciated that her work had finally removed an obstacle from my path. Learning the reason why, the true depths of what her family had suffered simply because my father had decided he wanted to play Realtor for a day and buy a house for a mistress who eventually became a wife, had added yet another layer.

Unlike many people, Juliette had played quite fair when it came to taking her revenge on my father, going after him for the sins he'd committed. She'd shown more strength and resilience than most people I've met.

They were all reasons for why I should never touch her again, all reasons that made me want to let down my guard for the first time in decades. If that hadn't been enough, her nonchalant words at dinner had been the final clue to the puzzle I'd been trying to solve since she added her own financial stipulations to the marriage contract.

Dessie. She had loved and supported Juliette in her time of need. And now Juliette was doing the same, selling herself to me to get Grey House back and provide a home for a woman who, despite being an incredible person, had nowhere else to go. My suspicions had been confirmed during a quick text conversation with my investigator on the ride back to the hotel. Dessie had been living with Juliette in that little cottage for over a year now. Or rather, up until her illness had relapsed and she'd gone to live at Catherine's facility. I'd bet my company that Juliette was footing the bill for it all.

The only question left unanswered was the amount of money she had spent on our wedding. Although I now had a pretty good guess what had happened there. The woman is a fighter. I can easily picture her taking my order to turn it into the wedding of the century and deciding to spend as lavishly as she knew how as pure revenge. It makes me like her even more.

Which leaves me at a crossroads. I like my wife. I respect her. I want her. I want her so badly it's a physical ache in my body, a compulsion that's getting increasingly harder to ignore.

But unlike this morning, when all we'd shared was a halfway pleasant conversation over coffee, a bond has been forged between us. Fragile, but it's there. Shared loss, overcoming adversity to succeed. Our mutual confessions reek of emotional intimacy. Something I want no part of, no matter how much I want Juliette in my bed.

Another sip of bourbon hits my tongue, the smoky flavor lingering as I stare out over the City of Lights. No one will negate my past, my inability to love. Three times I've risked caring for someone. My mother. My father. My brother. Being rejected time and time again could have left me like my mother: broken, defeated. That I not only survived but thrived is a miracle. I'm not risking it a fourth time.

Yes, Drakos Development is an anchor for me. It was the only thing I felt safe pouring myself into because whatever I invested, I and I alone was responsible for what came back. There was no trusting another person, no risking a change of feelings. No romance strained and then broken under the reality of parenthood, age and all the other surprises life dealt.

Her door opens behind me. I turn. My heart stops. She's still wearing that dress. Conservative compared to many. But I know now what lies beneath. Small, pert breasts that I've touched with my lips, my tongue, my hands.

My gaze drifts lower to her narrow waist and slim hips. She doesn't know the allure of her body, the sexiness of feeling the subtle muscle beneath her skin. I've never felt attracted to a woman before because of what she's capable of, the hard work she puts into something. But with Juliette, everything entices me to go just a little deeper.

Not too deep, I remind myself as I step closer.

Just one more step. I've kept my emotions separate from sex for years. I can do it again now, resist the temptation to share any more of my past while I enjoy what's building between us.

Except, I wonder as she joins me on the terrace, at what point will I take that one step too far and tumble over the edge?

"I didn't think you'd still be up."

"Not used to the change in times yet."

A bald-faced lie. It's not the travel keeping me up. It's her. Her and the selfish need to take her, to take and give pleasure for as long as I have her, even knowing that I can't give her anything but.

I hold up a glass. "Drink?"

She hesitates, and then smiles. Ever since I invited her to dinner and she surprised both of us with how much she opened up, she's been more carefree, relaxed. The feistiness is still there, the strength. But she smiled more in the past few hours than she has in the past month. I saw more unabashed delight toward things I take for granted, from the dessert that could have been a work of art to the private champagne toast I arranged at the top of the Tower after dinner. It makes me remember a time in my life I'd mostly blocked out. The moments of wonderment as I'd adjusted to a life of luxury after being crushed under the weight of poverty. I had lost that awe.

Now, as I watch her, I wonder what else I've missed by becoming just like everybody else. Focused on money, reputation, power.

I pour her a glass and hand it to her. Our fingers brush. Her eyes flare and stay fixed on mine as she raises the glass to her lips. I turn away when I realize I'm jealous of a damn piece of barware.

"I can almost feel how hard you're thinking."

I smile but keep my gaze fixed on the city. "What does it feel like?"

"Like it hurts."

I laugh. She joins in, the sound full yet silvery, a dash of bright against the night.

Silence falls. She gazes out over the city, her body relaxed, her face calm and serene like I've never seen her before.

"The two million you asked for."

The glass freezes halfway to her lips. Her gaze slides away from mine as she takes another sip but doesn't reply.

"It's for Dessie."

She hesitates, then nods once. I watch her, my eyes roaming over the hair falling freely now over her shoulders, then dipping down to her bare feet. The heels were sexy and gave me lurid daydreams of her wearing them and nothing else as I laid her out on the bed in my room.

But I like her this way too: natural, relaxed. She follows my gaze down to her feet.

"I did buy the dress. One set of shoes was for me."

"You don't owe me an explanation."

Another insensitive comment. I shake my head. "I don't think I've ever been cruel to a woman before. I have no excuse. I was an ass."

Juliette blows out a harsh breath.

"Thank you."

The simplicity surprises me, as does the genuineness. I smile at her.

"No reassurances that it wasn't that big of a deal?"

"No. You hurt me. Thank you for acknowledging it."

How am I supposed to resist this? A woman who knows her own worth, who stands up for herself yet gives grace? Who uses money not to further her own agenda but to help someone else? Her actions make me look exactly what I accused her of being: greedy and selfish.

"Don't look at me like that."

"Like what?" I ask softly.

I close the distance between us and reach up, doing what I've imagined doing for so long and brushing a stray strand of hair out of her face.

"Like I'm something good," she whispers. "I'm selfish. I want her close. I want to do something to pay her back for everything she's done for me." She bites her lip. "And you were right. I've done a lot of good things with my work. But it wasn't just a desire for justice that drove me. It was revenge, retribution." A shudder moves through her as shadows shift in her eyes. "I don't like who I've become."

I think of the first eight years of my life, the most vulnerable and painful years I've ever experienced. I think of those first few years in Lucifer's house, especially the initial days when I thought perhaps, just perhaps, I could turn myself into enough to gain my father's love.

I want to give her a fraction of what she has given me tonight. But I can't. The words become lodged in my throat. So instead of talking, instead of giving her trust and secrets, I give her the one thing I can.

I lean down and kiss her.

CHAPTER FOURTEEN

Juliette

NEED SLAMS INTO me as Gavriil molds his lips to mine. I don't bother to think, to acknowledge that this attraction is dangerous. Too dangerous.

Right now, I just want to feel.

This kiss isn't like the shock of unexpected desire from our wedding. Isn't the desperate hunger from earlier. This kiss is intimate, tinged with a surprising sweetness even as he takes charge and lays a hand on my bare back. I inhale, breathe in the taste of him as his fingers dance up and down my skin in a long, slow glide. More sweetness. Unexpected. It ignites the fire just as his ravenous touch did earlier.

Before I can think too deeply, his lips move from my mouth to the curve of my jaw, then down my neck. My breath escapes as he finds a previously unknown sensitive spot halfway down. He chuckles, the husky satisfaction trickling across my shoulder and down my spine. A pulse begins between my legs, a throbbing that makes me restless and try to press myself more fully against him.

"Patience, Mrs. Drakos," he murmurs against my back before gently biting the tender skin. This time, his use of my married name excites, arouses.

"No."

His chuckle turns to a laugh. He picks me up then, arms

about my waist, and lifts me so I'm looking down at him. Midnight moonlight kisses his face, making him look like an otherworldly being in the pearly light. Sharp lines contrast with the slight smile on his full lips and the brightness of his eyes.

"I'm taking my time, Juliette." His arms tighten around me. "This morning, I took from you. Tonight, I'm going to give, so don't you dare try to rush this."

The words shock me even as they wind their way through my veins, leaving behind a tangle of emotions I'm not ready to deal with.

Not wanting to lose this moment, I lean down and renew our kiss. He groans as my tongue teases his lips.

"Is this your answer?" he growls against my mouth.

When I nod, he deftly tosses me up, swinging my legs out and catching me in his arms before I can do anything but gasp. My arms fly around his neck and I hold on, my heart pounding. I look up and he's watching me with a smug smile. I can't help it. I throw my head back and laugh. I'm being held in the arms of a billionaire on a balcony overlooking Paris at midnight. If someone had told me six weeks ago that this would be my life, I would have told them they were crazy.

The amusement disappears as his eyes darken. If someone would have told me, too, that I would be willingly going to bed with Gavriil Drakos, I would have laughed until my sides hurt.

Now, there isn't a single other place on earth I'd rather be.

Gavriil carries me through to the living room, past the grand piano and the elegant couch where he had laid me earlier and into his room. Like mine, it's a mix of ivory, gold and deep blue. Ornate, expensive, yet regal, sophisticated. His bed is the same size as mine, slightly raised on a platform with another balcony that overlooks the Eiffel Tower. It's dark now, the iron glinting silver beneath the moon.

He sets me on my feet, captures my hand in his and brings my fingers to his lips. He kisses each one until electricity is humming from my fingertips through my arms and winding down to that pulse between my legs.

His hands slide under the straps of my dress and slip them down over my shoulders. A moment later I'm bared from the waist up. His eyes heat up as he gazes at my breasts for the second time that day.

"Beautiful."

I'll never hear that word again without thinking of him. Of earlier, when admiration melded with apology. And of now, when he makes me feel like the most beautiful woman he's ever seen.

He pulls me to him as he lowers his head to my breasts. My head falls back, hair brushing my bare skin as I moan. He sucks, kisses the tender skin, moves between them as he uses his tongue and lips to stir me into a storm of chaotic need.

Has it been mere seconds or long, delicious minutes since he started to undress me? Even as he continues to worship my breasts, his hands undo the zipper at the back. The dress falls in a soft whisper in a pool of periwinkle blue at my feet. The only thing giving me any coverage now is the scrap of white lace I pulled on earlier to give myself the boost of confidence, knowing I was walking the streets of Paris in sexy lingerie.

And now, as his lips part and he sucks in a ragged breath, I'm even more grateful I chose it.

He hooks a finger in the band and slowly, ever so slowly, slides the lace down over my thighs. A moment later, I'm naked under his heated gaze.

"Theós, eísai ómorfos."

I don't need to know Greek to feel the wonder in his voice. It banishes any lingering shyness, emboldens me to reach up and hold out a hand.

"I want you, Gavriil."

He strips off his clothing with deft, sure movements. My body burns as he reveals tantalizing golden skin, muscled arms, chiseled abs shaped by his daily swims. The bed dips as he kneels. When he covers my body with his, I can't stop the sound of satisfaction from slipping past my lips. I run my hands down his back, the first time I've touched him so intimately. I love the heat of his skin, the muscular strength beneath my fingertips.

"You feel incredible."

He kisses me as he places a hand between my thighs. I arch into his touch as he murmurs against my lips.

"Juliette, I don't want to wait. I need you."

I can only imagine what those words cost him. Gavriil isn't the kind of man to need anyone. But right now, in this moment, he wants me. Needs me.

My legs part. Steel presses against tender flesh. And then he slides inside my body and reality slips as a pleasure so intense it borders on pain charges my every nerve. He fills me to what feels like the breaking point. As he slides in, my body clamps down.

"Christ, Juliette." He sucks in a breath. "Don't move."

I realize just how close to the edge he is. Even though I'm drowning in sensations, I can't resist shifting my hips, savoring the feel of him inside me even as he glares down at me.

"What?" I ask with a teasing smile.

His answer consists of him pulling out and then sliding back in with one long, slow stroke that makes me bow off the bed.

"Tease," I gasp.

"Temptress," he replies before he lowers his head and consumes me again.

We find our rhythm as if we've been making love for years instead of just encountering each other for the first time. That incredible pressure builds again, pressing on my skin from the inside out, filling me with a burning tension that eclipses anything else I've ever experienced. Through the haze of desire, he kisses me as if he'll never get enough of the taste of me.

"Gavriil!"

My world detonates and I come apart in his arms.

Gavriil

I feel her body tighten around me as she reaches her peak. She cries my name again, her hands gripping my shoulders, head thrown back, eyes closed as a blush sweeps over her body. I can't hold myself back any longer, don't want to. I groan her name and follow her over the edge.

I manage to brace myself on my forearms above her and roll to the side so I don't crush her as I drift down from the most intense climax I've ever experienced. We lie there on the bed, our heavy pants mingling, sweat cooling on our skin. She turns her head and looks at me, her eyes barely open, a smile lingering on her lips. Satisfaction, yes. But also contentment. It moves me.

I reach out and smooth hair back from her forehead. Her smile deepens, her mouth curving up and making her eyes crinkle.

Emotions war in my chest. The same want that's been plaguing me, apparently unsated by what we've just shared. An unexpected thread of tenderness, one that I quickly smother as I kiss her forehead and give myself a moment to rein in my thoughts before I look her in the eye again.

I will never be able to give her anything but this. Moments of pleasure. Nothing concrete. Nothing permanent. Later I will remind her. Make sure we're on the same page. Given her feelings toward me before we went to bed, I doubt anything has changed for her either. But on the off chance our Paris confessions and frantic lovemaking shifted something between us, then we'll have to go back to the way things were when we first arrived in France. Organized outings in public, distance in private.

Not my first choice. But I won't be like my father. I won't pretend to be anything but what I am. I won't pretend to offer the world on a string before snipping it with casual cruelty and walking away without a backward glance. Juliette deserves more than that. So did my mother. So did the countless other women Lucifer used and discarded.

But as I pull Juliette's naked body closer to mine, I vow not to bring anything up tonight. To ruin the aftermath of our first time together with more unkindness. She's had enough of that from me. I may be damned tomorrow, but when it comes to the physicalness, I'm going to give into my every desire tonight.

As she curls into me, shock registers.

"What is it?" she asks.

"We didn't use a condom."

"I'm on the pill."

"I've never not used protection myself before."

The admission seems to touch her. "Well, I promise I'm safe. And healthy."

"As am I."

"Then stop worrying." She says it so matter-of-factly I

can't help but smile. She yawns and stretches her arms, then starts to roll away.

"Where are you going?"

"To my room. I didn't think…" Her voice trails off, and then she shrugs. "I just didn't want to make any assumptions."

I roll on top of her and pin her to the mattress.

"You've just been made love to in one of the most expensive hotel suites in Paris."

She smiles. "Every woman's fantasy."

"Exactly." I lean down and skim my lips along her jaw. "How can I let you go without seducing you at least once more?"

I'm using humor to hide that I want her again. That I'm not ready to let her leave my bed. Later, yes. I don't sleep with lovers. It's too intimate.

But I mean what I say. I can't let her go. Eventually, yes. Just not yet.

Her eyes widen. "Again?"

I shift my hips, let her feel my body already stirring again at the thought of sliding in and being surrounded by her.

A sigh escapes her lips. "Well, if you insist."

As she wraps her arms around my neck and presses her breasts against my chest, I banish the fear, the questions, everything but the feel and taste of my wife in my arms.

CHAPTER FIFTEEN

Juliette

I WAKE UP to an empty bed. I lie there in a sea of satin sheets and rumpled pillows, my body pleasantly heavy from making love with Gavriil.

I hadn't planned on falling asleep in his bed. Didn't want to risk further deepening the intimacy that had developed between us in just a few hours. Whether that was because I didn't want to get any more emotionally entangled or didn't want Gavriil to beat me to it and ask me to leave first, I don't fully know. Probably a combination of the two. But when he pulled me close and tucked me into the curve of his body after the second time, I promised myself I would just shut my eyes for a moment.

Long, caressing strokes awoke me sometime around dawn. He stirred my body to a fever pitch, teasing me with his touch even as he ignored my pleas for more. I finally took charge, rolling over and straddling him with a speed that stunned him long enough for me to grip his length and guide him inside my body. The pleasure, the heady power of watching his eyes flare as he gripped my hips and guided me up and down, was the most powerful aphrodisiac I've ever experienced.

It also, I remembered with a satisfied smile as I stretched my arms above my head, didn't last long. He flipped me onto my back and drove inside me with long, deep movements that sent me soaring over the edge. We fell asleep draped over each other as if it had always been this way.

I sit up and blink against the bright morning sun streaming through the windows. I grab one of the plush robes hanging in the marble bathroom and make my way out into the main living space. A clink of glassware on the balcony draws me to the doors with a smile growing on my face.

I freeze. The smile disappears. There's a butler setting the table with bagels, cream cheese, jellies, fresh fruit and boiled eggs. A traditionally light French breakfast. But it's the single plate and glass that catches my attention.

Gavriil's gone.

"Bonjour."

"Bonjour," I reply automatically, even though my heart is racing. "Is my...husband here?" I only hesitate for a second on the word.

"No, madame. But he did leave a note."

The butler gestures to a white envelope with the hotel's logo in the top corner. I wait until he's gone to sit and open it with trembling fingers. Written in a strong, bold hand, it simply says he's out for the day and he hopes I enjoy my morning.

I drop the note on my plate, my appetite gone. Not even the sight of Paris sprawling for miles can chase away the sting of disappointment, the burn of humiliation.

I told myself last night that I could handle a casual fling. I promised myself I wouldn't confuse sex with emotion. But apparently my heart hadn't listened. The dinner at the Eiffel Tower, his sharing of some of the mysteries and trauma of his past, of listening to my own hurts. All of it continues to peel back the mask Gavriil wore and reveal an entirely different man. One who could still be arrogant and flippant. But one who overcame incredible odds and horrible circumstances. One who, despite being hurt by his brother's indifference, still managed to have some compassion for what Rafael had probably gone through during his own childhood.

And our lovemaking…the way he pulled me back into bed. The way he held me afterward with such tenderness. I hadn't thought him in love with me. But I thought he might be starting to care.

I was wrong.

It doesn't matter, I tell myself firmly as I rub at the painful spot in my chest just beneath my ribs. His absence and the note are clear signs of how he views what happened between us last night.

I give myself a few minutes to sit, to hurt over how easily he withdrew this morning, to grieve what might have developed between us in another life.

Then I force myself to finish my breakfast. I shower, dress and set out on foot, this time without my camera. I wander down the banks of the Seine and eventually hop on a subway to visit Notre-Dame. I join the throngs of people and walk through the renovated interior. The soaring ceilings, the rows of pews and the dim alcoves filled with flickering candles bring me a peace I desperately needed.

The morning may have started out with pain. But it doesn't erase the good things that have come into my life. Financial independence. Dessie's healing. A chance to explore a city I've dreamed about for years.

I've been hurt before. I'll be hurt again. I'm not going to let it take away the joys I've been given. The gifts, both big and small, coming out of this contracted marriage. If I can focus on the gains that will come out of our arrangement, both for myself and for Gavriil, I'll be able to let go of this pain.

I leave the cathedral with renewed calm and spend the rest of the morning exploring shops like the renowned Shakespeare and Company, filling a tote with books I don't need but definitely want.

I arrive back at the hotel just after noon. As I contemplate ordering room service and dining on the terrace if Gavriil is still out, I see him. He's walking out of the lobby with a bouquet of white roses.

My heart drops to my feet. He swore to me on the bluff that cheating was not an activity he engaged in. A few days ago, it would have rubbed me the wrong way. It wouldn't have twisted me up inside.

But just hours after he left the bed we shared? That stabs deep, leaving a jagged, cold hole straight through my heart.

I tell myself there must be another explanation as I watch him near the doors. But where else would he be going with a dozen white roses?

I hesitate. It's not like our marriage is real. The day after our one-year anniversary, he'll file for divorce. But a combination of jealousy and my reporter's curiosity stop me from walking away.

I follow him. The summer weather has brought out locals and the usual horde of tourists. It's not hard to keep him in sight while keeping plenty of people between us. He doesn't even look back over his shoulder.

We walk for nearly fifteen minutes, passing bookstores, restaurants, and the Palais de Chaillot. Then I spy a large stone wall. Up ahead, he turns and disappears through a gate in the wall. I count to twenty and follow.

As soon as I round the corner, I stop. My heart drops

again, but not from petty jealousy this time. No, this time it's grief.

A mix of headstones, crypts and elegant statues fill the space in front of me. People drift among the graves, some snapping photos, some laying down flowers, others on their knees as they grieve. There's maybe a dozen people within sight. Far less crowded than the street just behind me.

It's not that hard to spot him. He's a few rows down in front of a white headstone, the roses at his side. My first instinct is to go to him, to lay a hand on his shoulder and comfort him the way he offered me comfort last night when I confided in him.

But we don't have that kind of relationship. I'm not even supposed to be here.

I need to leave. Go back to the hotel and never bring this up.

"Did you know that in order to be buried in a Parisian cemetery, one either has to have lived in Paris or died here?"

His voice is low, but in the quiet of the cemetery with the high walls muting a lot of the street noise, I can hear it loud and clear.

I approach slowly. He doesn't even look up.

"My mother lived here the first three years of her life. She talked about Paris as if she had lived here, but she would say other things, too. Things about my father and how he had promised he would come back for her. How one day he would divorce his wife and come back for the love of his life and his son."

He looks at me now. Despite the growing heat, he's wearing another suit. More casual than the ones I've seen him in; this one golden beige with a crisp white shirt and no tie. To a distant onlooker, he looks like a wealthy businessman paying his respects.

But when our eyes meet, I see the depths of anger and pain roiling behind the seemingly calm exterior. Feel it as if it were my own.

"When I made my first billion, I tracked down the cemetery in Santorini where she had been buried. A little patch of dirt and a stone that looked like a child had scrawled her name on it," he spits out. "My father knew exactly where she was buried. He couldn't be bothered to do anything more for the mother of one of his children. The only reason I even found out he knew was because the record showed that his company had paid for her burial."

Violence rolls off him in a vicious wave so strong I flinch.

"I contemplated killing him then." He glances back down at her grave, a cold smile lurking about his lips. "Obviously, I didn't. I thought even though she had died still living in that fantasy world where Lucifer Drakos would come to rescue her, even though she had said his name more than mine in the eight years I lived with her, she still cared for me as much as I think she was able to." His gaze sweeps the cemetery. "I petitioned to have her buried in Paris before I discovered she had been born here. I offered them millions. They didn't budge."

"You respected that."

Surprise flashes across his face.

"Yes. I make dozens of offers every year. Money, prestige, power. I don't have to lie or cheat or steal like Lucifer did. I simply offer people what they want. It's easy," he adds quietly, "to know what people want when you've grown up wanting and being denied time and time again."

I take a step forward. "And what do you want?"

He stares at me for a long moment. "I have all that I want."

Liar.

I don't say it out loud, not in his moment of grief. But I

know that something is missing in Gavriil's life. And despite everything that's happened between us, the good and the bad, I fervently wish that one day he'll figure out what is missing.

"And you, Juliette." He cocks his head to the side. "I thought at first you wanted to destroy my family. Then I thought you wanted a fortune of your own. I know you wanted revenge on my father, but you've succeeded there. So…" His voice trails off as he holds my gaze, his smile as careless as his eyes are hard. "What do you want now?"

I hesitate. Once I thought my career was everything. But somewhere along the way, or perhaps all along, justice and revenge had become synonymous. I'd become obsessive, vengeful, even power-hungry in my own way as I'd taken joy in the downfall of others.

A shiver creeps over my skin. If I was looking in a mirror right now, I would loathe what I see. What I had let myself become. And now, with Lucifer gone and Grey House back in my family once more, the driving force behind so much of what I'd done was gone, leaving me adrift.

"I don't know."

A family walks by, a man and woman with three little children in tow. The youngest can't be more than two, her little feet propelling her down the path as she looks up at the sky and lets out a giggle. I smile, the brief moment of joy that sounds out in a place of remembrance and mourning.

I look back at Gavriil to see him staring at me with narrowed eyes.

"Whatever it is you think you still want, I hope you're sensible enough to stay away from foolish ideas like true love."

He's trying to push me away, to remind me of the boundaries he's put in place. I don't need the reminder, not after this morning and his abrupt departure. But I also won't let him taint something that I want for myself. Something that's still possible down the road.

"What's wrong with love?"

"Love is unreliable." The words flow, cold and calculated. "It can bring happiness, yes. But it can also bring pain and grief like you've never experienced before."

My heart turns over in my chest at the thought of him loving another woman so deeply. All of my research never hinted at any one person, any grand love affair. But the venom in his words tells me that his views on love are rooted in something deeply personal and horribly painful.

"Who was she?"

When his head turns, the knowledge hits me with the force of a train. He crouches down and lays the roses in front of the headstone.

"I loved my mother with everything I had. She chose her grief over me. Chose to lie on a mold-soaked mattress and stare at a wall, wallowing in the pain of loving a man who never returned her affections." He stands, shoving his hands forcefully into his pockets. "Or she'd drink until she drifted into some fantasy world where it made sense for her to persist in her ridiculous beliefs."

He turns and walks to me, stopping mere inches away. When he leans down, it's not the intimate movement of a lover, the closeness of a friend about to confide a secret. It's for me to see his pain, to feel the depth of his belief that being alone is preferable to risking his heart for anyone ever again.

"I will never make her mistake."

I tilt my chin up, refusing to be cowed.

"You made it perfectly clear when you proposed what your expectations were for this arrangement."

He blinks as if surprised by my response. He leans back slightly but keeps his eyes focused on mine.

"I wasn't sure how you would feel after last night."

"We had sex. Really good sex. But you needn't worry about me imagining that there's anything else between us."

I say it so convincingly I almost believe it myself. Telling him now that what happened between us last night did mean something, did make me wonder if there could be more, would only create more friction. It also would accomplish absolutely nothing. I have no desire to try and change a man, to bend him to my will. When I get married again—and I will—it will be to someone who loves me and accepts the love I have to offer in return.

I break eye contact and glance up as a light breeze dances through the leaves of the chestnut trees scattered throughout the cemetery. When that happens, it will also be when I'm not in the middle of a personal crisis, trying to figure out if I want to continue the work I've dedicated my life to.

"Relax, Drakos." I give him a small smile. "I won't fall in love with you."

Instead of relief, there's a quick flash of anger. Before I can say anything else, he nods once and then strides past me and out of the cemetery, leaving me alone amongst the headstones.

CHAPTER SIXTEEN

Gavriil

THE WATERS OF the Rhône lap gently at the hull of the boat. On the nearby bank, a bird sings softly to its mate hidden somewhere nearby. The sky is streaked with shades of brilliant pink and vivid purple. My computer sits open on my lap with the latest report on the Paul Properties deal, including an email for an official meeting to discuss pricing and terms when I return from France. A bourbon rests within easy reach. With the press of a button, a butler will be by my side in a minute, available to answer almost any question I have or retrieve anything I want. I have everything.

But in this moment, knowing that the master suite behind me is empty, as is the guest suite on the floor above, I feel like I did right before the wedding ceremony: hollow.

It's an uncomfortable feeling, one I haven't experienced this deeply before. Every deal I made, every dollar I added in profits, brought me happiness and a sense of fulfillment I had never found in my life. What I put into Drakos, the company gave back. The finer things that had eluded me in the early years of my life were available with a snap of my fingers. People who would have looked down on me when I was begging on the streets of Santorini now begged for me to consider their properties, their proposals. For the first time in my life, I had respect. Power. Control.

But right now, as I stare out over the water, I feel powerless for the first time in years. It's been three days since Juliette found me in the Cimetière de Passy. Three days of cool politeness and, on the few occasions we spoke to each other, bland conversation. No repeats of the incredible night we shared.

We spent the night after she followed me in our separate rooms and checked out of the Shangri-La the following morning, traveling by limo to the departure point of the second phase of our honeymoon: a private boat trip down to the French Riviera. It met my requirements of luxury with the opportunity for photos that could be shared on Instagram, reinforcing the illusion of a happily married couple. The limo ride was almost entirely silent, reminiscent of our flight over from the States. Except now there was an added tension. We knew each other far better, physically and emotionally. Knew there were depths beyond the faces we presented to the world. And at least for me, craved what we had shared for one starlit night.

It was for the best, I remind myself for the hundredth time, to stay away from each other. When we made love, I knew as she'd come apart beneath me, as I'd lost myself in her, that I had gotten too close. When I'd woken the next morning, my arms wrapped around her waist and my face buried in her hair, I allowed myself one moment to simply enjoy the indulgence of waking up with a woman I greatly respected and genuinely liked.

Then reality had set in. I had made love to her not once, not twice, but three times. All three times, I'd pulled her close and fallen asleep with her in my arms. I'd wanted it.

Too much. Too much too soon.

So I'd slipped away, beginning the process of putting distance between us. It was necessary. No matter how enjoyable that night had been, no matter how much I had discovered about Juliette and the woman she was, I couldn't do it. I couldn't risk my sanity again.

Her following me to the cemetery had been a sign. It gave her a chance to see why I would never be the kind of man who could let himself love, who could provide her with the things she obviously wanted, like a family of her own.

The way she'd looked when she'd watched that child dancing down the row in the graveyard had made me ache for something I'd never longed for before. Something I have told myself time and again would never happen. How could it when loving a woman, let alone creating a family, was out of the question?

Yes, her full assurance that she would not be falling in love with me had stung. But shouldn't I be grateful for it? Instead of tears or begging, she acted exactly as I'd hoped she would, for the reasons why I chose her over the numerous other women who would have jumped at the chance to marry a billionaire. It should have reassured me. It should have calmed the turmoil in my chest.

But it didn't. I found myself missing the intimacy we discovered at the restaurant. On more than one occasion, I had nearly gone in search of her as the boat had passed one of the numerous landmarks viewable from the river, just for a chance to watch her face light up the way it had when we'd crossed the Pont d'Iéna.

Instead, I focus on the one thing that has always brought me pleasure: work.

For the first day, I convinced myself that things were just as they had always been. The back-and-forth between Drakos Development and Paul Properties. Reviewing the reports, analyses, opinions from my executives as we progressed forward. Yet even completing the tasks that had once made me feel in control now felt hollow. Years and years of building one of the largest fortunes in the world. And how had I spent that money? What had I done with it? My few attempts for community investment feel like a drop in the bucket. I had years to make a difference. Instead, I focused on myself.

Like father, like son.

By day two, as the boat slipped past a magnificent castle that made me wonder if Juliette had managed to snap a photo of the turret, I'd stopped pretending and acknowledged I wasn't as hard-hearted as I wanted—or needed—to be when it came to her.

When the boat had docked this afternoon near a village renowned for wine, lavender and its twisting maze of stone alleys, I'd wandered the decks with the poor excuse of stretching my legs. I only encountered the crew.

It has now been over forty-eight hours since I last laid eyes on my wife.

I glance down at my watch. It's well past dinnertime. I drum my fingers on the railing. This is ridiculous. I'm letting myself get bent out of shape because for the first time in years, possibly ever, there's an extra layer to my relationship with a woman. I manage billions of dollars in assets, oversee hundreds of properties around North America, and survived a man Hell probably spat back out when he arrived at the gates.

I'm more than capable of handling a few emotions. Especially if it means enjoying time with a woman like Juliette. A woman who came apart with a trusting abandon that has lingered in my blood ever since I slid inside her wet heat.

I press the button. Thirty seconds later, Renard appears.

"Bonjour, monsieur."

"Bonjour. I was thinking about having dinner on the top deck with my wife."

"Madame Drakos has gone into the village."

I try and fail to quell my irritation as my plan to seduce Juliette into bed while dinner was being prepared falls apart. "I see."

"Shall I still have dinner served on the top deck?"

"No. No, *merci*, Renard."

"*Merci*, monsieur."

Renard is almost to the door when I call him back.

"If I wanted to surprise my wife, how would I get to the village?"

Twenty minutes later, I'm walking through a fairy-tale French village at twilight. The houses and shops are smooshed together, the buildings made of brick and stone, the narrow alleys strung with lights and bursting with blooms that pour from containers on the streets, mounted to the walls, dripping from windowsills.

I can't remember the last time I wasn't surrounded by glitz and gold. But there's elegance here, evident in everything from the well-placed signs advertising the various shops and establishments to the quaint iron lanterns lining the roads. There's history, too, from the placards noting the years various structures were built to the well-maintained but worn cobblestones beneath my feet. It's like stepping into another world. I pass shops featuring everything from glass-blown sculptures to artisanal crafted pastries.

I pass a small restaurant, then pause and double back. Juliette is sitting at a little table on a small patio. My eyes devour her. She's wearing a pale green shirt and a white skirt that falls just past her knees. She's flipping through her camera, a small smile on her face. I wait a moment, making a mental note of details like the strand of hair framing her face, the spark of happiness when she sees something on her camera screen.

I want to stop time. To freeze this moment and have her be this way forever. Happy. Content.

Slowly, I approach. I don't know what to expect. The way she confided in me that night at the Eiffel Tower, the way she curled into me after we made love, I thought her just as affected—if not more—than I. But with her casual dismissal in the cemetery, I don't know what I'm more afraid of: her indifference or her affection.

She looks up as I approach. I see surprise in her eyes before a veil drops over her face and she gives me a polite smile.

"Gavriil."

"May I join you?"

"Of course."

A waitress appears moments after I sit. I order a glass of merlot and a plate of assorted cheeses, crackers and fruit.

"What are you looking at?"

Juliette freezes, her hands tightening on her camera. I watch the myriad of emotions cross her face: uncertainty, pride, fear.

Then, slowly, she hands me the camera. I don't tell her how much it means to me that she's trusted me with whatever has captured her attention.

I toggle through the photos, not bothering to hide my surprise at the quality of the images she's captured. The most recent ones are of the village, tourists examining the wares in various shops. An elderly shopkeeper grinning at the camera, the missing tooth adding a touch of character to her broad grin as she gestures to a wall of colorful scarves. Photos of the castle I had noticed the day before, the lighting just right to give the battlements an ethereal touch. Then further still, to Paris. The landmarks are beautiful. But it's the people she's captured that impress me the most. Raw yet powerful, personal yet professional.

"You've been hiding something from me."

She tenses, tries to mask it by picking up her glass of wine.

"Like what?"

"Your photography."

Pink colors her cheeks as she murmurs a soft thank you, trying to pass it off as casual. But I've come to know her better than that. I know these photos mean something to her. I take a risk.

"Is this part of that new project you've been alluding to?"

She stills. Her eyes dart from side to side as if she's trying to seek an escape.

"Et voilà!"

The waitress appears with my wine and the charcuterie tray, setting it down alongside a bowl of colorful ratatouille and another glass of wine for Juliette.

After she leaves, Juliette's gaze flicks between me and the camera.

"Yes."

The one word sounds like it's been dragged out of her. Given our last serious conversation, I don't blame her. I all but pushed her as far away from me as possible. Asking her to share something so personal makes me a bastard.

Before I can tell her she doesn't have to share, her fingers wrap around the stem of her wineglass and she sighs.

"Did you read my article on the Walter human trafficking case?"

I nod. Peter Walter, renowned hotelier, suspected of smuggling priceless artifacts out of Central and South America. But it wasn't just art he'd been dealing in. He had been using his network of luxury hotels to smuggle in people, primarily women, with the promise of work, only to turn them over to a network of sex traffickers.

I suddenly remember the report airing on the evening news of a raid at one of Walter's warehouses in Dallas. The priceless Incan and Peruvian artifacts had been nothing compared to the women found in the back of a truck, half of them close to the point of starvation. Juliette's article had been published a few days later.

She holds out her hand for the camera. I hand it to her, watch as she types something into the screen. She hands the camera back to me.

My throat tightens. Even though I know exactly what I'm looking at, it takes a moment for my brain to catch up. The empty shackles hanging from the roof of the van. An officer with his arms wrapped around a woman facing away from the camera, the hunching of her shoulders and desperate curl of her fingers in the folds of his shirt hitting me like a train.

"You were there."

Her eyes glint for a moment before she turns away.

"Yes. I'd been tracking Walter for months. There was plenty of evidence to suggest he was engaged in the smuggling of artifacts. But that night..." Her voice trails off. She blinks, as if trying to banish the image of whatever she saw. "I was the one who called the police. One of the editors threw a fit because I phoned it in instead of going to the paper first."

The idea of Juliette even being close to something so heinous, so evil, makes my blood run cold. My fingers curl into fists so I don't reach out and touch her, reassure myself that she is truly sitting in front of me, safe and sound.

"I'd gotten a reliable tip that he was getting a shipment delivered that night. Took my photos, matched a license plate to a robbery that had taken place in Mexico City a week prior." Her eyes grow distant. "The last truck. It took me a while to realize why it bothered me. The other trucks were enclosed. But that last one had vents all along the top." She presses her lips together and looks me straight in the eye. "I knew something was wrong. I knew and I almost walked away so that I could have the exclusive on Peter Walter for art smuggling."

She looks away, and I know the admission had cost her. I reach out, cover her hand with mine. I don't know if she notices with how far back into the past she's retreated, how deeply she's sunk in her own guilt.

But I'm there. I won't have her thinking that I'm judging her, that I'm finding her wanting. Not after what she risked, what she gave up to do the right thing.

"If I hadn't listened to my instinct, if I hadn't set aside my ego and my pride, those women would be lost to the network of sex trafficking."

Revulsion hits me straight in the gut. The depravity of what humans are capable of, along with how close Juliette came to encountering monsters. I wait for a moment, trying not to let her see how much I'm affected by what she shared.

"But you didn't."

"I thought about it though." She bites her lower lip. "I thought about ignoring that instinct because I wanted that exclusive."

She suddenly sets her glass down so hard on the table I'm surprised it doesn't shatter. I smile reassuringly at a nearby couple who are watching Juliette, as if wondering if she's about to burst into tears.

"I wanted to be the one to unmask him. My pride nearly condemned those women to a fate worse than death. I was so blinded by my own past that I failed to see the people who were truly the heart of my work."

I don't even bother to question the compassion I feel for her in that moment. I simply offer it because I want to.

"And I thought about killing my father. But I didn't. Just like you didn't abandon those women."

"No, I didn't." The shadows in her eyes make my chest ache. "But I hesitated. I hesitated and ignored what makes me a good reporter because for a moment, I did exactly what the people I hunt do. I put myself and my career first."

"Thinking and doing are two very different things," I counter.

"You were right, you know." The look she gives me is full of a sadness so profound it takes everything I have not to stand up, sweep her into my arms and carry her back to the boat where I can hold her and comfort her. "I told myself for so long I do what I do so that what happened to my father doesn't happen to someone else. But the more I published my work, the more I felt...powerful."

She spits out the word. I hate the loathing in her voice. I hate hearing how much time and energy she has wasted beating herself up when she is worth so much more. She's a far better person than the people I've rubbed shoulders with and sought the approval of for over twenty years.

The thought stops me cold. That hollow sensation rears up, widens. More than wealth, more than prestige, I've wanted power. Survived on what shards I could grasp as a child, then thrived on the steady streams that flowed in as I rose up the ranks. I considered it synonymous with control, with everything I'd dreamed of and been denied in my childhood.

But at what cost? Juliette's not the monster she believes herself to be. Yet I can't help but wonder what I would see if I looked in the mirror, if I looked at everything I've done to get where I am today.

My grasp on Juliette's hand tightens. "You called the police. You published your story days later, giving up an exclusive so those women could be rescued. You did the right thing."

She watches me for a moment, hope flaring in her eyes, before she looks away.

"It still made me question everything. All the stories I've written, the people I've ruined."

"They ruined themselves."

Rafe and I suspected for years that Lucifer was at the very least flirting with the edges of the law, if not outright breaking them. And we did nothing. It took one slip of a girl from the Olympic Coast to bring the devil to his knees.

As I watch her, berating herself for one moment where she contemplated pride over doing the right thing and still made a choice that saved the lives of the women trapped in that truck, as well as future lives who would have been consigned to a fate worse than death, I realize that I can't even come close to being the kind of person Juliette is in her heart.

But I want to try. For the first time in my life, I want something more than wealth. More than fame.

I want to do something good.

She runs a hand over one cheek, wiping away a tear. "You didn't, though."

I falter. "What?"

"I tried. I tried to pin something on you and your brother. These last few months, I knew about Lucifer's diagnosis. I tracked down everything I could on you and Rafael and came up with nothing." She rolls her hand over in mine, squeezes my fingers. "I'm sorry. I wanted to believe that you both were like him, to continue on this quest for vengeance. I think a part of me hoped it would fill the void I was experiencing after Texas. After realizing I'd based so much of my work on your father and what he did to mine. Renew my motivation for my career. But you're nothing like him," she adds softly.

"That's the nicest thing anyone has ever said to me."

Her laugh is surprisingly light against the darkness of our conversation.

"Were you relieved? When you realized Rafe and I were not like our father?"

"Not at first. I was surprised. Then I was angry." She sucks in a deep breath. "And then I was angry with myself for being angry. For wanting you or Rafe to be like him."

She looks at me then, straight on. I respect her for telling me all of this, even more so knowing how much it cost her. I also feel myself slipping closer and closer to that edge that I came so close to that night in Paris when I realized the kind of woman Juliette Grey truly is.

"Why did you want me to be like Lucifer?"

Her eyes glint with unshed tears, but she doesn't look away.

"When you live for so long with a single purpose in life, it's hard to live on the other side of it." A shuddering sigh breaks from her lips. "I've been so incredibly blind. So selfish."

I nod toward her camera. "Is that what this photo project is about? Trying to find something new?"

"Sort of."

She picks it up, presses a few more buttons, and then hands it to me. Images of women fill the screen. Most of them young, a couple of them closer to middle age. All of them with a darkness in their eyes that speaks to the horrors they've lived through.

But in many of them, there's also hope. A sense of pride as they meet the gaze of the camera lens.

"Some of the women from Walter's warehouse wanted their story told. I'd always focused on the perpetrators before. Never the victims." I look up and she flushes. "I've been working on their stories for the past six months. I don't get the same joy out of investigative reporting that I used to. But telling their stories..." Some of the tension bleeds from her body. "It's not just fulfilling, it's inspiring."

"There's a difference to you as you're talking about this."

She tilts her head to the side. "How so?"

"A softness. The same softness I saw when you looked at Grey House. Contentment."

I don't add that I saw the same emotions on her face after we made love. Knowing what I had in my hands, what I pushed away out of fear, makes me sick to my stomach.

She smiles then, a movement so uninhibited and bright it chases away the pain. Juliette is not perfect. She's human. But right now, as I watch her, I know that she is the most incredible human I've ever had the privilege to know. She has more humanity in her so-called selfish heart than I have in my entire body.

Is it even right for me to still want her? To try and convince her to spend the next year with me, in my bed, when I can't hold a candle to her integrity? When I've used people's desires to achieve my own without a second thought?

"I've been wondering for months if I needed to refocus my career. It's torn me up inside. Ever since I moved in with Dessie, I've been fixated on taking down your father. Righting wrongs. But even after I published my first story on your father, there was this...emptiness. I thought maybe the next report would bring me closer finding some peace, some resolution. It wasn't until after Texas that I started to realize nothing would ever resolve what happened to my family. That I was chasing the unattainable."

My chest tightens. It's as if she's reading my thoughts. Experiencing the emotions that have been growing increasingly tangled over the past few months.

She nods toward the camera in my hands. "But this...this feels different. This feels right."

"You have a talent."

I'm not lying as I hold up the camera, the screen depicting a young woman with fatigue in her eyes but hope in the tiniest of smiles. It's a face I saw time and time again in the poor sections of Santorini. But where I merely glanced on my way to pickpocket the nearest gullible tourist, Juliette has captured a story. She's brought attention to the faceless, the nameless.

"I told you before, Juliette, that I admire your work. I didn't lie then, and I don't lie now when I say this has the potential to be a new beginning for you."

This time her smile is small, soft. It fills me with a fierce sense of pride.

"Perhaps I've found my new calling after all."

It turns into one of those evenings that drags on for eons yet speeds by in the blink of an eye. We dip into cheese and roasted vegetables as Juliette shares stories of her days at a college in Missouri and I counter with my experiences at Oxford. We laugh, smile, bond over shared memories and an intimacy I've never experienced before. Our hands brush, linger. The heat that has existed between us ever since that moment in the hotel grotto, a moment that feels ancient and new, simmers, deepens with the confidences we've shared, the vulnerabilities we've bared.

It's nearly midnight when we leave. The walk takes us through the village, then past fields of lavender, the heady scent wrapping around us. I give into impulse and pick a sprig. I tuck it behind her ear, my fingers lingering for a heartbeat in the silky tendrils of her hair. The smile she gives me winds its way around my heart. This time I don't fight it. I enjoy it. I grasp her hand in mine as we walk down the star-dusted path.

Mine.

My fingers tighten on her as a need surges forth. Not just a need to feel her bare beneath me, surrounding me. But a need to be with her.

When she stops and turns to me and lifts her face to mine, my body stills as moonlight paints silver light across her face.

"Kiss me, Gavriil."

I'm not strong enough to resist that. But when her arms slide up my chest, when she presses her body against mine in an obvious invitation, I stop her. She pulls back.

"If you don't—"

"I do." I hold her against my body, her eyes widening as she feels the evidence of my arousal against her hips. "But I want to do this right."

She sighs. "It's hard not to like you when you're so noble."

I scoop her up into my arms, savoring her delighted laugh as I carry her across the gangplank onto the ship.

"Not completely noble."

I carry her to my suite. I ignore any lingering whispers of why this is a bad idea, why I should take her to her room instead of mine.

I've spent too many nights with her just out of reach. I don't know what tomorrow will bring. But for tonight, at least, my wife is where she needs to be. In my arms.

CHAPTER SEVENTEEN

Juliette

I BARELY REGISTER the opulence of the two-story suite Gavriil carries me into. Not when I'm focused on the man holding me in his arms like I'm the most precious thing he's ever held. Not after he listened to every single doubt, every insecurity I've ever had, and accepted me for it.

He sets me on my feet. I reach out, grab the string on his pants, and pull. He doesn't flinch, doesn't move as the pants fall, leaving him naked. I trace my fingers over him. Pure feminine satisfaction rolls through me as he hardens under my touch. His sharp inhale makes me look up. His face is calm, smooth.

Except for his eyes. His eyes burn.

"You're a tease, Juliette."

I prove him right by kissing the pulse throbbing at the base of his throat. My lips drift down over the ridges of his chest as my fingers trace teasing circles on his thighs. Every tensing of muscle, every sharp inhale, fills me. Seduces me.

I know, as I move lower still, that I've completely surrendered to him. My husband. One year from now I have no doubt my heart will be shattered. But I can no more stop my desire, my feelings for him, than I could stop the moon from crossing the sky. Not when he has given me so much in just a few short days. A man who has known hell and yet encouraged me. Believed the best in me when I couldn't see anything but bad.

I swallow past the lump in my throat as I wrap my fingers around him. My hand moves down, up, then down again. I lean forward and take him in my mouth. His groan fills me. His hands sink into my hair. I feel like a goddess as I move my lips over him, feeling the effect my touch has on him.

Suddenly, he steps back and kicks his pants away.

"My turn."

He scoops his hands under my arms and moves me back to the middle of the bed before I can utter a protest. He has me on my back in seconds. He covers my mouth with his, another possessive kiss, but one with a touch of sweetness that makes tears burn beneath closed eyes. For a moment, I wish. Wish for more than this night, for more than a year.

One hand settles on my breast, gentle yet firm. I arch up beneath his touch. Whether we have just the remaining nights of our honeymoon or the rest of our contracted time together, I will take everything he has to give and never regret surrendering to him.

He moves farther down my body, worshipping my breasts with tender kisses and teasing strokes of his tongue that send me hurtling to the edge of reason. I shift, moving my thighs, my body seeking him out.

When he finally lifts his head, I sigh in relief, ready for him to finally end the agony he's created. But instead, he smiles at me before he grabs my hips and slides down my body. I clench, waiting. His lips graze my inner thigh, the tender flesh, the spot just above.

But only grazes, kisses, light nips, until I feel like I'm about to burst.

"Gavriil."

"What?"

I can hear the smile in his voice.

"Please!"

"Please what?"

"You—"

He moves then, a deep kiss to the most intimate part of my body. I arch up and cry out, my hands grasping, sliding through his hair, over his shoulders. He makes love to me with his mouth, keeping me in a frenzied state as he alternates between short, teasing kisses and long, slow dances of his tongue across my skin.

One minute pleasure is spiraling through me. In a second, it shatters, leaving me trembling. He moves up my body and slides inside before I can catch my breath. Still shaking, I wrap my arms around him and hold on as he moves inside me. Slow strokes at first, deep ones that I feel all the way to my soul. His eyes hold mine, the emotion reflected in those pale blue depths enough to obliterate any lingering doubts.

I whisper his name as I lift my hips to meet his thrusts. His gaze darkens as he groans, his hips quickening as I hold on to his shoulders, the peak inside me building until I know I'm going to explode, break apart into a million pieces unless he—

He covers my mouth with his. It sends me over the edge. I cry out as I crest. He follows a moment later, my name on his lips as we shatter together.

Gavriil

I wake to sun filling the suite. Juliette and I lie together, pressed against each other as if we can't get enough. I wait for the uneasiness to settle in. But it doesn't. Lying here with Juliette in my arms feels right.

She stirs and smiles up at me with sleepy eyes.

"I could get used to this." Her eyes widen and her cheeks pale. "I just meant…good sex."

She wrinkles her nose and tries to roll away. Laughing, I grab her arm and pull her back.

"You've never had good sex before?"

"I've had good sex," she mumbles against my chest.

I frown into her hair. I've never been the jealous type before. But the thought of any other man touching her incites an anger I've never experienced before. One that includes vivid images of me planting my fist in their face. Completely unfair, especially given the numerous women I've entertained over the years.

But I don't care. I don't like it.

"I just haven't had mind-blowing, spine-tingling, sleep-inducing sex."

The jealousy dissipates. I arch a brow down at her. "Are you trying to stroke my ego?"

She narrows her eyes at me. "Your ego doesn't need any stroking." Her hand drifts teasingly down my stomach. "Now other parts of your anatomy…"

"After breakfast. I need my strength if we're going to spend all morning in bed together."

Her eyes brighten. "All morning?"

My arms tighten about her. Last night, she opened up again. Except instead of confiding secrets from the past, she shared something even greater: her fear. The one thing holding her back, something so personal she hadn't even shared it with the people in her life who loved her and she them. The gift of her trust, the deeper understanding of everything she had been through and what had spurred her to investigate Rafe and me in the first place, had wiped away the last lingering bit of resentment I hadn't even realized I'd still harbored.

It also left me wanting to do the same. To share with her. Not just my bed, not just my body, but myself. I had resisted it before in Paris. But now, for the first time in my adult life, I wanted to share a piece of myself.

I don't prepare her. I just speak. If I try to explain, to give any context, I don't know if I'll be able to get through this.

"My mother and I lived in squalor in Santorini."

Her hand stills for a moment, then resumes tracing slow, reassuring circles over my chest. I stare up at the ceiling, eyes wide-open but not seeing anything except a dirty apartment with a single mattress on the floor and broken windows that didn't stand a chance against the sweltering heat of summer.

"My first real memory was when I was about four. We didn't have anything to eat. My mother sat on the mattress, holding me, crying and telling me how sorry she was."

"She cared about you."

I hear the question in her voice, the confusion.

"She cared for me as much as she could." I swallow past the resentment I can feel building even now as I tell my story. "Dessie knew you needed a mother's touch, a steady influence in your life. So she drove hours to see you at least twice a month. When things got bad, she made a home for you. Provided for you.

"My mother turned to alcohol. She just drank more until there was nothing left. I have my suspicions about how she earned the little bit of money she brought in, but I never asked."

I had come home to the occasional scent of too much cologne or the faint whiff of a cigar. Nothing concrete. But I grew up too fast to not know how some people earned their meager income.

"The one good thing she did was never let me see that side of her life."

Juliette's palm flattens on my chest and rests over my heart. The weight is comforting, steadying.

"When she was sober, she would make plans on how to finally get Lucifer's attention. She tried reaching out multiple times, but he had instructed his staff to rebuff her. He didn't want his wife, Rafe's mother, knowing he had another child."

"I always knew I hated him." Juliette's voice is a vicious whisper. "But I had no idea how truly hideous he was."

"He seduced an eighteen-year-old hotel maid, kept her in his penthouse for a week and gave her a taste of the kind of life she had never imagined. When he left, someone reported her for fraternizing with a guest. She was fired. When her family found out she was pregnant and unmarried, they kicked her out."

I feel Juliette's breath catch, but she stays silent.

"It's possible, I've come to realize, to have pity and compassion for her, and still be angry with how things turned out."

"I wonder if things would have been different if her family would have taken you both in."

I shrug. I used to ponder the same thing as a child. Now, it doesn't matter.

"I came home one day from running around the neighborhood, picking tourists' pockets, and discovered her dead on the mattress we shared."

There's no gasp, no strong reaction. There's just Juliette, her hand over my chest, her head warm against my shoulder. She knows exactly what I need and, for the first time as I revisit the past, there's no anger for my mother. Just a bittersweet pain of knowing what could have been but wasn't.

"How did Lucifer find out about you?"

"The police. I found a neighbor, who called them. My mother had written a letter she had entrusted to a friend in the event of her death. The friend gave it to the police when they came to our flat."

I can still remember the look of incredulity on one of the officer's faces when he had opened the letter and read my mother's claims.

"They took me away kicking and screaming. I had overheard my mother trying to talk to Lucifer's staff on and off over the years. I didn't expect a limo to pull up outside the police station and take me to a nearby dock. One of his security guards took me on the boat over to his private island."

I still remember walking into that palace of an office, shelves two stories high and arranged perfectly to feature awards, rare books, works of art. Even to an uneducated eight-year-old, Lucifer's private study had screamed wealth.

"He looked up, saw my eyes, and leaned back. He said, 'So she was telling the truth.'"

"That's it?"

"No." This part I still cannot remember without anger, without fury against a man so cold and so selfish that he couldn't even have a moment of compassion for a grieving child. His grieving child. "He approached me and looked me up and down. Then he smiled and said I might be related to him by blood, but he would bet that I would prove to be more like my mother than him."

"What?"

"Weak. Unmotivated. A failure. He told me those words himself."

The little sliver of heart I had left, the secret longing to finally meet and perhaps be loved by the father I'd always heard about but never met, had shriveled up and died that day. In its place, though, anger had been planted. Anger that just a month later, once Rafe had walked by me and dismissed me with such casual indifference, had twisted and morphed into determination. Determination and a vow to never let anyone close enough to break me again.

"He told me he would support me until I was eighteen. After that, I was on my own. I could either take advantage of the opportunities he offered me or live the good life until he turned me out on my ass."

Juliette gives a huffing little laugh. "And look what you became."

There's pride in her voice. It moves me in a way I can't put into words. I wait a moment before I speak again.

"I'm proud of what I've accomplished."

"As you should be."

I can't help but laugh as I gather her close, slide a finger under her chin, and kiss her firmly.

"Just a little over a month ago, you thought I made at least part of my fortune through illegal means."

She winces. "I don't even know if I fully believed it at that point. I didn't want to miss something."

"I still don't like it. But," I add as her look of guilt deepens, "I understand it better now."

"As I do your drive to be the best." She tilts her head to the side. "Although, I'm curious. Why this deal in New York? Normally your projects seem bigger, splashier."

Pride fills my chest. The deal with Paul Properties has evolved in the last couple of days to include more investments in the community. A targeted recruitment plan for locally owned businesses. Grants to fund said businesses. Future meetings with some of the neighborhood organizations to have them be an active part of the development process.

"One of the things I've been trying to incorporate into

the deal is development not only for the sake of the deal, but for the neighborhood and the people that it impacts."

She freezes. "What?"

"The slum I grew up in in Santorini made an impression. There were good people there, some of them through no fault of their own except circumstance. Fate. I watched so many of them struggle. Once I realized I was actually going to make a success out of Drakos North America, I started taking on the occasional personal project."

"The project in Los Angeles," she murmurs. "I remember reading about the high crime rate in the area, the lack of housing and restaurants that might attract workers. It surprised me that you would push for that property."

"Which is why that project included guarantees from several local business and franchise owners to put in said restaurants and shops. It also included funding for a year for a private security firm and donations to renovate some of the houses in the area."

"You did all that."

"Yes. It's good business."

And not enough.

Not nearly enough when I have so much at my fingertips. I want to tell her more about the spark she's created in me to use my wealth in a way I never thought about. But before I can, she sits up, eyes flashing, color filling her face. She doesn't even seem to notice that she's bare from the waist up with a sheet tangled about her hips. She's magnificent as she leans forward and pokes me in the chest.

"Don't you tell me that line if it's just business. You care. You're doing good things."

"Yes, but don't tell anyone. I could lose my reputation."

She buries her face in her hands and groans. "How did I miss all of this?"

I grab her hands and pull them down from her face. "Because you weren't looking for it. Juliette, I'm going to say the same thing to you that you said to me. Don't turn me into a saint. I only started making this a priority in the last year. I still make a lot of money off these deals. Money that, as you can see, I use in very selfish ways."

"But you're doing things for others," she insists. She cups her hands on either side of my face. "You don't have to be perfect. But you're so much more than I ever realized. I have to wonder that, if not for your father and this ridiculous will, if I would have ever seen that."

I'm lying to myself every time I think her words don't matter. They matter a great deal, more than anything that matters to me in recent memory, including Drakos North America. I'm not quite ready to fully accept that yet. Just a little more time. A little more time to process these newfound emotions, figure out exactly what I feel for Juliette and how far I want it to go.

She leans down and kisses me. Her naked breasts brush my chest. Blood pumps through me. I'm hard and grow harder still when I brush against her thigh. She laughs against my lips and makes me want her even more.

"What about your breakfast?"

I pull her to me and roll, pinning her body beneath me. "It can wait."

Whatever else she is about to say is lost as I grasp her hips and slide back into her wet heat. As we start to move together, as I surrender even more of my control and let down my walls, emotion surges with the lust already pounding inside me. I realize, as our breaths merge and her cries grow louder, that I feel like I'm home for the first time in my life.

CHAPTER EIGHTEEN

Juliette

I SIT ON the deck outside Gavriil's stateroom. Hills teeming with lavender spread out before me. I lean back in my chair, wearing nothing but a silk robe, holding a mimosa in my hand with a bright red cherry nestled in the bottom of the glass. The scenery, the delicious breakfast we just shared and the events of the past twelve hours have left me happy. Content.

I don't know what all this means for our future. We still have fifty-one weeks left in this so-called marriage. Plenty of time to figure it out.

I glance back over my shoulder. He disappeared inside a couple minutes ago to check with the captain on our itinerary for the day. He mentioned an art museum set inside an old quarry, with projections of classic works of art on the stone walls. It sounds like a wonderful adventure to have on my honeymoon.

A honeymoon I've decided to fully commit to. Shortly after Gavriil left to speak with the captain, I texted my contact, Jared, to tell him to pause the investigation into Louis Paul. I need to have that conversation with Gavriil myself before I proceed any further. To give him what little I know and let him make what decisions are best for him and his company. To trust him to be the man I've come to know as

I move on to the next phase of my career. One that I know will bring both purpose and joy to my life while giving a voice to those I've looked over for so long.

My phone dings a moment later. Aside from some good-natured ribbing and a detailed invoice of what I owe Jared for his time, he includes a quick summary of what he found, which is thankfully nothing.

There's a reason for the trips to Texas. But nothing professional. It's personal.

I'm not even tempted to follow up on that. If Jared says nothing illegal is happening, I believe him. And I have no interest in looking deeper into someone's personal life. I just want to move on.

I sit there on the deck, breathing in deeply, savoring the feeling of peace for the first time in over two decades. I'm hopeful. I have so much hope I feel like I'm about to burst.

Footsteps sound behind me. I turn. Unease cuts through my happiness at the frown between his brows. I stand.

"Gavriil? Is everything all right?"

"Louis Paul just called."

I frown. "And?"

"The deal is suspended."

Something starts gnawing on the inside of my stomach, a horrible dread of what Gavriil is going to say next.

"Suspended?" I repeat softly.

"Someone has been looking into Paul's personal life. Asking questions about Paul and his friendship with Peter Walter. About the time he spends down in Texas."

He walks toward me, his jaw tight, his eyes more apprehensive than angry. I realize he doesn't want to ask, doesn't want to know. I stare back at him, fear and hopelessness building in my chest with such strength it robs me of breath.

Then I square my shoulders and prepare myself to do the right thing. The right thing I'm terrified will snatch away something I held in my hand for mere moments.

"It was me."

Gavriil

The sound of water trickling by, the wind stirring through the lavender on the hillside, the gentle hum of the boat's motor, all of it fades away, replaced by a roaring in my ears that smothers it all.

I trusted her. I trusted her with everything. She knows why Drakos North America means what it does to me. Knows the kind of impact doing business with someone who has links not just to scandal, but to the selling of actual human beings could have on my company.

"You knew as soon as you saw his name on the file in Paris."

Her single nod breaks me. Just an hour after she straddled me and held my face and told me things I had never thought I would ever hear, making me believe that she truly cared for me...

I share some of this responsibility. I was so distracted by her, so caught up in the mystery and allure of Juliette Grey, that I didn't do my usual due diligence. Didn't dig deep enough into Paul's background to uncover this potential link to Peter Walters.

But Juliette knew. She read the file, and just hours later she gave herself to me. She told me that I was more than she had ever imagined. Just not enough to trust with the information that the man I was dealing with could ruin my reputation and rip my company's status to shreds. Invite scrutiny and gossip as to whether or not Drakos North America was involved in the trafficking of innocent women.

She moves to the railing, silk draped over her body, hair flowing past her shoulders. And her face. Her beautiful face, looking like she actually regrets what she's done, is a knife to the heart. I wonder if what I accused her of in Paris has been right all along. I have no doubt she's supporting Dessie and moving her back into Grey House.

Yet just because someone does good things, doesn't mean they're a good person. Right now, I have no idea who the woman standing in front of me is. If her motivation truly faltered in Texas and died with my father, or if that was just a ruse to kick-start the next phase of her career after she didn't have the ruins of Lucifer Drakos at her disposal anymore.

I imagined that I could let myself care for her. That over the next year, we could forge something between us. But without trust, there's nothing. Nothing but a flimsy illusion built on sex and a few midnight confessions.

I walk to the table where we dined just a few minutes ago. I sit and pour myself coffee. I sit back and gaze at her over the rim of my cup. I give her no emotion, no sign of the fury clawing inside me.

"Explain."

Her hand tightens on the rail. I find myself curious as to how she's going to spin this. Will she simply own up to the fact that when she reacted with such theatrical offense back in Paris, she had just been baldly lying and doing exactly what I had accused her of? Using our marriage to further her career? Or would she try to play it off, come up with an excuse for what she has been doing behind my back even if she slept in my bed?

"When I saw Louis Paul's name on that paperwork in your suite, it brought Texas back."

I stay silent. She hesitates, her throat working as she swallows, before she continues.

"I found the timing of his visits to Walter odd. I couldn't find anything and as I started to focus on my other project, I decided to drop it."

"Until I provided you with the perfect opportunity to continue your work."

She flinches. My anger multiplies at the tiny sliver of guilt for hurting her. I should feel nothing. She is the one at fault.

"It wasn't like that."

"Of course it wasn't." I take a sip of coffee. It burns its way down my throat, gives me something else to focus on. "Tell me, Juliette, how was it?"

She looks away then. I thought my heart already crushed. But the sure sign of her trying to come up with an excuse, of continuing to lie to me, grinds it from tiny shattered pieces into dust.

"I reached out to a couple of my contacts. Not for a story," she insists as she looks at me again. "I just wanted to make sure I hadn't missed something again."

"So altruistic reasons then? Nothing to do with a future story, another lauded investigation by the infamous Juliette Grey?"

She looks at me with heartbroken eyes. In that moment, I despise her for it. For making me care. Making me think that I might have a shot at happily-ever-after.

"You know I was considering giving up investigative reporting."

"You said you were. I have no way of knowing if that was just another lie you told me or had any basis in truth."

"It's the truth." She releases the railing and stalks toward me. "You saw my photos. I told you everything."

"Everything you wanted me to think and believe."

She stops then, looks at me as if I'm the one who's caused all of this.

"Is that what you really think?"

Her words catapult me back to Paris, to that moment when I felt lower than dirt for jumping to conclusions and accusing her of using our marriage to advance her career. That moment, and my subsequent apology, led to our dinner at the Eiffel Tower, our lovemaking after.

"I think you're far more dedicated to your career than I gave you credit for." I sit up then, lean forward, pin her with my gaze and let her see the depth of my anger. "You lay next to me in bed this morning when I talked about Paul Properties. When I unburdened my soul to you. You didn't think to mention that you were looking into him then?"

"What was I supposed to say, Gavriil? Oh, thank you for sharing the worst possible moments of your life and all the great things you're doing despite the trauma you've suffered. Oh, by the way, did I tell you that the man you might be making your next big deal with is suspected of trafficking?"

"You could have told me in Paris. You could have told me numerous times. But you didn't. I had to find out from someone else. Had to find out by having the deal I've been working day and night on yanked away from me." I can feel the next words building in my throat, know deep down that they're wrong. But I can't stop them. "I think in your desire for revenge on anyone worth over six figures, especially the offspring of Lucifer Drakos, you decided now was the time to kill two birds with one stone."

She rears back as if I've slapped her. I almost hate myself for what I've said, for voicing my deepest fear as fact. But I also know it doesn't matter what she says in rebuttal. Nothing can fix what she's done.

The words are cruel. But they will sever all ties. I need that. I need to never, ever have hope that something could change.

Her eyes glint. Her lashes sweep down. She inhales deeply, then looks up at me. I don't trust the sadness I see in her dark brown gaze even as I can feel something inside me wanting to reach out, wanting desperately to grab at that last thread that might somehow make this all right again.

"I hid something from you. I'll apologize for that, and for what it's caused. My contact has always been reliable, so I didn't think twice about asking them for more information." Her shoulders sag, as if the weight of the world has been dropped on them. "Louis Paul is clean. Whatever he's doing in Dallas is personal."

Beneath the betrayal, I can at least respect Juliette's ability to ferret out information. But I don't trust a single word she says right now. If Paul has any connection to Walter's human trafficking ring, I need to know about it. Not only can I not risk Drakos doing any dealings with him, but I will personally do whatever is in my power to put him in prison where he belongs. If he is innocent, I will be working night and day to get this deal back on track.

She breathes in a deep, shuddering breath. "Believe it or not, I didn't say anything to you in Paris because I was afraid it would look exactly like this. Like I was trying to use you to get to a story. I didn't want to potentially sway a monumental decision with supposition from an old case. A case where I failed once already to make any connections."

"And after we slept together?"

Her chin drops.

"You could have come to me."

"I should have."

"But you didn't."

"No." The word is barely a whisper. "I didn't."

There it is. We've trusted each other with so much. Something so small shouldn't have such an enormous impact on what we've shared the past few days.

Except it does. She didn't trust me. I can't trust her.

Won't trust her, a little voice whispers.

I silence it, quickly and ruthlessly. This is what comes from opening one's heart. The high is enjoyable as long as it lasts.

But inevitably, it come crashing down.

She starts to walk past me.

"Where are you going?"

"To pack my things." She stops on the opposite side of the table and looks down at me. "Drakos needs your attention now."

I surge to my feet, coffee sloshing over the rim of my cup and splashing the snowy white tablecloth. "Of course it needs my attention." I plant my fist on the table and lean forward. "How could I focus on anything else when the future of the most important thing in my life is at risk because you hid things from me?"

Silence falls like a death knell.

I don't know how long we stand there, me with fury pumping through my veins and her with grief echoing in her eyes.

Finally, she moves. The smile she gives me is so heart-wrenchingly sad that a perverse part of me wants to reach out and pull her into my arms, to offer comfort. To apologize for the unforgivable thing I've said.

Except it's true. Without Drakos, I have nothing. I thought that Juliette might care for me. That I could risk caring for someone again. That we could be more than just names on a contract.

But she didn't trust me. Just as I no longer trust her.

The pain drains away, leaving me feeling like I did the day I met my father. Hollow, hopeless.

"I did. And I'm sorry I put your company at risk."

She glances down. I see her reach for the rings on her left hand, but she stops.

"I will still honor our agreement. But if you decide that we can no longer continue—"

"We will continue. You signed a contract. I expect you to honor it."

"I will." Her voice is soft. Heartbroken. "Goodbye, Gavriil."

She walks away, the sound of her bare feet on the deck fading as she moves inside. I look down at the table, at the coffee still spreading and scarring the tablecloth with an ugly brown stain.

I know this is the right thing to do.

This is the right thing.

Water laps at the side of the boat. The breeze brings the faintest whiff of lavender. Two birds soar overhead, twisting and dipping in a coupling ritual. I sit down, listening to the addition of the slow, steady drip of coffee sliding off the table onto the deck.

CHAPTER NINETEEN

Gavriil

I WANDER TO the window and gaze out over the golden sands of Malibu. It's a place I've stood countless times since I bought this house. The view of the beach, the ocean, the glimpses of the mansions on either side of mine, used to bring me joy.

Right now, though, all I feel is alone. Alone in a massive house filled with priceless treasures that once meant everything, and now mean nothing.

It's been a week since Juliette left. I learned from the captain that she had arranged for a car to take her south to the nearest airport so she could catch a flight back to Washington. She told the captain it was a family emergency. Whether or not he believed her, I didn't know and didn't care.

I stayed on the boat, drifting down to the coast, passing the stop at Les Baux-de-Provence where we were supposed to get off and tour the quarry together. Once we arrived in Marseille, I took up residence in the suite at Le Petit Nice I had reserved for the final phase of our honeymoon. I spent almost every waking hour on the phone or on the computer, instructing my security team to dig deeper into Louis Paul even as I tried to persuade him to meet me across the negotiating table.

His secretary deferred my calls. My attempts at contacting him through his personal phone were met with voice-mail. Losing the contract would not hurt Drakos North America. Given that it appeared Paul had something to hide, it was doubtful he would talk about our falling-out with others.

But it was the only thing I could focus on right now. The only thing that distracted me from the fact that Juliette was not in my life.

The first few days, it was easy to hold on to the anger, the betrayal. It wasn't until I was flying back to the States that the first doubt appeared. The image of her standing on the stern of the boat, looking like I'd crushed her, played over and over in my mind until I could swear the image was embedded on the back of my eyelids. It bothered me enough that I reached out to Michail of all people. I hadn't been satisfied with our security firm for a long time. As much as I didn't care for my newfound half brother, his firm had grown rapidly over the past couple of years. He was re-nowned for finding out the exact kind of details I needed to know. I was surprised when he agreed to take on my case.

I told myself it was simply confirming that doing busi-ness with Paul would not darken the Drakos name. My fa-ther had done enough of that when he was alive. I would not enter into a deal, no matter how potentially lucrative it could be, if Paul had been engaging in criminal activity.

I turn away from the window. Juliette hasn't contacted me. I've checked her social media more than I care to admit. There's been nothing since her last photo of the village where we shared wine and secrets. I've revisited that mo-ment often, too, of how truly conflicted she sounded, the genuine pleasure in her eyes when I complimented her pho-tography.

As I moved past my initial hurt, truth has been slowly edging out my rancor and leaving a gaping hole in my chest.

Did Juliette use my file? Yes. But not in the way I had accused her of. It had simply been seeing the name that had reignited her need to know and fully close a painful chapter in her life. What she had done had been a continuation of her own work, her own insecurities and self-doubts. Yes, she had kept things from me. But I had done the same, keeping so much of myself away even as she tore down the walls between us and bared herself to me.

The more I recognize this, the more I realize just how much I let my past speak that day on the river, the more I want to sink to my knees and scream up at the sky.

I haven't called her. Haven't reached out, even as I've uncovered this epiphany in slow, agonizing moments. Because it doesn't matter that I've realized she was telling the truth. In a moment that mattered, I failed. I let my own doubts take over, my own fear of getting hurt override any rationality, any emotion but self-preservation. If that is my go-to at the first sign of crisis, how can I possibly be worthy of someone like her?

It doesn't stop me from glancing at my phone, from hoping she'll call. I do this now on my way out to the pool. There are plenty of text messages from members of my team. A voicemail from my secretary letting me know that Paul has finally agreed to a face-to-face meeting next week in New York to revisit the deal. What once would have brought a surge of triumph brings nothing.

I ease into the warmth of the heated saltwater lap pool. I swim as often as I can. But since I've been home, I've been swimming as if the devil were chasing me. That if I swim hard enough, fast enough, I'll outrun the mistake I've made and somehow be able to return to the life I had before I proposed to Juliette Grey.

I've just completed the second lap when something bounces off my head. I stand up and rip the goggles off my head. Michail stands on the pool deck, legs spread as if he's a cowboy headed into a gun battle. He looks down at me, sunglasses shielding his eyes. A tennis ball floats in the water next to me.

"I didn't realize you made house calls."

Michail holds up a file. "Got what you were asking for."

I run my hand over my face, dislodging the water still clinging to my skin. Then I grab the tennis ball and lob it in his direction. He dodges it, but barely. I smirk as he swears. I get out of the pool and towel off.

"How did you get in?" I ask as I hold out my hand for the folder.

One corner of his mouth tilts up. "My company manufactures your security system."

"Comforting."

I rip open the seal and slide out a document. Louis Paul, I read, has a son in Texas. A son born from a brief affair during a tumultuous time in his marriage to an Austin oil heiress. While Paul and his former mistress are no longer intimate, he makes multiple trips a year down to Texas to see his son. From what Michail's firm has been able to determine, his wife knows nothing about the affair or the child. Given that she's stated multiple times she never wants to have children, along with an ironclad infidelity clause in their prenup, Paul has plenty of reasons for not wanting this to come to light.

There are several pictures in the file, too. One is of Paul and his son sitting high in the stands at a baseball game. The boy can't be more than nine or ten years old. He wears a baseball cap. So does Paul, along with sunglasses and a casual T-shirt I never would have believed he'd wear if I hadn't had the evidence right in front of my face. But there he is, smiling down as the boy cheers on whatever happened on the field.

My chest tightens. "All of this because he's trying to be a good father."

Michail snorts. "Apparently it can happen."

I glance at him. "You truly didn't know who our father was?"

"Nope." Michail shifts as if he is suddenly uncomfortable. "Mom told me he was a bastard and I was better off not knowing him."

"Smart woman."

"The best." He glances down at his feet for a moment. "I expected you and Rafael to be exactly like him."

"Why?"

"You had his last name. You worked for his company."

"Drakos North America is my company." The steel in my voice is ice-cold. "I won't lie and say that I got to where I was solely on my own merit. But everything that Drakos North America is, it is because I built it that way."

"I know." Michail shrugs. "I read up plenty on the two of you after that will-reading. And," he adds slowly, as if it almost pains him to say, "I realized you two were different."

"I think that's a compliment."

"It is." He glances back at my mansion. "Even if you live like a damn peacock."

I grin. "Now that I will take as a compliment."

Michail makes a sound that almost resembles a chuckle. He glances around.

"Where's your wife?"

My brief moment of good humor evaporates.

"Not here. I assume she's at Grey House."

Michail stares at me for a long moment.

"I hadn't planned on showing up to your wedding."

"Why did you?"

I almost missed the slight tensing of his shoulders.

"Changed my mind. I thought you were just marrying for the money." He smiles wolfishly. "But then I saw your wife and that kiss you gave her during the ceremony. Sure was something."

"It was."

It had been the start of everything. Perhaps the moment I'd started to fall in love with her. And I'd let it slip away.

Michail tilts his head. "Which makes me wonder why she suddenly departed from the south of France before the end of your honeymoon and is now up on the Olympic Peninsula."

I entertain the idea of planting my fist in his face. I've never engaged in a brawl with a sibling. Perhaps it's time I finally experience that family tradition.

"You've been busy."

"Curiosity."

"We had a fight on our honeymoon."

"Must have been some fight."

"Is Sullivan Security now offering marital counseling as well?"

Michail makes that rumbling sound again. "In my early days, I did plenty of investigations for marriages, both the before and after. Vetting potential spouses, seeing if the loving husband or wife had someone on the side. My business tends to rip marriages apart, not mend them."

So do I, I think gloomily as I glance back down at the report. Juliette had had a feeling that Paul was hiding something. But she had been trying to do the right thing by finding out more before pursuing him, before losing herself in the investigation and intentionally ruining someone's life. I stare down at the photo of the boy, a child who has a father who, despite his faults, loves him very much.

Juliette did the right thing. She did the right thing, and I still pushed her away without even contemplating that there was a reasonable explanation. I caved to my own insecurities, to my intrinsic beliefs that I would never be enough for anyone, and used it as an excuse to withdraw, to pull away from something raw and frightening and beautiful. Something that was far more important than Drakos North America will ever be: the woman I loved. The woman I wanted a future with.

I'd already known I'd made a mistake. But seeing the evidence in front of me, the confirmation that she had made the right call while I regressed into old habits, kills me.

"You're not the only man who's suffered a setback with a woman."

I glance up. I'd almost forgotten Michail was still there.

"If we're going to start talking about relationships over a glass of wine, you know where the door is."

He rips off his sunglasses. There's still that smoldering anger I saw back in Alessandra's office. But in those all-too-familiar pale blue eyes, I see something else. Uncertainty. Frustration. And above all, apprehension.

"You're not an idiot, baby brother." He grins as I bristle. "Don't let someone like her get away."

With those parting words of wisdom, he leaves. As much as I wanted to pitch him into the pool while he was here, I prefer his company to the silence.

I've known for days now that I spoke too harshly to Juliette. That she didn't walk out of my life; I all but pushed her out with my fears and doubts. I should have walked away, given myself time to calm down, then go back and talk to her. Yes, I was hurt. But love doesn't mean never getting hurt or being hurt by loved ones. What I've realized, perhaps too late, is that loving someone includes being willing to forgive, to focusing on and trusting who they are at their core, even in the moments when they mess up.

And I do love her. I love her so much, the thought of never seeing her again, of never seeing her face light up, of hearing her voice or seeking her out at the end of a long day, nearly kills me. The thought of never building a family together, of never knowing the magic of all the things I've denied myself over the years, fills me with an even deeper fear, one that threatens to choke me.

No. I have fought for what I wanted for years. I'm not going to give up now. I'm going to make mistakes. Chances are high I will hurt Juliette again. But I love her. I love her and I will never stop trying to be the man I want to be, the man she deserves.

I make several phone calls. Then I start packing. Tomorrow, I will tell my wife how I feel and pray that I haven't broken her heart so much she's incapable of returning my love.

Juliette

I stare out over the ocean. It's the end of the day. The workmen have left.

But Grey House is coming to life once more.

The house itself has been maintained. I might curse Lucifer Drakos for many things. But his care of Grey House is not one of them.

When I first stepped foot inside, it hurt. The refinished floors. The repaired walls. All things my father had dreamed about doing. Lucifer took that away from him, too. But, especially in light of what had happened in France, it was also one less thing I had to pay for.

I shove thoughts of my husband away. There's no need to spend time or energy thinking about something that's lost to me. Instead, I need to be thinking about the future. Things like the plans Gavriil's sister-in-law Tessa emailed over for making the house more welcoming for Dessie. We've talked a lot the past week, ever since I emailed her asking her opinion on making Grey House accessible for Dessie and the possibilities that come with her multiple sclerosis. I'd forgotten that she had started her own interior design firm with a focus on accessibility.

But once I'd arrived back in the States, I'd recalled our brief conversation at the wedding reception. I'd desperately needed something else to focus on. Remodeling Grey House had been an immediate solution, one that brought both Dessie and me joy. Collaborating with Tessa, someone who understood the difficulties of traditional home construction for those with mobility challenges, had given me something else to focus on.

I hadn't expected Tessa to come up with the plans so quickly. I fell in love with them, as did Dessie. Tessa truly has a talent, combining her inner knowledge of the accessible touches needed to make a house a home for someone with mobility challenges with a sense of style.

There will be about two-thirds of the money left after the project is completed. Some of that has already been earmarked for a donation to Catherine and her facility for renovation and expansion. The rest will go into a high-yield savings account that will give Dessie and me enough to live off of as I work on rebuilding my career.

I circle my arms around my knees and stare out over the ocean. It will be enough. I will make it enough.

But every now and then, and moments like these when I'm alone with nothing but my thoughts and regrets, I can still hear Gavriil's voice from that day in the cemetery.

And you, Juliette? What do you want?

I want to turn back time. I want to go back to the penthouse in Paris and tell him about my suspicions about Louis Paul. I want to go back to that little French village where we had wine and cheese, tell him about Paul then before we went back to the boat and tumbled into bed.

It had been the perfect opportunity. To tell him my lingering fear as I confessed one of my darkest moments. But it had slipped by me until it was too late.

I miss him. On more than one night, I've reached out for him, only to have my fingers grasp cool sheets. It doesn't matter, though, how much I want him. He doesn't trust me. Can't trust me. I can't blame him for the conclusions he jumped to. For the hurt I caused.

I lie back in the grass and close my eyes. When he'd looked at me with betrayal haunting his face, I felt like someone had grabbed my lungs and squeezed all the air out. It wasn't just that I'd hurt him. It was that I had realized in that moment how deeply I loved him. How much I'd been hoping that our time together might result in him feeling the same way.

But instead of trusting him, I'd given life to my doubts. Let them rule when I'd chosen not to tell him my suspicions. I knew how much Drakos North America meant to him, knew better still after everything he had shared. Yet I hadn't given him critical information that could have affected the most important thing in his life.

My heart twists at that memory. The moment when he confirmed that, despite his hidden depths, his company would always be the only thing in his life he allowed himself to care about.

But it doesn't stop me from loving him. From respecting the man who built so much out of nothing. Who can still have compassion for people like Rafe. People like me. Who can realize he's not doing enough and change it.

Tears bead on my lashes. I love so many things about him. So many things I'll never be able to tell him.

"You were right."

My eyes fly open. Did I imagine that voice? I sit up and look around. There he is. Still too handsome, with his dark hair blown wild by the wind, that slight smile curving his lips up.

His pale blue eyes shift from mine to the ocean behind me.

"It is beautiful."

"What are you doing here?"

"Michail did some additional digging on Louis Paul."

I barely stop myself from slumping. He's here about business.

"But even before he showed up, I knew I'd made a mistake."

I suck in a shuddering breath. "Oh?"

"I told you the most important thing in my life was Drakos." He stares at me like we haven't seen each other in centuries, devouring me with every shift of his eyes. "But I lied. Both to you and myself."

He crouches down in front of me. I don't want to hope. I don't want to think that there's possibly some way we could fix this. I thought I would never see him again, unless it was on the cover of a magazine or a news report. If this is to be the last time we see each other, the last time he touches me, I want to savor every moment I can. I've apologized for my role and what happened. I've grown a lot in the last few weeks. But if he can't change with me, we have nothing.

"I don't want an arrangement, Juliette."

The pain is swift, sharp. He's going to ask for a divorce. Not even the prospect of losing Drakos North America is enough for him to want to stay married.

"I see."

"I want you."

My head snaps up. "What?"

"I want you as my wife. As my partner. As…" His voice falters. "As the mother of my children. I lied when I said Drakos was the most important thing." He reaches up and smooths my hair away from my face. I can't help but lean into his touch. "It's you, Juliette."

I blink rapidly, trying to keep the tears at bay. "What?"

"I've known for a while that Drakos North America was not the answer to my life. It's a big part of it. But it's nothing compared to you. The acceptance you've given me, the trust you've placed in me—"

"I wasn't trying to hurt you," I break in. "I wanted to do the right thing. To take my time and make sure I had the facts—"

"I know." He cups my face in his hands. "I know, Juliette. You did the right thing and I pushed you away because of it. I hope you can forgive me. That you want me in your life just as much as I want you in mine."

I stare at him, my heart thundering so loudly I can barely hear my own racing thoughts as a door opens to a future I never thought possible.

"Juliette?"

"Yes," I whisper, "I want you."

"Thank God."

He wraps one arm around my waist and pulls me onto

his lap. He crushes his lips to mine, then kisses my face, my neck.

"I pushed you away. I pushed so hard I was afraid I would never get you back. It hurt even more because I finally started to accept I was falling in love with you."

"You love me?" I whisper.

"I love you. I admire you. I like you." He punctuates each statement with a kiss to my forehead, my cheeks, my lips. "I enjoy spending time with you. Your writing is phenomenal. I hope to God that what happened between us hasn't derailed your plans for your career, because I know, Juliette, you're going to make a difference."

A tear slips down my face, but not one of sadness or heartbreak. One of hope. He cups my face.

"I never thought I was capable of letting myself love again. Perhaps it was seeing you dance with Dessie at our wedding, or realizing how much you overcame to get where you are today. Maybe it was seeing your face as you looked through the pictures you took, or watching how much you enjoyed the things I took for granted, like a limo ride in Paris. Or maybe," he says with a smile so beautiful it makes my chest ache, "it was everything. Everything that made me love you." Pain darkens his eyes. "And then I pushed you away."

I shake my head. "I should have told you. I let my doubts get in the way. I didn't want to be wrong again."

"You did the right thing. You told me about how I hurt you before. That you deserved better. Don't do yourself the disservice now of thinking you deserve any less."

I smile through my tears. "You did hurt me. But I hurt you too, and I'm sorry."

"We both have work to do." One thumb wipes away a fresh tear. "But I'd like to do that work together."

"Together sounds wonderful." I loop my arms around his neck. "Especially because I love you, too."

He smiles then, a real smile that lights up his face.

"I can't pinpoint the moment it started. But I know by the time it hit me I was so deeply in love with you the thought of getting divorced nearly tore me apart."

I cup his face with one hand. "No divorce. Not now, not ever."

He grabs my hand and pulls it away, looking down at my bare ring finger. "That's a shame."

I wince. "It's back at the house. I can put it back on—"

"I have something better in mind."

He pulls out another ring box. My heart speeds up as he flips the lid open. Inside is a silver band with an emerald in the center and two small diamonds on either side. It's simple, elegant, a far cry from the ring he slipped on my finger at almost this very spot six weeks ago.

"I bought the first ring to make a statement to the world. When I bought this one, I bought it for you."

He shifts to his knees. My heart thunders in my chest.

"The first time I proposed, I didn't have the words I do now. I love you, Juliette. I love you and I want to spend the rest of my life showing you just how much you mean to me. Will you do me the honor of being my wife?"

I smile through hot tears. "I'm already your wife."

"In name. But I'm asking you now, Juliette, will you be my wife in the ways that count the most? Will you stay with me, create a family with me?"

"Yes. Yes, Gavriil."

He swoops me into his arms and spins me around. I throw my head back and laugh moments before he seals his proposal and the beginning of our new life together with a kiss.

EPILOGUE

Juliette
One year later

THE VIBRANT BLUES and bright yellows of van Gogh's *The Starry Night* light up the wall in front of me. It is a stunning sight, one I'm finally glad we were able to see. Gavriil surprised me with a re-creation of our honeymoon for our first anniversary. We celebrated that first night in Paris by tossing the contract I'd signed into the fireplace.

The rest of it has been a blur of good food, exploring the sites and long nights spent losing ourselves in each other. The few times I've managed to tear myself away from him, I've been out wandering, snapping photos, jotting down ideas.

I smile. In the next town over, I'll be sitting down for an interview later today with a survivor of the French Resistance from World War II. My human-interest stories have been well received this past year. I'm open to taking on an occasional investigative story in the future. But these interviews, bringing attention to not only the survivors of trauma like the women rescued in Texas, but the average person one passes on the street, has brought me a sense of fulfillment my investigative work never did.

My hand slides down to my still-flat belly. My new line of work is also far less stressful. Something I've been grateful for the past ten weeks as exhaustion has settled in, along with severe bouts of nausea at night. I always thought morning sickness occurred in the morning. However, as I learned the hard way, it can happen at any time. It didn't stop Gavriil from insisting I go to the doctor to get checked out and make sure everything was well. The one positive was that we got to hear our baby's heartbeat again.

Our baby. It still doesn't seem real. I'm married to a man I love and who loves me deeply. I'm doing a job I love. Dessie, who's now going on almost a year with no relapse, is thrilled that she's going to be a grandmother. That Gavriil and I have been splitting our time equally between Malibu and Washington has also made her very happy.

Grey House has a nursery set up, along with renovated guest quarters to accommodate the growing Drakos family for family events and holidays. I've told Gavriil I want to spend as much of the baby's first years there as possible, reclaiming some of the innocence of childhood that I lost. He's come to love Rêve Beach, too. He still prefers the finer things, and always will, as evidenced by the teddy bear he already bought from Tiffany & Co.

But he's happier, more content. He's still very involved with Drakos North America, especially now that the deal with Paul Properties went through. Just like Gavriil predicted, the neighborhood is experiencing a resurgence, with Gavriil's property in high demand. I love watching him work, appreciate that he comes to me and asks for my opinion, my insight.

It's not perfect. There are still moments where he hesitates, when he struggles to share and open up.

But he does it. He does it and we make it through all of the good and the challenges.

The lights on the wall shift, making it appear as if the

stars are falling straight from van Gogh's painted world into ours. An arm wraps around my waist and pulls me back against a solid, muscular chest.

"I wondered where you'd wandered off to."

"Worried about the baby?" I tease as I turn in the circle of his arms.

"My child and my wife."

He says this with unmistakable pride.

"I'm here," I whisper. "Always."

He smiles down at me, his eyes warm as his hand settles on my belly.

"I know."

We share a kiss and then walk hand in hand on to the next chapter of our lives.

* * * * *

Were you swept off your feet by Deception at the Altar? *Then you'll love the next two installments in the Brides for Greek Brothers trilogy, coming soon!*

And don't miss these other stories by Emmy Grayson!

Cinderella Hired for His Revenge
His Assistant's New York Awakening
An Heir Made in Hawaii
Prince's Forgotten Diamond
Stranded and Seduced

Available now!

MILLS & BOON®

Coming next month

ENEMY'S GAME OF REVENGE
Maya Blake

Jittery excitement licked through Willow's veins as she watched Jario stride to the edge of the swim deck. Like her, he'd changed into swimming gear.

She tried not to openly stare at the chiselled body on display, especially those powerful thighs that flexed and gleamed bronze in the sunlight.

She sternly reminded herself why she was doing this.

He'd finally given her the smallest green light, to get the answers she wanted. Yes, she'd jumped through hoops to get here but so what?

'Ready?'

Her head jerked up to the speaking glance that said he'd seen her ogling him. Face flaming, she shifted her gaze to his muscled shoulder and nodded briskly. 'Bring it.'

A lip twitch compelled her eyes to his well-defined mouth, and her stomach clenched as lust unfurled low in her belly. God, what was wrong with her? How could she find him—yet another man bent on playing mind and *literal* games with her, and the one attempting to destroy what was left of her family—so compellingly attractive?

Continue reading

ENEMY'S GAME OF REVENGE
Maya Blake

Available next month
millsandboon.co.uk

COMING SOON!

We really hope you enjoyed reading this book.
If you're looking for more romance
be sure to head to the shops when
new books are available on

Thursday 16th January

To see which titles are coming soon, please visit
millsandboon.co.uk/nextmonth

MILLS & BOON

LET'S TALK

Romance

For exclusive extracts, competitions and special offers, find us online:

f MillsandBoon

X @MillsandBoon

⊙ @MillsandBoonUK

♪ @MillsandBoonUK

Get in touch on 01413 063 232

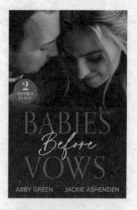
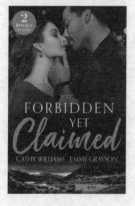

afterglow BOOKS

Afterglow Books is a trend-led, trope-filled list of books with diverse, authentic and relatable characters, a wide array of voices and representations, plus real world trials and tribulations. Featuring all the tropes you could possibly want (think small-town settings, fake relationships, grumpy vs sunshine, enemies to lovers) and all with a generous dose of spice in every story.

♪ @millsandboonuk
⊙ @millsandboonuk
afterglowbooks.co.uk

#AfterglowBooks

For all the latest book news, exclusive content and giveaways scan the QR code below to sign up to the Afterglow newsletter:

SCAN ME

afterglow BOOKS

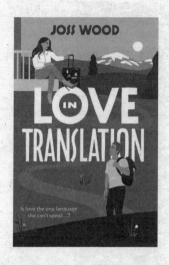

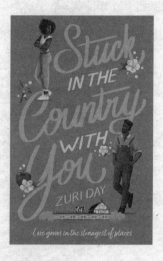

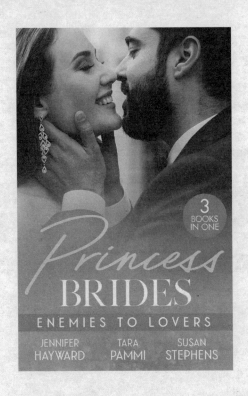